PENGUIN BOOKS

DORIAN

Will Self is the author of three short-story collections, *The Quantity Theory of Insanity* (winner of the 1992 Geoffrey Faber Award), *Grey Area* and *Tough, Tough Toys for Tough, Tough Boys*; a dyad of novellas, *Cock and Bull*, and a third novella, *The Sweet Smell of Psychosis*; and four novels, *My Idea of Fun*, *Great Apes*, *How the Dead Live* (shortlisted for the 2000 Whitbread Novel of the Year Award) and *Dorian*. Together with the photographer David Gamble, he produced *Perfidious Man*, a sideways look at contemporary masculinity. There have been three collections of journalism, *Junk Mail*, *Sore Sites* and *Feeding Frenzy*. Most of his books are published by Penguin.

Will Self has written for a plethora of publications over the years and is a regular broadcaster on television and radio.

Dorian
AN IMITATION

WILL SELF

PENGUIN BOOKS

PENGUIN BOOKS

Published by the Penguin Group
Penguin Books Ltd, 80 Strand, London WC2R ORL, England
Penguin Putnam Inc., 375 Hudson Street, New York, New York 10014, USA
Penguin Books Australia Ltd, 250 Camberwell Road,
Camberwell, Victoria 3124, Australia
Penguin Books Canada Ltd, 10 Alcorn Avenue, Toronto, Ontario, Canada M4V 3B2
Penguin Books India (P) Ltd, 11 Community Centre,
Panchsheel Park, New Delhi – 110 017, India
Penguin Books (NZ) Ltd, Cnr Rosedale and Airborne Roads,
Albany, Auckland, New Zealand
Penguin Books (South Africa) (Pty) Ltd, 24 Sturdee Avenue,
Rosebank 2196, South Africa

Penguin Books Ltd, Registered Offices: 80 Strand, London WC2R ORL, England

www.penguin.com

First published by Viking 2002
Published in Penguin Books 2003
6

Set in Monotype Dante
Printed in England by Clays Ltd, St Ives plc

For Ivan

And with thanks to Jack Emery and Joan Bakewell

There is an unconscious appositeness in the use of the word *person* to designate the human individual, as is done in all European languages: for *persona* really means an actor's mask, and it is true that no one reveals himself as he is; we all wear a mask and play a role.

Schopenhauer

PART ONE

Recordings

I

Once you were inside the Chelsea home of Henry and Victoria Wotton it was impossible to tell whether it was day or night-time. Not only was there this crucial ambiguity, but the seasons and even the years became indeterminate. Was it this century or that one? Was she wearing this skirt or that suit? Did he take that drug or this drink? Was his preference for that cunt or this arsehole?

These combinations of styles, modes, thoughts and orifices were played out in the gloom of the Wottons' dusty apartments and the brightness of their smeary water-closets, as if artefacts, ideas, even souls were all but symbols inscribed upon the reels of the slot machine of Life. Yank the arm and up they came: three daggers, three bananas, three pound signs. At the Wottons', three of anything paid out generously – in the coin of Misfortune.

But such was the particular correspondence between the year our story begins, 1981, and the year of the house's construction, 1881, and such was the peculiarly similar character of the times – a Government at once regressive and progressive, a monarchy mired in its own immemorial succession crisis, an economic recession both sharp and bitter – that a disinterested viewer could have been forgiven for seeing more enduring significance in the fanlight and the dado, the striped wallpaper and the gilt-framed mirror, a reproduction bust of Antinous and a very watery Turner, than in the human figures that actually stood in the mote-heavy beam of light which fell to the runner.

Upper-class people – that much was clear. Anyone would've judged Henry Wotton to be so by his hauteur alone, by the way his arrogant, supercilious face was looking past its own image in the mirror, as if searching for someone more interesting to talk to.

Someone who didn't have reddish curly hair, and eyes like the buttons of an undertaker's suit sewn on to an expanse of waxy pallor. There are those for whom all existence is the first hour of a promising cocktail party, and Henry Wotton was one of them.

If any further confirmation were needed, it was provided by his tailoring: Wotton was swaddled in class. His immaculately-cut three-piece Prince of Wales-check suit bagged slightly at the knee; his off-white butterfly-collar linen shirt frayed a tad at the cuff and the link holes; his red knitted silk tie was casually knotted. But only a slice of this costume was on view, a long stripe from his knobbly Adam's apple to his scuffed loafers. (An English gentleman never polishes his shoes, but then nor does a lazy bastard.) The rest of his finery was hidden beneath a full-length black Crombie overcoat; a garment that was also perfectly crafted – if, that is, you like the skirts of overcoats to be overfull, and distinctly epicene.

Behind Wotton stood a scarecrow woman, black hair flying away from her broad brow, which was buried in the hollow between her husband's shoulder blades. He was sorting through the mail, mostly a stack of pasteboard invitations, some inked, others engraved. Wotton tapped these together on the credenza in front of him, with disconcertingly fleshy and spatulate fingers, then riffled them as if he were shuffling a pack of cards. His wife, Lady Victoria, snuffled at his back. Her skinny arms, like animated pipe-cleaners, writhed in the stale air. Wotton laid the invitations down among overflowing ashtrays, empty bottles, stained wine glasses, crumpled bits of this and that. On the floor at their feet, tumbleweeds of dust sauntered in a febrile draught.

It's worth remarking at this stage on the precise character of the Wottons' house unbeautiful. Please don't let it be misunderstood that this was a filthy mucky home. Like any marital estate it had its ebb and flow of order and disorder; it's just that this disorder was extreme by anyone's standards. The ashtrays were huge, as big as geological features. Cigarette and cigar butts were buried in their cones of ash like the victims of a volcanic eruption. As for the empty

4

bottles, these were so numerous that their ranks formed a kind of anti-bar, offering up a fine selection of dregs, lees and spiritous vapours. And the many glasses which accompanied them were so casually abandoned as to suggest the recent dispersal of a considerable body of people – yet no one had visited the house in days.

Lady Victoria, whose family and friends knew her by the sobriquet 'Batface', was still attired for this long-gone party in a girlishly tiered ra-ra skirt of navy crushed velour. Her hair was a mess and so was she. She wove, her arms snaked, she was so irrefutably aristocratic that she was allowed to do almost anything – short of pissing herself – while remaining altogether acceptable.

And, truth to tell, she *could* have pissed herself as well – nobody would've judged her. Her father, the Duke of This or That, was a dandified bully, a preposterous little popinjay of a man who privileged his children with his superfluous anger. He had so much of everything that there was plenty to spare. When he first came across the infant Victoria, who was by then aged three or four months (His Grace having spent the preceding year – after having mounted the Duchess in the enclosure they kept for rare goat breeds – gaming at Biarritz and game-pie-eating in Caithness), on seeing her vast eyes, her triangular face and her elegantly enlarged ears, he had exclaimed, 'Batface!' Naturally, she adored him, both ultrasonically and stridently. The way her body and her mind both jibed with the world, the way she wriggled and writhed and gurned, all of it derived from his rejection. Lady Victoria stunted herself so as to tenant the queer space of the Duke's contempt.

'Lots of oblongs –' she squeaked on this occasion. They were the first words she had spoken to her husband for some hours. Not that they had been asleep – far from it. In their separate portions of the house – he below, she above – they had spent the hours of darkness secreted in their own ways, observing silence in lieu of repose.

'Sent out by squares.' His tones were deep and cold, a contaminated reservoir of inky disdain.

'We hardly go anywhere . . . any more . . . at least not together.' But there was no captiousness in her tones; Lady Victoria cared entirely for Henry, and cared for her own caring for him. Thus she did the sympathy for both of them.

He felt for her, too. He lay down the oblongs, and one of his hands first went to his eye to remove some wakey dust, then came groping behind her, to where one of the tiers of her skirt had become caught up behind the waistband of her tights. This he untangled and set to rights, before turning to face her. 'I don't give a shit about going to any of them, just so long as they keep inviting us.' He kissed her lightly on either eyelid; then, releasing her, he glanced around as if looking for a briefcase or a newspaper or some other staff of workaday righteousness, but finding none he opted instead for a bottle of Scotch within which a couple of inches still remained, and, tucking the furl of glass under his arm, he swivelled to depart.

'Have a good day, darling . . .' Lady Victoria trailed off. She was always trailing off.

'Yeah, fuck, whatever – you too.' They kissed again, this time on the lips, but sexlessly. He opened the front door and descended the front steps to the street, scrunching up the pocket of his coat to feel for his car keys.

It may have been the beginning of the Wottons' day, but outside morning had passed. It was noon, a noon in late June. The street, although bathed in sunlight, had no freshness about it, but was baking to a harsh monochrome. For this was an impossible late June, with the fruit trees in blossom as well as the flowers in bloom. All along the terrace of off-white four-storey houses, cherry and apple trees were bowed down with their gay burden, like willowy brides, their veils scattered with confetti. In window-boxes and the crowded little front gardens, a thousand stems effloresced: tulips, magnolia trees, desert orchids, snowdrops, daffodils, foxgloves. It was a veritable riot of verdancy against the urbanity all around, and above it spore hung like a mist of blood over an ancient battlefield.

Wotton hung over his own front railings, as if speared by them, like an overdressed St Sebastian. He pulled the folds of his overcoat about him and shivered. His pocket trawl had resulted in the netting of two pairs of Ray-Ban Wayfarers. Levering himself upright he clamped first one pair and then the second on to his face. 'It's perfectly all right to stare into the abyss for days at a time' – he addressed the empty street – 'so long as you're wearing two pairs of Ray-Bans.'

This was the manner of man he was – supremely mannered. A collector of *bons mots* and aperçus and apophthegms, an alfresco rehearser of the next impassioned, extempore rodomontade, whose greatest fear in life was inarticulacy, or worse, *esprit de l'escalier*. Henry Wotton might have professed an indifference about his position in society, but in truth, like all those who have ascended too high and too fast, he had failed to acclimatise, so he gasped desperately for the next inspirational acknowledgement that he existed at all.

'Gaaa . . . ! Christ – Christ!' Wotton fought for breath while lighting an outsize filterless Virginia cigarette. Even this suffocating outside was too exterior for him. He longed for the night, for con-fining drapes, for silky sheets and silken cuddles. He pushed himself up, and like a tree falling in the forest collapsed towards the door of a dark-green late-model Jaguar saloon, which was parked near to – but not exactly by – the kerb. It was a filthy luxury vehicle, the green paintwork furry with dust-upon-sap and maculate with bird-shit. Having finally located the keys in his waistcoat pocket, Wotton admitted himself to the car as if it were a vault, then pulled the door to with a moneyed clunk. The whisky bottle he aligned carefully between the upholstered grooves on the passenger seat.

Wotton organised his two pairs of shades, and stabbed at the ignition with the key. Despite being half-blinded by his ridiculous eyewear, he still adjusted the mirror so that he could see his own face. Turning this way and that he seemed to take a particular satisfaction in observing the white rheum that had gathered at the corners of his cruel mouth, like sea froth on anfractuous rocks.

Once Wotton had shackled the Crombie to the car's cream leather and begun dickering with the controls of the radio, he realised how muted the world's soundtrack had been. His wife's voice, his own footfalls, the avian din, and even the distant roar of the traffic on the King's Road, all were muffled. When he depressed a button on the car radio he recoiled from a blast of pure, stentorian, ordinary news. Information concerning a parallel world in which people walked and talked and brawled and died. A radio announcer blurted, 'In the wake of the disturbances the Government is considering setting up an inquiry under the chairmanship of Lord Scar –' and Wotton – having had quite enough – punched another button, which brought synthesised pop music, thudding and peeping into the car's interior.

Vigorously tapping, Wotton's black loafer burrowed into a slurry of opera programmes, discarded cocaine wraps, biffed cigarette boxes and empty hip-flasks, beneath which his sole felt for the accelerator, so he could jam it to the floor. The Jag pulled away and raced up the nearside lane of the straight residential road. After four hundred yards it veered back to the kerb and stopped. Inside the smoke-filled booth, Wotton extinguished one Sullivan's Export and lit another. The pop still peeped and he sang along with the mincing front man, 'Oh-woh-woh tainted love!' for a few bars before summoning himself, killing the engine and exiting the car. The Scotch went along for the ride.

Entering a narrow door in a brick wall, Wotton followed a path that ran obliquely through a patch of thick shrubbery to the door of a two-storey, purpose-built Victorian artist's studio. Using another of his keys, Wotton opened the door of this charming building, still yodelling, 'Take my love but that's not really all!'

It was dark inside. Very fusty. Terribly gloomy. The shrub-choked windows and leaf-pressed skylight of the studio admitted hardly anything of the day, as if this were – bizarrely – of little importance to the artwork undertaken here. And what creation could this have been? For this studio was patently a disordered brushed up against his butt in the hall when I last paid the rent on this place. He's just left Oxford, and now he's helping your ma with that Soho project.'

'Silly bitch.'

'He isn't very intellectual, if that's what you mean.'

'No, I meant Mama, but anyway I don't want want to mount some encephalitic *thing* – its brain swelling like a *bubo*.'

'Yeah, fuck, I dunno why I bothered with the whistle, her house is overrun with renters, tarts and social workers. But this kid is absolutely divine, he's a true original, he's *gorgeous*, he's next year's model – take a look at the stuff we did last night.' Baz headed over to a bank of video recorders which were connected to the monitors by coiled creepers of cabling. He fiddled intently with these while Wotton prowled. After a while he located a spoon, a glass of water, a two-millilitre disposable syringe, and a drug wrap on a windowsill. Then the two men's conversation assumed a common purpose.

'Is this gear?' Wotton held up the wrap.

'No, give over, Wotton, it's charlie – and it's my last.'

'Yeah, well . . .' Wotton considered this proposition while unbuttoning the cuff of his overcoat, his suit cuff, his shirt cuff. 'Ach! All this buttoning and unbuttoning. This is my *last* hit for this hour. This is the *last* summer of the dormouse. Moments, Baz, are dying out all about us, we are in the midst of a great extinction to rival that of the Cretaceous era . . .' He concocted the fix precisely, rapidly and elegantly. 'You dare to speak of your last charlie, when I am irrefutably the last Henry. The last with such a rare combination of gung-ho drugging . . .' he used the bunched-up sleeves in lieu of a tourniquet, and pushed the Ray-Bans up on his forehead so as to see his swollen main line better in the green light from the window – 'and *comme il faut* tailoring.'

But this supramundane rant remained unacknowledged, just as the peculiar sight of Wotton's aureole of red hair and flushed works full of green blood – as if he were a junky Pan – remained unobserved. Baz's attention was wholly caught by the first monitor, which zigged and zagged into life. It showed the naked figure of a beautiful young man, posed like a classical Greek kouros: one hand lightly on hip, the other trailing in groin, half-smile on plump lips. A naked figure that turned to face the viewer as the camera zoomed in. The second monitor came to life and this displayed a closer view of the still turning youth. The third view was closer again. The sensation imparted as all nine monitors came to life was of the most intense, carnivorous, predatory voyeurism. The youth was like a fleshly bonbon, or titillating titbit, wholly unaware of the ravening mouth of the camera. The ninth monitor displayed only his mobile pink mouth.

Wotton's rictus responded to this as it quivered and grew a moustache of sweat. 'Time flies when you're watching replays, eh Baz?' He drew the needle from his arm, licked up the gout of blood, grinned.

'Whaddya think, Henry?'

'I thought you'd found yet another epicene swish, Basil, but this boy looks tough –'

'But tender, yeah?' He laughed.

'I like bodies better than minds, Baz, and I like bodies with no mind at all better than anything else in the world.'

'If all I'd wanted was flesh, Wotton, I'd've gone to a butcher or a meat rack –'

'Yes, well, whatever other things you can accuse my mother of being, a pimp isn't one of them.'

But it was Baz who was agitated now, who paced about from screen to screen, before heading over to where Wotton stood by the windowsill. 'Your mother remains incredibly helpful, and very understanding . . . and as for him, *he's* interested in my work, *he* wants to help. He's unashamed – not like us. He belongs to a totally new generation, the first gay generation to come out of the shadows. That's what I've wanted to get with this –' he gestured towards the monitors – 'that would be perfect.'

'Unashamed? *Gay?* What the fuck're you talking about?'

'Of being a faggot, Wotton. A queer, a bum boy, an iron-bloody-hoof. Of that. And in your case, as a result, of being married to a Duke's daughter who you treat like a convenience store. That.'

Wotton, despite his snobbery and his affectation, liked nothing better than a proper joust. 'Baz, Baz,' he cooed, 'our proximity makes it essential that we be strangers to each other, Batface and I.'

'Whatever. Perhaps you can't see the hypocrisy you're mired in, but don't you have some responsibility for your wife's feelings?'

'Don't be absurd, I've never misled Batface for an instant concerning my sexual inclinations.'

'Maybe not – so I s'pose she just goes along with the fraud because she finds it perfectly natural. But I want a different kind of relationship. I want truth and beauty and honesty, but the world wants to destroy that kind of love between men. I think Dorian could be these things for me – but he'd probably mean nothing to you.'

'That's too many buts,' Wotton sneered. 'Better stick to buns – *Dorian's* buns. What is this, Baz – in love with *Dorian,* are we?'

To Wotton's surprise Baz shovelled up this facetiousness with great seriousness. 'I dunno. Y'know what I'm like, Henry, always getting hurt, and Dorian already seems to sense this. He's sweet and charming and naïve on the surface, but I expect he'll turn out to be a vicious little bitch like all the others.'

'He's here now, isn't he? Not that I give a shit, it's just that if he's making you into this much of a bore I'd better leave – it must be serious.'

'Yeah, well, serious enough for the work, at any rate.' Baz waved at the televisions. 'It's called *Cathode Narcissus,* and it'll be the last video installation I make. The whole fucking medium is dead. Fuck, it was *born* decadent, like all the rest of conceptual art. First it was Nauman, then Viola and me, now it's finished. From now on, conceptual art will degenerate to the level of crude autobiography, a global village sale of shoddy, personal memorabilia for which video installations like this will be the TV adverts.'

Wotton, grinning, stoked up his friend's little furnace of ire. 'What, with special offers on bottled piss, canned shit and vacuum-packed blood –?'

'That's all been done already!' Baz expostulated. 'When I was with Warhol –'

'When I was working at the Factory with Drella – with And*ee* . . .' Wotton was a superb mimic, a master of the accented caricature, and his Baz was a whining, preening, mid-Atlantic hipster. 'Well, *maan*, and Billy Name and Edie and – oh gosh! Doc-tor Robert – well, we all *did speed*, you know . . . It was part of the scene, *maan*.'

More unexpectedly, Basil Hallward could do Henry Wotton just as well, exaggerating the lisp, turning up the affectation as if it were the contrast knob on one of his television monitors. 'We ate at Harry's Bar and then wepaired to the Gwitti Palace, where I quaffed quails' eggs from her carefully coifed cunt –'

And he would've gone on and on and on with this, had it not been for Wotton breaking back in with another impersonation – complete with acoustic air guitar – of Baz doing Bowie doing 'Andy Warhol': 'Baz Hallward looks a scream, standing on his silver screen/ Baz Hallward looks a scream, can't tell him apart at all, at all, at all . . .'

In a cubbyhole of a bedroom hidden behind successive dark, membranous curtains, the object of Baz's affections and his latest muse lay, only just now awoken from the easeful slumber occasioned by weed and wine and mutual wanking. Dorian Gray had been seduced thus far by Baz Hallward but no further. He'd been impressed by his connections and excited by his air of debauchery. He'd been beguiled by Baz's suggestion that he model for this video installation, but there were limits. So during the videoing it was weed not coke, and afterwards he let Baz take him in hand, not mouth or arse. For now, Dorian was just young enough to want to go to bed with his elders out of a sense of being flattered by their attentions.

Dorian could hear the two older men hooting and railing. He

stirred himself and thought he perhaps ought to find out what was going on, but it was difficult to get motivated and so much more pleasant to lie in a tatty pile of sheets and blankets, stretching luxuriously and admiring the way the tendons and arteries writhed in his own wrists, or the way his brown legs – twined in white cotton – assumed this or that angle.

Liquid blobs of light shimmered on the wall above Dorian's tawny head. On the bedside table stood a half-empty glass of whisky and beside that was a metallic cigarette lighter, and beside that a pair of nail-clippers. Like the rest of the studio the cubbyhole was oak-panelled. Here and there a bronze-effect spotlight had been insensitively inserted. In each of these reflective surfaces Dorian Gray sought himself out, while lip-synching to the narcissistic soundtrack that played in his empty head. 'She's a model and she's looking good, I'd like to take her home it's understood . . . She plays hard to get, she smiles from time to time . . . It only takes a cam-er-a to make her mine . . .'

The cackling voices of the two older men in the studio kept cutting into Dorian's reverie. So, in one sinuous movement, he arose from the bed. From the floor Dorian retrieved white boxer shorts; he pulled these on and then sheathed them in white chinos which he fastened with a snake-buckled belt. *Cathode Narcissus* was no contrivance; this young man moved with the performer's zeal which assumes an observer even when none is present.

Dorian jived a little as he pulled on a T-shirt. He began to pay attention to the voices in the next room. 'She's a one' – Wotton was in raconteur mode – 'a real card. Have you seen her back room?'

'Yeah, man.' Baz was only half-listening.

'It's worth scoring off her just to see it – row upon row of new clothes, all still wrapped in polythene. Then electrical goods stacked up – all still in their boxes. She's even got five fucking Corby trouser presses – showed them to me with great pride.'

'Yeah, I know, man.'

'It really proves that drug-dealing should be legal – not, you understand, for any of the usual reasons, but simply because the likes of Honey don't know how to dispose of such outrageous profits tastefully . . .' Baz Hallward may have heard about the trouser presses, but Dorian hadn't. He wanted to know more, and to see who was describing them. On bare feet he padded towards the drawl, which continued, 'I don't suppose you have anything much more than a list to contribute to this shopping expedition, eh Baz? Everything gone on trying to pump yourself up enough to satisfy little *Dorian*, hmm?'

Dorian stood in the doorway, swivel-hipped, blank-faced, floppy-fringed. Wotton fell silent, feeling new eyes upon him. The two older men turned to regard this Adonis, and in their heated appraisal and Dorian's cool appraisal and their more fervid reappraisal of this and his more frigid reappraisal of that was the most exacting and timeless of triangulations: Baz would always love Dorian, Wotton would never love Dorian but would want him consistently, and Dorian would betray Baz and would never love anyone at all.

'I'm incredibly sorry' – Wotton, misinterpreting Dorian's disgusted pout, began secreting charm – 'you must have heard that. I didn't mean anything by it at all – I only said it because I was hoping to upset Baz, I do so like him when he's aggrieved . . . I'm sure that if your association persists you'll soon find out how comical it can be to wind him up until he positively twangs with stress and indignation . . .' Wotton advanced, his hand out, his many flopping cuffs adding to the cavalier impression '*Ça suffit*. You must be Dorian Gray. I understand *you* know my mother; *I'm* Henry Wotton.'

'D'you mean Phyllis Hawtree?' Dorian took the hand, held it for second while exerting no pressure and would've let it fall, but it held on to him.

'Quite so,' Wotton snapped. 'She will insist on changing her name every time she changes her bed partner.'

'I'm sorry . . .' Dorian floundered ' . . . I've just woken up . . . Um, yeah, I've . . . Your mother –'

'Warned you against me in no uncertain terms, told you of profligacy, drug addiction, sodomy, and even more exotic vices? Am I right? Of course I am.' Wotton, still retaining Dorian's hand, led him to the centre of the room and drew him round so that they faced each other, like dancers frozen in a minuet.

Baz smiled at this exchange in a twisted way, while Dorian summoned himself to play his part. 'No no, she said you were a brilliant –'

'Mistake? I daresay I am, but we weren't talking of me, we were discussing you, your hopes, fears and most intimate, most quavering desires. Tell them to me. Now. All of them. But make it snappy!'

'Wotton –' Baz began a teeny admonition.

'"Wooot-ton," he cries, like a fucking maiden aunt with a maidenhead the size of Maidenhead! But I mean it! I want to know your intentions now you've been exiled from the groves of academe. Your willingness to associate with my philanthropic mother suggests that you're well on your way to becoming a man of the people, *Mister* Gray.' He let Dorian's hand fall as if the very idea were contaminating. 'Or have I got it wrong, do you intend devoting yourself to Baz's bizarre art fetishism? He's been showing me *Cathode Narcissus*.'

'Isn't it fantastic –'

'Fantastic, absolutely. Quite fantastic that any medium – let alone one as shallow and transparent as Baz's – should be allowed to traduce *your* beauty.'

'I dunno.' Dorian moved off, gifting the two older men a view of his feral prowl. 'I try not to be hung up on the looks thing –'

'Hung up? *"Looks thing"*? I reel with the impact of these heresies.' And, as if choreographing such a reel, Wotton pivoted, stooped, yanked up his Scotch bottle from the floor, uncorked it with a 'plop', hoisted it to his mouth, drained it, gasped, lit a cigarette, then continued, 'You should remember, *Mister* Gray, a nude body requires no explanation, unlike a naked intellect.'

Dorian shrugged, unimpressed. 'People are always coming on to me about acting or modelling or whatever. But I think it'd be chronically dull. You may think your mother's ridiculous, but there's nothing funny about the Youth Homeless Project she's fundraising for.'

'There's certainly nothing funny about *youth*' – Wotton smiled, replete, for he loved a good feed line – 'a *youth* is the one thing worth hanging on to.'

'It's not much, but I feel I'm doing something. I go into this place in Soho three afternoons a week and talk to the guys there about art. It's as good a use as any for an art history degree, and I get to meet some amazing characters . . . Even if I'm just turning them on to a different way of seeing things, surely that's worthwhile?'

But Wotton wasn't thinking of value judgements – he was still feeding. 'Art for the underdog, eh? Thrown like a titbit from your high table. Pity they can't jump up enough to reach it –'

'Look, Wotton,' blurted Baz, who'd been agitating to get in, 'd'you wanna sit on the terrace and have a coffee with Dorian, or what?'

'Terrace? Coffee? We're not in fucking *Naples*, y'know –'

'I know. What I'm trying to say is I want to get on with the editing and sequencing, Dorian's moving into a new pad and this installation is the centrepiece for it, right? Now I don't object to you two rapping but it'd be cool if you gave me some space . . .' And as if responding to the doggy way Wotton and Dorian were sniffing around each other, Baz Hallward began to shoo them out of the studio. 'C'mon – scat! I'll bring you some coffee out. I'll come to Honey's with you in a bit, Wotton; for now, keep the client entertained.'

Outside in the garden, Wotton took Dorian's arm. He could do this – casually take someone's arm. It was odd that such a caustic character should have such an easy physicality – but no odder than the garden itself, for here, as in the street, the dense and overgrown foliage was oppressively, queerly diverse. The presence of so many different plants and flowers from so many different regions of the world would in and of itself have been disorienting, but since they were all simultaneously in flower and in fruit, the effect was deranging.

Not that Dorian Gray noticed; he allowed Wotton to lead him by the arm into this upsetting thicket. They paused in front of a carnation and Wotton pointed out the peculiar green shade of the flowers. 'My mother cultivated plants before she moved on to humanity,' he drawled. 'I'm not altogether sure which is the higher life form.' With a flourish he lit yet another cigarette and blew brown scrolls of smoke among the green leaves and brilliant blossoms. In the mid-distance traffic rumbled, while at their feet insects pulsed and chafed and buzzed. 'You see that man?' Wotton snapped after a while.

'Sorry?'

'There . . .' His naked arm – cuffs still flapping – hailed the sky overhead, and the tip of his fag pinpointed a window five storeys up in a block of flats next to the garden. 'You see the jiggling man?'

'He's more swaying back and forth like a metronome,' Dorian corrected him. And it was a better description of the odd sight, this ordinary man in a V-neck sweater and an open-neck shirt, hands stuck in his pockets, rocking sideways, from foot to foot.

'He does it all day,' Wotton continued, 'and all night . . . and in the early morning. I once came out here at five-thirty a.m. just to make sure he hadn't knocked off. I'm convinced that it's he who's really meting out the minutes. He'll probably cease when the apocalypse begins. I call him the jiggling man, and I suggest that if you want to dub someone "metronome man" you find your own fucking loony!'

'Actually,' Dorian said, 'that's not something I want –'

'Ah, exactly, but what is it that you *do* want?' Wotton rounded on him. 'D'you know? Do any of us? I've a terribly fey friend who swears that he isn't really a faggot at all, it's just that he has these vivid dreams of being buggered – which, as we all know, is perfectly normal, even for the most red-blooded of heterosexuals – and when he awakes he finds it terribly hard to shake them off. Now what, *Mister* Gray, d'you say to that?'

It was unclear whether Dorian understood Wotton at all, or comprehended him only too well. 'I'm happy enough . . .' he replied. 'I've only –'

'Only what?' This was another of Wotton's myriad techniques of seduction, the continual interruption as a means of making up another's mind. 'Only spent the one white night with poor, washed-up Baz, who's not so much hip as a hip-fucking-replacement? I congratulate you. Did he seduce you with potions and rub unguents on you?'

'We smoked a bit of grass . . . I'm not sure about hard –'

'Hard what? Hard talk? Hard cocks? Hard labour? Hard drugs? Hardly anything? You should remember, my young friend, if you don't know what you want to do, at least do something. There's no other cure for indecisiveness.'

'Henry,' Dorian demurred, 'look, we've only just met, I don't know why it is you're being so intense . . . Actually, that's what your mother said about you, that you're a brilliant talker. But I don't want to be cured of anything, any more than I'm obsessed by looks – least of all my own – they're such a superficial thing.'

'You say that Dorian, you say that, but we are in an age when appearances matter more and more. Only the shallowest of people won't judge by them.'

There was a terrace, of sorts, by the door to the studio – if you call twelve bird-shat-upon Portland paving slabs a terrace, which in London most do. This Wotton and Dorian now regained, still arm in arm, and both of them felt as if the interlude in the bijou jungle had been significant, although in Wotton's case this was partly because it was the longest walk he had taken in several weeks.

It could have been a Neapolitan terrace, because there was a small, round, metal table and two folding metal chairs. Baz had managed to assemble a tray of coffee, complete with matching white china cups and saucers, sugar bowl, cream jug. The whole ensemble was ridiculously elegant and bright in the dull, oppressive afternoon. They scraped their seats to sit, and Wotton was mother, while Dorian became his vain daughter, twirling a teaspoon between his fingers, so that he might admire the way his face ballooned then hollowed, ballooned then hollowed. 'I've no idea what I'm going to do,' he said after a few slurps. 'I've come down from Oxford with an indifferent degree and too much money – hardly a recipe for success.'

'*Au contraire*,' said Wotton, 'if you've got it – and you have it all – you must use it, and you must use it all. Before this jaded century is utterly exhausted, at least one individual should've pleasured it thoroughly. I'm prepared to be your pandar, I'll take you under my ample wing . . .' at last he noticed the bloodied, flapping cuffs and began to button them '. . . today!'

'Today?' Dorian saw the blood and prevaricated, but the people who had warned him about people like Wotton should, in turn, have themselves been warned about. 'Look, I'm – I'm not sure, I said I'd drop in at this reception your mother is giving – for her donors.'

'Fine.' He was not to be deflected. 'I'll accompany you.'

'If you're sure . . .' Dorian warmed to the idea; Wotton might be disturbing, but at least he wasn't boring. Wotton might want to fuck him, but at least he didn't make Dorian into an object of veneration as Basil Hallward did.

Baz, who at this point emerged from the studio, and having overheard the last exchange, snapped at Wotton, 'I thought you were going to Honey's, to score?'

'I am' – Wotton was unperturbed – 'I shall go *en route* to the reception and take Dorian with me; I doubt he's seen five trouser presses in one place before –'

'But I need Dorian for the sequencing.'

'Really? I thought *you* were coming with me to score,' Wotton sneered, 'but anyway, Baz, no buts, I warned you about them.'

'Whatever you say, Wotton – besides, I s'pose I can do without you, Dorian; *Cathode Narcissus* is about done –'

'I want to see it!' And the way Dorian rose from the table and headed impetuously for the door was a reminder for Baz and Wotton of how much younger he was than them. As if they needed it.

Inside the dark studio the nine monitors were sharply outlined. Across their faces, hissing with static, the fluid images of Dorian presented a cascade of motion. There was a soundtrack as well, an insistent thrumming beat entwined with a breathy fluting. Dorian was transfixed for a few moments, but then he moved closer and began to sway in time with his own televisual images. Nine naked Dorians and one clothed. In synchrony, youth and the images of youth waltzed to the heavenly and eternal music of self-consciousness.

'Well, whaddya reckon?' Baz blurted out from the shadows, and Dorian turned to see him and Wotton, their faces soiled with lust.

'He's absolutely superb,' Wotton answered, 'and this afternoon has become remarkable since I encountered your faun.'

'I think I've caught him at just the right point –'

'Oh, indeed you have, Baz, he's like a ripe grape dusted with yeast.' Wotton made as if to pluck one of the monitors and eat it.

Dorian felt uncomfortable with the way the older men were speaking; was it at cross-purposes, or did they regard him and the video installation as entirely interchangeable? 'How long will these tapes last, Baz?' he asked.

'It's hard to say . . . Certainly years, if not decades, and by then they can be transferred to new tapes, and so on – for ever, I guess.'

'So, these' – Dorian gestured – 'will remain young for ever, while I grow old, then die?'

'Yeah, well,' Baz snorted derisively. 'You can't copy bodies – yet.'

'I wish it was the other way round,' Dorian said, and to support the throwaway nature of the remark, he picked up a black wind-cheater which was slung over a chair and headed for the door, calling over his shoulder, 'You coming, Henry?'

'Er . . . yuh.' Wotton stirred himself, as did Baz.

'What about the piece, Dorian?' he pleaded. 'I need to do two more recordings for the soundtrack. I *must* do them.'

'Well, if you must.' Dorian's whole tone had hardened since he'd seen the installation. 'Personally I'm jealous of the bloody thing – it's already hours younger than me.'

Baz took this as the acceptable petulance of the patron who's also a model. He smoothed his hair, hooking strands behind his ears, and began moving from monitor to monitor, switching them off. 'As soon as the recordings are done,' he told Dorian, 'and the sequencing and editing are finished, I'll bring *Cathode Narcissus* round to your apartment and set it up. Then you can do whatever you want to your several selves. Scratch their eyes out, or jerk off with them. Whatever.'

'OK.' Dorian paused in the doorway, and Baz, thinking of him at dawn – screaming with delight, trussed in a sheet, his erect cock arched like bow, a pearl of his semen on Baz's tongue – couldn't play it cool any longer.

'Come tomorrow, Dorian, please, at around noon?'

'All right, Baz.' And withdrawing the psychic knife from between Baz's ribs without troubling to twist it, Dorian left.

*   *   *

It was, apparently, a tactical withdrawal, as if he wanted his rivals to fight over him forthwith. This they obliged him by doing: 'For fuck's fucking sake, Wotton!' Baz howled. 'How long are you gonna go on shooting me down like this?'

'Only as long as you go on shooting up at my expense' – Wotton was straightening his tie, patting down his clothes – 'and poncing this studio off my mother.'

'I like him,' Baz near screeched.

'And I like him too.'

'You don't like *anything*, Wotton, you're poison running in the gutter.' Baz walked over to Wotton and taking a wad of currency from his jeans pocket, peeled ten notes off and stuffed them into the top pocket of his friend's overcoat. 'Get us one of each, willya?' he snarled.

'What's this – in funds, are we Baz?'

'Dorian paid me for it – for the piece. Cash down.'

'Oh really?' Wotton sniggered unpleasantly. 'Something makes me think he'll have to go on paying indefinitely.' And without waiting for Baz's reply, the vile fop turned on his heel and departed.

2

Henry Wotton drove his five-litre Jaguar around central London as if he were at the wheel of a powered lawnmower, and the city itself but a rough oblong of lawn, to the rear of a romantically ruinous country house. A lawn planted with stucco models of famous metropolitan buildings, perhaps one-tenth scale, between which he piloted his vehicle at once lazily and wildly. He seemed to have no concern for either the Highway Code or the sensibilities of other drivers. Indeed, if there was the remotest awareness of a danger, it was merely that he might tip over the ha-ha.

Dorian Gray understood this about his new admirer as soon as he buckled himself into the car's cream interior. Clearly, to be in Henry Wotton's Jaguar was to be in Henry Wotton's capricious and cruel embrace. At first he stole the occasional sidelong glance at his chauffeur, who guided the car with three fingers of his left hand on the lower rim of the steering wheel, while trailing his cigarette hand out of the window and lolling his reddish curls against the headrest. But soon Dorian surrendered to the lurches, surges and drifts of the big car. He began peering at the detritus on the car's floor, a veritable midden of discarded material from which much information on the Wotton culture could, undoubtedly, be gained. Pop music purled from the car radio, as if a sonic brook were running between the two men.

The car was at the traffic lights at the top of Exhibition Road when Dorian exhibited his first find, a brace of opera programmes. 'D'you like the opera?'

'My wife does,' Wotton drawled. 'My main pleasure at Glyndebourne is counting the homosexuals in the audience and seeing if they outnumber those on the stage.'

'What about these?' Dorian held up a flyer for a stock car race at the White City Stadium. An old drug wrap was stuck to it.

'I adore destructive spectacles; they are the last refuge of the creative.' The lights changed and a loafer came down on the accelerator; the big car gathered its massy inertia under its whale's back of a bonnet, and then slid smoothly past the Albert Memorial. By the time the Jag reached the bridge over the Serpentine it was travelling at sixty. It swiped to the left, then to the right, weaving between two lumbering vans, before tucking into the chicane that led up towards Lancaster Gate.

Dorian knew intuitively that it was profoundly uncool to mention Wotton's driving, but he couldn't help himself. 'How d'you manage to get away with it?' he asked. 'You had no way of knowing if there was a car in the oncoming lane.'

'I have an aerial view, Dorian. I see the whole situation from above.'

'Are you serious?'

'Never more so.'

'But how? It's not possible.'

'I don't expect *you* to comprehend it' – Wotton peeked slyly out at him from under his four brown lenses – 'but my father buggered me relentlessly when I was a young child. While he was doing it I found myself becoming curiously disembodied, floating up to the ceiling of the room where my child-self lay as he heaved and panted. I occupied this point of view – in the region of the cornicing, although occasionally revolving around the chandelier – on a regular basis between the ages of five and eight. For so long, in fact, that I have retained it into adulthood.

'You, my dear young friend,' he continued, 'are condemned to a seventy-millimetre, windscreen view of the city. You are a mere corpuscle, travelling along these arteries, whereas I have a surgeon's perspective. I float above it all, and see Hyde Park as but a green, gangrenous fistula in London's grey corpse!' And with this flourish he yanked on the handbrake, for they had arrived in Marylebone High Street.

Henry Wotton adored drugs and he adored buying them. He understood, of course, that the aesthetics of drug-dealing left much to be desired. This painfully *petit bourgeois* little flat, marooned eight storeys above Marylebone High Street, its chintz-wrapped windows looking out over the Westway flyover, was no mud-bricked stall in the walls of an ancient citadel. No, this was no caravanserai, or souk, and nor was Honey – a stringy blonde, in loose white smock and tight black leggings – a noble spice merchant, with a scented beard and indigo robes. Her conversation with her customer displayed no elaborate courtesies, nor alluded to prices with great subtlety, hiding them in invocations of the Prophet. On the contrary, the two of them sat rapping in front of a glass-topped coffee table, upon which she unceremoniously weighed up the product using jewellers' scales.

'Yes,' said Wotton, 'I remember that fifty quid owing, but I sorted it out with you the day before yesterday.'

'Nah,' Honey sniffed, 'your mate came by and racked up a g on your slate yesterday evening.'

'Christ – I've got to take more drugs than I want just to keep up with that bastard. All right, here's a hundred and seventy.'

Dorian turned from his careful examination of a modular wall rack, which contained compartments for picture books, pot plants, pen pots and potpourri, to see Wotton laying notes down on the table, while Honey poured powders into envelopes and neatly folded them.

'Not these two.' Wotton stayed her hand, took two of the envelopes, deftly married their contents, withdrew a small capsule from his capacious pocket, unscrewed it, poured in a tiny dun cascade, screwed it up again, and dropped it in a waistcoat pocket; the drug wraps were tucked in another. All these actions were neat, precise, focused. They spoke of concomitant thought processes – fold, wrap, tap, snort, shoot, walk, pay – going on in the Wotton psyche, while the sweat simmered on his brow. 'Right,' Wotton rapped, 'that's that. But before we go, *chère Miel*, my young friend would love to see your splendid collection.'

Honey rose, and, gums smacking, nails scratching, she led them out of the room, down a short corridor stinking of air freshener and into a back bedroom. The entire room had been crammed full of stuff. On three freestanding Dexion shelving units reposed irons, televisions, stereo units, tape recorders, kettles, food blenders, and all – as Wotton had said – still in their packaging. There were also rails hung with polythene-wrapped clothes, and many many stuffed animals. Honey garbled a wired commentary on this materialistic superfluity, while massaging the shoulders of a trouser press. 'Not that I need all of 'em, yuh, but these Corby ones only have three pressing settings, whereas these Danish ones have five . . .' While she rattled on, Wotton felt for Dorian's hand and took it, a gesture the younger man found simultaneously tender and subversive.

Back in the car, as they barrelled down Park Lane, Wotton yanked the little capsule out, fiddled with it, stuck it up his nose, honked noisily, repeated the fiddle, then passed it to Dorian. 'Just hold it up your nostril and sniff – go on.'

'I'm not sure –'

'Go on, I insist. It would be bad manners not to.'

'Oh, all right.' And he did, he sniffed. Dorian had decided to absorb as much of Henry Wotton as possible through whichever membrane presented itself. He knew his own limitation: he had money but no real style. His upbringing had been here and there, on the fringes of film sets, in foreign hotels, in transit, sitting at tables with hired, pan-European staff. It had given him polish but no shine. He lacked the deeper lustre of someone like Wotton, who by remaining *in situ* had acquired cultural verdigris.

The Jaguar coasted to a halt at some traffic lights. The stereo was cranked right up and belting out 'Too Drunk to Fuck' by the Dead Kennedys. It was amazing that the duo weren't in the process of being righteously busted, so flagrant were their activities, but through the tinted windows, surrounding drivers could be seen, stalled in every sense, eyes front, sitting mindlessly, eating a late lunch out of their noses.

'Hnghf – oof! That stings.' Dorian passed the capsule back.

'But you're not losing your nasal virginity?'

'What?' Dorian near shouted, frantically rubbing his nose.

Wotton killed the Dead Kennedys. 'You've done gear before?'

'Gear?'

'Horse, scag, smack, H, *he-ro-in.*'

'Oh, I thought that was charlie.'

'I always add the merest whisper of smack to take the edge off. The merest.'

Dorian changed tack. He pulled down the sunshade to reveal a vanity mirror, and spoke while observing his own pupils. It was as if he'd been snorting vanity mixed with cocaine and heroin. 'I thought you liked Baz.'

'I love him. He's a fucking genius.'

'But back there?'

'I love him, but he's becoming sentimental – that's bad. That means he isn't *simpatico* – and that's worse. That I can't abide. Worse still, he repeats himself – all that avant-garde bullshit, the hamster wheel of the Manhattan art world, how he scored with Burroughs on Avenue B, and "*William*" threatened the spade with a sword-stick – you've heard all that, yuh?'

'Well, yes.'

'That was me.' Wotton flashed an unexpected smile. 'With the fucking sword-stick, you fool – although it wasn't New York, it was Marseille. I don't *do* America.'

Wotton parked the Jag in Savile Row and they walked around the corner into Piccadilly. The afternoon heat was fierce, so Dorian took off his jacket, but Wotton ploughed on in his overcoat regardless. Dorian resolved to be measured for a three-piece suit as soon as possible.

The charity reception for the Youth Homeless Project was being held in the restaurant of a cavernous hotel which had grown seedy and unprofitable in the recession. Its grey flanks were pitted, its reception rooms smelly and its staff surlier than ever. 'Naturally we're extremely late,' Wotton declaimed, leaving his coat in the cloakroom, 'but then punctuality is the fucking thief of time, burgling precious seconds which we could've spent getting higher.' The woman behind the counter scowled at him, and he smiled back while handing her a pound note.

The interior of the restaurant was vernal in the extreme: great tubs full of blooms stood about, connected by troughs full of shrubbery. The carpet was floral-patterned, the drapes the same, the lighting in this painforest was noonday equatorial. From between two pointy-shouldered PR girls – their dumpling bodies unsuitable for such sharp suiting, their blonde sausage curls and retroussé noses making them altogether spaniel-like – came Phyllis Hawtree. She set off gamely towards Dorian and her son across the trackless waste of carpeting, but the distance was so great they had plenty of time to appreciate quite how mad and ethereal she appeared, with her coiffure so stiff it vibrated with each arthritic step, and her knee and arm both surgically braced. As she drew nearer they could see that her creviced cheek was so powdered that a careless air kisser might find themselves tumbling into her face.

'My mother,' Wotton whispered, 'is an intelligent woman who views the distressing of the social fabric with the very real emotion she withholds from all those around her. Like Schopenhauer, the more she loves mankind, the less she loves men.' Dorian was going to say he thought this was unfair, but it was too late, he was caught in her bony talons.

'Oh Dorian,' she fluted, 'I'm *so* glad you're here, there are so many people who want to meet you.' She ignored her son and he took this as his familial due, merely following in her wake as she led Dorian into the throng of superannuated debs, professional faggots and off-the-peg suits – a flat company leavened only by a handful of the requisite donkey-jacketed roll-up smokers (just as a charity event for multiple sclerosis sufferers would have its wheelchair users, or for sickle-cell anaemia its blacks).

Eventually, after traversing the trench between two buffets, where glistening kiwi fruit cascaded and miniature sausage rolls were piled up like some novel form of ammunition, they reached their target. He was a florid politico in a suit with wide chalk stripes and a yellow waistcoat. He had an impressive lick of chocolate hair over a bulbous brow, and those out-of-control eyebrows which only men firmly within the British Establishment can carry off.

'Dorian,' Phyllis cooed, 'this is David Hall, the Member for Bexleyheath, he's on the Housing Committee. David, this is Dorian Gray, the young man I told you about, the one who's putting the shelter on a computer . . . And this is my son,' she added as an afterthought. Then she evaporated, leaving only the stench of her perfume.

'Are you working voluntarily at the shelter, Mr Gray?' Hall's accent was as fruity as the buffet.

'Dorian, please – and yes, there wouldn't be money to pay me, and I've no need of it anyway.'

'What're you doing, exactly?'

'Oh, this and that, computerising the client list, the donors and so on. I also muck around a bit with some of the regulars . . . muck about with art materials.'

'Is it a career path for you' – Hall was amazed – 'social work?'

'I dunno – I shouldn't think so.'

'There's obviously a need for such people, but I wouldn't have imagined you one of them –'

'Which is all by way of saying,' Wotton scythed in, 'if you sympathise too much with pain, you become one.'

'I'm s-sorry?' Hall spluttered.

Dorian wasn't surprised that the MP was taken aback, but more shocking than Wotton's intervention was his appearance. He looked entirely at ease, his complexion warm, his hair neat, his cuffs shot. It was as if he were a chameleon, assuming the protective coloration of respectability simply by standing in front of it. 'Bluntly,' Wotton continued, 'I'm trying to warn Dorian off this man-of-the-people act. Hypocrisy won't suit his nature.'

'Do you think . . . ?' Hall left a gap that begged for the insertion of a name.

'Wotton.'

'Mr Wotton, that all philanthropy can only be for show? Surely it's only an "act" when viewed with an eye for acting, a cynical eye.'

'I'm sure, *Mister* Hall, you would agree that the most honest of socialists couldn't give a toss being poorer, so long as nobody else is richer.'

'D'you think there were any such honest socialists among the youths rioting the other week?'

'Probably, but I know there were definitely some ballet dancers *manqué* – marvellous, lithe young black guys. I saw them on the news, shattering the windows of shoe stores with the most delicate of high kicks, then selecting the training shoes they wanted, then off they went through the wreckage *en faisant des pointes* –' Wotton broke off as a thin, nervous woman approached their group. She was in her forties, prematurely grey, wearing loose trousers and a top which appeared to be woven from a fine hessian. 'Hello, Jane,' he said.

'I'm sorry,' she replied through cracked lips, her brown eyes downcast.

The apology was not just for the interruption – it was for *everything*. For colonialism and racism and sexism; for the massacres of Amritsar and Sharpeville and Londonderry; for introducing syphilis to Europe and opium to China and alcoholism to the Aboriginals; for the little Princes in the Tower *and the Tower itself*. This was manifestly a woman who viewed sackcloth as *de rigueur*. But Hall saw her as an opportunity to escape, and grabbed on to her with both hands. 'That's all right, Jane – we need to talk. I'm sure these blokes won't mind . . .' And he whisked her away.

Dorian was left with a spluttering Wotton. 'Christ, he's awful, a serial realist – the very worst kind.' He got the capsule out, fiddled, took a snort, then passed it to Dorian.

Dorian followed suit then asked, 'What about her?'

'The Duchess? Not that she uses the title – she's extraordinary. She wove those drabs herself in some godforsaken mud hutment in Uttar Pradesh. She has the finest Palladian house in the world, Narborough, and she's trying to throw it – along with the rest of her husband's staggering wealth – into the void.'

'The void?'

'Nirvana, that which is beyond all illusion, the eternal substratum. It's true that the best kind of woman has an empty head and donates it willingly, but that isn't Jane's particular vapidity; she's genuinely lost in Turgenev's white void, the only alternative Buddhism offers to the black void of Christian damnation, or materialist extinction. And her house – which would offer a great deal of shelter for a great many youths – is in the process of going the same way.'

'But is she happy?'

'Happy? My dear Dorian, she's fucking furious. The Buddha is the patron saint of the passive–aggressive.'

'Does she go out in society much?'

'Of course, she's a fucking duchess. No amount of eccentricity debars her from her own kind. Aristo punks sniff glue together, just as aristo Buddhists meditate together. She'll be in St Paul's next month, along with the rest of them. She'll probably be wearing a special Royal Wedding hair shirt.

'I hate this doghole.' Wotton suddenly changed tack.

'This' – he made as if to spit out a gulp of the white wine they'd acquired – 'is the decoction of the bile of the livers of splenetic Communist Party bagmen in Lyon. These people' – he gestured at the debs, the suits, the faggots – 'can't even make proper use of their own homes, let alone provide shelter for anyone else. That cunt over there is screwing me out' – it was true, an intense type with spiky hair and wire-rimmed spectacles was staring at Wotton – 'I want to break free!' He turned on his heel and made for the distant double doors.

Dorian remained where he was, and the intense man – who was

the volunteer co-ordinator at the project – joined him. Who's he? the man spat in the direction of Wotton's retreating back. His own name was a classless John.

—'Enry Wotton, Dorian sneered, despising himself for the way he automatically dropped into Mockney. 'E's Phyllis's son.

—Why're you hanging out with him?

—Friend of a friend.

—He looks fucking dodgy – John looked Dorian in the eye – like a junky as well as a toff.

—And a queer – you forgot to say queer.

—What?! John was nonplussed, but Dorian was gone.

*　　*　　*

Meanwhile, Wotton had run into the Ferret, an old crony, by the entrance. The Ferret was staring at Dorian. 'He's amazingly beautiful, the one natural flower in this plantation of artifice.' The Ferret himself was small, and his wrinkled pinhead was liver-spotted. He wore an obvious toupee.

'Yes, well' – Wotton gave a bashful moue – 'I'm going to mount him like a butterfly until he whimpers like a hog.'

'You'll do no such thing,' the Ferret giggled indulgently. 'All that heroin and cocaine and alcohol and nicotine and marijuana makes your penis very small and completely limp.'

'I tell you, Fergus,' Wotton said with some seriousness, 'I'd give up doing drugs altogether, if I wasn't afraid of other people taking them without me.'

A waiter was passing and the Ferret took a glass of Perrier before replying, 'No one's suggesting that you stop dissipating yourself for one minute, Henry. The IMF are being called into Rome – fiddle on. How's Baz?'

'I don't mind discarding any lover – as long as they stay discarded.'

'You're unnecessarily cruel –'

'And you're ridiculously old.'

'And he . . .' the Ferret chose to disregard the insult, preferring instead to ogle Dorian, who was hovering nearby '. . . he is *most* lovely. He reminds me of somebody . . . Can he talk?'

'Who cares. Dorian, this is Fergus; Fergus, this is Dorian. That's all that it's necessary for either of you to know now. You'll both know everything else so soon it's sickening. Bye.' And he strode out, obviously expecting Dorian to follow.

Dorian – with a feeble 'Excuse me' to the Ferret – complied.

In the street, feeling stoned and strange and oddly exalted among the office fodder, Dorian found himself loitering with Wotton in front of a tailor's window. They contemplated a model gentleman, who was perfect in every way save for being headless. 'Who is Fergus?' Dorian asked, for want of any other thought to enunciate.

'The Ferret is immensely rich,' Wotton obliged, 'from property deals. He's also immensely queer; he has his own resident catamites. He's fairly posh – his father was Lord Rokeby. He's also nearly psychopathic – he killed a man once in an alleged skiing accident. Quite a feat, as I'm sure you can imagine.'

And with this, Wotton took his now somnolent and opiated acolyte by the arm and guided him in the direction of the Jag. It was time to take Dorian Gray somewhere else for more intimate and mysterious instruction.

3

A week later Henry Wotton called on the Ferret at his maisonette, which was high in one of those blocks on Chelsea Embankment that impart an almost Dutch feel to the view from across the river. It was another hot morning in the city. That summer Britain was in the process of burning most of its remaining illusions, which was why, perhaps, Henry Wotton felt more obliged than ever to drape his warped sensibility in the straightest of garbs. For this particular elevenses he opted for the green corduroy bags, the brown brogues, the powder-blue Pringle sweater, and the check Viyella shirt – what had been, still was and would remain the uniform of the seriously retarded country gent.

It was difficult to secure an invitation from the Ferret, who had that foible of men who have inherited a fortune and managed to multiply it: he was staggeringly mean. He didn't want to invite any-one round for a meal because he wanted it all. He wanted to gobble and be gobbled by a procession of Dilly boys. He wanted to snack on warm, free-range coddled eggs, lopped open and dusted with beluga caviar, while drinking the finest Champagne. And it was these vic-tuals that he was obliged to share with Henry Wotton, along with the sanctuary of his equally opulent rooms. Rooms that were like a calm pool of urbanity tucked behind the waterfall of the city.

The Ferret had serious taste. There were good Persian rugs on the parquet floors, fine modern paintings on the silken yellow walls. The place had an apian smell. Pollen, wax, royal jelly, honey. There were proper bookcases which appropriately sequestrated the Ferret's serious collection of weighty tomes. Outside, the sweep of the river was unusually glittery in the sun. Inside, all was furtive, comforting gloom.

The Ferret and his guest were being imperfectly served by the current catamite, yet another Dilly boy, Jon. He was a big, crop-headed bruiser who lent a tin ear to his silver service. Each time Jon offered the rack of toast, Wotton observed the word 'FUCK' tattooed on the knuckles of his right hand, and each time he charged Wotton's glass, the word 'CUNT' was manifested on the knuckles of his left. 'Thank you, Jon,' said the Ferret; 'now put it back in the cooler – the *bucket*, that's right.'

Wotton exhaled cigarette smoke over a small silver dish of truffles. 'I've taken a shine to that boy Gray,' he purred.

'I know,' his host slurred with fatigue.

'It's disgusting the way you know everything, Fergus – perhaps you're God?'

'That would be a turn-up.' The Ferret appeared to be genuinely pondering the ramifications; at any rate his old, lizard eyes were being occluded by near-transparent lids.

If the Ferret had been God it would have explained a lot. The occurrence of evil, for one thing, and the extent to which it thrived, because for much of the time he left the world to its own devices and slumbered, a curiously willing victim of narcolepsy. So it was on this occasion: the window of the Ferret's consciousness was slowly pulled to, and his brow declined towards the smoky truffles. 'Perhaps, *pour m'sieur un petit cachou?*' Wotton mimed pill-popping for Jon's benefit.

'I was gettin' one, mate.' He went to the sideboard and selected a pillbox from a display of bibelots and knick-knacks.

'What's he on nowadays?' Wotton adopted the hobbyist's tone he used for serious drug talk.

'Same as ever, five-mil Dexies in the day, tombstones or bombers if he's out on the razzle.'

'Spares?' A twenty-pound note appeared in Wotton's hand and was exchanged for the pillbox less the required dosage.

'C'mon, Fergus me old love . . .' Jon cradled the Ferret's head with surprising tenderness, and as the jowls sagged open, deftly inserted a couple of Dexies '. . . 'ave a little shampoo to wash 'em down . . .'

'Gaa! Oh – gaa! This is bitter.' He came round abruptly.

'It's always bitter – when you crunch 'em.'

'But I *like* crunching them – more Champagne . . . ah, better . . . much.' As the Ferret slurped, Jon continued to cradle his warty head. The lizard eyes flickered, opened and then focused on the twenty, which was still tucked between the 'N' and the 'T' on Jon's left hand. 'You young people imagine money will get you everything,' the Ferret said, without rancour.

Wotton reflected that he was a noble queer of the old school, who rather than paying his servants preferred that they steal from him with panache. 'And old ones like you know it full well.' He ostentatiously munched a Dexy of his own and snapped the box shut.

'You still here?' said the pocket Morpheus.

'I'm not going until you tell me what you know about Dorian Gray.'

'That would take simply hours . . .' the Ferret disengaged himself from Jon's arms '. . . I'm not prepared to have you remain for a fraction of the time necessary – you consume so much, Wotton, it's like having elevenses with a high-class bloody renter. Still, I was right about recognising him, I knew his bloody father – I know his bloody mother too. As a matter of fact he lives virtually next door to me . . . across the river behind Battersea Park –'

'Fergus, I know where his flat is, what I want to know doesn't appear in the *A–Z*. He's distinctly cagey about his family.'

'As well he might be.' The Ferret yawned expansively, stretched, rose and walked to the mantelpiece, which, instead of leaning upon as any average man might, he tucked himself beneath. 'Dorian's father was a peer and a curly-wurly. An habitué of the Grapes, he liked a bit of scarlet as we all did in the war –'

'The war?' Wotton was incredulous. 'Which war – the Crimean?'

'No, the Second. You youngsters take so much for granted, you know nothing of the way we were, the tenderness that can exist between men from quite different stations in life . . .' Reaching up above his head, the Ferret selected a photograph in an ornate gold and ivory frame from among many similar. It showed a young man in pillbox hat and frogged jacket. 'Ah well' – his eyes grew misty – 'I'm wandering. Dorian's father, Johnny Gray. He was a gambler and a drinker, part of the set around Lucky Lucan. What passed for a man of the world in the days when the world – for that sort of man – was the size of a schoolroom globe. He put on a grand show, indeed he did. Very upright, didn't want any whispers –'

'So how did you know he was queer?'

'Like I say, we had similar tastes. Must I elaborate? Anyway, he married Dorian's mother – Francesca Mutti – for what? Show, certainly, and I daresay issue as well. Although he already had an heir from a previous marriage, these types like a spare. I've heard it said he was vicious to the boy before a friendly aorta took him from us.'

'And the mother?'

'You've never heard of her, my dear! She was a thinner, more elegant Lollobrigida. Very beautiful, very sexy – if you like a pudendum, that is . . .'

*   *   *

For much of the time Henry Wotton wasn't altogether sure which human gender he preferred, or even if he liked sex with his own species at all. Pudenda? Pricks? Petals? What now?

It was true that his raving, rampant and still rambunctious drug addiction took up much of his energy, but he wasn't impotent – yet; and there was a deeper, stranger ambivalence at work in him than straightforward and manly homosexual self-hatred. Henry Wotton was prone to saying – to anyone who would listen – that 'the chameleon is the most significant of modern types'. And while his outer appearance – the suits from Savile Row, the accessories from Jermyn Street and Bond Street – would seem to belie this, the truth was that beneath Planet Wotton lay a realm of complete flux. He was a Mandarin intellect who had calluses from annihilating Space Invaders and a social climber who revelled in the most dangerous class potholing. He professed no politics other than revolutionary change – for the worse. In the context of such a comprehensively contrary temperament, his conflicted sexuality was almost superfluous. Or so he liked to imagine.

He also liked to imagine that what he looked for in a lover was not so much this face or that figure, let alone *style*. (Yech! How *poofy*, how *precious*, how *twee*, how *bide-a-wee*. Style – the very word could trigger the telling of another hundred decades on his internal rosary of contempt.) No, what Wotton sought was mortal clay to be moulded and shaped with a degree of definition that he felt lacking in himself. Henry Wotton wanted only to be *anybody* by proxy.

Basil Hallward, with his talk of being 'unashamed', his proselytising for 'gay' rights (another word that couldn't exist in the Wotton lexicon, save in so far as it applied to bunting), proved all too resistant to Wotton's project. But it wasn't on account of his pink militancy that he'd been discarded. Wotton didn't mind if his doppelgänger was a campaigning homosexual, in fact it suited him. It was rather because Baz clung on to such exalted notions of his own artistry that he had to go.

Baz would keep trying to reassert himself as a flamingo when Wotton was seeking to employ him as a croquet mallet. Not that Wotton thought of himself as a player – after all, what could he possibly do *were* he to be an artist, save price up piss bottles, and stack more shit cans on the shelves of the personal memorabilia mart? He knew Baz was right about the direction conceptual art was taking, and as for art that depended on more than craftiness, well, he had not the craft for that. People who met him at the square cocktail parties advertised by oblongs assumed that he styled himself as some contemporary dandy, *flâneur*, or boulevardier, and that he saw himself as a work of art. Whereas people who met him in squats, or at underground clubs, took it for granted that he had a private income. But neither lot was correct.

Wotton lived off his wife, Batface, and he had no other creations besides those, such as Dorian, whom he met and manipulated. Like some royal matriarch, Wotton himself displayed none of the grosser symptoms of misogyny; rather he was a carrier. No one – *avant la lettre* – could credit the idea that the Wottons had sexual intercourse. She seemed too vague and he too disengaged for them to bring their genitals into sufficient proximity with each other at the right time. If tumescent simultaneously, it was to be supposed there was a wall or a floor between them.

Still, if Wotton could achieve intercourse through solid surfaces, his imaginative gifts were equally magical. It took him only a short time in his lovers' company for him to be able to picture their doings with unbelievable accuracy. Henry Wotton could have written a brilliant book about the life and times of . . . Henry Wotton, but as he himself said derisively, 'The only circumstances in which I would write a *roman à clef* would be if I'd lost my fucking car keys.'

* * *

After a week's acquaintance with Wotton, which included a single night in the blood-red-painted bedroom he kept on the ground floor of his Chelsea home, Dorian found himself suffering from a florid bout of woman-hating. He despised their shape, their smell, their genitals, their gooey secretions – lachrymal, vaginal, emotional – their hair, their faces, the lilt of their voices. All of which was particularly unfortunate for the young woman he had been been making love to during his last term at Oxford. 'Making' in the sense that he was making it up as he went along, while she was assembling a prefabricated illusion for herself to inhabit. 'Love' in no sense at all.

She came to see him in London after a two-week lapse in phone calls. On his part. She went to his penthouse, which was on the posh, park-facing side of Prince of Wales Mansions. He let her in and she kicked off her sweaty sandals so as to feel the tiled floor cool beneath her hot soles. It was the fetid mid-morning of the same day Wotton rendezvoused with the Ferret. Dorian made tea for her in the splendidly-appointed kitchen, while she padded around the main room, combing the deep pile with her paws. She was feline and blonde, her name was Helen and she too was beautiful – if you like pudenda.

—What're all these monitors? she said.

—It's a video installation, a kind of TV sculpture.

—I know what that is.

—It's by this guy Baz I met.

Dorian went to a niche in the wall and dickered with switches. The monitors fizzed into life. On the screens the naked Dorians effervesced. Helen stared at the gorgeous bodies. Baz Hallward's piece was most cunning; it forced all who looked upon it to become involuntary voyeurs, Laughing Cavaliers, compelled to ogle the young man with eyes pinioned open.

—Is he a poof ? she spat out.

—What?

—You heard. Is the man who made this a poof ? You know what that is, right?

That's how it went, possibly. It's a mistake altogether to write off young women of Helen's sort, scions of the upper-middle-class Hampshire convent-school set, who go wild when they discover what's between their dewy thighs. She was smart enough to read theology, and perceptive enough to read what was in her tea leaves once she'd drained her cup.

—Why the Earl Grey?

—What?

—Why're you drinking Earl Grey? It's such a cliché.

—Oh . . . I dunno . . . this guy I know . . . he makes it . . . and he says the flavour's incomparable.

—Is that the artist?

—No, a friend of his, the son of the woman who's the benefactor for the Youth Homeless Project.

—Does *he* have a name?

—Wotton . . . Henry.

The silence between them wasn't awkward – it was boorish and stupid. Like a drunk, drooling student it bumped about the trendy minimalism of the penthouse, knocking into the blocky blue divans, the huge coffee table, the varnished wood pediments that supported *Cathode Narcissus*'s nine monitors. Dorian was so easily influenced – they both knew this. He took on other people's styles, modes and even habits the way kitchen towelling sopped up spilt milk. And was there any point in crying over this? When he'd begun fucking Helen he'd taken to drinking Lapsang Souchong – now he was getting infused elsewhere. *Of course* she'd known he was a poof, but only in the way we all know we're going to die.

Still, she unbuttoned the front of her dress, which was a hundred per cent cotton, and had a pattern of loose grey and black squares, like a plaid drawn by a preschooler. It had a vaguely 1920s cut – mid-length, with a tight bodice and a low waist. Remember, divide the decade of the original style by the decade of its revival to discover how many times it's been revived before. This equation holds good for the entire twentieth century, which was an arithmetic cultural progression of modal repetition. We digress.

She unbuttoned her dress to reveal bull's-eye breasts, brown on white on brown. Brown nipples on white flesh on brown ribcage. She hadn't broken with her background enough, yet, to sunbathe topless. She unbuttoned her dress to reveal the gentle landscape of her body, its soft loam and softer thickets. She let the dress fall from her warm, mole-seeded shoulders, and staying in the same decade adopted an art deco pose, by running a hand through her Eton crop before swallow-diving into the here and now of the penthouse. She held her position – her arms held back, chest thrust forward, like a static bonnet mascot.

Dorian – who appeared tightly buttoned into a Delphic

charioteer's suit even when he was stark naked – had never looked more wrapped up than he did now. He propped himself against the wall, white shirt cuffs turned up over smooth forearms, tea steaming, chest gleaming.

—You won't see me again, then, not ever? Helen's innocent gambit had failed and she sat with the lumpy inattention of a woman who has no modesty or allure, both having been stripped from her.

—Yes I will. We're friends. We were friends before we started screwing. Good friends, I hope.

—But it means you don't love me, doesn't it?

—Helen, I masturbate but it doesn't mean I'm in love with my hand.

—You used to do it with me *and* enjoy it. What is it? Aren't I *boyish* enough for you?

Exactly. She wasn't boyish at all. Furthermore, the cropped hair, the straight lines of her period modern dress, they only hoodwinked us momentarily, and once the ruse was revealed we felt worse than cheated by Helen's strident femininity: the ample breasts, the stippled aureoles, the healthy hips, all the generally insulting curvaceousness of her.

—Henry Wotton isn't boyish – Dorian spoke with some authority – he's a man.

—What – what d'you do with him? Does he . . . does he *sodomise* you? She did her best, but the term still sounded ridiculously technical when uttered in her plummy, pony-club accent.

—Actually, I bugger him. He prefers that. It's amazing, Helen – and this animality animated Dorian – when I fuck him he becomes completely pliant and emotional, like a strait-laced lady who's lost her head. It's an astonishing transformation.

It was an astonishing transformation in Dorian as well, but paradoxically the utter callousness with which the intimacies of her successor were flourished won Helen over. She realised – as so many women have before in such circumstances – that this new liaison was of a different order altogether – non-equivalent, inaccessible – and that the change wrought by this in Dorian was irrevocable.

—It all sounds perfectly revolting to me. Yucky.

—Oh believe me, Helen, it isn't, it just isn't.

* * *

Later the same day Dorian fetched up in Soho. Soho was, at that time, just gay enough but not yet the flagrant village it was to become. Janus the flagellators' boutique had recently opened, while the Swiss Pub was going strong, and other brittle, night-time hang-outs clustered like snails beneath the flat, stony sky of the city.

Dorian Gray felt this. He also sensed the quivering shaft of Eros's arrow as it was loosed and flew up Shaftesbury Avenue, a deathly love missile aimed by the renters straight at the junkies who huddled outside Hall's the chemist. The junkies caught it, transformed it into a hypodermic and flung it right back down again.

Dorian Gray stood outside the shabbily inconspicuous door of the Youth Homeless Project. It was late afternoon and the commuters clattered past him on their way home. However, Dorian wasn't going home, he was coming for the homeless youth he'd spent most time talking to, mucking around with, fancying. Coming to prey on this black chicken. But just as his hand reached for the buzzer, the door slammed open and out he came – at speed – pushing past Dorian.

He was unstoppable, as twitchy as an antelope – and as swift. His hair bounced on his electric head like a neat hank of black flexes, his bed-roll was slung over his shoulder and his elbows and knees stuck out, pumping. He was a conical mop-top of dusky fury, in among the piecrust white cotton collars of sub-Sloane Ranger office girls. Dorian managed to snag the black man as he paused to let the 19 bus plunge past.

—Herman . . . ! Man! Where you going, man?

—What the fuck's it t'you? He rounded on Dorian. He was belligerent, this Herman. Terribly aggressive. He was also the same height and build as Dorian. Lither, true, and more effeminate as well. Like a queer Oedipus, always threatening to scratch either your eyes out or his own.

—I'm sorry, I don't mean to piss you off. It's just – we were talking, and I thought you were staying –

—I can't stay in the fucking shelter, *I can't stay in it*. Herman wrenched himself away from Dorian and resumed weaving down Shaftesbury Avenue.

—But isn't that the whole point of the place –

—What? What!

—To stay the night.

—Listen. He stopped again. I can't stay in the shelter 'cause I can't fucking score in the shelter, an' I can't have a hit in the fucking shelter, an' if I can't have a hit I can't work, an' if I can't work I can't score. An' if a ponce like you, *Dorian*, is crawling up my fucking arse I can't do fucking either. Now walk, man – you're in my light.

—I don't mean to be – I thought we were getting on. We were talking.

—Shit! Talking.

—Look, if it's money you need, I'd be happy –

Dorian couldn't have spoken at a more opportune moment, for at that very moment, limping down the road came a pedlar legendary on the Front Line, and so closely associated in his clientele's minds with his produce (which, when you come to think of it, is exactly the same as with many retailers, fishmongers in particular), that he was known simply as the Dikes and Rits man. Or even just DR, or the Doctor.

This was eminently suitable, for the Dicanol and Ritalin that the Doctor sold were stolen or defrauded – or even received on legitimate prescription – by addicts, who used them as a cut-price version of the heroin and cocaine they craved. How fitting too that Ritalin should have become, in another decade, the drug of choice for pacifying those the medico-education establishment deem to have 'Attention Deficit Disorder'. Does speed really calm these hyperactive children, or does it merely allow them to become healthily fixated by the minutiae of our tiny society, with its toy cars and play buildings? Taking the long view, perhaps the West End junkies with their Dikes and Rits were the obsessive psychic abscess that, once burst, spread this poison throughout the body politic. Surely socialised medicine has always been a covert means of ensuring that all society is medicated?

The Doctor had the old street junky's trick of being able to project his voice directly into one's inner ear, so that his sales pitch was tossed several yards in front of the man himself.

—Dikes an' Rits, Dikes an' Rits, Dikes an' Rits, five'll get you three of one, ten'll get you two of the other, twenny gets you lucky dip. Dikes an' Rits – there's no gear on the Front Line, jus' Dikes an' Rits . . .

A folk dance of concealment then followed, as Dorian and his new sweetheart promenaded in the Doctor's trench-coated train, listening intently to his sleight-of-mind commentary, which was improvised for their sessile ears.

—I see you there, young Herman my lad, I see you there, I see you hungry. Hungry for Dikes an' Rits. Back from the West Coast, Cal-i-for-ni-a, an' wiv a massive fuckin' habit wot your sugar daddy given you. I see you there. Wot you want, eh? Gear? There's no gear on the Front Line. No amps neevah – jus' Dikes an' Rits. Thass all there is if this little chicken don't wanna do turkey. Cluckin' already, are you? Wossat, forty? Forty gets you twenny. Kosher, very kosher. Nice doin' business with you Herman, very nice indeed . . . Dikes an' Rits, Dikes an' Rits . . .

So it was that Dorian learned the facts about his bit of rough, and they only endeared Herman to him the more. After Helen and Oxford and sub-flapper dresses and japes and diving off bridges in the May morn and sucking dicks under dining society tables and all of *that*. This . . . this . . . he figured was life as it *must* be lived. Life as Henry Wotton lived it, foreshadowed by death. By death and degradation as well, for within minutes Dorian and Herman were

47

ensconced in the room of another of the black renter's admirers, a pudgily unthreatening skinhead dubbed 'Ginger' for his unpleasant furze.

Ach! Such astonishing filth and mess in this place. To have said 'room' would've been to dignify it, would've been to assume a recognisable floor, walls and ceiling in place of this peculiar, upended shoebox, which was poised atop four storeys of grime and grout, while being slowly strangled by rusty external drainage. Dorian reclined beside a half-open sash window on a bank of organic detritus. Filthy clothes, rotting banana skins, used syringes, stale crusts of bread. He stared up past the wan sun of a forty-watt bulb, dangling on its furred fifteen-foot length of flex, to a postage stamp of ceiling which sweated toxins.

Dorian had known that there was squalor like this in London, but never conceived of himself as part of it. Beside this – this *stinking entropy* – the mere messiness of Henry Wotton and Baz Hallward was just that: the wilful refusal of naughty boys to *tidy up their rooms*. This – this *infective moraine* upon which he lay was, Dorian realised, truly sordid. And this – this *ringside seat* as he watched Herman first do the laborious home chemistry required to syn- thesise a fix of Dikes and Rits, and then – then *punch holes* in his suppurating calf as he searched for a vein. This – this was something emphatically *not to write home about*. Not that there was anywhere to write to, unless you consider a Palm Beach hotel homy; nor anyone to read the missive who wasn't too addled by vanity and Valium to comprehend it.

Dorian watched Herman and Ginger watched Dorian.

—Aww fuck, that's evil shit, that is, said the gingerhead.

—I've no money for gear.

—I gave you the money. Dorian staked his claim. You could get some gear with that.

—Oh yeah? An' who's gonna get the nex' fix, anna one after that, an' that, an' that? What're you, a fucking chemist?

—Nah, he's another fuckin' sugar daddy Herm. Where you

48

taking him to, pretty boy? He's done the United States of Arsehole already.

What an awful compression they all experienced as Herman thrust the plunger of the huge five-millilitre syringe home, sending chalk and poison and Christ knows what other crud into his leg. They all felt it – Dorian, Herman, Ginger – the giant plunger of darkness pushing down the weeping sides of the space over their heads, the pressure boiling their blood, then popping their skins, so that their puréed bodies mingled with the grime and muck and the shit to concoct an ultimate fix: the filthy past injected into the vein of the present to create a deathly future.

—I don't need no more fuckers, fucking me an' then despising me. Herman grunted with the exertion.

—But what if they didn't?

—What?

—They didn't despise you? Herman finished fixing and with his index finger wiped the ribbon of blood wrapped around his leg. Dorian stared at him, green into brown. Herman was so beautifully suitable for patronising, like a buggered-up personification of Third World debt.

—That would be worse.

In one fluid movement Herman rolled forward on to his knees, grasped Dorian by the shoulders, and kissed him. Such suction. They were like two flamingos, each attempting to filter the nutriment out of the other with great slurps of their muscular tongues. Adam's apples bobbed in the crap gloaming.

4

It's little wonder that once the pressure built up and the melting-pot boiled over, the Metropolitan Police felt that radical sartorial changes were required. By the middle of the 1990s they were resplendent in Kelvar bulletproof waistcoats, submachine guns dangling across their chests like the ornate breastplates of modern primitives. But in 1981 they were compelled to enter the hail of glass vessels (some half empty, others half full of *parfum de fracas*) wearing knee-length blue macs and tit-shaped helmets. Their phalanxes had a makeshift appearance, as if the individual members had been press-ganged from the village greens of thirty years earlier, then bolted together to form usable squads.

They advanced – these naïvely-painted matchstick coppers – up Brixton Road, while the glass – which is itself a slow-flowing liquid – hard-rained down on them. They sheltered beneath their plexiglass riot shields as if they were flat, oblong umbrellas, and the Molotov cocktails promptly set these on fire. A couple of miles away, safe in his penthouse, Dorian Gray sipped his vodka martini and enjoyed the spectacle on one of his nine televisions. It was night-time and the treetops in the park across the road murmured dark green. The reflection of the riot flickered yellow and red on the smooth tan screen of his perfect face as he stood, legs apart, giving the correct formal shape to his immaculate Japanese kimono. Nearby, slumped on a sofa, was Baz Hallward, his shirt sweat-streaked, his hair lank, his leather trousers rank. So rank they might have only just been cut from some still more unfortunate beast. He too held a martini, but clearly this was a far from perfect moment for him. Is this live? he enquired of his host.

—No, you fool, it's a tape. Some friend of Henry's got it off a news cameramen he knows. Cool, isn't it?

—Fucking marvellous.

—I caught some of the action.

—You what?

—I saw some of the rioting, the action. I drove over to Brixton, but stupid squad turned me back at Acre Lane. Still, I got the scent of it –

—Stupid squad! Scent of it! You sound like Wotton.

—And what if I do?

Dorian had achieved more intimacy with Wotton in a two-week relationship than Baz had managed in two years. Baz felt shouldered out by a phalanx of Dorians. I suppose you haven't shown *Narcissus* much then? He tried, but casualness did not become him.

—To tell you the truth, Baz, looking at myself looking at myself looking at myself isn't exactly my idea of a turn-on, even if it's yours.

—That's not the fucking point, Dorian, it doesn't matter what I or anyone else wants to do with you. In the piece you aren't *you* – not in that way. You achieve a bit of fucking transcendence –

—Transcendence!

—Is that so ridiculous? Look – you can mock me, but you can't mock my work. I'll buy it back off you if you've no other use for it than *this*. He slopped alcoholic droplets at the screen.

—No . . . No, don't do that. It may be art for you, Baz, but for me it's . . . it's an alternative me. I said it when I first saw him – I'm jealous of myself; and now he's almost a whole month younger than me – and such buns!

—You're still laughing at me. I shouldn't give a shit – cruising queens and romance don't exactly mix – but I did try and say a true thing in all this . . . Baz did more slopping . . .'bout you, me, 'bout bein' gay, 'bout . . . stuff.

—Baz, you're wandering.

—Fuck it, Dorian. I'm all washed up, man. My habit's so chronic I wake up in the night with a hand at my throat and it's my own

. . . He slumped back, his head hanging . . . I'd go back to the States but they probably wouldn't let me in . . .

Dorian had begun to display talents in the only two areas of human life that are worth considering: he was becoming a seducer *par excellence*, and he was transforming himself into an artificer of distinction, a person who is capable of employing all of the objective world to gain his own end. If Dorian had been some Jacobean Machiavel, he would have swiftly acquired the means by which to introduce belladonna into a victim's eye. As it was, he dabbled in drugs.

He knelt in front of poor Baz, unwrapping just two of a succession of envelopes he'd bought from Honey. He withdrew the injecting equipment and a bottle of distilled water from a small Chinese cabinet set in a niche. No addict, Dorian was able to make good choices in bad faith, and so he had stockpiled. Have a hit if you feel like one – he said heavy things with great levity – I've white and brown. Have a speedball. A little of what you fancy does you good.

—What is this, Dorian? You're not doing all this shit, are you?

—No, not really. I've a friend . . . Dorian rose and sauntered over to the darkened picture windows. On arrival he peered at his own reflection . . . He's got a bad habit. I'm trying to help him. Actually, he'll be coming along tomorrow evening. I'm having a little *vernissage*.

—*Vernissage*? For what?

—For *Narcissus* – what else. Henry will be coming, naturally. He's asked me to invite a person called Alan Campbell – perhaps you know him?

Dorian had acquired Wotton's matter-of-fact tone for discussing facts as if they didn't matter. This was creepy enough, but creepier still was the lust with which he watched Baz take the hit. The pumping in and sucking out of the hypodermic – which both resembles coitus and also is experienced by the injector as a series of mounting waves of orgasmic intoxication – was what particularly aroused him. Yeah, Baz groaned, I know him. Australian. Bent doctor. Bent in every fucking way.

—Henry says he's very amusing. Anyway, my young friend needs connections of all kinds – *I* think he's rather talented. He does a sort of painting based on the ghetto graffiti. Picked it up in LA. *You* could be of help.

—Listen . . . Dorian . . . I don't wanna be a wanker –

—Then come, and don't be.

—But Wotton – Henry; and Campbell. I know what it's gonna be like. A lotta fucking drugs, rags out, amyl out, then circle-jerking . . . It'll all end up in a conga line of fucking buggery. You want that for your young friend?

—You want that for yourself, Baz?

In a few three-day weeks (forty hours awake, sixteen asleep – drugs and sex are not merely socially liberating, they secure a release from the calendrical straitjacket as well), Dorian had moved from ingénu to omnivore, which is always a delightful metamorphosis, especially when achieved at a grotesque, galumphing pace. Now, with the countervailing heroin and cocaine making him spuriously lucid, Baz succumbed to Dorian's advances with tense speed. Hands went to crotches, legs entwined. The vitreous perfection of Dorian's beauty shattered in Baz's mouth, and his acid saliva bit into Baz's tongue. On screen, on carpet, in Brixton, in Battersea, on videotape, in reality, men thrashed and bashed about in the violence of abandonment.

*   *   *

In Henry Wotton's childhood the years were inseparable and their events were confused. JFK stood trial in a glass booth in Tel Aviv and was sentenced to orbit the moon. In Henry Wotton's boyhood it was the seasons that were mashed, so that the boy Hal tobogganed down grassy slopes, or picked daffodils from among drifts of fallen leaves. But in 1981 it was *that* summer, the impossible one that budded and blossomed and fruited at once. It was perpetually a sunny mid-morning in the vicinity of Henry Wotton (as if time's arrow were a record player's sapphire stylus, to be picked up and returned to the same groove, over and over and over), and at a large bay window to the rear of his house (a window stinky-fringed by thick-stemmed amaryllis and thicker still arum lilies), Consuela, a stolid Filipino woman, could be observed banging a rug out on the windowsill. She was doing it unconsciously and yet with great physical concentration. If a tidal wave had hit she would undoubtedly have kept on going, her light-blue nylon housecoat whistling slickly in the sticky heat.

Behind her a tidal wave had hit. A tidal wave of debauchery. It was a room of substantial size and unnecessary length, with two entirely separate seating areas, one based around facing leather settees, the other centred on a group of armchairs. All of the furniture – and there was a lot – failed. There was expensive modern stuff that looked about as comfortable as a colonoscopy; there was spindly early-nineteenth-century clutter, evocative of mounting hysteria; and there were even some overstuffed Edwardian pieces, which lay about on the tawdry purple prairie of the carpet, as if they were recently slain buffalo. All this, together with a colour scheme notable for its sky-blues and lemon-yellows, produced an overall effect that was at once chilly and cluttered. A high level of indifference to their own habitat was integral to the Wottons' willed extinction.

More obvious pathogens took the form of occasional tables castellated with bottles and glasses, and ashtray after ashtray set upon surface after surface, all shedding cigar, joint and cigarette butts. The ash in one particular chair lay so heavily – on the back, the seat, the arms – that the outline of where someone had been sitting was clearly visible. It was as if a latter-day Pompeian had been extinguished by the eruption of a cigarette.

How sublime it is to eavesdrop on the rendezvous of spies, or to be a peeping Tom who specialises in watching voyeurs. The finest, most exquisite acts of betrayal are those of the double agent. Lying on a tubby sofa, in a towelling robe with 'Waldorf Astoria' sewn over the breast, was the lean form of Dorian Gray. He was reading *Against Nature* by Huysmans, the Penguin Classics edition with the portrait of the Comte de Montesquiou on the cover. He was surrounded by plumped-up cushions and appeared indecently comfy. His hair was wet, his adorable chest glistened in its fluffy housing. The uneasily dreamlike music of Debussy, or possibly Respighi, twined its strings and harps and cymbals in his blond waves. This allegorical scene – Industry in Opposition to Repose – demanded to be ruptured.

Batface could always be relied on in this capacity. She spun across the room and crash-landed next to Dorian. 'Whoa! Whoa! I'm most awfully sorry, Dorian, I didn't realise you were here,' she shouted over the violins. She was wearing a dress comprising several layers of translucent peach material, which was a ludicrous choice for a thirty-year-old such as herself. Poor Batface, with her strong features, which would have been so handsome had they not been permanently twisted into an asinine upper-class moue, and her straight limbs ever kinked by the puppeteer of embarrassment. 'Golly,' she gibbered on, 'I mean – *are* you here, anyway?' apparently confusing the real present with an undergraduate philosophy seminar from the not so distant past. 'I mean – oh, of course you are, silly, silly – what I mean is, what I mean is . . . y-you and Henry must . . . m-must *sleep together*!'

Batface spat it out at last, although she didn't mean it euphemistically and Dorian didn't take it that way. It was only the third – observing but unobserved – party who found this shamelessness on his part and her monstrously clashing horns remotely upsetting. She got up and began pacing, her floral dress trailing behind along with her words. 'Oh look! The jiggling man is jiggling in time to *Pini di Roma* and Consuela's beating. Oh, *do* come and see, Dorian.' Her frightened hands spread about her frightened face, a gesture that was her anxious essence. Dorian detached himself languorously from the sofa's embrace and joined her at the window. It was true, the jiggling man was up there, and he *was* in time. It was awful and claustrophobic, this Planet Wotton, with its grossly abbreviated growing season, and its tight orbit around the fixed sun of the jiggling man.

'It's odd,' Dorian said, as the beating and the jiggling and the violins all continued, 'Henry pointed him out from the studio garden when we first met.'

'He's quite obsessed . . . He thinks it's a portent, but it's more likely someone with Tourette's – they tic, you know. I myself don't believe in p-p-portents . . . but I d-do. Bother! I do in c-onnections . . . For example, this, here. Th-this cover picture on *A Rebours*. Henry gave it to you, I daresay. He fancies himself as de Montes-quiou, the real-life model for Des Esseintes, the decadent hero of Huysmans's novel. Incidentally, there's a copy of Baldini's original in the Langham Hotel of all places. But what interests me is that de Montesquiou was also one of Proust's models for the Baron de Charlus in *A la recherche*. Not that his period interests me *per se*, but Proust was ob-ob-obsessed by Madame de Sévigné and she does interest me . . . really . . . really . . . she . . . does.'

At last, her hesitations outlasting her words, Batface had stopped. Meanwhile the violins, the jiggling man and Consuela's beating all continued relentlessly. Dorian stared at Batface. He could see no attraction in her face, he had no compassion for her bonsai of self-esteem, and he had no real intellect himself to speak of, yet he could discern – and marvel at – the hidden order in the Batface world view.

'B-but,' she stuttered up again, 'I'm not talking about what I should be talking about, w-which is to ask you where Henry is – have you seen him?' Having at last managed to utter the query, Batface went over to the turntable, yanked the stylus off and scratched out the *Pines*. Consuela stopped beating, the jiggling man kept on making the pace for entropy itself. 'Yes, that was it. Very definitely.'

'Actually, he's with the police.' Dorian glossed this supremely Wottonish remark by filching one of his mentor's cigarettes from the pocket of the robe and lighting it with a gold Ronson.

'Oh dear – nothing boring, I hope?' It was Batface's major accom-plishment to render ignorance and insouciance utterly indistinguish-able. 'Henry does *so* dislike the police – he cannot abide them.'

Dorian was impressed. 'It's not exactly boring –'

'It's fucking murder – a murder inquiry.' To enter in *such* a theatrical fashion – through double doors, in full, midnight-blue, sharkskin-suited fig, and holding a bunch of white shirts (some of them prominently bloodstained) in his crooked arm – implied that Henry Wotton had been awaiting a cue. At any rate his lines were well prepared. 'Stupid squad snapped into action when the laundry service reported me for consistently dispatching claret-soiled clouts to them, and sent two of their finest round to interview me.'

'You mean,' Batface was intrigued rather than appalled, 'they don't actually have the *corpus delicti*?'

'Absolutely not. It's more a case of them adducing random evidence and then seeing if there's a crime that relates to it. Trouble is, if they look hard enough they'll probably find a victim, and then where will we be?'

Presumably not where Wotton currently was, namely floating upon a pink fluffy cloud of amused forbearance. He'd had *such* a good anecdotal feed, and so early in the morning. He thrust the bloodied shirts at Consuela, together with two or three rusty Spanish phrases, and turned to his wife. 'I trust the jiggling man's all right?'

'No one's murdered him, if that's what you mean.'

'Dorian is holding a little *vernissage* this evening, darling. For the video sculpture that Basil has made of this loveliness.' He was standing close enough to his lover to accompany this information with a brazen caress.

Predictably, Batface ignored it. 'Will there be talking?' she asked her rival.

'I dunno . . .' Dorian felt childish in the face of this mature indifference. 'I s'pose . . . some, at any rate.'

'Talking. Not my thing. Must demur. You won't mind? So kind . . .' And Batface wafted away, back to the seventeenth century.

Once she was gone, Wotton lost no time bearing Dorian into the tense present of the room behind the double doors. Such was the congruity of their home with the Wottons' relationship that this was Henry's bedroom, or, more properly, his fuck pad. Two tall parenthetic pier-glasses made whatever was said in a big bed eminently quotable. The counterpane was red, the silk bolster was red, the walls were red, the velvet curtains were red, the lampshades of the standard lamps were red. Only the carpet had escaped the massacre.

While Dorian resumed lounging, Wotton crossed to where a table-top fridge resided on a gilt-painted escritoire. He opened it and retrieved a hypodermic, its plunger extended, its barrel full of red blood. 'As if in anticipation, I was actually having a hit when the constabulary called on the related matter. I popped it in here to stop it clotting . . . there!' With one fluid motion Wotton commenced injecting the room's colour scheme into his main line. 'Ah!' he grunted. 'Fixing coke is the perfect modern pleasure, because even as you do it you want to do it again. It's like powdered greed dissolved in desire. All of human striving is here – measured out in millilitres.'

Dorian affected to ignore Wotton's moustache of chemical sweat, just as he blanked the Z of pink water that the bandit sprayed on the wallpaper with his hollow épée. He examined his cuticles and drawled, 'Why didn't you tell me, Henry, that the only boys worth loving are black boys?'

'Because I've loved so many of the ragamuffins myself. I presume we are discussing your friend Herman?'

'Naturally – he fills my waking hours.'

'But he hasn't been within your budding grove yet, now has he?' Wotton prowled jerkily over to where Dorian lay and groped his flanks for fags and lighter. He lit up and blew a perfect smoke ring, which was curiously substantial as it trundled across the subdued room.

'He's uptight,' Dorian mused. 'He'd fuck if I paid him to, but I don't want him to take me for just another trick. So we snog. I sort of like the idea of him, Henry, as a courtly figure. What was the fairy-tale lady in the tower called, the one with the long hair?'

'Rapunzel.'

'That's it. I like the idea of Herman as a black Rapunzel.'

'Come now!' Wotton snorted. 'You're being absurd – what are

you going to do, shin up his dreadlocks? My dear Dorian, if love is every man's psychosis, you're crying out for a major sedative.' Wotton leant in to Dorian still more, so that the contours of their bodies fitted. 'More pressingly,' he breathed, 'are you sure you want to expose Herman – sensitive renter flower that he is – to the likes of burnt-out Baz, and flame-grilled Alan, on an evening that I trust will be more than *outré*?'

'Why not? We could help him, Henry. After all, he's got nothing – nothing but a huge drug habit.'

'Now that is something I can entirely sympathise with. Being poor would be an absolute tragedy. So poor that you had to be straight. The poor may take the occasional cheap day return to oblivion, but only the rich may maintain a villa there.'

Dorian struggled to keep afloat in this turbulent repartee. 'But he isn't straight, Henry, not at all . . . But – look – I do hope you won't all be *too* decadent –'

'*Too* decadent? Who gives a shit about being too decadent, when to be contemporary is to be absolutely so? Besides, it's up to you whom you invite, it's your *vernissage*.'

'That's why I invited the artist –'

'I suppose you had to.'

'Why are you so down on Baz? He's really in quite a bit of trouble now. He says his habit's out of control.'

'Ridiculous.' Wotton set off on a prowl around the room, picking up and adjusting drug paraphernalia the way a dowager dusts picture-frames. 'And I'm not down on Baz, I simply object to his wasting things – you boys, my drugs, his talents – he should take more pleasure in these things. Pleasure is Nature's credit rating. When we are happy we are always good, but when we are good we are not always happy.' He fetched up back by Dorian.

'Baz said he thought he might die for love of me.' Dorian sounded entranced . . . by himself.

'*Encore ridicule*, but so what, to die for the love of boys would be a beautiful death.' However, immediately after saying it Wotton realised that this had been a *mal mot*, an anathema, or worse some reflexive juju. He felt the breath go out of himself as if he'd been punched in the solar plexus. He staggered, reached for Dorian, grabbed for the lapels of the robe as if they were the ropy rails of a makeshift bridge swinging over an abyss.

'Henry!' Dorian grasped the slick-suited shoulders, felt the cold, damp weight of the man against his own bare chest. 'Are you all right?'

In pulling himself upright Wotton succeeded in pulling the robe off Dorian altogether. They stood, the one clothed, the other naked, and in becoming aware of this contrast both became lascivious – hands groped for groins, fingers grasped, throats groaned. With one arm Wotton stripped off his tie, shrugged out of his jacket, peeled away his shirt, all the while tightly embracing Dorian. His kisses were avid, his movements precise and clinically sexual. But as soon as he had entirely disrobed – to reveal a body surprisingly slight, its marbled skin pebbledashed with red freckles – Wotton transformed, becoming pliant. Dorian assumed the dominant role, led him to the big bed, peeled back the covers, pushed Wotton down, reared above him. Dorian's penis was curved, red and gnarled with veins like the dagger of an alien warlord.

*   *   *

In Soho ten hours later, the deathly and dying boy ran up Old Compton Street, breasting the solid citizens as if they were a fluid element. They scattered – these plump Americans in search of musical theatre – but in Herman's wake came Ginger, singing out discordantly, Her-man!

On the corner of Dean Street he caught him, and Herman rounded, spitting, Get off, man!

—What you doin'?

—Get off!

—What you doin'? Ginger wouldn't let go. Passers-by assumed it was a racial assault and hurried on.

—I'm going somewhere –

—You're fucking meeting 'im – aren'tcha?

—What if I am?

—He's a sicko, a perv, a fucking nonce.

Herman shucked Ginger off and plunged up Dean Street, shouting back, He said he was gonna help me – he's an artist, after all. He's gonna introduce me to his friends.

—Oh yeah, like fuck; it'll jus' be another gang of rich poofs who wanna fuck you.

—Yeah, and that'll be a first.

—I'm warning you Herm, the pudgy skin sob-shouted, If you go with this one I'm not gonna fucking be here when you get back. That's it mate – it's fucking over!

At the corner of Meard Street, Ginger gave up. He stood in stolid pain, his suety face shredded with the love of Herman, as his lover escaped down the narrow passageway between the old house fronts. Halfway along, Herman realised he was alone and turned back.

—Don't go, Herman! Ginger choked on the words, and his cheeks, his brow, his lips shifted and twisted as anger vied with pain. Herman turned back the other way, to see, across the far end of Meard Street, a substantial limousine pulled up by the kerb. The door was open, and seated in the back, his gold hair effulgent in this jewel-box setting, was Dorian Gray. I've seen you, Prince-fucking-Charming! I've seen you!

This outburst decided Herman. Propelled by the force of Ginger's emotion he ran towards the car, jumped in and immediately embraced Dorian. The door clunked and the car pulled away. Ginger was left screaming after them in the gathering London dusk. Her-man! Her-man! Her-man!

5

The soles of your feet snagged and scratched by twigs, sap smearing your calves, you proceed on tiptoes over the treetops of Battersea Park. Occasionally your passage disturbs a nesting pigeon, which burbles with sleepy alarm. This portion of London is an old shambles, where stagnant water once lay and gypsies encamped to render horseflesh down for glue, which is why bad air so adheres to the place. No amount of imperial landscaping can cover up this malodorousness, the swamp that lies beneath the pleasure gardens and the miasma percolating up through the run-down ornamental terraces.

You pause in the clearing between one stand of trees and the next, hovering above the boating lake, looking down on its brown lapping of pondweed and sweet-wrappings. No, this is not an era for municipal grandeur. The city, feeling itself to be moribund, is simplifying its routines, deaccessioning its most solid and durable possessions in favour of sentimental trinkets and plastic gewgaws. It wants to move into a gigantic granny flat, where – while still preserving the illusion of independence – it can have all of its practical needs taken care of.

In the mid-distance, bright yellow pinpricks indicate the dark liner of the Prince of Wales Mansions, as it slides through the inky urban night.

In memory arrivals were always made of this: the oblique and the impossible, as one tunnelled up from below into the brightly-lit burrow, or swung in through a skylight on a flying trapeze. But even if it cannot be recalled, it must be assumed that Henry Wotton arrived for Dorian Gray's *vernissage* by means of his car. Because that was how he arrived almost everywhere in those days, the car being, he said, a kind of mobile potting shed in which he might sit and muse and infuse. Smoke, mostly.

Wotton drove south over Chelsea Bridge, circled the roundabout once, looking for the exit, but decided not to take it for magical reasons. He circled it again and again and again, until forced off by dizziness and fear of the police.

Despite being extremely late – the result of car keys hopelessly lost in the domestic forest – Wotton parked the Jag in Lurline Gardens and sat there for a full three Sullivan's Exports. He smoked the unnaturally fat and white cigarettes while grimacing into the rear-view mirror, squeezing blackheads and smearing their yellow-white lode across the piebald areas of the windscreen the wipers had failed to reach. Eventually he got out, locked the car and walked up the street. Fifty yards further on he couldn't remember whether he had locked the car, so he returned to check it. He repeated this exercise five more times before he realised that if he were to continue in this fashion for much longer he would, *de facto*, be insane. So he wrenched himself around the corner to the front door of the block, and pressed the buzzer. He muttered into the intercom, entered the vestibule and ascended in the lift.

Ah yes! But in Wotton's recollection it was always an ambulatory arrival that he'd made, sixty feet up in the sky, sliding smoothly from the dark verglas without on to the icy pile of the carpet within. *Vernissage* – such a great, glissading word – literally 'a varnishing'. It was, in every sense. That night, every encumbered soul in the minimalist apartment was completely stripped and then thoroughly coated.

Wotton took the view that such orgies were no less than the shucking off of the threadbare constraints of contemporary morality, and yet, even at the time, he also understood that in some crucial yet indefinable way (was it for solace alone?), a slave's morality *might* be preferable to the whips and chains of a mastery that was already becoming little more than attitudinising.

Perhaps it was this division within himself that explains why

Wotton was so dilatory in even arriving. As the brass booth rattled up five floors, he thought of fascistic chic, and how his companions' sense of history was savagely concertinaed, like a speeding limousine that's hit a concrete pillar. Was it any wonder that in place of any real ceremonial or culture of their own, they'd sooner watch the expensive charades invented for a German ruling house by a nineteenth-century popular novelist? Namely:

'The royal-fucking-wedding! What's this?' He had found the door on the latch and banged through it to confront Dorian, Baz, Herman and Alan Campbell grouped around one of the *Cathode Narcissus* monitors, watching a videotape of the ceremony.

'I think it's quite amusing,' Dorian drawled. 'I love all this ancient pomp.'

'Ancient pomp! Repro charade more like it. The whole ghastly business was dreamt up by these Krauts when they got the regime in the last century. Perhaps a more honest ceremonial would've been for them to broadcast the results of the virginity test the future brood mare was compelled to undergo.' And Wotton, sloughing off his overcoat as a lizard abandons his skin, grabbed for a Champagne flute from a tray that stood atop the monitor. He would've continued – having warmed to his theme – but Baz, who was sweating and twitching, saw fit to add complaining to his roster of active verbs.

'I thought this was a *vernissage* for *Cathode Narcissus*.'

'No no, it's a *vernissage* for this – this *black* Narcissus . . .' Wotton advanced towards his quarry, hand outstretched. 'You must be Herman – Dorian has told me fabulous things about you.'

'Yeah?' Herman neglected to take it.

'Oh yes indeed. He says you are beautiful and talented, and Dorian is too wise to be foolish in such matters.'

'Yeah, an' he wants to fuck me.'

'You are direct – very direct. But I rather think you're mistaken. The way I understand it – and I hope Dorian will support me – he would far prefer it if you were to fuck him.'

'Who cares about fucking anybody?' Baz broke in. 'Let's see the fucking installation.'

To forestall any more of Wotton's attempts at seductive badinage, Baz went over to the niche where the video recorders were stacked and began changing the tapes.

'Whatya gonna do with the thing now it's done, Dorian?' Alan Campbell said. Campbell was a man it was easy to avoid bestowing attention upon. He was, Wotton averred, 'far too evil to be seen in close-up'. Older than the others – perhaps as old as forty – wiry, dapper, with salt-and-pepper hair and a neat moustache, he was dressed conservatively in dark slacks, a brown pullover shirt and a tweed jacket. His accent was that particular kind of emotionless Australian that suggests a willingness to do anything to anyone. In Wotton's wonky circle his notoriety rested on two, equally contaminated grounds. First, his willingness – as a medical doctor – to prescribe with great liberality; and secondly, his attempt to hang Francis Bacon.

It was in the mid-sixties. Bacon – together with the photographer John Deakin – was cruising the roughest of the West End spielers looking for the roughest of trade. They found Campbell and his crew, who abstracted the master of the figurative back to a basement in Dalston. 'I dunno what possessed me, but I thought, if he wants it he can have it. So I flipped this length of clothes-line over a beam and went to get the end round his neck. I'll tell ya this for nothing, when he realised it was for real he fought like a fucking tiger. Only a little bloke, but he fought like a fucking tiger . . .' And got away. Campbell had been making a killing out of the murderous anecdote ever since.

Dorian gave Campbell's question serious consideration – engendering a charming pout-and-eyebrow-cleft combination – before answering, 'I hadn't thought. I don't *think* I shall allow it to be exhibited, not unless Baz demands it. Perhaps instead I'll hold an exclusive *vernissage* like this one every decade, and we can all meet up again to see what odd lines time has inscribed on our faces, while this *Narcissus* has remained permanently in flower.' As he was speaking the monitors pranged into the present, the Dorians pirouetted and pranced. The five men ranged in front of the nine monitors stared at their cathode partners. The sophisticated music of a lobby orbiting the earth floated through the lunar apartment, and Dorian, showing no aversion any more to contemplating his own loveliness, was obviously smitten.

Everyone who isn't a pseudo-intellectual loves television – it's so much *realer* than reality. That night was a television night. You could say the tempo increased when the poor sweet Herman got in on the act, but it demeans him to speak of good acting, which is such a tragi-fucking-comic oxymoron. But while sex undoubtedly melted the social ice, it was drugs that really heated the water then ripped out the thermostat altogether. You can always rely on drugs to do that, although their exigencies can be a tad extreme.

Herman understood what was required of him as linked arms became caressing hands. He moved to embrace Dorian and slid his own brown ones up under his host's tight white T-shirt. Their tongues slid out and in, but at that point Wotton imposed himself once more as the conductor of this sinister gavotte. 'Hold it! My dear fellows, you must desist until Alan has given us his ultimate fix. It's absolutely key to the whole tempo of the evening.'

It was a tempo that accelerated as Campbell got out his doctor's bag and lined up ampoules with professional precision. He snapped them open and sucked up their contents with a vast syringe, as if he were an artilleryman loading intoxicating ordnance. His delight in such gunnery extended in a continuum between work and play. It was all a bit of a blur for Alan, shooting up friends and fucking them, shooting up patients and fucking them as well. His piquant cocktail on that night was five cc of heavy derangement for five apocalyptic jockeys – although there was some bridling in the paddock.

'I'm not sure about this, Alan,' said Dorian. 'I've never injected before.'

'Dorian,' Wotton admonished him, 'no cultured man ever refuses a new sensation, and no uncultured man even knows what one is.'

'I'm more concerned with what the cool man does.'

'Cool is a semantic concept, Dorian – since when have you been a semiotician?'

'What're all those amps, anyway?' Baz broke in.

'There's some methylene-dioxyamphetamine' – Campbell rattled out the synthetic syllables – 'it was called the love drug in the sixties; this batch is straight from Sandoz. Then there's some ketamine, which is an analogue of phencyclidine – PCP to you guys. The main effect of the MDMA is to increase psychic empathy, while the ketamine makes you confused about whether you have a body or not. Then there's just good ol' diamorph', good ol' Methedrine, and a few dampers and buffers to make sure our rigs stay in shape.

'We're gonna have to share this works by way of making it a thoroughly co-operative venture,' the bad nurse continued, 'and that means precise flushing by everyone, gentlemen. One cc each. Now, I've tested you two for hep' already' – he ruled out Baz and Wotton with the needle's tip – 'Dorian doesn't need testing and I know I'm clean – but I don't know nothin' 'bout you, soldier, no offence.' The needle transfixed Herman.

'I'm clean, man, I ain't even been shooting up.' Herman was hungry for that hit and he meant to be first. He unbuttoned his shirt-sleeve and rolled it up to show the assembled company how free of track marks his arm was.

'We believe you, man,' Baz said. He was hungry too – he was constantly ravenous. Shouldn't Dorian have said something? He'd seen Herman fixing in his pox-ridden legs, he'd seen the ruckled pus-scape, which was like some miniature terrain, an awful environment perfect for viral propagation. But Dorian said nothing.

It was a strange blending of the essences of the five men. One cubic centimetre out of that arm and another into this arm, arm upon arm upon arm, black upon white upon brown, while the transparent proboscis probed. 'It suck'd me first, and now sucks thee / And in this flea, our two bloods mingled bee'. And when it was done, the tempo didn't so much accelerate as disappear altogether around the chicanes of their collective consciousness. Like Muybridge men, the five moved to engage, each appearing to the others to trail behind him a series of more solid after-images, while the music tinkled and thrummed and howled and thudded over their bodies. Love! the doomed boy sang, Love will tear us apart!

Half-naked they swayed in a loose thicket of wavering arms, rubbing crotches. Their fluttering tongues agitated the smoky air, while the amyl-soaked rag circulated. They were all awesomely high, as Dorian eluded first one and then another's grasp, until he manoeuvred himself into his desired position in what can only be described as a conga line of buggery. But it was to be his last contact with Herman for that and all succeeding evenings, because after a few staggering lunges, Dorian jumped out of the sodomites' queue, then lurched across the room and in through a darkened doorway.

Herman was abandoned and he was deranged. His eyes were vacant, his blue-black cheeks flecked with white foam. The host having departed the proceedings prematurely, it was left for his guests to essay the many different and pleasing combinations that occurred to them. Which they did – indeed they did – until that busy old fool the unruly sun arose, and Cinderella's carriage turned into . . . a Jaguar.

Just as Herman was picked up, so was he dropped off at the end of Meard Street in the crap gloaming that was his natural lighting. Wotton sat at the wheel of the car, his sharp profile etched against glass, awful rheum at the corners of his saturnine mouth. He turned to Herman. 'Since Dorian appears to have taken on the role of your patron, I think it only civil to reward you handsomely for an evening of such enchanted theatricals.' From his waistcoat pocket Wotton withdrew a drug wrap that was fatter than it was broad.

'Yeah, whatever.' Herman took it and quit the car. Before

shutting the door he leant down to say 'Fuck off' to Wotton – in the most robotic and unfeeling voice the older man had ever heard.

After Herman had gone, dragging his sore, stinging legs off up the alley, Wotton sat for a few minutes, savouring the desperation. Then he flicked the car into drive.

*   *   *

Back at Ginger's upended room, the tenant had been driven away, leaving behind his static car seat. The remains of last night's supper – Tuinal and Special Brew – were scattered on the festering mulch like strange fruit. Herman crouched down unsteadily on this jungly floor. As he got out his works and cooked up a fix, an observer would have been acutely aware of the harsh noises floating up through the open window – traffic, sirens, shouting – and the harsh light in the trashed room. Wotton had tipped him with a big mound of beige heroin, and Herman was intent on taking it all. He didn't even bother to mix citric acid – or even vinegar – with the gear, so it wouldn't dissolve properly, and he siphoned it out of the cruddy spoon without troubling to filter it.

When he rolled up his sleeve to take the fix in the main line, his whole attitude was one of broken despair. An observer would've noted at this point the glimmer of tears on his cheeks and realised that he was intent on suicide. But what could any observer have done? It was too late already, surely? If Herman wasn't to die that day, he was to die another not long thence. It would be folly, wouldn't it, for a hypothetical onlooker to blame himself for this inevitable – and not even premature – demise. Wouldn't it?

The mammoth syringe-load was rammed home and Herman pitched forward into his final abyss. The blood rushed and thudded in his inner ear, like the electronic beat of a synthesised drum machine. Herman's death – was it a peculiar form of tocsin? Instead of London calling – was this something calling it?

*   *   *

At home, in Chelsea, Wotton was already ensconced, such was the insane alacrity of his driving. He was in the drawing room, morning fruit juice in hand, staring up at the jiggling man. In the mid-distance a power tool was drilling holes so as to attach the world more securely to the present. 'Death,' Wotton mused aloud, 'is first and foremost a career move.'

*   *   *

Beached on a futon, on the far side of the river, lay Dorian in all his loveliness. Could he hear the thudding blood in Soho? Certainly his face twitched in time with its awful rushing rhythm. If only it would stop – but it wouldn't; instead it woke him up. He rose, with the pained recognition of last night's fun smeared over his handsome chops. He stalked into the main room: the blinds were wide open, the detritus of druggery and buggery spread across the carpet brightly illumined. What a night! His guests had departed without remembering to turn the nine monitors off. Yes, there they were, so many cathode Narcissi, all prancing and pirouetting in time with the gross thumping of his hangover. He moved towards the screens, and the banging against his temples rose to a crescendo, as if some soul burglar were attempting to escape. Then Dorian saw it: the faces on the screen had all changed – and for the worse. An exaggerated moue twisted his formerly flawless mouth. A distortion of a perfect symmetry such as his was far worse than a harelip on an ordinary face. He grimaced and drew closer – surely there must be some grease or fluid on the screens? But no. Closer and closer he drew, until all he could see were lines of dots leading into the future. His temples rang like a bell as his conscience clapped at their insides.

Dorian's face. Wotton's face. Herman's face. Dorian's face. Wotton's face. Herman's face. Eyes wide open. Eyes wide open. Eyes wide open. The reels came to rest. Vomit on Herman's chin. Vomit on Herman's chin. Vomit on Herman's chin. Three of anything paid generously – in the coin of Misfortune.

PART TWO

Transmission

6

Rear up and pull away from Herman's dead face, because, hey, that's what everyone does. They rear up and pull away from the faces of the dead. They reel back – and in so doing they cast away the years. Recency is its own reward – and so much better than the Regency. Only a very few of the dead are vouchsafed the ability to reach a wraith-like hand from beyond and tap somebody they have known on the shoulder. Some warm body who's hurrying up a crowded street, in the full light of day, on his way to an important encounter with an old friend.

Ten long years. A camera stealing the several souls of the city, capturing perhaps an image every hour, what could it tell us about the passage of time? Only that this or that building has been replaced by another without our even noticing. Best not to meddle. Never mind. Days and nights strobe past, the traffic is a river of light and time is a tidal bore.

In Charlotte Street ten long years had passed. The newspaper headlines held aloft by hands at café tables shrieked 'Civil War in Yugoslavia!', and 'Body Count of Milwaukee Murderer Reaches 18!'.

Among the countless heaving bodies of the crowd, there was one hurrying figure that forced itself out of the mass, as a card is forced by a sharper. It was Basil Hallward. He was ten years older, it was true, and he looked thin and wan – not at all well generally – but it was also evident that he was straight: scrubbed in appearance – with his grey, single-breasted suit, white shirt and leather shoes – and clean from drugs as well. His eyes were clear and direct behind rimless spectacles, and he strode along with lively purpose, as if health and vigour could be achieved by bad acting alone.

Baz made his entrance to the 1990s marching between an honour

73

guard of gays – if that doesn't sound too absurd. Here, in Fitzrovia, close to both the hospital complex and the burgeoning gay village, there was a preponderance of homosexual men. They sported greased head hair, pencil-line facial hair, earrings and white vests, the better to show off their easy-to-wipe skin tones. Some were gaunt-jawed and slope-shouldered, others were pumped up and overly active.

Turning the corner into Goodge Street, Baz came face to face with a policeman and a security goon. The latter had come in kit form, complete with snap-on dark glasses and a plastic pigtail connecting his red ear to his blue collar. They were staunching a small flow of pedestrians, while in the roadway another cop arrested some traffic.

—Would you mind waiting for a moment please, sir?

—Is there anything the matter, officer? Baz was amused by the cop's courteous manner; it wasn't what he was used to.

—Nothing to worry about, sir, just be a few more seconds 'til they're clear. The goon's ear squawked and he barked at his two colleagues in an American accent, OK, let's roll it up now gentlemen!

The cop in the street directed the traffic to pull over to the kerb. There was a short siren yelp and two motorcycle outriders came from the direction of the Middlesex Hospital travelling surprisingly fast. They were followed first by a Lincoln Towncar bearing the Stars and Stripes, and then by a customised Daimler with the royal crest poised on its roof as if it were a petrified floral tribute.

The other bystanders craned to look through the tinted glass of the cars. In the first sat Barbara Bush, who, in common with every First Lady since Jackie Kennedy, closely resembled a male-to-female transsexual. In her case, rubicund features and a white smoke cloud of hair suggested she would be more comfortable on the front step of some Appalachian log cabin, corncob pipe in puckered mouth, whiskey jar to hand. In the Daimler, the pale profile of the Princess of Bulimia sluiced through the street. There was a chorus of 'Ooh's and 'Ah's in their wake, but Baz wasn't paying any attention. He powered on through the loosening cordon in the direction of the hospital. There he strode across the forecourt, which was empty save for a knot of medical staff enjoying a post-royal-visit cigarette.

Inside, Baz paused to enquire where Broderip Ward was, then followed these directions along corridors, through hallways, up staircases, past all the usual traffic of a workaday hospital: patients on trolleys, patients in wheelchairs, posters advertising diseases, auxiliary staff, uneasy civilians. Everywhere he went was spick and span and therapeutically colour-coded. The interior designers had been summoned when the Royal Fag Hag began to take an interest in the gay plague and came to open the Broderip. Yet just inches away from where Baz strode were ventilation ducts choking on infective fluff and stagnant puddles of mop wipe, each with its own malarial vector. But he wasn't to know, old Basil, zooming forward with his missionary zeal.

On the fifth floor he skated across the polished floor to a blond-wood desk beside a plate-glass window, where a blond nurse with wooden features sat smouldering with anger. Like so many of the nursing staff on Broderip he would soon be burnt out altogether. He fixed Baz with an appraising eye; if called upon to, he could've given his T-cell count to within ±10. Do you know where you're going? he asked.

—I'm looking for a Mr Wotton.

—Henry's got his wife with him at the moment. Is he expecting you?

—I called this morning and said I'd be coming.

—Oh, *you're* Baz Hallward . . . It seemed as if the nurse was going to add to this, but he didn't.

—That's right.

—Yes, he's definitely expecting you – in fact, he's looking forward to seeing you, said you'd be an antidote to our royal visitor –

—I'm sorry?

—Princess Di, she was here a few minutes ago – didn't you see the kerfuffle on your way in? It's a pity she had to bring that warmonger's wife with her.

The nurse – whose name was Gavin – might have been about to add to this as well, but at that moment Batface appeared by the nursing station in a gyrating tangle of plastic bag, handbag and car keys. As if only ten minutes had passed, she was in the same purposeless dither as ever. She looked older, certainly, but none the worse for wear. In fact, her rather more matronly habit – a well-cut scarlet two-piece, dark tights and serious pearls – acted as a visual sedative, making her daffy delirium much easier for onlookers to bear. Um yes, Gavin, sorry to bother you . . .

—Yes, Lady Wotton?

—Quite discomfited by Diana Spencer – not that we know her, excepting *en passant*, but still, not ex-pec-ting her. No, not at all. Wanted to curtsy, but Henry's so against such deference. Calls curtsying 'waterless peeing' – vulgar but apt. Anyway . . . Henry says it's quite all right with you people if he discharges himself tomorrow . . .

—That's OK.

—I'll pick him up after lunch, seminar in the morning, have to bring Phoebe, Nanny's got the dentist . . . It's of no interest to you, Gavin, of course . . . but Henry insists on a little smackerel from F-Fortnum's for supper, his friend Bluejay will bring it by – at around nine?

—Now Lady Wotton, you know we don't like Henry's friend Bluejay on the ward – for obvious reasons . . .

—Oh, absolutely, I quite understand, he can be rather silly. I'm not keen on him at home, either, but Henry is most insistent, says he'll discharge himself before the ward round if Bluejay can't call by. Asked me to ask you most especially . . .

—As far as I'm concerned this will be entirely for your sake – not Henry's. Do you understand me, Lady Wotton?

—Oh, ab-so-lutely, Gavin, f-fully comprehended. Most grateful, many thanks, must go now . . . meter . . . Batface was about to depart but then she noticed Baz. Is it Basil Hallward?

—It is. He went forward to her and their cheeks collided drily.

—It must be five years since I've seen you.

—I'd say more like ten.

—Henry told me you were coming; he's very much looking forward to it – he only wants to see his old friends now he's got this b-b-bug . . . He told me you'd given up on the art world, taken another direction, quite changed your life . . .

—That's right, Batface. I'm hoping I can help change Henry's as well.

—Oh, too late for that I should imagine, ha ha, still . . . She whinnied nervously, sensing she'd said too much, then cantered on. You'll be in London for a while, won't you? Have you somewhere to stay?

—I'm all right.

—Oh, well, but you'll dine with us . . . tomorrow? And most days . . . Henry will want that, I know. He's just the same as ever – anyone he wants with him he wants with him all the time.

—I should like that, Batface.

—Good good, settled then, tomorrow. Bye Basil, bye Gavin, must dash.

And she was gone, although to describe her egress as dashing would have been a mistake – she clunked off on court shoes, pigeon-toed, arms akimbo. The two men exchanged looks, each warning the other not to mock.

—So, Baz, Henry's free now. He's in Room 6, and you'd better go and see him before bloody Bluejay turns up.

There were small cuboid rooms ranged along the mind-numbingly magnolia corridor, and divided from it by waist-to-ceiling windows with embedded wire graticules. Here and there a carpeted ledge supported a desiccated magazine rack or a succulent pot plant. The atmosphere was one Baz had come to expect; he'd been in many similar places. But what he'd never come to accept were the jerkily animate versions of Munch's *The Scream* that thronged the corridor.

Of course, this was a sight that many others never even bothered to *admit*; and which those who did managed to banish entirely, from the arrogant vantage of having read newspaper articles about effective combination therapy. If such stick-figure vistas existed anywhere any more – they thought – it was in Kinshasa or Kigali or some other sub-Saharan K-hole.

But in the Broderip Ward on that day in 1991, there were whole squadrons of young men with Bomber Command moustaches who had been targeted with the incendiary disease. Their radiator-grille ribcages and concentration-camp eyes telegraphed the dispatch that this was less a place for the mending of civilian injuries and quotidian wounds than a casualty station near the front line with Death. And if further confirmation were needed, it came in the form of the ongoing triage that accompanied these men. They clumped along on Scholl's and Birkenstocks (natural footwear hardly alleviating their neuropathy), pulling their drips with them on wheeled stands. Their faces were studded with Kaposi's sarcoma, and every third eye was patched. Some had the obscene, flesh-coloured, plastic plugs of Hickman lines clearly visible in their gaunt cleavages. Baz was compelled to slow down in order to negotiate these walking wounded, so, having had a lovely canter along Charlotte Street, he now entered Room 6 as if hobbled by the disease.

To find the same amazing squalor that was always associated with Henry Wotton. The familiar rankness infiltrated Baz's nostrils, an acrid braiding of cigarette smoke, alcohol fumes and stale sweat. But this was underlain by hospital disinfectant, just as the over-flowing ashtrays and stained glasses sat upon a hospital bed, a Formica-topped locker and a tray table rather than the mismatched pieces of furniture in the Chelsea house.

Still, there was a half-full bottle of Champagne and two red-wine empties; there were crumpled newspapers and cracked-spine books aplenty; and a silk scarf had been draped over an Anglepoise lamp, which was bent back so that it suffused boudoir light at the ceiling. Someone had also imported a trouser press, and draped over this were items of Wottonesque apparel: the Crombie, a suit jacket, a silk tie, a linen shirt with bloodied cuffs, and so forth. Without, on a tiny ledge snowed under by bird-shit, a pigeon stood on fungal feet coo-coughing in the eternal gloom of a light-well. In the top corner of the boxy room a television was wedged. It was on, the volume turned right down, and a female newsreader was whimpering about the collapse of the Soviet Union. In vases of coloured glass, expensive cut flowers were silently screaming as they smellily expired. Their demise served only to make the sickroom still more sickly.

Wotton himself was supine on the bed, Ray-Bans clamped across his eyes like the mask of a cartoon bandit. Perversely, Baz felt a reawakening of his thraldom, as, contemplating the waxy features, he was reassured to see that not only was Wotton not looking too bad, he was even looking better than Baz himself. 'Henry?' Even now he felt uneasy with the first name, as if he were employing slang with some dowager duchess.

Wotton undulated on the mattress and his dry tongue slitted open his thin mouth. 'Ah, Baz,' he croaked. 'Like the poor, the pretentious are always with us. You never say goodbye, you only say *au revoir* and retire for a while to recoup your feigned seriousness.' He undulated some more. 'How are you, old friend?' Baz found even this degree of warmth chilling – Wotton *was* ill, after all.

'I'm not so bad. I keep moving –'

'You'll forgive me,' Wotton's voice rustled on the ferny floor of his throat, 'if I neither strive to be upright, nor attempt a *vis-à-vis* – my mollusca, you see . . . they proliferate laterally. Recently they've been frozen out, but my teats, you see, they're *so* hospitable, soon the mollusca will come clustering back . . . I must be lactating this bloody virus.'

Baz removed a ball of shirts and cardboard kidney-dishes from a chair and seated himself. 'How's your sight, Henry?'

'My inner vision is clearer than ever, my dear Basil, it's just the external correlate that's becoming a little difficult to corral. The old cytomegalovirus has a way of gifting me the most Vaseline-smeared view of the world. A nice irony, really – now it obscures my peep-holes I can't smear it on anyone else's holes, hmm? Still, this affliction has at least saved me this very day from a worse one.'

'Oh, what would that be?'

'Having to kowtow to Princess Nightingale and her fat Yank friend, or, worse, give her the opportunity to rock me in her arms like that poor fool next door.'

Baz rose up to regard the fool in question, but through the reinforced glass he witnessed only a sight that should have aroused anyone's pity – let alone that of a fellow sufferer: a man utterly emaciated and completely trussed up in a macramé of life-maintaining medical technology. 'The poor man's dying, Henry – surely you wouldn't deny him whatever comfort she had to give?'

'It seems a shameful, constipated way to go, if you – as he patently has – have looked at life with your cheeks wide open. Anyway, it's absurd, the deference that's paid to Fatty Spencer; after all, it's looking increasingly unlikely that she'll *ever* be a queen, whereas there're oodles of them in here.'

Baz decided to ignore this badinage; he was here with a purpose. 'I met Batface in the corridor.'

'On good form, I trust?' Wotton might have been speaking of the remotest of acquaintances.

'She was having to put pressure on the duty nurse to allow a man called Bluejay in to see you.'

This got a rise out of Wotton; he levered himself up on his pillows. 'And did they accede?'

'She had to *crawl* to the nurse, Wotton. He only agreed in order not to make her feel still worse.'

'Ah well, it doesn't matter if they're compelled, as long as they do what I want.'

'I assume Bluejay is a dealer?'

'Yes, but in ephemera rather than antiquities.'

'You don't seem to be taking any of this seriously, Wotton – Henry. You've got AIDS, something your wife seems in total denial about. You're bullying the medical staff and her into enabling your drug use . . . Don't you care about Batface? Don't you care about yourself?'

Wotton removed the Ray-Bans and began to conduct a tutorial, using one of their arms as a baton. 'Let's answer your prosaic questions ordinally – it's all they deserve. First, I have not, as yet, been diagnosed with AIDS, my symptoms merely describe an arc' – he described a parabola with his crooked pointer – 'secondly, the medical staff are adequately recompensed for all of the licence they allow me, and thirdly you do Batface a grave injustice if you imagine she's one of those women who think they love too much. On the contrary, she's a woman who loves to think too much, and that is why our marriage has lasted so long.'

Still Baz wouldn't be drawn. 'Who's Phoebe?'

'Our daughter, of course.'

'And how old is she?'

'Six, seven, somewhere in that region.'

'Don't you realise, Henry, I'm HIV positive, you're HIV positive, I've heard Alan Campbell is too. I don't know about Dorian Gray . . . but I'm almost certain that I know when we were infected and by whom. I know when I seroconverted and I bet you do as well. It all happened on the night of Dorian's *vernissage* – don't you see what that means, Henry? There's every chance that Batface and your daughter are HIV positive – don't you think you have a responsibility to at least *tell* her so she can find out for herself?'

'Oh Baz, you're so morally pedantic, but if you will insist on this rote religion I'll tell you. I've had blood taken from both of them – by Campbell, as it happens – on the pretext that they should have a flu jab. He had it tested and they're negative. If it pleases Batface to think of this' – he gestured at his etiolated form – 'as an inconvenient malaise of some sort, then you must allow her that liberty.'

'And what liberty is that, exactly? Does she have lovers?'

'Baz!' he guffawed. 'Don't be preposterous!'

'But I'll bet *you* do.'

'Monogamy is to love as ideology is to thought; both are failures in imagination.'

'Do you practise safe sex?'

'Don't be absurd, Baz – what could that possibly mean? Orgasming under medical supervision?'

'Jesus, Henry, you'd take the whole fucking world down with you if you could arrange it.'

'And you, Baz – are the wings of your desire quite so clipped? The last I heard of your' – he savoured the word – '*activities*, it was back to the same old Baz brown-nosing, putting it about with Bobby Mapplethorpe and And*ee* and the whole, tedious Manhattan coterie.' As if to fumigate the thought of such a *passé* scene Wotton groped for a cigarette, lit it, puffed.

But Baz, not to be ruffled so easily, maintained his inquisitorial role: 'I suppose this came from Dorian?'

'Well, he has rather been the goer between us, wouldn't you say? I've witnessed some of his activities on this side of the Atlantic, but as I understand it you were privy to his entry into New York society.'

'For a while, I s'pose – I was useful to him in the early eighties. His looks and his money opened every door, but first he had to find them, and for that he needed me.'

'Well, Baz' – Wotton leaned towards him – 'we no longer have time to kill, but there are still a few minutes to while away before Bluejay arrives. Wouldn't you agree that one of the most useful by-products of the increased commercialism of the past decade has been the "we deliver" ethos among drug dealers? I understand the practice originated in Manhattan. Tell me about it – and incidentally you can tell me about Dorian. But before you do either, pour me a glass of that flat 'poo.'

7

'Yeah – Manhattan, Henry. Yeah, y'know – no. You can be dismiss-ive – you do that very well. You think you have all the angles on dissolution, don't you? Now you're dying I guess that's true, but New York in the early eighties was at the very peak of a great mountain of depravity. It was *so* extreme, Henry, so totally uncon-strained, that it almost had an aura of innocence about it.

'Not that I was innocent of anything. I had to be insane going back there, but the shit I'd got myself into in London was worse than the shit I'd got myself into over there in the late seventies. I'd fucked up all my connections in NYC before I left to come back to London. Story of my life – shifting from one city to the next with no money and a roaring smack habit. Now I was back in NYC with no one to . . . ahem . . . assist me, it was a habit I couldn't sustain, so I kicked, painfully and messily, in a roach hotel I shared with three not-so-gorgeous she-males off Avenue B.

'Once I could stand without shitting myself, it was payback time, and I became one of the lowest fucking gophers ever seen. I swear, Henry, if I'd known how low I could go . . . ah well, perhaps it was the only way. Still, at least I had a proper routine: up at two in the afternoon and out to the grocery store for Pop Tarts and grass. Yeah, everyone delivered in the East Village, Henry – they still do – but my she-males didn't need a delivery boy; they had me to fetch for them instead.

'Bangles, the guy who served up in the grocery store, thought I was hilarious. I remember him, playing Grandmaster-fucking-Flash on his boom-box and pushing me closer and closer to the edge. He'd dole out his dime baggies of weed and wheedle me at the same time. He couldn't believe this dumb honky junky limey fag fallen from another planet. Flicking his fucking jeri curls and jangling his wrist-wear and giving me this jive. Almost every day I'd tell him: I've pulled myself out of worse holes than this one, Bangles; and he'd say, yeah, but they had Crisco round them. Because that's what they'd use, Henry, the Stateside heavy-hitters, not Vaseline – fucking *lard*.

'It was eleven flights up to the pad I shared with the three graces, and even if the lift was working it wasn't too safe a bet to use it. I didn't care, I was on a health kick, and like the involuntary monk I'd become I was also cultivating a fucking *tonsure*. As for the scene, for the time being the only door in Manhattan that would open for me required about eleven fucking keys.

'My patrons were Désirée, Little Rhea and Lady Di, respectively a rangy Southerner, a Brooklyn Jew and a black kid from the Chicago projects. Not that you'd know them as such when they were dolled up for their act at the drag club in the meat-packing district. No, they were a class act, these girls, and they took plenty of time getting ready every day until they looked just like dolls. I learned the secrets of assembling a Blanche Dubois doll, a Barbra Streisand doll and a negative of our very own Princess of Wales. Not that this Lady Di had ever even heard of Wales; all she knew was the schtick worked, make 'em laugh – wouldn't you agree, Henry?

'You think you know about messiness, you think you *do* squalor? You know nothing, Henry, even at your worst all you do is toy with disorder and affect a little dishabille, whereas these three *revelled* in filth. Every day when I got back to the apartment I was overwhelmed again by the great sea of discarded pizza boxes, crushed soda cans and filthy fucking underwear in which the three of them lay – buck-naked and sweat-shiny in the summer fug, like great beached seals, two white and one black, with grimy mattresses in place of granite rocks.

'On the windowsill the air-con unit gargled and spat out tuberculous air, while the roaches looked up quizzically from their lunch.

They always do that, New York City roaches – look up quizzically. It's as if they're constantly being reminded by each human arrival of the injustice of their position, caught with their mandibles rasping the cardboard trash, instead of ordering their own fucking pizza on the phone. These three gouache trannies, last night's slap all smeared about on their flaccid faces, Henry, they were something else. I'd step into the desperate cubbyhole of a kitchen and roll their get-up joints on the fly-infested worktop . . .'

*　　*　　*

He didn't do a bad job of evocation, our Baz; besides being a Grand Inquisitor he'd also become a bit of an Ancient Mariner. Henry Wotton thought so, as he drifted into an unpleasant reverie, compounded in equal parts of mild heroin withdrawal, low fever, and flat 'poo. He could well imagine the festering pad and the slumbering female impersonators, Baz shaking their shoulders, their pachyderm eyelids ungumming, their thick mitts reaching out for Styrofoam coffee cups and ready-lit joints.

All at once they were upright and babbling.

—I swear that's the last time *him* treat me like that, Little Rhea said; no fuckin' class, that man.

—Did he –? Désirée put in.

—No way – came backstage after the second set, stuck his hand upside my fuckin' butt, tried dry-humpin' me in the dressin' room like I'm some grimy fuckin' hooker. More coffee please, Basil.

—I think he's just a fag stag, Rhea – leastways he's never come on to me.

—And why should he, sweetie?

—I don't know –

—No, you don't. You lit out quick – where to?

—The Eagle's Nest. I had a date.

—A date! Who with, the entire friggin' Marine Corps?!

—No, jus' a few of 'em.

There was general merriment at this quip; even Baz joined in.

Lady Di, who'd been in the can, reappeared with a Ziploc bag of cosmetics. He sat back down on his mattress, took out cleanser and cotton wool and began removing his make-up.

—How 'bout you, honey? said Little Rhea.

—I ain't doin' no bath-house scenes no more, replied the big black Sloane Ranger; you know that.

—Well yes, but you might be feeling better.

—I ain't. If anythin' I feel worse, don' feel like eatin', don' feel like drinkin', sure as hell don' feel like makin' no bath-house scene. An' I got these. He indicated a scatter of angry red pimples that zigzagged between his nipples, marking his shaven chest as if he'd encountered Zorro's sword tipped with infective matter.

—Oh honey! Désirée went over and gave him a hug. It'll clear up. You put that stuff on like I told you?

—Yeah, I dunnit, but that ain't gonna do nothin'. I *know* what this is about.

There was a strained silence for half a beat – then it snapped. Basil, babe, get me my duds, willya? said one; then the other two chimed in as well: Me too! Yeah – and me.

'At times, Henry, living with these three, I thought of William Buckley Junior's characterisation of gay men as "the sex that will not shut up", but that was just the you in me, because the truth was that Di, Rhea and Désirée pulled me out of the fucking gutter. They let me cluck on their floor, they fed me, and so what if I had to run errands for them and act as their dresser? The truth was that they showed me a little love, which was a lot more than anyone else had for a very long time.'

—I think the halter neck today, Basil.

—My falsies and bra please, Basil.

—Be so good as to pass over that slip, Basil. Baz brought razors and foam and hot water. Cocks and balls and legs were shaved, then sheathed in satin and fish-net. Wigs were donned, gowns and blouses and skirts brushed down. Baz proved a most efficient and capable dresser, smoothly assisting them to assume their mantles of exaggerated femininity: the gold-lamé-dusted vamp, the chiffon-muffled Southern belle, and the blonde-wigged, piecrust-collar-bloused *über*-nanny.

There was a banging at the door.

—Didja order pizza, Basil?

—No, you girls have got a matinée, I didn't think you'd have time – ' The banging continued.

—You better check it out, Basil, said Lady Di.

He undid bolts and slid the door open with three chains on it. Outside there was a strip of leather cowboy boot, blue denim, white cotton and blond hair. A strip of Dorian.

—Who is it, honey? called Rhea.

—It's . . . it's . . .

—A friend, Dorian mouthed.

—A friend.

—Now Basil, said Désirée, you know you don't have no friends no more besides us three queen bees.

—No really, it is a friend – a guy from London.

—Oh ferchrissakes, Rhea bawled, let the guy in, let's get a look at him.

'And in came Dorian, right over the threshold and bounding into the false bosom of the family. The great thing about Dorian is that he can always assume this air of puppyish good nature. He also looked the same age as a puppy, which the Avenue B trio thought was just *too* peachy. He stepped over their trash as if it wasn't there. I guess it was hanging round with you, Henry, that gave him the idea of incorporating camp courtliness into his act; well, it went down a scream with the she-males, the hand-kissing and the "Charmed to meet you, ladies".

'Even so, they were suspicious – God bless them – they knew what I'd been through. They knew that no one who'd been as down as me had any friends left worth the name. Still, they ran with Dorian's formal act and questioned him as if he were a suitor and they three maiden aunts guarding my virtue. Eventually they had to go, but they made me promise to be back the next day. I wasn't. Nor the one after.

'I was powerless to resist Dorian, Henry, I always have been, and anyway, I didn't want to resist him – I simply wanted him again. As long as I didn't go back on the fucking gear I thought everything would be OK; it was that – as far as I saw it – that was the problem. Not Dorian. So, that day in the summer of '82, he picked me up, he dusted me down and he took me shopping.

'We zoomed uptown, leaping from cab to cab, in and out of stores. It was like a parody of every naïve-hick-comes-to-New York movie you've ever seen, Henry. Dorian wanted to take Manhattan by storm; I was to provide his entrée, and for that I needed clothes and grooming, I needed what Dorian freely gave. I did feel a genuine gratitude to him. I still do, despite everything that came afterwards. He plucked me from Avenue B and set me down fifty blocks north in the Palm Court of the Waldorf Astoria. You know how good that kind of transition can feel, Henry, don't you?'

Indeed.

*　　*　　*

In the Palm Court of the Waldorf Astoria, a string quartet whittled away at the afternoon, paring off shavings of time. At round, glass-topped tables women with big hair and egregiously padded shoulders were sipping tea or martinis. The mismatched duo – one a gilded youth, the other a sweaty wreck – were ushered by a white-jacketed waiter into the presence of a little old man in a tiny contemporary suit. The collar points of his seersucker jacket rose almost to his pixie ears, and his lined pinhead was liver-spotted. He wore an obvious toupee. It was the Ferret. But Baz wasn't remotely surprised to see him; he merely acknowledged the way the titchy world spun thus:

—Fergus.

—Ah, Baz, my young friend here has managed to locate you – we had only the most *oriental* of whispers as to where you might be. Bob had told Doug, Doug had vouchsafed it to Steve, Steve passed it on to Captain America, and so on, and so forth . . . so fatiguing. The Ferret sniffed noisily and dabbed at his dribbling nose with a square foot of silk.

—He was way downtown, Dorian put in, on the Lower East Side. He's become a kind of ladies' maid, Fergus!

—Confirm, Baz?

—It's true enough. These three drag queens took me in and looked after me – they've helped me kick the smack.

—Oh jolly good, such a *bore*, smack. Or rather, that kind of it.

The waiter reappeared and asked Dorian and Baz if they'd like anything. Dorian confined himself to a glass of Badoit, but Baz began as shamelessly as he intended to go on, requesting a quantity of sandwiches that amounted to a meal.

—In New York for any special reason, Fergus? Baz asked, when the waiter had clicked off across the tiles.

—No, no, usual shopping expedition. It may be hot at this time of year, but it's quiet. Naturally I shall take Dorian out to the Hamptons to meet a few people, but I shan't be able to truly launch him until the season begins.

—So where do I fit into this picture?

—Well, his dear parents having abandoned him so woefully in this regard, I shall have to take care of his uptown début, but we rather felt that in the meantime you could facilitate his entry into the downtown milieu.

—I don't know, Fergus, I've got to stay clean, and the gay scene here – well, it's saturated with drugs and a hell of a lot rougher than it is in London. The people I know play hard, and Dorian's too tempting a plaything.

The Ferret first sniffed at this, then blew into his silk hanky. He certainly found what Baz said interesting; it was just that the Schubert was perfectly slumberous and the ambience absolutely torpid and he couldn't quite forbear from allowing his head to nod towards the damask. Still, he did manage to make a few remarks on the way down . . . My dear Baz, I'm under no illusions as to how *louche* things can be in New York.

—There's some kind of new disease around; it's killing gay men on the west coast, and I've heard of a few cases here in NYC as well.

—*Gay* – must you employ the term quite so widely? It's a ludicrous sobriquet, I *so* prefer 'queer' . . . I'm well acquainted with this new malaise . . . They say it's a function of too many poppers . . . or some such *déclassé* drug-taking. Not the sort of thing we expect from dear Dorian . . . Anyway, Baz, you'll be around to look after him, *won't* you m'dear . . . ? Too kind . . . I'll be here for a couple of weeks . . . You'll keep me posted . . .

And Baz and Dorian strained for a few seconds to hear the pinhead drop, which it did, with an audible 'clank' on to the glass table. As if this were a prearranged signal, one of the Ferret's heavyweight boyfriends materialised, pushing a wheelchair. He was a swarthy Mexican; an old knife scar across his Hispanic cheek had let out a little of the Amerindian stuffing. He gave the duo a cursory nod, manhandled the Ferret into the wheelchair, and pushed him away between the palms. The egregiously-shouldered women sent the little parcel of a man pitying looks as he passed by.

—Jesus, said Baz once they were gone, that was a quick flake-out even by his standards.

—Well, he can't get the speed he likes here for some reason, so he's doing cocaine instead. Pablo handles giving it to him, and even here at the Waldorf they take a rather a dim view of their patrons' engaging in such practices in the public areas.

The waiter returned with a silver stand laden with ditsy eatables; he poured them tea, distributed plates and retired.

—So, how about it? Dorian said, rubbing his hands together with childish glee.

—How – *nyum-nyum* – about what? Basil was stuffing the sandwiches in three at a time, poor Gulliver at the Lilliputian court.

—How about introducing me to Warhol and Burroughs and that photographer guy? Y'know, all the people you told me you hung out with here? I've got the money, I'll even set you up in your own studio again – we can create a scene together.

—Oh . . . well . . . I s'pose we can give it a try.

A pathetic rejoinder: 'I s'pose we can give it a try.' Difficult to conceive of this as the beginning of one of the great avant-garde scenes: 'I s'pose we can give it a try.' Hard to imagine that this inauspicious beginning ('I s'pose we can give it a try') will none the less become a rallying cry for disaffected youth from all over the eastern seaboard and then the wider world; or that this downbeat encounter will, in time, come to be deemed as significant as the first meeting between Rimbaud and Verlaine. Hard – because it won't. By the early 1980s the avant-garde was busy being franchised and sold off to a series of designer labels and purpose-designed emporia. Halston, Gucci, Fiorucci. Only somebody as staggeringly ill-informed as Dorian Gray could have imagined that there was still a 'scene' to be created in Manhattan.

Oh no, what happened to flagrant queers and uppity blacks and defiant junkies in America was that they got absorbed, then packaged and retailed like everybody and everything else. In America in the 1980s the counter-culture became the over-the-counter culture with sickening alacrity, and Andy Warhol – poor Basil Hallward's name-dropping nemesis – was the acned acme of it all. When the domestic market was brand-saturated they re-exported it all back to Europe, just in case there were any little pockets of resistance that needed mopping up.

A 'scene'. Laughable. Impossible to imagine Baz Hallward, with his mouldering collar-length hair and mildewed pate, strutting his stuff on the dance floor at Studio 54. No, it was too late for those lofty heights; Baz only just about had the cachet to infiltrate his beautiful protégé into the loft of Bobby Mapplethorpe, who, when all was said and done, would say anything and do anyone.

'Naturally,' Baz grabbed his tale back and brought it twisting into the cubicle, 'Bobby wanted to photograph Dorian in poetic positions. Dorian erect, Dorian among the nightingales, Dorian penetrated by black cocks and arms, while his face betrayed nothing save wry amusement. But while he made an impression, securing invitations to soirées of artists and intellectuals, he was quite as taken . . . by being taken. He seemed, Henry, to positively enjoin the people he met to handle him without care, to fold him, to spin-dry him . . . it's a wonder, considering the way he put himself about, that he wasn't mutilated.

'To begin with I'd go out with him at night, down to the Mineshaft on 12th Street. It was strange the way he not only adopted the typical clone costume of biker jacket, white T-shirt, and jeans, with greased-back hair under a peaked cap, he even made it his own. All the clones I've seen since then – even the ones I saw walking through Soho on my way here – seem to me to be clones of Dorian. The streets of downtown New York were fucking rough, full of homeless guys, and crack was beginning to cut its swathe through the city. On 12th there'd be empty coke vials crunching under our boots. It was the meat-packing district, so the air smelt of blood and the paving stones were sticky with it and worse. I tried to warn him . . .'

'I can imagine . . .' Wotton drawled from the bed.

'Imagine? Imagine what – the Mineshaft?'

'No, not *that*, I never went there' – he groped for another cigarette – 'but I bet I could write your dialogue so that it had greater authenticity than when you actually spoke it in Manhattan.'

'Don't they ever object to your smoking in here?'

'They object to just about *everything* I do in here, Baz. It's peculiar how terminal illness is so constrained; it explains what martyrs mean when they describe death as a "liberation", hmm? Pass me that ashtray and I'll get on with my imagining. You tell it how it was, Baz – I'll listen to how it should've been.'

The two men stood outside the Mineshaft, feeling the heavy heart of the city beat in the darkness. Listen, Dorian, Baz admonished him, you can play catch-as-catch-can in the bar, but even if you pair off, downstairs and in the back anything can happen, it's a fucking meat rack in there – I can't keep up with you . . . I won't –

—And I don't want you to, Baz. I'm a big enough boy – you know that – and I can look after myself.

—You can't, Dorian; this isn't Bobby's playpen, this isn't a controllable situation at all –

—Shut up!

—What?

—Shut the fuck up! Shut up! You don't understand anything, Baz, you don't *know* anything. I can do what I please – I can do what I bloody well please. I'm inviolate, Baz – I'm fucking immortal! And Dorian began to laugh wildly, before grabbing Baz by his jacket and dragging him into Hades – or at any rate some realisation of it art-directed by Hieronymus Bosch but cast by Kenneth Anger.

At the top of a short flight of stairs stood a grim apparition, a leather queen so withered and ravaged he might have been Old Father Rim, the primordial sodomite. He was vetting the queue, beckoning some in, while rejecting others who had failed to observe the dress code with the petulant squeal, You can't come in! Disco drag! Disco drag!

Dorian and Baz passed muster and entered the main room. It was gloomy, and through its slimy confines gusted the hysterical, chemical stench of amyl nitrate. In one corner a makeshift bar had been knocked together out of plastic crates and wooden boxes; behind it stood a shaven-headed giant serving liquor and beer. In another corner a crude canvas sling swung back and forth, its bare-assed occupant yelping as he was buggered by a fat trucker type. The clientele – to a man – were mustachioed leather queens, pumped up in every way. The only sound was a disturbing susur-ration; there was no music – and besides, the bar-room had no dance floor, only space for a freeform ruck. The beetle men in their leather carapaces grabbed at each other's shoulders; they tossed back shot glasses of vodka and bourbon, while wheeling around in an aggressive parody of sociability, closer to a football scrum than any other interaction. There was the reek of sweat and the creak of leather, there was a drunken intensity of leering, and a veritable spumescence of testosterone hovered over the whole scene, as shaven heads clashed and the acrid clouds of cigarette smoke were pierced by spotlights.

Dorian sprinted straight into this garden of unearthly delights. He not only accepted the hands grabbing at his crotch, the drinks shoved in his mouth and the tongues pushed into his ear, he revelled in them. Baz struggled to stay by his side. Don't forget, Dorian, Bobby said he'd take us to meet some friend of his uptown if we were back at his studio by midnight.

—Don't be ridiculous, Baz – he who makes a beast of himself gets rid of his watch! And that's what he did: he loosed the strap of his chunkily expensive diver's watch and thrust it into the hand of a deranged clone, who was so taken by Dorian's beauty that he licked the face. Baz gave up; he shouldered his way to the bar and stood there contemplating his own worn features in the mirror behind it, his own runty figure crushed between flanking Visigoths.

Baz felt a tug on his trousers at the back of his knee. To begin with he ignored it, but it persisted until eventually he turned and looked down. It was a tiny leather dwarf, complete in every detail of chains and jacket and trousers, but no more than three feet tall. The leather dwarf had a five-dollar bill tucked in his hand, which he poked up towards Baz with the pathetic entreaty, Can you get me a drink?

'Well, Henry.' Baz paused, and with a profound shudder of relief and revulsion he took a sip of cold tea from an apparently unsullied beaker. 'They say now that those few short years between the Stone-wall Riots and the arrival of AIDS were characterised by a mounting sense of liberation, that we gay men felt the time had come to be ourselves, to express ourselves, to live as we truly wanted to live, free of guilt, free of convention, free of interference. They say now that the disease is a ghastly, one-off, one-act play. A piece of incomprehensible dramatic irony, inflicted on us happy Arcadians by a god who doesn't even exist. They say now that those damp bath-houses and fetid gyms, the bloody meat racks and the shitty cottages were the perfect places for the virus to fester, to replicate, to pump its own iron. The glory hole turned out to be a gory hole. They say HIV may have been present for years in the West, and that it was only this ever lengthening conga line of sodomy – with jet travel connecting cock from San Francisco with asshole in NYC, cock from NYC with asshole in London – that allowed it to get so out of control. They say a lot of things, but for those of us who were there it was simple. Simple to observe that for men who were meant to be free, how readily they draped themselves in chains . . .'

They were draped in chains, the men who jostled and clinked in the Stygian chambers beneath the bar-room at the Mineshaft. Dorian penetrated this sphincter of darkness. He stopped to try his cock in a glory hole, he paused to watch while two men fucked a third at either end, he moved to join a circle of happy flagellators, he critically pissed on a naked performer in a bathtub. On and on he went; darker and danker it became, as wonkily partitioned room succeeded warped vestibule, each filthier and ranker than the last with the odour of faeces and semen and poppers. All around was the thwack of flesh on flesh, with its ragged accompaniment – the grunts and groans of effortful coition.

But as Dorian progressed from one rigorous knot of men to the next, there was always a trio who peeled away to accompany him. Their leader was an ultimate leather queen, a big moon-faced man complete with the craters. With him were two snickering incubi, both chubby, both shaven-headed, who affected the same Gestapo uniform of full-length leather coat and chain choker. When at last they reached a zone of near-privacy, this trio surrounded their victim. One of the incubi offered Dorian a popper, the other caressed his crotch. The two of them helped him out of his jeans and encouraged him to his knees. While they kept his head occupied, Moonface moved in on his rear. But when one huge hand – replete with studded wristband – grasped Dorian's golden oiled curls, he suddenly reared up and, getting hold of the incubi by their thick necks, cracked their heads together.

—Why, you piece of shit, screamed one, I'm gonna have to cut you! And he had the knife for it, an evil six-inch switchblade.

—On the contrary, Dorian snarled, if there's to be any evisceration, I think you'll find that you lack the guts for it. He wrenched the knife away from the man, reversed it, and in one bravura act of savagery sliced him clear across his belly. Blood gushed from flaps of cloth and flesh. The incubi retreated, keening like terrified dogs. From somewhere Dorian had got a handful of poppers; pirouetting round, he rammed these into the Moonface. Then it was the leather queen who was hobbled by his trousers, the leather queen who was being forcibly sodomised by the pretty blond boy. Dorian smashed the man's head against the floor with his hand, again and again, until there was a pink mist of blood in the air. In Dorian's fevered head the blood beats doubled up, tripping over one another until this cardiac timpani reached a crescendo. His whole consciousness of the world swelled and whooshed and wobbled and dilated as amyl nitrate swirled in a vast anticyclone over the face of the earth.

8

The mid-afternoon sun beat down on a small but perfectly-formed Riviera harbour. Within the semicircular quay there was the brittle rasping sound of the mistral agitating metal rigging on the yachts, flapping their canvas and slapping wavelets against their hulls. Light rays bounced off the aquamarine water and coruscated from every reflective surface – windows, glasses, bottles and forks.

Specifically the upheld forks of some late lunchers at an opulent party. A repast that had been set out a long while before, on white linen, on the terrace of a restaurant which was exclusive in the way that only a French restaurant can be, namely, by virtue of content as much as form. True, there was a hefty *prix fixe* and a haughty maître d', but it was in the great middens of Crustacea shells that the evidence of full-blown luxury lay. In these, and in all the myriad shiny implements required to poke, probe and scour the flesh from them; and in all the ice buckets containing bottles of *premier cru* white wine and Champagne; and in all the overflowing ashtrays; and, of course, in all the diners themselves. Diners who, while hailing from more northern climes, still looked considerably better than they did in their usual habitat, once they'd been tanned and masked with sunglasses, then draped in cream linen and creamier silk.

'I'm absolutely certain, Batface,' said Henry Wotton, who was sitting at the head of this table, 'that I have no inclination to visit the Principessa. Why ruin a perfect day by hammering in this heat all the way into Toulon on the bloody *péage*? Besides,' he continued, puffing expansively on a Cohiba, 'what's a Medici doing in Toulon? Nobody *lives* in Toulon, it's where the French Navy *docks*.'

'Um . . . w-well . . . yes, you say that, Henry,' Batface replied from the foot of the table, 'but she's not at all what you expect from a M-Medici, no . . . er . . . air of power about her at all. Incorrigibly bourgeois, in fact. Lives in a little apartment with far too many cats. Incorrigible gossip as well . . . but only about her neighbours. I did say to Mummy that I would look her up –'

'Well, you do that then. But I'm going to Aqualand. No, correction, I'm going to drop some acid, then I'm going to go on that mini-submarine trip over to the island, *then* I'm going to Aqualand, where I shall ride the big twister chute. What's it to be, Dorian' – he turned to his protégé – 'the revolutionary big twister chute or the *petit bourgeois* Principessa?'

For Dorian Gray's European sojourns he still needed Henry Wotton – or perhaps that was something his one-time lover imagined. Maybe Dorian simply liked Wotton, or had the need of a refresher course in the older man's mastery of *bons mots*, which, like boomerangs, invariably returned to his mouth, so that they might be hurled forth once again on some later occasion. Certainly, by the mid-eighties Dorian was moving in the most elevated and catholic of circles – Claus and Sunny, Mick and Jerry, Donald and Ivana – whomever he wanted to associate with wanted to associate with him. None of these luminaries could have said exactly what it was that they found so agreeable about Dorian Gray, because to have mouthed 'money' and 'beauty' would have had the prosaic character of the truth, something they avoided at all costs. As for Dorian's charm, it existed, true enough, but then there's nothing more charmless, ultimately, than charm alone.

Whatever the reason, during those years when the Wottons retreated for the summer to a villa set among the dusty vineyards in the back of the Côte d'Azur, Dorian would often happen along. Usually he'd have a titbit on his arm, a beautiful straight boy he was in the process of subtly warping, or a respectable wee wifey whom he'd encouraged to slip the noose. In the course of becoming who he truly was, Dorian had reacquired a prodigious sexual omnivorousness.

He told Wotton about the man he had killed in the Mineshaft, except 'killed' wasn't how he put it; rather he asserted that he'd murdered him. This Wotton was disinclined to believe. While he considered that Dorian was one of those unusual beings who make a reality out the fictions they cannot write (so much more diverting than those poseurs who write the fictions they dare not realise), he very much doubted that the incident was anything more than some rough-housing gone wrong. Wotton liked to think that Dorian intended his boasts to be found out for what they were, and that like him, his protégé had far too much *amour propre* not to thrill to being ridiculed.

That particular afternoon at Cassis, in his summery incarnation, Dorian affected the palest nicotine shade of linen suits, the softest of silk shirts, the floppiest of spotted foulard ties. With his golden hair frothing from beneath an immaculate panama, and his profile imperious yet elegant, he sipped a glass of wine, cracked the claw of a lobster and thrust the filament of white meat at his companion, who was an ethereally lovely thing, all ash-blonde locks, scattered freckles, tip-tilted nose. 'Suck it!' he exclaimed.

'What?' She was charmingly aghast.

'Suck it – suck the claw, it's the only way to get out all the flesh.'

Jane Narborough, whose white beach weeds and prematurely grey hair gave her a shipwrecked air, broke in, 'I shouldn't do any such thing, my dear. These creatures are sea rats, complete scavengers – '

'But nevertheless,' Dorian baited the vegetarian, 'scavengers with souls, Jane, that's what you believe?'

'Yes, of course, with soul substance.'

'Is that like soul food?' said Wotton, who liked nothing better than a good tease.

Dorian refused to admit him and continued, 'D'you think, Jane, that lobsters have the soul substance of human scavengers with bad karma?'

'I'm not . . . er . . . I don't . . .'

Batface came to her rescue. 'I don't think metem-metem-metempsychosis works quite like that, Dorian.'

But Dorian had never intended this to be a discussion. He addressed himself once more to his companion, thrusting the white prong right into her mouth. 'Suck it, Octavia . . . suck it and find out.'

'I rather think' – Batface began collecting up her impedimenta – 'I better *had* go and see the Principessa. Why don't you come with me, Jane? We can stop at Cap Ferrat on the way back –'

'Oh yes, if you say so, Victoria.'

'And you, Octavia?'

'I'll stay with the boys.'

The florid figure of David Hall, the politician, was set down next to Batface, his lick of chocolate hair gently irrigating his bulbous brow, his barely-in-control eyebrows dewy in the afternoon heat. For his transplantation to the Côte d'Azur he had managed an MCC blazer and cricket whites. He swilled, then swigged the remains of his wine and said, 'I'll come with you, Lady Victoria. I haven't been to Cap Ferrat for twenty years.'

Wotton muttered to Dorian, 'Not since he gave Willie Maugham a blowjob on his deathbed.'

'In that case I shall have to take the Jag, Henry – will you three fit in the Volkswagen?' Batface looked down at her husband with genuine concern.

'Of course, if Dorian doesn't mind sitting on Octavia's lap.'

'Good, well, we'll see you back at the house for drinks then.'

Hall and the two women left the table, strolled along the terrace and were gone. Wotton beckoned to a waiter and ordered three glasses of *marc de champagne*, three double espressos and the bill. He studiously relit his Cohiba. When the drinks arrived, he and Dorian knocked them back with gusto, but Octavia was more ruminative – so far as that was possible for a young woman like her, who looked as if a strong breeze might carry her off. 'Are you and Batface in love, Henry?' she said at length.

'When you fall in love, Octavia, you join the league of the self-deceived' – Wotton waited a beat – 'and by the time it's all over you've enrolled everyone else.' She didn't understand what he said, though, merely hearing it as a neutral sort of burble.

'I thought I was in love with Jeremy,' she mused, 'but perhaps I don't have the right kind of personality to be successful at marriage.' And in return Wotton didn't pay any attention to the substance of what she said, merely listening for his cue.

'Marriage has definitely been good for my personality,' he drawled. 'Since marrying I've acquired at least four more personae.'

'D'you love me, Dorian?' Octavia touched his dimpled chin with the tips of her fingers.

'I'd like to make love to you right here' – he took them and buffed them with his lips – 'right now. I adore you.'

'*Quelle bonne idée,*' Wotton put in, 'but why not wait until these kick in?' He had three acid blotters tucked in the palm of his hand, which he exposed to the other two as if they were stigmata. 'They're Tetragrammatons – see, the name of God is written on them in Greek, Latin and Hebrew. They're incredibly strong – but mellow too. Just the thing for Aqualand.'

'Oh, I don't know . . .' she prodded the cardboard squares as if they were alive '. . . it's acid, is it? I've never taken it before.'

'Have half, then.' Wotton was emollient. 'Half of anything never hurt anyone. Trust me.' To almost anyone who knew Wotton even slightly this would have been an absurd proposition, but Octavia knew nothing at all about anyone whomsoever, so she took the proffered half that Wotton tore off, while Dorian had the other. Needless to say, Wotton himself washed a whole blotter down with the dregs of his *marc*.

Shortly, the mismatched trio found themselves in a strange kind of interior. They were caught up, like three Jonahs, within the iron ribs of the miniature submarine that plied a five-minute course across the harbour to the artificial island protecting it from the Mediterranean. The submariners sat in a row, on a metal bench which spanned the hull of the vessel, swinging their legs. In truth, it wasn't much of a submarine, more of a demi-sub dabbling its nether regions in the ocean. Through the upper portholes there were splashed-upon views of bikini-clad yacht girls and kids mucking about in inflatable boats; while through the portholes in the bottom of the hull could be seen weedy outcrops of old Evian bottles set in sludge. The Nemo who piloted this clip-joint *Nautilus* one twenty-thousandth of a league under the sea was poised on a bench up in the bow, his tanned legs dangling, his espadrilles kicking. Octavia concentrated on the straw whorls as they appeared in the green gloom, first the right, then the left. First the right, then the left.

'Are you going to stay at the villa?' Wotton asked Dorian conversationally.

'I'm not sure that would be wise, Henry – can Hall or the Duchess be trusted?'

'They can be relied upon to be dull.'

'Why the fuck d'you put up with them?'

'Simple. Batface likes them – they talk history and religion and politics together – and they're good front – Hall's a minister now – and their being here makes it curiously less punitive undergoing the necessary health regime.'

'Are you off smack, then?'

'I always kick in the summer hols, Dorian – you know that. No drugs at all to speak of, just a little weed, a few hallucinogens and some fine wines. Self-control is always easier to practise in the country, after all – there's nowhere for the self to escape to.'

Octavia's periscope spotted what was bearing down on her and she resurfaced into the conversation. 'Hall knows Jeremy – they belong to the same club.'

'They're certainly both clubbable,' Wotton said.

'Dorian,' she pressed on, 'perhaps it would be best if we stayed at a hotel?'

'Nonsense,' Dorian huffed, 'we're here perfectly legitimately. We're friends. Jeremy's flying down to join you in a couple of days;

you decided to visit Henry and Victoria with me. We'll occupy separate rooms. For Christ's sake, Octavia, anyone would think this was the eighteen- rather than the nineteen-eighties.'

'You and Henry have no idea what people say about you, have you?'

But if she had been about tell them she was denied the opportunity, for the hull bumped then grated on concrete, and the Captain sang out, *'Nous voici, Madame, Messieurs; l'Île de Bendor. Nous sommes arrivés.'* They ascended through a hatch, and the cinematically dim interior of the miniature submarine was eradicated by the flashbulb intensity of the afternoon sun. The three stood on the dock, teetering and momentarily stunned, while the craft bumped and grated about, before churning its way back.

Dorian and Henry adored Bendor. They often took guests there to savour its utterly chichi falsity. The islet was a mere crenellation of concrete, encrusted with mock-Moorish pavilions and implanted with palms. Tennis-court-sized courtyards were overseen by hidden balconies, and there were niches within grottoes within turrets. The folly was the creation of a pastis millionaire and it was a load of aniseed balls. But then that's the French, simultaneously the most stylish and the most gauche people imaginable.

Not that there were any French in evidence on that particular afternoon; the trio had the pseudo-place to themselves. Which was just as well, because as they frolicked up into its tiny interior – holding hands, cavorting, the two men swinging Octavia between them as if she were a child – it became increasingly obvious that the acid was getting a grip on them. They came to a halt, giggling with the unaccustomed exertion, and propped themselves along a balustrade in an archway which looked down on a little enclosed courtyard.

'I feel awfully peculiar,' Octavia said.

'So do I,' Wotton added, getting out a packet of Boyards Maïs and sticking one of the thick, bilious cigarettes in his thin, pale lips.

'You always feel peculiar,' Dorian put in.

'Excepting . . .' Wotton emitted smoke and twisted self-regard in equal measure '. . . when I feel someone more peculiar than me.'

Octavia was examining her outstretched fingers intently, as if seeing them for the first time and puzzled as to their function. 'D'you think . . . ? My hands . . . they feel like skin gloves stuffed with meat . . .' Even in the harsh sunlight her pupils were monstrously dilated, completely eclipsing her green irises. 'Are we all simply skin suits stuffed with meat?'

'Don't tell that to poor Jane,' Wotton chortled; 'she wouldn't like the idea at all. Far better that you tell her we're stuffed with grain – then she can slit our bellies, decant the stuff into sacks and send it to the poor Ethiopians.'

'Yes, that's what they need . . .' Dorian had pulled up the front of Octavia's dress and was blatantly caressing her naked belly '. . . belly-aid.'

'I feel so strange . . .' she moaned. 'Everything's too big or too small, and it's all sliding in and out of itself, as if the world were a trombone.'

'That's very good, my dear' – Wotton also patted her belly – 'a very nice image.'

'I never knew before' – she slumped a little, groping for Dorian's hand – 'that the world has a pulse.'

'Perhaps, Henry' – Dorian fastidiously removed Wotton's hand from Octavia's belly – 'it would be sensitive of you to leave us at this point?'

'Perhaps . . .'

It would have been entirely in character for Wotton to have insisted at this juncture on a grotesque form of *droit de seigneur*, as if, having brought Octavia to Bendor, he had first claim on her hallucinogenic hymen. Instead, he wandered off without a backward glance, strolling through the deserted courtyards, past the mini-minarets, and down some steps to a rocky shoreline, where he squatted and, clearly hallucinating madly, became wholly focused on the wavelets breaking at his feet. In Wotton's inner ear great whirls and skirls of electric guitar slashed and meshed and crashed, as if a vast orchestra of Jimi Hendrixes were playing the *Siegfried Idyll*.

Back at the balustrade, events took a nauseating course:

—Most people are dead, aren't they, Dorian?

—They're certainly a rotten bunch. He was still caressing her, but at the same time encouraging her out of her silk briefs. He wound her dress up around her armpits and fastened it there with a firm twist. He lightly touched her exposed breasts, as if they were objects.

—But you're not dead, Dorian; you're so beautiful – you're so alive. She was fixated by his face – seemingly his beauty was the one thing checking the very dissolution of her ego. Which was why it was all the more cruel when Dorian turned her away from him, and bent her upper body over until she was face down across the balustrade. Her vacant visage was now in a position to babble at some lichen, You're green and small and slow and so old, so very old.

But then, as Dorian did things at the other end of her, Octavia's face became contorted with awareness, and her spaced-out vacancy was overwritten with the most earthy of violations.

*   *   *

It was twilight in the hospital. Wotton stubbed out his umpteenth cigarette, twisting the stub as he twisted the end of his tale. 'It certainly wouldn't have been my wish to bridle Dorian's instincts in any way. I concede, she did seem distressed, but there was nothing untoward about that – it was bloody righteous acid. You have to remember, Baz, at that time the disease was very much the new kid on the viral block. There'd only been a few score actual deaths in Britain, and as far as we knew they were all renters and street junkies. I had no reason to connect her demise – it was pneumonia, I believe – with Dorian.'

'But it *was* connected, wasn't it?'

'*And* we never made it to Aqualand that day. I had to dose the poor waif up with brandy and Valium before we could even get her into the mini-sub.'

A large plump Rastafarian came into the cubicle, bearing a Fortnum & Mason's bag in one hand, while the other clamped a handkerchief across his nose and mouth. His dreadlocks were fastened in a tricoloured sweatband (red, yellow and green); he sported dark glasses with Lion of Judah hinge bosses and wore a lucent tracksuit.

'Ah, Bluejay!' Wotton exclaimed delightedly. 'Come here and show me what you've brought for my little picnic.' He yanked the Anglepoise round so that it shone down on to the apron of covers between his parted legs.

But Bluejay displayed a marked unwillingness to advance any further than the door; instead he merely tossed the bag over. It fell limply on to the bed. Seizing it, Wotton emptied out five or six nodules of heroin and crack cocaine, all tightly wrapped in plastic. Baz rose and went over to the ghastly little window, the better to ignore the transaction.

'Excuse me, my dear Bluejay, while I arise from this semi-recumbent position.' Wotton struggled up on an elbow.

'Don' get nowhere near me, man!' He warded Wotton off with a be-ringed hand and partially retreated out of the door.

'Oh come now, Bluejay, you cannot be so credulous as to believe that I'll infect you with my touch or . . .' he gently exhaled '. . . *poof* . . . my breath?'

Bluejay recoiled still further. 'I dunno nuffin' 'bout that Henry, I jus' don' want you near me, man. Take the fuckin' gear an' gimme the dosh. Dis place gives me the fuckin' 'orrors.'

'I don't think you'd find many who'd dissent from that. So be it, here's your *dosh* . . .' he chucked a sheaf of notes on to the bed and Bluejay retrieved them with a flinch '. . . and I trust when we meet again it will be in more salubrious circumstances.'

'I ain't comin' here again, Henry.'

'Well, you and my medical gaolers are in concurrence then. *A tout à l'heure.*'

As soon as the Rasta had left, Wotton, with trembling hands, began to unpick one of the nodules. Baz turned from the window. 'I can't believe you're still using drugs, Henry – don't you realise how severely they compromise your immune system?'

'Compromise? What an absurd expression – how can my immune system be compromised? It's not an adulterous husband caught with its trousers down in a bedroom farce. Really, Baz.'

'Listen Henry, your only chance of staying alive is to live as healthily as possible, eat organic food, drink pure liquids, exercise regularly. You must understand that.'

'Oh, but Baz, I assure you, I *do* regard my body as a temple. It just happens to be one where the ceremonies are orgiastic and conducted using mood-altering drugs.' Wotton remained a punctilious officiating priest at these ceremonies: despite his tremors he'd already managed to chop out a couple of lines of smack on a handy plate. 'Baz, you'll indulge?' He looked up at his old friend with an eyebrow arched interrogatively.

Basil Hallward shuddered. 'I haven't touched the stuff for five years, Henry; I'm not about to now.'

'I see; well, I suppose it would be remiss to chide you for a sin of omission. You'll have a drink, though?' He sloshed the remains of the 'poo.

'I haven't drunk alcohol for five years either.'

'That's absurd . . .' he snarfed up first one line '. . . incomprehensible . . .' and then the other.

Baz pressed on with his inquisition. The only way – he reasoned – to keep his sobriety in this den of disease and derangement was to focus on what mattered. 'But you didn't see Dorian only on the Riviera, did you, Henry?'

'Oh no no, I saw him in town as well. Not that he's *always* been pleased to see me. As I know you appreciate, Baz, Dorian is a social chameleon, adapting himself perfectly to whatever background he finds himself standing against. In London that Christmas – as he has been for every subsequent one – Dorian was at the very epicentre of what passes for a season. He'd moved to a mews house off the Gloucester Road, and acquired a silly little sports car to jiggle over the cobbles. He drives it with superb recklessness – as if he were immortal – and with the top down whatever the weather. But his real *coup de théâtre* has been to infiltrate the select little circle of faggots who stack themselves around the Windsors' stake. Not, you understand, that Dorian's on anything but curtsying terms with the Queen herself, but he has managed to ingratiate himself with Her Royal Regurgitation, the Princess of Clothes.

'Dorian has always been a harlot high and low. Whether he's in the darkness of a box at Covent Garden, or the darkness of a toilet stall underneath the Strand, his behaviour remains the same, intriguing and besmirching. He's developed a particular affinity with Thickie Spencer, because like her he's a psychological parvenu. After all, both of them have bona fides aplenty to be themselves in the beau monde, yet they prefer to act. They find acting so much more *real* than reality.

'Personally, I'd never allow myself to kowtow to the Windsors. Ridiculous. But Dorian's intent on being the ultimate fag – and she's the ultimate fag hag. There's that, and also, to his credit, he understands how her particular act – her grazed heart crying out for a Band-aid, while she shops 'til every last equerry drops – constitutes the very *Zeitgeist* itself. Remember, Dorian can be whatever you want him to be – a punk or a parvenu, a dodgy geezer or a doting courtier, a witty fop or a City yuppy. I tell you, Baz, the eighties was Dorian's decade – he revelled in every opportunity that London offered him to assume an imposture. Sometimes I think,' he snorted, 'that it's Dorian who's the true retrovirus. Because throughout everything, his true self has remained inviolate . . . Yes . . . If Dorian has a heart, I envision it as being like this . . . this dear little iceberg of . . . crack . . . cocaine.'

Baz, despite himself, had ended up sitting on the edge of the bed, looking down at Wotton, who was nodding out, his chin on his chest, the ash from his cigarette falling in grey flakes. He held the little iceberg of crack aloft, turning it this way and that, so that the glare of the Anglepoise glissaded across it. 'Jesus, Henry' – Baz betrayed a grudging admiration – 'you're smacked out of your fucking gourd.'

'Ah, that's more like the old Baz, the Baz we hate to love. Wouldn't you like to join me here, Baz? Smacked out of Henry's fucking gourd. It's a fine place to be, yes indeed.'

But instead of replying, Baz took the dying cigarette from Wotton's mouth and dropped it with a fizz into the dregs of his friend's 'poo. 'You're too stoned now,' he said, 'to come up with anything worth hearing.'

'I both resent that, Basil . . . and accept it . . . But light me another gasper and I think you'll find I'm still a very capable listener. Tell me what happened in the States, Baz, because he kept going back and forth, didn't he?'

9

This sun didn't so much beat down as hammer the wide sand beach, choppy ocean, tussocked dune and distant pines into two ductile dimensions. A strip of reality that was wound around the bronzed shoulders of a group of near-naked young men, who, like the good Prometheans they were – this was, after all, Fire Island – tended a small conflagration of driftwood, oily planks haloed green and blue. An old radiator grille propped in among the embers did service for a barbecue.

Dorian Gray, his hair a flaming aurora, his skin flawless, came tripping up the strand. Even here, in this open-air festival of self-love – the pecs oiled and shaven, the abs burnished and buffed – he still stood proud of the rest. His every carefree movement blazoned the fact that he – unlike them – wasn't even trying.

He joined the colloquy of modern Platonists with their modest picnic. A ghetto blaster tootled out Bowie, who weedily inveighed at the company, 'Let's dance.' They rearranged themselves to accommodate Dorian, but only grudgingly.

—What ho, Dorian, said one of them, Roy, a beetle-browed chap, whose heavy shoulders and Gaulish mustachios gave him the appearance of an epicene walrus.

—I'm sorry? Dorian was blithe.

—I said 'What ho', old man – isn't that your Brit jive?

—Yeah, whatever you say, Roy.

—Are you going to the party tonight, Dorian? put in Stan, who was rawboned and nervy; his right-angled ears were sunburnt, while patches of rough hide at elbow and knee suggested eczema or worse.

—And what party would that be?

—The wake, man, the fucking wake for Brucie – Stan convulsed himself upright – he was only one of the guys who *made* this place, Dorian, who created the fucking scene here. Jesus, you *knew* him, man. I saw you talking with him – I even saw you boogieing with Brucie, making love with him, Dorian.

—I'd hardly describe it as making love, Stan; what most men around here do is copulate to avoid violence. Without asking, Dorian detached a can of beer from its plastic webbing, cracked the ring-pull, took a pull and began to expatiate in the manner of his mentor: When any group of aggressive predators are confined together, a hierarchy rapidly emerges; dominance and submission rituals ensure order. Mock mating is often one of them. The only peculiar thing about the homosexuals of Fire Island is that there's nothing mock about *our* mating. May I have a chicken wing? He took one anyway, seemingly oblivious of the simmering aggression his remarks on aggression had provoked.

—I dunno what you're saying, man – Roy took up cudgels – but I don't like the way you're saying it. It's a wake, Brucie's dead; we're commemorating his life, saying who he was.

—It all sounds a little too morbid for me, Roy; I'd sooner say who I am and remain in the tense present.

—You don't give a damn about anything, do you, Dorian? Stan was appalled. You don't do anything for anyone who's sick, you don't seem to care about how you behave – what is it with you?

—You're all delicate little flowers, aren't you, boys. The whole death thing shakes you up so, and that *nasty* moral majority saying it was all your own minority fault. That it was all that rimming and writhing and buggering you did, which upset sweet Jesus and his sour daddy. Now he's not going to let you sit on his right hand so he can slip a finger in. But I'm not like you boys, not like you at all. I don't shudder to think – I think to shudder. Dorian, the very picture of health and vitality, did shudder. He chomped into the greasy, flame-grilled limb and gave a delicious writhe to his perfectly-proportioned shoulders.

This was too much for Roy, who jumped to his feet, fists raised. I'm not so much of a faggot that I can't fight. Get the fuck outta here, Dorian – get the fuck out! The other loungers were upright as well, making a petrified tableau of muscle and sinew.

Dorian was, of course, amply confirmed in his zoological analysis of Fire Island society, and chillingly he preserved his cool: I know when I'm not welcome, boychicks, and that's a decided improvement on you, who welcome not knowing. He threw the half-eaten chicken wing on the fire, slowly rose, and sloped off along the beach.

Even as the others watched him go, shimmering into the heat haze, they saw him pause by another colloquy, exchange a few words with another young man, extend an arm and pull him upright. So, it was as one of a couple that Dorian wavered into insubstantiality.

*   *   *

It was night-time now on Broderip. Gavin had been by to say goodbye and the incoming duty nurse had come to say hello. Neither, on seeing the two men in earnest conversation, had felt inclined to interrupt, and besides, there were nebulisers, and drips, and pumps aplenty to change. There was workmanlike dying going on.

'As the gays in NYC fused into a closer community,' Baz continued, 'the better to deal with this awful scourge, so Dorian managed a rare feat. Despite being rich, beautiful and seemingly eternally youthful, he became a pariah. People got to hear about him, Henry, and his name became associated with all the guilt and shame surrounding the old bath-house scene. It was even rumoured that Dorian was the AIDS Mary, the malevolent and intentional transmitter of the virus.'

'But what of you, my dear Baz? Did Dorian create a little scene for you, as he said he would?'

'He set me up in a studio in the Village – if that's what you mean. He even threw money around, got me to assemble a little coterie of artists to put on group shows and the like. But I was fucked up on drugs again within a matter of months; the mid-eighties were just another smear on the windscreen so far as I was concerned. By the time Andy died at the beginning of '87 it had all gone bad. Fucking dreadful.'

To be precise, it had gone bad in a loft on Mercer Street. A loft that had high windows with the requisite vast fanlights, through which all the dizzying vertiginousness of downtown Manhattan could be seen rearing up into the heavens. The twin towers of the World Trade Center, like the severed legs of a brutalist robot god, were having their feet kissed by lesser buildings with neoclassical façades, featuring not one or two but twenty or thirty friezes. Manhattan – like Ancient Rome with a pituitary disorder.

Inside, the large, foursquare, whitewashed room looked superficially trendy and tidy, but this was no more than arty camouflage thrown over the very real patina of grime that coated the fixtures and the two slashed leatherette sofas which were the only fittings. As if there weren't enough filth *in situ*, small drifts of trash had built up in all the corners and crannies.

Baz and Dorian stood in the middle of this shabby atelier. The former was – once again, as in the beginning – a sweating, shaking, stuttering morass, all the chemicals agonising and antagonising inside him. Dorian, on the other hand, was poised in midnight-blue velvet, a Hermès scarf frothing out of his breast pocket. He tapped oval-rimmed fashion eyewear against his oval lips. They were contemplating a plywood pedestal, upon which sat a sculpture made from a welded tangle of bent and burnt spoons. It looked like the model of some undeniably complex but for all that dangerously unstable molecule.

On one of the sofas sat a black kid with his hair bound into sloppy antennae. He was moodily cooking up a fix in a spoon that had become detached from the artwork. A brittle Hispanic girl in a little bloodstained dress contemplated him with hungry eyes. From a single giant speaker – devoid of a cabinet and lying on its side – came peculiar hurdy-gurdy music, as if this sordid scene were some fairground unattraction.

—It looks like it took him about an hour to make.

—Don't be crazy, Dorian – look at the sheer number of welds involved in the thing.

—OK, it took him a hundred hours and he's truly untalented.

—No, I don't think you're right there, Dorian. You never get Manhattan do you? You don't quite grasp how far image and aesthetic are the same thing here. This is the city where the multiple sets the standard for the artefact. Why paint one portrait when you can print a hundred? Why bend one spoon when you can bend a thousand?

—Yeah, and why ponce one dollar off me when you can ponce ten thousand, eh?

—The point is that Gary here is very much of the moment – he's a pal of Jean-Michel's, he's got a show coming up in Chelsea, at Gallery 7. He is, to all intents and purposes, the toast of the town.

—He's a plaything of And*ee*'s – that's what you mean.

—He's been doing some collaborations with Andy, that's what I mean, exactly like Jean-Michel.

—Titivating the King Queen of Manhattan – that's what I mean. Jesus, Baz, when I heard you going on about And*ee* five years ago in London, I thought there might be a certain cachet to him and his precious scene, but now I've seen them and they're as dull as any gaggle of old faggots anywhere in the world. Bloody wizened old stick, with his acne scars and his white Rasta wigs and his tape recorder and his dumb Polaroid. Lisping on about this celebrity and that celebrity: 'Gee, Dorian, don't you think so-and-so is fantastic . . .' Fan-fucking-tastic – when it's some Z-list TV actor he's salivating over.

—You just don't get it, Dorian.

—Get what? That he's dead already but won't lie down? What was that bullshit TV show he was in last year? *Love Cruise*?

From the fake depths of the sofa, Gary, who'd had his hit and was now disposed to look favourably upon everything, said, *Love Boat*, man, *Love Boat* – an' he was awesome in it. Yeah, the dude is the man.

—The dude is the man? Baz, do I *have* to listen to this crap?

—You have to've been here in the sixties and seventies, I suppose, Dorian – things have moved on.

—Yeah, right, moved straight into the fucking morgue.

—People aren't well, Dorian, they're dying. But I've heard that you keep right on doing all kinds of stuff, riding bareback –

—Well, what d'you expect me to be like, Baz? And*ee*, who has a hissy fit if his telephone hygienist doesn't clean the receiver properly?

—He has his foibles.

—Foibles? He's like some hideous mad old maid, who's terrified a roach is going to crawl into her piss flaps.

—Dorian, you've become somebody I don't recognise any more.

—You mean I don't resemble your stupid, lousy, derivative installation?

—Well, if you wanted to revitalise the gallery you could always exhibit *Cathode Narcissus*. With your reputation on the scene it would be a big hit.

—Bigger than the hits of smack and coke you've ponced off me?

—What is this, Dorian, this vituperation? Not even Henry is as big a bitch as you've become.

—Not even Henry is as big a ponce and a junky as you are, Baz.

Then Baz went and spoilt all this fabulously nasty repartee by saying something silly, like, I thought we had a relationship, Dorian . . . Unbelievably, he was on the verge of tears . . . Fuck it, we used to m-make love . . .

—In order to enjoy having sex with you, Baz, I had to become a masochist. Dorian circled the spoons, putting thirty-odd more between himself and Baz.

—Bring over *Cathode Narcissus*, Dorian – that'll make things right with us, with everything.

—I couldn't even if I wanted to, Baz. No, it's over between us. Over the years I've come to loathe your sensitive face. I'll tell you another thing, Baz. When you clear out of this joint – because I've given up the lease and you've got to be gone by tomorrow – do me a favour, and take the fucking cutlery with you. With this Dorian grabbed one of the spoons protruding from Gary's sculpture and yanked it out, which brought the whole clanking pile tumbling down.

—Hey! yelled the artist. You've bust my sculpture, man – you can't do that!

—Can – and I bloody well have. So what're you gonna do about it, *man*, make a distress call to And*ee*?

Gary lunged up out of the squashy embrace of the sofa and the two men began to circle it, both of them in fighters' crouches. Then Dorian went and spoilt it all by laughing uproariously. He chucked the spoon in Gary's face and bolted out of the door. His cackling and his footfalls retreated down the stairs. Gary sat back down. The Hispanic girl sobbed. Baz sank to the floor. The hurdy-gurdy music swelled, encompassing the futility of it all.

*   *   *

Tenderly, Baz removed the cigarette butt from Wotton's lips and dropped it into the teacup. There was another fizz. He looked down at the waxen face. The ill man's veined eyelids twitched and his lips parted to reveal yellowed incisors. He whimpered, as might a sleeping dog that was hunting in its dreams. 'I wonder if you heard that, old friend, before you gouched out?' Baz murmured. 'I say "friend", Henry, because I think of you as a friend, whatever it is that's happened between us. I think of you as a dying friend, someone just like me.'

Baz sighed, rose and went over to the glass partition. He peered through into the next room, where the remains of another young man's life were being meted out by the mechanical 'choof's of a respirator. He returned to his bedside vigil. He ran his hands over his crew cut and ground his fists into his eye sockets. He felt he had to appease the ghosts of his and Wotton's tumultuous past. He felt he needed to protect himself from his old friend's madness in the present. The future was simply terrifying. He felt – and that was the worst thing of all. A swollen emotional dyspepsia, compounded in equal parts of love, pity, fear and a desire for self-preservation that – all things considered – seemed ludicrously out of place. Still, at long last Basil Hallward had a measure of calm; there was nowhere to race to or escape from any more. He readied himself to soliloquise.

'Perhaps it's worth speaking to you now, Henry, speaking to you in a way that I'll probably never have the guts to when you're awake. Who knows, maybe you'll hear me. Fuck it – believe me – I'm not doing it for you or me, I'm doing it for us both.' Baz took a deep breath. Even when he was unconscious, Wotton's expression was mocking. 'Look, I think I know you, I think I know what that mask of cynicism obscures – a child, desperately frightened of his own capacity to feel and to be felt, to love and be loved. I was like that, and the mask had to be picked away at, and picked away at . . . as if . . . as if it were a hard scab protecting my raw features, until the vulnerable Baz underneath was exposed.' He got up again and began to pace around three sides of the bed.

'I escaped from New York, Henry. Or rather, one of the guys who'd been on the fringes of the scene, a wealthy gay guy with impeccable ethics – yes, such people exist – paid for me to go to rehab in the Midwest. I'm not saying it was easy – it fucking wasn't – but it was the beginning of my recovery. When I got there, Henry . . . it was as if I'd woken up in a surreal orphanage . . . All these people wandering around . . . They'd been devious fucking addicts and brawling drunks on the outside, but in this place they were children . . . Arrogant children screaming defiance – I want my sweetie drugs! As you can imagine, I was one of the loudest.'

Wotton's eyelids moved more rapidly. Was he asleep, or merely dreaming that he was – his opiated visions interleaving themselves with Baz's word pictures to create a flick-book that could be viewed only from an exact angle? From a point in between him and Baz, here and there, now and then.

*   *   *

It was a wooden room full of splintered people. There was pitch-pine cladding and polished pine floorboarding. Outside, evergreens shaded in the mid-ground and cancelled out any background altogether. In the foreground crouched more hutments, obviously part of the same camp. In this one there were slogans on the walls – 'I Can't – We Can', 'Keep It Simple', 'Just for Today' – that cumulatively implied the marketing of a suspiciously intangible product, such as invisible snake-oil. The strip lighting, the fire extinguisher, the laminated card printed with directions saying where to point the squirty foam, everything in sight screamed 'Institution!'; and while everybody in the room had their mouths shut tight, nevertheless their fidget language was strident. The motley collection of ten deadbeats sat in a loose circle of plastic stacking chairs, scratching, picking, jiggling and rubbing. Clearly, shit had been going down, and the one who appeared most dumped upon, most curled up in his chair, was Basil Hallward.

Billy, who had hair pressed into frizzy earphones by his baseball cap, and acne the same red as the fire extinguisher, felt moved to speak. You're full of shit, Baz, all you wanna talk about is the celebrities you've hung out with, an' all the ass you've had –

—Ass y'may've 'fected yo'sel' with AIDS. Y'wanted t'bring the whole fuckin' world down widya? Was that it, Baz? added Bear, a man who justified his moniker by reason of his size, his colour and his bushiness of beard.

Ashley, a preppy Percodan abuser, felt prompted to pipe up, You say you've loved people, Baz – I don't think you can have loved anyone ever, not even this Dorian guy you're so obsessed with. I don't think you know what love is.

Sven, the counsellor running this group, was, with his clipped sandy hair and smooth sandy beard, suitably Nordic in appearance. He looked very fit, absurdly fit, so fit it was difficult to believe that he too was a recovering addict. What substance could he possibly have abused – wood? OK, he said, that's enough, people; we've heard Basil's life story and you've read him your peer evaluations.

What I want you to share with us, Basil, is – how do you feel about what your group is saying to you?

—What do I feel, Sven?! I feel faintly nauseous, and if it weren't so absurd to imagine that these people are my peers, I expect I'd be offended by it. Very offended. But forgive them, Lord, they know not what they do. Baz's bravado was belied by the tears that leaked from his eyes.

It never failed, Sven thought, the peer evaluation. It didn't matter how smart or savvy an addict thought they might be, it was impossible for them to escape the verdict of Judge Junky. Do you think you're like Jesus, Baz? he said. That you're a martyr to your disease?

—And which disease would that be, Sven?

—The disease of addiction, Baz.

—Ha! That bullshit again. Where's the fucking virus that gives it to you then?

—Not all diseases are caused by viruses, Baz, you know that.

—OK, Sven, in that case what's the cure?

Before answering, the odious Odin flexed his mighty biceps in a luxuriant motion evocative of complete and healthy embodiment. There's no cure, Baz, you've been here long enough to know that. But maybe if you got offa that cross you're dangling on you might find what it is we here have to offer you. We can't cure you, Baz – but we can help. Am I right, people?

*   *   *

'Who knows whether any kind of treatment really works, Henry. Treatment for the disease of addiction or AIDS. I don't want to sell you on the idea of rehab. Looking back, I'm not so sure I didn't stay clean *despite* rather than because of it. But it did give me the opportunity to put things in their correct place.' As Baz spoke, *sotto voce*, he was putting things in their correct place. He emptied the ashtrays into the bin and the dregs from the bottles into the sink. He stacked the hospital crockery on the hospital tray, and folded

Wotton's clothing over the trouser press. If nothing that Baz had softly said could convince a cynical onlooker of his change in character, then these actions at least spoke pleasantly of practical alterations.

'It's language that you'd find laughable – repugnant, even – if you were conscious, but I had a form of spiritual awakening in rehab. Naturally' – he nearly chuckled – 'finding out you're going to die a fuck of a lot sooner, rather than the hoped-for hell of a lot later, does help. You also make intense friendships in those places, Henry; you're thrown together with all kinds of people, and either you learn to like them or you end up going mad with hatred for yourself. I made friends with a guy called Bear. He'd been a fucking gangster, he'd killed, he was from the Chicago projects, he was black. Shit, he was even a straight guy who'd *raped* queers in Federal Pen – but he was the one who helped me when I was diagnosed.'

As in some promotional film for a cancer hospice, two men walked beside a lake, the brilliance of the sunlight on the blue water rendering them insubstantial. Baz was walking with Bear in this suitably sylvan setting, and the big black man had his arm tight around Baz's narrow shoulders. Listen, Baz, he said, there ain't nothin' no one can say to make this one good.

—You're fucking right there, Bear.

—I remember when they tol' me, I jus' cried an' screamed. It called to mind every goddamn time I'd cranked up in my whole sorry life. All them spikes diggin' inta me, like spears or arrows. I hollered so much they hadta put me in County for a night. Counsellor drove me there himsel' –

—What? Sven?

—Yeah, an' I tell you, Baz, that man cares. He really does.

—Yeah – whether he cares or not, we're still gonna fucking die, Bear. We're still gonna die – what's the point in staying clean, working a programme, all that shit, only to die at the end of it? And Baz broke down.

—'Cause you're worth more than that, Baz, you're worth more.

We're all worth more . . . He cradled Baz's head in his big hand, as a mother might protect the skull of a baby . . . I'm gonna do what they say, he continued, I'm gonna stay clean. I ain't gonna die hatin' mysel' for jus' another dumb motherfuckin' junky.

*   *   *

Done with the housekeeping, Baz sat on the chair beside the bed, looking down at his friend. In keeping this vigil Baz was freed to speak of earlier vigils, because that was the temper of the time. Wotton himself lay sinisterly calm. But maybe he wasn't sleeping, merely lying stock-still, for fear any admission that he could hear what Baz Hallward said would make his own bravura in the face of death quite untenable.

'He did die, Henry. I was there. It wasn't in a ward like this one either, with hip nurses and halfway decent doctors. It was a run-down Medicare ward on the south side of Chicago. A joint where the orderlies zipped guys with pneumonia, and covered with fucking KS, into body-bags days before they died, because they knew they were going to and they didn't want to fucking *touch* them. Those guys wailed and screamed, lying in their own piss and shit. But I and guys from Bear's group sat vigil with him, we cleaned him up, we hassled the medics for pain relief. We looked after him. And I tell you, Henry, that man died with *dignity*. He died with *grace*. A fucking no-hope ghetto boy, an addict, a fucking crack dealer, a killer. He died with dignity because he could love himself a little – and let others love him too. I wonder if it can be like that for us, Henry? I have my regime. I spend an hour and a half every fucking day boiling up Chinese herbs and drinking the vile broth. I shove selenium suppositories up my arse – the only thing that gets shoved up there nowadays. I do the acupuncture, I take other prophylactics. But every year the virus gets a little stronger, outwits me a little faster. Every year I end up in hospital for longer, like you, with a drip pumping AZT and DDC and DDI into me. And every year the mollusca – as you so coyly put it – proliferate, while the shingles sprout in my fucking colon and my weight falls. We've been lucky enough already Henry, you and I, but no one dies lucky.' He leaned forward and snapped off the light; the room was plunged into the unquiet grave of a night-time hospital. 'Well, goodnight, Henry. I'd like to say I don't envy you at all, smacked out of your fucking gourd, but at times like this . . . I do.' And at last, Baz left the room. But perhaps if he'd paused outside for a few moments he would have heard some snuffling, evidence that his words had been heard. Perhaps.

10

Car horns were hooting and ambulance sirens were singing from the concrete rocks in front of the Middlesex Hospital. The worn-out brakes of black cabs squealed, and pneumatic drills hammered exclamation marks into the margins of streets. The city bowed down to the east, expressing all its robust matutinal reverence – for itself. In the immediate vicinity of Henry Wotton's little cubicle of a room there was the squeak of rubber tyres on linoleum, the rattle of crockery being stacked in plastic crates and the 'chink-chink' of an approaching drug trolley. Wotton ungummed his eyelids to see the doorway packed full of medical students and junior doctors, who, like any class of adolescents, were affecting the manner of their pedagogue. The pockets of their white coats bulged with radio pagers, stethoscopes, Biros and chewing gum, while their eyes were bugged out by the attempt to mask prurient curiosity with professional detachment.

As Wotton's own eyes reached their maximum aperture, he saw that two men had ventured right inside and were louring over him. With devilish cunning they must have advanced under the cover of one of the grey patches that floated across his visual field. But now he saw them for who they were: Spittal, the consultant, an oncologist by bent, and Gavin Strood, the senior duty nurse. 'My, my,' Spittal purred, '*Mister* Wotton, how tidy it is in your lair today.' He was tall, stooped, round-shouldered. His prognathous jaw drew charcoal grooves across his papery face. It was amazing that he believed himself enough of a pussycat to affect a purr.

Wotton stirred. 'Is it?' He goggled around him at the order imposed by Baz during the night. 'Oh . . . It is.'

'Did you or the auxiliary staff do this, Gavin?'

'No, Doctor.' Gavin folded his arms. 'It must've been Henry's visitor.'

During this exchange Wotton was heeled over, frantically opening drawers in the bedside cabinet and rummaging inside them. Evidently he found what he was looking for, because he collapsed back on to the pillows with a sigh.

'Looking for your ssstash, are you, *Missster* Wotton?' Now Spittal was snaky and sibilant.

'Unfortunately, unlike you I haven't been provided with a convenient trolley for my drugs.'

'Can you give me one good reason why I shouldn't call the police, *Mister* Wotton?' This threat was studiously ignored. Wotton had found a hand-mirror, in which he now examined his ravaged features. 'I said, *Mister* Wotton, why the hell shouldn't I have you arrested?'

'Still here, Spittal? I'm sorry, I always find myself checking a mirror after someone's accused me of being bad – a guilty conscience is *so* narcissistic.' This was *so* impertinent that the students gave an anxious susurrus – what would Spittal's vengeance be?

'Apparently you're to be discharged this morning. In view of this I'm going to let you go . . .' a sigh of student relief '. . . to put it bluntly, you'll be dead within weeks anyway, given your drug abuse, but otherwise I'd refuse to have you back on this ward again.'

There was a murmur of dissent – this wasn't what the young Hippocratics were going into the healing business for, and unlike their consultant they weren't inclined to view mass forcible castration of homosexuals and drug addicts as the solution to the AIDS epidemic. But they needn't have worried, for Wotton merely struck a further attitude. 'In that case you condemn me to the London Clinic, where I shall have to die beyond my means.'

'You can die anywhere you please,' spat Spittal, 'so long as it isn't on my AIDS ward.'

'Yes, we wouldn't want to queer your statistics, now, would we?

You don't mind that all your patients die, as long as a hundred per cent of them die pliant and contrite and stupefied on *your* morphine.'

'What the hell are you saying, man?' Spittal was starting to turn an unpleasant, vinous purple. 'This isn't some restaurant where you can bring your own bottle.'

'Oh yes you bloody can,' Wotton snorted, 'but the corkage is extortionate.'

'Are you implying' – Spittal was now muted with barely repressed rage – 'that you've been bribing my staff?'

However, visibly buoyed up by this rebarbative exchange, Wotton was content to lapse into silence, leaving Spittal, in a final metamorphosis, to gulp like a landed fish.

'I don't think,' said Gavin, judiciously sensing a shift in the balance of power in the room, 'that you can tell a patient he won't be readmitted.'

'What!'

'He'll have to be taken in here or at St Mary's, and if he goes there he'll tell them what happened here.'

'Don't tell me what I can or can't do on my own bloody ward!'

Wotton observed the way the conflict was widening with considerable satisfaction. 'When the doctors disagree,' he mused aloud, 'the patient is in accord with himself.' He would have said a lot more on the subject, but at that moment Baz appeared, his cropped head nodding along the corridor. 'Ah!' Wotton exclaimed. 'This looks like my lift.'

Taking this as an opportunity for face-saving, Spittal drew himself up to his full height and stalked out of the room. The little herd of future physicians trotted dutifully after him.

'Have you come to take me away, ha ha, ho ho, hee hee?' Wotton said to Baz once they'd gone.

'Yeah, I called Batface this morning and she asked me to – she has a seminar at the University. I went and got the Jag from Chelsea; it's outside.'

'Well, let's be off then.' Wotton began dumping drugs and

cigarettes from the bedside cabinet into an exaggerated sponge bag. 'My wife is a better doctor than this lot.'

'Yes, but her PhD's in history.' Baz gave Wotton the feed line as he helped him up out of the bed.

'Indeed, but neither death nor vulgarity is likely to be cured by modern medicine.'

A decade is a long time in hubcaps, and three of the Jag's hadn't made it. The exposed bolts gave the car a constructivist air, as if a mechanically-minded child might at any moment pick it up from the roadway and remove the wheels with sticky fingers. Possibly the same child had been playing with the Jag in a sandpit, because the car, once merely unkempt, was now filthy, covered not only with the action splatter of bird-shit, but also by another hardened and excremental substance. An envious, infantile person (although envious of whom exactly – the imaginary child?) had savagely keyed the Jag's flank, gouging out long streaks of the paintwork. Inside the car, ten years had flowed over the upholstery, depositing several further layers of silt. The poor Jag, once as securely proud of its era as a portly Edwardian gentleman sporting a shotgun and standing behind a mound of fresh game, was now stuck at traffic lights by the Dorchester on Park Lane (lights that hadn't existed in 1981), and hemmed in on all sides by boxier, sleeker, more modular vehicles. It was as if cheap and flashy mafiosi had joined the pheasant shoot.

At least Wotton himself, although emaciated, still affected three pieces of tweed, even if today he couldn't quite manage the driving. 'You'll see *him* tonight,' he confided to his chauffeur from the front passenger seat.

'Tonight?' Baz didn't require a name.

'Absolutely, together with the old crowd – the Ferret, Campbell, Jane Narborough . . . It was to have been a little homecoming party for me, but *you* may share it . . .'

'I – I don't know.'

'Oh, come on, Baz, you said there was a favour you needed to ask him. Besides, I'm sure you're intrigued to see him in his current manifestation.'

'What will that be, then?' The lights changed to a flashing orange; Baz shifted into drive, and with laudable caution piloted the expensive wreck down to and around Hyde Park Corner, then off along Knightsbridge.

'Who can say?' Wotton said. 'The late eighties were a real efflorescence for Dorian; his petals fluttered in the breezes that blew during that hot, hot summer of love. He's so capacious that the new bagginess of the era suited him just fine. He yakked on the mobile phones, he twirled the baseball hats, he twitted the teenagers and, of course, he took a muckle of ecstasy. You have to hand it to our Dorian, Baz, he threw on the sweaty threads of contemporaneity with his usual casualness, exposing himself to all the same risks as his impulsive peers. I believe he even adopted the moniker "Dor", and encouraged them to believe him incubated in a perspex carport and born of Maidstone. A child of the London periphery exactly like themselves.

'He told me of diabolical nights beneath the sodium glare of the streetlamps around the Oxford ring road. Together with his hooded posse he would stake out the forecourts of petrol stations, waiting for the foolishness of a key left in an ignition. A sprint, a scrabble, a squeal of tyres and they'd be gone, leaving the idiotic previous owner screeching in their wake. They'd drive for hundreds of miles around the Midlands, from this field full of fucated flamingos to that marquee of madness, always accompanied by the tweet and thud and thrum of techno.

'Ah, Baz, we were born too early, *n'est-ce pas*? Would that we too could have swum among the bodies of a thousand sweaty youths, as they synchronously waved like seaweed fronds beneath the sea of pheromones and sweat. Like Dorian, we too could have whirled in the solid mandala of flesh, sweat arcing from our brows like the sperm of a Hindu deity!' Wotton timed this rhetorical flourish to coincide with a slim cigarette's being tucked between his thin lips.

To his surprise, Baz said, 'I'll have one of those, Henry.'

'What? I assumed you no longer smoked, either.'

'Well, perhaps I need at least one cheap kick.' He took the pack.

'There's nothing cheap about those, Baz; they're Turkish State Monopoly cigarettes, the most morally costly tobacco in the world. Every time you light one up – a Kurd dies.

'I digress. Dorian was perfectly tailored for this off-the-peg youth cult, with its pre-millennial cocktail of stimulant drugs and dance music. How he cavorted, how he smarmed, like a cat in a thicket of knees . . . So much of a fixture did he become on this "scene" that its other tenants imagined he had no other. But that's the way of smooth diamonds like Dorian; every face they show to the world is simply a different facet. Think of him, Baz, lying on a disordered duvet, in some parental bedroom at the end of a Barratt cul-de-sac, garlanded in teen flesh! Who could begrudge him this – when, after all, youth is no stranger to friction.'

They were at the lights, alongside Harrods, that vertical Babylonian souk. Baz stared into the inert eyes of a mannequin squeezed inside a thousand-pound tube of Versace. Its rigid digits beckoned to him, summoning him behind the plate glass. He turned back to Wotton, handed him the cigarette packet, took the lighter with his own rigid digits. Lighting up, he tried hard not to think of himself as setting a touch-paper to his own explosive nature. 'You mean to say, Henry . . .' he concentrated on the matter in hand, although the cigarette smoke made him feel as if a pyre had been ignited in his mouth, and he didn't dare inhale '. . . that none of these kids ever found it creepy – this man, in his late twenties, fiddling with their flies?'

'He doesn't *look it*, Baz – that's the point. Time may have etched our faces, like acid biting into copper, but Dorian's visage is an Etch-a-Sketch; no smear of dissipation or leer of venality – let alone marks of ageing – remains upon it for long. *De temps en temps* I wonder who's twiddling the knobs and then shaking away the Dorians they draw.

'But you also have to remember, Baz, that along with HIV another plague hit our sceptred isle in the mid-eighties, courtesy of your American friends. This was a pandemic of pecs and an outbreak of deltoids. Every underemployed faggot in town began to "work out", as if to raise a sinewy standard against the wasting disease. No one was more adept at aerobics than our Dorian – he positively glowed, as if he spent nights disco dancing in a wind tunnel. And in the season he's always to be seen schussing in the vicinity of Klosters, where the House of Windsor swaps their speedy decline for a spot of downhill racing. Yes, he has his legs tightly wrapped around the greasy pole, does Dorian. His social and his sexual promiscuity have had the same bewildering effect – that of making him incomprehensible and unknowable. Is he gay or straight? Is he nob or yob? Incidentally, how old is he, exactly?

'He's carried all of this off with a most astonishing sang-froid, Baz. I might've wanted to view Dorian as my protégé, but he far exceeds anything I could have *dreamed* of creating. After all, it was widely touted that the homosexual community were in danger of dying of ignorance, but in Dorian's case he was more likely to expire from being too *knowing*. Yes, he's *always* been in the right place at the right time. I remember being at some avant-garde event and watching Leigh Bowery mimic a miscarriage on stage. It struck me then that it was Dorian who was truly orchestrating the mental couvade male homosexuals felt they were enacting in the late eighties. If Bowery was the mother, then Dorian was the mother of all mothers, showing us how to give birth to our own images.'

Fittingly, as this speech concluded they arrived. Baz squidged the Jag's wheels against the kerb, then switched off the engine. It was silent save for the deathwatch ticking of contracting metal, and utterly oppressive. Outside the car, the impossibilist season that always embowered Chez Wotton was in full budding, flowering, fruiting and falling swing. Supernature's own couvade. Cherry and apple blossom drifted across the pavement, while everything in the gardens – from snowdrops to roses, to lilacs and delphiniums –

was in bloom. The wistaria, which ten years previously had only sprouted halfway up the first storey, now covered the entire façade like a vegetative beard. The grey clowns sat in the green car, quietly contemplating this harlequinade.

'C'mon now,' said Wotton, 'let's get inside. I didn't discharge myself from the Middlesex to sit in a car.'

'In good time, Henry –'

'This *is* good time – I want to go in the bloody house. I w –'

'Henry, you're holding out on me.'

'What d'you mean?'

'You're not telling me everything – everything about Dorian.'

'I thought I'd made myself tediously plain, Baz; I don't *know* everything about Dorian. Hardly anyone knows that much. I know a bit, you know a bit, doubtless others know bits, but no one knows the lot. Probably not even Dorian himself.'

'Does Dorian know about Herman – about what happened to him?'

'Herman?'

'Don't come the fucking ingénu with me, Henry.' Without asking, Baz took the pack from where it lay between them and shook one out. 'You know bloody well who I'm talking about. Herman, the black kid Dorian was carrying a torch for, the one who fucking burnt us all!'

'Ah, *that* Herman. Yes, well, I believe he's no longer with us.'

'The virus, right?'

'Erm . . . no, not exactly. As I understand it from Dorian, young Herman, seeing his personal defeat in the War Against Drugs, took the noble, Roman way out.'

'Henry! What're you saying, that the kid killed himself?'

'Precisely – shortly after the *vernissage* for your installation. Now give me my cigarettes back.'

The two men sat in angry, pained silence and smoked. They smoked a lot. Baz would've liked to cry for Herman, but this death was a decade old, and there were so many others jumbling up the intervening years, so many skeletal young men shot with each other's guns, their corpses shovelled into time's trenches. 'How,' he muttered eventually, 'did Dorian find out?'

'Ah well' – Wotton visibly brightened at the opportunity for anecdote – 'there lies a tale. Dorian went to enquire after Herman at the hole he slunk into occasionally to shoot up, but it turned out there was a snake in this hole. A skinhead snake, a vicious little fucker who also had a thing for our Herman. He didn't so much tell Dorian about Herman's demise as scream it at him while giving chase through Soho brandishing a knife. After that Dorian was *very* circumspect. This character – his name is Ginger – had no way of finding Dorian, but he averred that if he could he would wreak all sorts of mundane nastiness on that heavenly body.

'The thing is' – Wotton flicked his butt out through the car window – 'that wasn't the last Dorian saw of Ginger.'

'No?'

'Oh no, he's seen him around, on the scene, as it were. In clubs, at raves, here and there. Every time Ginger claps eyes on Dorian, he goes for him like a Rottweiler . . . Dangerous dogs are all the rage in Britain at the moment, Baz. I myself have thought of acquiring one, if only in order to add a little *frisson* to my relationship with Bluejay . . . Suffice to say, if *this* Cerberus ever catches up with our Orpheus that'll be the end of him. Not even Dorian is immune to a knife, or a fist or a gun.'

If Wotton had sought to provoke Baz, he was disappointed. The prospect of Dorian being done did nothing for Baz. He stared out through the windscreen at the mid-morning calm of this moneyed embayment. A crocodile of schoolboys in antiquated corduroy knickerbockers passed by, shepherded by a teacher with an umbrella for a crook. A postwoman slogged up the steps of the Wottons' house, unlimbered her canvas sack, withdrew a sheaf of oblongs, stuffed them in the brass slot and then withdrew herself.

Without a word, Baz got out of the Jag and went round to the passenger side. To tug Wotton up and out by the velvet lapels of his Crombie, to feel his body like a bundle of struts sheathed in tweed, to smell the sick sweat on his stippled cheek – none of this was bearable. Baz levered him upright and leant him, like a coat-tree bought at an antiques fair, against the furry haunch of the Jag. 'Jesus, Henry,' he panted, 'I'm no stronger than you, I shouldn't be dragging you about. You could do this yourself if you'd. Just. Stop. The. Fucking. Smack.' Each word was another heave in the direction of the front door.

'Steady, Baz . . .' Wotton addressed him as if he were a groom – or a horse '. . . steady – we're not late for a business meeting.'

'Really? I would've thought you'd already arranged for a morning conference with Jah Bluejay. When I put your stuff away last night you only had a couple of rocks and a trace of smack. That's not going to last you for long, is it?'

'Oh, I don't know, Baz, even my flesh feels a little unwilling nowadays. As for Bluejay – he's no Rastafarian; he affects all that clobber – the dreadlocks and what have you – so that stupid squad will think he's a holy ganja smoker.'

'Unbelievable.'

'You say that, but it seems to work. Still, you're right, he'll be here soon enough. I *am* his oldest customer – and seniority has its privileges. Last year he baked me a cake for my birthday.' They'd gained the front door and Wotton was groping under the skirts of his coat for his keys. 'Bloody keys!' he expostulated. 'Fucking bloody stupid keys! Always the keys!' He was more distressed by this than he'd been about anything else, and seemed close to weeping.

'Calm down, Henry,' Baz admonished him. '*I've* got the keys, *I* drove.' He admitted them to the house and, dropping Wotton's bag in the hallway, followed him as he limped on into the drawing room. Wotton slumped down on the chaise-longue and Baz settled awkwardly by his slippered feet.

In the ten years since Baz had last seen the room it had changed, although not as much as could have been reasonably hoped for. The uncomfy seating areas had been winnowed out a little, as if subjected to a decade-long game of musical chairs, and in their place two separate cultures had emerged at opposite ends of the long room. One was centred on an ornate Second Empire escritoire and had an advanced paper economy comprising piles of books, file cards, and yellow legal stationery. The counter-culture was based around a modern reclining armchair and was devoted to entertainment and medicine in equal measure. A huge television and VCR cabinet was set six feet in front of the recliner, its top and shelves stacked with tapes. By contrast, the mantelpiece above the fireplace and the shelves of two adjoining bookcases were lined with medicaments of all descriptions, both conventional and alternative, prescription and proscribed. In between these two sites wended a trail of children's toys, here a teddy or a doll, there a picture book.

'So,' said Baz, 'no one here to greet you at all?'

'Well, as you know, Batface is at her seminar – she's teaching part-time now at University College and writing a book as well, about Madame de Sévigné . . .'

'You're proud of her?'

'Of course. I respect knowledge; its possessors are usually a little less stupid than the ignorant.'

'You're weird, Henry. Totally weird. What's mellowed you? Are you happy together?'

'A man can be happy with any woman as long as he doesn't love her.'

'Ha! No – still the fucking same bitter man. Still slicing everything up with your bloody epigrams.'

'I wouldn't do it, Baz, if life weren't a chance meeting upon an operating table between a sadistic surgeon and a patient with Munchausen's.'

Baz looked about at the toys. 'And Phoebe, who you care about just enough to get her HIV-tested – how old did you say she was? Six? Seven?'

'Perhaps minus sixty or seventy would be closer to the truth, since Batface seems intent on raising her in the inter-war period, complete with ringlets, singlets and a Norland-fucking-nanny.'

As if responding to this rantlette, the nanny in question came into the room. She was following the trail of toys, picking them up as she went. She certainly looked the part, with her thick blonde hair cut in a dead straight fringe, across a brow of such pink clarity that every single one of her eyebrow hairs was distinctly visible. In the middle of each plump cheek glowed a warm red spot, and every item of her apparel – velvet Alice band, pleated skirt, powder-blue tights, quilted sleeveless anorak and candy-striped blouse – could have been chosen with parodic intent. 'Oh golly!' she brayed upon noticing them. 'Henry . . . Mr Wotton . . . sorry . . . I didn't realise you were back.'

'Yes, Claire, I'm back, back from my exciting sojourn in town, to this charming but parochial backwater. This is Mr Hallward.'

'How d'you do.' She offered a hand well shaped – for a trowel – and well used to mucking out, both horses and humans.

'Oh, all right I s'pose –' Too much time spent in the States meant Baz took her greeting as a genuine request for information.

'He means,' Wotton put in, 'all right given that like me he has the dreaded lurgy. Better not get too close, Nanny Claire; he might get you with his death breath.'

If Wotton had hoped to freak Claire out with this sally, he was gravely disappointed, for she merely clapped a trowel hand to his forehead and observed brusquely, 'You're running a fever, Henry, I'll help you into your chair. Is the medication from the hospital in that overnight bag in the hall?'

'Yes,' said Baz, 'I packed it.'

'I'll get that first then.'

While she was gone, Wotton tried to give Baz a conspiratorial look, which said, can you believe this sham caring? But Baz was comforted by Nanny Claire's competent manner and ignored him. He got up from the chaise-longue and wandered over to the bay window, where he stood, looking up and away from the sickroom. Behind him he dimly registered another bout of nannying.

'C'mon now . . . that's right . . . honestly, your shirt is wringing wet, I'll help you out of it. Is it still the Cidofovir three-hourly?'

'I'm not having that shit – it's evil. Bluejay will sort me out when he arrives.'

'Not with anything that'll deal with the herpes virus in your eyes.'

'I don't want to be so sick that I shan't enjoy my dinner party.'

'You won't be having any dinner party at all if you don't take your medication.'

It was astonishing, Baz mused, how Henry managed to maintain the most compliant set of people around him. Any other gay man who'd lived his life in this fashion – sham marriage, rampant drug addiction and now the virus – would've found himself at best abandoned. But Henry simply carried on as before; he seemed to view the whole deathly débâcle as merely another opportunity to *épater* the bourgeoisie he so detested. Was there perhaps a certain nobility in this? Or at any rate a level of philosophic detachment? Yes, Henry had always been detached, not only from society but from the entire epoch as well. It wasn't merely because of his sexuality and his drug addiction, either. What was it that he had adopted as a fetish of time itself? Something – or rather someone – whom he used to view from this very window? 'That was it,' Baz muttered as his gaze zeroed in on the fifth storey of the flats opposite, 'the jiggling man.' It *was* the jiggling man and he was still at it, rocking and hopping from side to side like an autistic imprisoned in his own head, or a disturbed bear trapped in a zoo cage.

Baz stared at the jiggling man with horrified pity, while the bickering continued behind him. Christ! It had been a long time, a long, long, lonely time for the jiggling man. It would've been comforting if this urban anchorite hadn't aged as quickly as the outside world, but the reverse was the case. Jiggling for the past decade had really taken it out of him. His hair had gone grey, his face had become lumpy and blotched, his V-neck pullover was sadly raddled. Baz stared and stared as the jiggling man simply jiggled. What was it that Henry had said? That the jiggling man was meting out the very seconds allotted to the world? That he was a sibylline metronome prophesying the day they all would die? Well, judging by his worsened appearance, this now lay in the not too distant future.

II

Dusk fell over the summertime city like a hunter's net weighted with the threat of night-time. London mewled and thrashed, then, becoming completely entangled, lay still, awaiting its chance to lash out again. In the Wottons' asynchronous establishment lights were switched on prematurely, in order to ward off fear of darkness as much as darkness itself. Basil Hallward, after distracted hours of watching Wotton ride the rollercoaster of intoxication, found himself back in front of the bay window.

The jiggling man's lights were also on, and although Baz hadn't been watching him the whole time, he still found it difficult to believe that he'd stopped jiggling for long enough to gain the switch. How did he eat or sleep or shit? How did he incorporate any of the normal functions of life into this ceaseless motion? Was there a ministering angel, a Nanny Claire who was always there for the jiggling man? Who would darn his unravelling woolly or twine together the frayed ends of his unravelled psyche? One thing was for certain, guests were assembling for a party at the Wottons' house and the jiggling man wasn't invited.

Baz turned away from the window. Standard lamps and wall brackets, dangling fitments and daringly unshaded bulbs, all gushed wanness. The guests stood about in a variety of heraldic conversational poses, from couchant to rampant. It was the cocktail tourney and Baz felt highly vulnerable. He had failed to pack his character armour. What was he doing? He had intended to spend at most a day with Henry Wotton, to pass on the message of recovery and discuss their mutual friend. He knew that this environment was poison to him – one dose might just be bearable, but to expose himself further was to risk the most dangerous emotional anaphylaxis. And he was smoking cigarettes again! He huffed. How absurd was this? He puffed. The most useless, damaging and addictive of drugs – what was the *point*? He huffed again.

A smallish girl of eight or nine, wearing an old-fashioned muslin frock and with her brown hair in ringlets, materialised by Baz's elbow. She broke the surface of his pool of self-recrimination with her alarmingly undershot jaw and goofy teeth. She was skilfully bearing a tray of Champagne flutes. Would you like a glass of shampoo, Mr Hallward? she piped.

—No thanks, Phoebe, I don't drink, you see.

—What d'you mean – are you a robot?

—No no, I mean I don't drink alcohol.

—My father says that fizzy drinks don't count as booze.

—Perhaps not for him, but they do for me. Can you find me an orange juice?

—Oh, all right then, if you insist.

She tripped away, to be replaced by another figure almost as diminutive. But this one was mannish and old, wrinkled and psychically malodorous. It was the Ferret. Well, Baz, long time no see. I understand from our host that you've become quite the clean-liver queen.

—I'm dying, Fergus, just like Henry, and I've no time left for being stoned.

—Ah yes, Baz, but you've *always* insisted on calling a spade a spade, so it's no *wonder* that you've managed to dig your own grave.

—Are you suggesting it's my literalism that's killing me rather than AIDS? Even as he did it Baz regretted being drawn into this banter.

—I wouldn't know, the Ferret snuffled; I haven't qualifications in either philosophy *or* medicine. Have you met Gavin?

It was the nurse from the Middlesex Hospital, which explained to Baz his air of familiarity with the whole Wotton coterie. With his blond good looks and affable manner, he was an altogether planed-down version of the Ferret's usual bits of rough. Now that he was suited and booted as well, he floated in the prevailing social current rather better than his two interlocutors. I'm pleased to meet you again in a social context – he addressed Basil – I know your work.

—Really? Basil found it impossible not to be flattered.

—Yes – I did a foundation course at St Martin's; my tutor was an admirer of your installations. You've become very influential, a sort of British Viola – but I'm sure you knew that.

—Well . . . yes . . . Baz blustered. Still, it's different hearing it to reading it in some mag. So, what happened to *your* art?

—Oh, I dropped out. Gavin affected the inertia common to all drop-outs at all times and in all places.

The Ferret said, To care for me, the love.

—No, that's not right, Fergus, and you know it. I left to do nursing, but the NHS doesn't pay a living wage, so I take on the odd private patient.

Very odd, Baz thought, then remarked aloud, You seem altogether more sprightly than I remember, Fergus.

—Yes, the homunculus tittered; nowadays I have no difficulty in being distinctly chipper and alive to the world – why, I'm always up at the dawn of crack.

—D'you see much of Dorian?

—Oh, no no . . . My dear boy, Dorian is *far* too popular for leathery old queens like us; frankly, I'll be amazed if he turns up this evening. Which is just a little bad of him, because Henry quite *created* him. Still, how the butterfly despises the pupa, hmm?

There was a little hubbub by the door to the drawing room, and Wotton and Batface loomed up from their respective pits of conversation to welcome in David Hall, who was limping heavily, despite being supported on the one hand by a three-pronged aluminium walking stick, and on the other by a willowy, fortyish blonde.

—Ah, said the Ferret, the Minister for Housing, you know him of course, Baz?

—No, not really. What's wrong with him?

—Oh, he had a stroke last year. You could say a lucky stroke, since it's done *wonders* for his popularity. Now the way he limps towards the future makes him the perfect personification of the regime.

—Isn't that Hester Wharton with him?

—Yes – they say she married him for his crippled cachet as much as his bulging portfolio. Pity is a *beastly* perversion, wouldn't you agree?

Despite himself Baz found he was being swept away by this snide cataract, for it was exactly as it had always been in the vicinity of Wotton, with quipsters vying for opportunities to torpedo meaningful conversation with their *bons mots*, and stooges such as himself providing them with the set-ups for their cheap shots. When I knew her, Baz said, she'd slept with half the men in New York –

—And now she's sleeping with half a man in London, said a silky-voiced interloper, whereupon all three men turned to confront –

—Dorian! Baz despised himself for his enthusiasm.

—My dear, dear Baz . . . It took until the second 'dear' for Baz to realise that this salutation wasn't dripping with venomous sarcasm, that in fact it was genuinely affectionate. Baz had also forgotten how charming sheer beauty could be; or rather, he had done his level best to recondition his sensibility, so that it could no longer affect him. However, this availed him naught – he was caught once more in Dorian's seductive web . . . *Enchanté*, breathed the beauteous one, kissing him on either cheek; he then confirmed the specialness of this intimacy by merely turning to the Ferret and Gavin and saying, Fergus, Gavin.

Baz stared at Dorian, who was resplendent in the sharpest of *à la mode* suiting, his lapels mere stilettos, ready to cut to the quick whosoever might grasp them. Dorian's hair was a golden cap on his flawlessly brown brow. Set beside the Ferret – whose skin was so wrinkled it appeared as if his eyes were peering out through a shattered windscreen – or even Gavin – whose stripped-pine features nevertheless exposed his own peculiar dendrochronology – Dorian's complexion was porelessly smooth. It's been nearly five years, Dorian, Baz exclaimed, and you haven't changed a bit!

—Oh, the product has changed, Baz, believe me; it's only the packaging that remains the same. But you – you're altogether a different man. My informants tell me that like crystal dunked in Fairy Liquid you're squeaky clean. Congratulations.

—I didn't do it by myself, Dorian.

—Nonsense, Baz, *you're* a true artist, and artists always create themselves to begin with; then the more wildly inventive you are, the more you feel called upon to reinvent yourselves –

He would have gone on, but at this point a rental major-domo entered via the double doors at the furthest end of the room and declaimed, Ladies, Gentlemen, dinner is served. Without more ado the guests unfroze their heraldic poses and began to make their way out. Baz hung back, watching as Dorian encountered first Wotton and then Alan Campbell, who was struggling up from a large leather hassock. Campbell, while as dapper and bloodless as ever, bore the fatal taint upon his smooth features. Baz noted that his now scraggy neck was wrapped in a voluminous cravat, and suspected that beneath such a sartorial solecism would be found embarrassing KS medallions. Put next to Wotton and Campbell, Dorian appeared to belong to a different order of being. While he might not have been able to acknowledge this at any conscious or rational level, Baz sensed that Dorian had not only escaped the clutches of the virus, he had also freed himself from all the dreary claims of the body. Pausing in the doorway, Dorian offered his arm to the ever absurd – but always pitiable – Batface. He turned briefly towards Baz and smiled in a cheesy, feline manner, such that his grin remained after the rest of him had passed on through.

An hour later one course had been served, chewed and removed, and a second had taken its place and been half consumed. The Wottons' board was long and serpentine; it snaked awkwardly along the length of the basement-cum-dining room, kinking here to avoid a buttress, and over there to skirt a chimney breast or a fitted bookcase. White damask was thrown over this concatenation of sub-tables, which meant that adjoining diners found themselves sitting at slightly different heights, as if the one were set up on a small stage for the other's entertainment. The cutlery, the crockery and the glassware were as rented as the major-domo, who, assisted by two other hirelings, was charging glasses and circulating platters.

Perhaps the most surprising thing for a visitor unfamiliar with a milieu such as this would have been the discovery that the Wottons were one of those upper-class families who tended towards being hypertrophied bourgeois. Down here in the basement there were kiddy daubs and snapshots pinned on cork boards, while the furniture was the same overstuffed and spindly freak show that had been mounted in the drawing room. There was some unavoidable mingling, but mostly it was Wotton and his pals who occupied the dining-room end of the table (warped old boys flanked by upstanding tallboys), while Batface and her friends resided in the more rational and uncomfortable milieu of the kitchen.

All along the length of the table limped a procession of Badoit bottles, wine bottles, beer bottles, flower vases and candlesticks, as if they were soldiery fleeing the mouths of the diners, which, like the barrels of guns, sent forth volley after volley of conversation. 'Nowadays,' said Wotton to Jane Narborough, who was sitting on his right, 'I want my sins to be like sushi – fresh, small and entirely raw.'

'I shouldn't imagine you'd say that, Henry, if you looked at some sushi through a microscope.' She spooned up a blob of her individual cheese soufflé for emphasis. 'They're absolutely *crawling* with bacteria.'

'So am I,' he replied succinctly.

Meanwhile Dorian was putting his even bite on the new Mrs Hall, Hester Wharton. She was a distinctly chilly and exiguous blonde in a grey silk shift dress the consistency of water vapour.

Her nipples stuck through the material like chilled glacé cherries in a freezer cabinet. 'Of course,' he drawled, 'the Gulf War never *really* happened . . .'

'What the hell d'you mean?' She had married Hall for his apparent straightforwardness and was finding his compatriots' extreme facetiousness very hard to take.

'Please,' Dorian damped her down, 'I can see I've offended you –'

'You haven't! I just wanna know, what the hell d'you mean?'

'I mean that the Gulf War didn't happen.' Dorian held up his hands and began telling off the fictions on his manicured fingers. 'There was no invasion of Kuwait, no tense standoff, no coalition-building, no Scuds falling on Tel Aviv, no bombs smartly singling out Ba'athist apparatchiks in Baghdad, no refugees on the Jordanian border, no Republican Guards buried on the Basra road, no Schwarzkopf, no dummkopfs, no tortured RAF pilots, no victory, no none of it. No Gulf War. Can I make myself any clearer?'

'I bet you wouldn't say that,' she said, 'if it was one of your kids who'd died in the Allied bombing, or been wiped out by one of Saddam's Scuds.' Like all liberals she had a goat-like ability to gain the high moral ground of other people's suffering.

'Do you know anyone who lost a kid in the war?'

'Whaddya mean?'

'As I say, do you know anyone who lost anyone in this war?'

'Uh – *no*, but that doesn't mean it didn't happen.'

'D'you know anyone who knows anyone else who lost someone in the war?'

'Ferchrissakes –'

'For anyone's sake. Look, the point is, Mrs Hall, you may well be at more than six degrees of separation from this "conflict", and that means it barely exists at all so far as you're concerned.'

'You're crazy' – Hester grabbed for her wine and took a bar-room slurp – 'we could get up from this table, go to the airport, get on a plane, fly there and see the actual evidence of this war in the goddamn flesh.'

'Could we? I rather think that all the parties concerned have conspired to prevent that from happening. But anyway, let's talk no more about it; if one doesn't talk about a thing it never happened. It's simply expression – as Henry says – that gives reality to things.'

Meanwhile, further along the table, the Ferret was brightly declaiming, while poking at the blunt lapel of his own sharp suit, 'I don't always wear this AIDS ribbon, y'know.'

'Because what?' snapped his companion, Manuela Sanchez, a Hispanic art dyke of formidable sterotypy, complete with cheroot, monocle, red huntsman's coat and black tie.

'Because, my dear Manuela, it sometimes doesn't quite *go* with what I'm wearing – you can appreciate that.'

'I am thinking this ribbon has nothing to do with the fashion – it is a political statement, yes?'

'Ah, but Manuela, the late-twentieth century requires of us that all political statements be fashionable, just as all fashion statements must be political. In time I predict there will be a whole spectrum of these little ribbons, each one professing the wearer's solidarity with this or that cohort of the diseased, or tribe of endangered indigenes.'

'Pah!' She spat cigar smoke at him. 'You English never say what you mean.'

'On the contrary,' he sniffed, '*I* say what I mean, although I seldom mean what I say.'

Still further along the table, Gavin was telling Baz about life and death on the wards. 'His gut,' he said of one patient, 'was punctured by some guy fist-fucking him.'

'Jesus Christ!' Baz exclaimed. 'Did this character have talons, or what?'

'No,' Gavin sniggered grimly, 'unless you believe that marriage makes you soar like an eagle. The fister was married and hadn't thought to take off his wedding ring.'

And at the far end of the table from Wotton, his wife was addressing David Hall on matters of more global import. 'Great nations aren't established b-b-by n-negotiation, M-Minister,' she spluttered claret, 'b-but by f-f-fiat. History tells us this.' Her hands waved in the air so as to express the idea of vast empires collapsing into the dust of ages.

'So, what are you saying, Lady Victoria?' He moved a cruet towards her as if it were a battalion of bureaucrats. 'That the EU should send an expeditionary force into the Balkans?'

'Golly, no, I mean, golly, no, mine is not a p-prescriptive statement – merely an observation.'

'Well, it is perhaps your right as a historian to indulge in such observations, but my colleagues and I have to decide what it is that we, as a nation, should actually *do* in this conflict. That the Balkans are revolting is not, any more . . .' he paused to give emphasis to one of his biannual witticisms '. . . a matter of taste.'

Batface, out of politeness, affected not to notice. 'I'd r-rather thought that i-i-inertia was deciding the i-i-issue,' she clumsily iterated.

It would have been interesting to remain with this exchange (which was the most interesting dialogue at the table by far), but like any other circumnavigation this one cried out to be completed. Beside David Hall sat Chloë Lambert, who wasn't so much a girl-who-painted (as were so many of her high class and low ability) as a girl who rag-rolled skirting boards. She was *tête-à-tête* with Alan Campbell, describing for him the location of a friend's weekend retreat. 'I like his place; it's absolutely isolated in a wood at the far end of the estate. I think it was built as a folly or something.'

'And didja say there were two roads into this place?' Coming from Campbell's mouth, twisted with ill will, this sounded like an unpleasant insinuation, as if he were planning a murder and had lighted upon this as a good place to dump the victim.

Next to Campbell sat two highly disparate characters, yet they both sported dreadlocks and were discussing a region of common interest. One was Angela Brownrigg, another posh foal soused in privilege, who, in a misguided attempt to appear hip, had braided her lank yellow locks with multicoloured wooden beads. 'Yes, I *love* Jamaica,' she trilled, 'although there's hardly *anywhere* to stay in the Caribbean nowadays, so if you do open your hotel . . . Mr . . . ?'

'Bluejay,' said her dour and heavyset neighbour, upon whom dreadlocks appeared far more convincing, 'jus' Bluejay.'

'Bluejay, then – well, *tout le monde* will flock there, believe me. Mustique is *so* uncool now.'

'I dunno no fucking Lamonde, but if 'e toot, well, thass easy done.'

'And tell me,' Angela said, persisting in her life at cross-purposes, 'will you have an arboretum?'

A small head bobbed by Bluejay's tracksuited shoulder. It was Phoebe, who cowered away from the lugubrious gaze of a whole monkfish which lay across her plate.

'It's not looking at you, Phoebe,' said her nanny.

'It *is*, Claire,' the little girl protested, 'even though its eyes are all dull and dead – it's still looking at me!' Holding it at arm's length, she prodded the fish with her knife.

'Well, you would've done better to have nursery supper this evening.'

'But I wanted to see Daddy and Mummy's guests.'

'You've seen them now and it's a schoolday tomorrow, so unless you're going to try with the fish, it's up to bed.'

'You should've had a soufflé like me, Phoebe,' Jane Narborough said. 'It's quite all right to think of all animals as your friends, y'know. *I* do.'

'You can afford to, Jane,' said Wotton; 'you've a big enough establishment to maintain an ark-load on full board.'

'You say that, Henry' – she manifested the weary resignation of those who have to bear the awful burden of great wealth – 'but truthfully, running costs at Narborough simply get higher and higher.'

'Unlike that' – he gestured at her soufflé – 'which looks distinctly soggy. I'm sure even zero-rate inflation would be no compensation for a collapsed soufflé.'

'C'mon, Phoebe.' Claire rose up, a solid bulwark against all of this brittle persiflage. 'It really *is* your bedtime now.'

'Oh, all right,' the little girl conceded, 'but I want to kiss everyone goodnight first.'

Round she went, from her father to Hester to Dorian to Manuela to the Ferret to Gavin to Baz to Batface to Hall to Chloë to Campbell to Angela to Bluejay to Claire to Jane and back to her father. Round and round, kiss after kiss, the imprint of lewd lips, lascivious lips, leftover lips, pink-lipsticked lips, all on her white brow. Eventually Claire persuaded Phoebe to peel off and head upstairs, but the giddy rondo continued after she was gone, the mouths pouting and opening and closing, expelling smoke and babbles while the candles guttered; faster and faster until all there was was this sociable blur. Then, at last, the fateful wheel slowed down as the gravity of true night-time exerted itself.

It was way past everyone's bedtime now. The candles had melted down to Gaudíesque finials. Plastic crates full of the rental ware were stacked in a barricade by the stairs. The hired men had long since departed. The dinner party had completely resolved itself into the two cliques that were at its core, and these had repelled each other, so that they ended up inhabiting either end of the long table. Around Batface were gathered David and Hester Hall, Jane Narborough and Gavin. Their talk was earnest, full of the names of people not personally known to them – Yeltsin, Gorbachev and Rajiv Gandhi – and referring to places they would be disinclined to visit, such as Moscow, Sarajevo and New Delhi.

At the other end of the table, grouped around Wotton, were the Ferret, Alan Campbell, Bluejay, Dorian and Baz. The latter – for reasons of self-preservation – was keeping an empty place between himself and the rest, but really the Urals would have done the job better. The chatter among this little posse was perverse, cynical and brittle, incorporating the names of people they knew only too intimately and referring to places where they would far rather be.

'Have some more brandy, Baz,' Dorian said provocatively,

offering a slopping decanter. Whatever enthusiasm he'd evinced earlier in the evening for Baz's sobriety seemed to have evaporated.

'I can't have any *more* because I haven't had any at all,' Baz replied.

'You're an awful prude now, aren't you, Baz,' said Wotton. 'Since you've swapped one kind of needlework for another and become a Victorian miss, you can help me with Quilty.'

'Quilty?'

'It's my AIDS quilt.' He pulled a tattered bit of cloth about the size and shape of a bar-mat out of his pocket and waved it aloft.

'What the fuck is that?' Baz was genuinely distressed; the others were authentically indifferent.

'Quilty. It's a bar-mat with the names of everyone I would like to get AIDS sewn on to it. Everyone else has an AIDS quilt – why the hell shouldn't I?'

'Let me have a look, Henry . . .' Wotton passed it to Dorian '. . . ooh, you've put *her* on, I didn't know the little bitch was in such disfavour.'

'Well, of all the people who gossip about me *she's* the worst, because everything she says can be verified.'

Alan Campbell broke in on this badinage. 'Let's move round a place,' he slurred; 'my glass has got dregs in it and there's a clean one over there.' They all rose to move round a place, even Baz, who had no need of anything clean save his personal cordon sanitaire. 'No, Bluejay,' Campbell admonished the fake Rasta, 'don't take that spliff with ya, it goes to the man who takes yer place.' He duly acquired it and began puffing expansively, his Adam's apple bobbing up sharply from behind his cravat as he gulped down the smoke. Baz saw the lesions he'd suspected.

Dorian resumed. 'And you've put *him* on, as well – mind you, there's not much chance of him getting it, he hasn't shot up in his life; he isn't even a switch-hitter.'

Baz could stand it no longer. He raised his voice to get the attention of all of them. 'A report this week says forty million people will have the virus by the end of the century, and heterosexual transmission is an established fact, so there's every chance – '

'Oh Baz, *must* you be so prosaic?' Wotton cried.

'Oh Henry, must you be so brainless?'

'To live life with true artistry is to perform a successful brain-bypass operation – on yourself.'

'Anyway, Baz,' Dorian drawled, 'what's happened to *your* artistry? Surely you'd claim to be the only true artist among us, or has your clean-up campaign erased your talent as well as your sense of humour, hmm?'

But Baz didn't get to reply immediately, because the Ferret piped up at this point in a strangled little disembodied voice, 'So sorry, so sleepy, so very sleepy . . .' then slumped face down into some leftover *tarte Tatin*.

Wotton, who was sitting next to the Ferret, reached over and peeled back one of the little man's eyelids. He released it and it rolled down like a roller blind. The sight was cartoonish in the extreme. 'Give the Ferret some crack, will you Bluejay?' Wotton said. 'Best take him into the lavatory to do it; we don't want to upset my wife and her ministerial friend.'

'You payin', Henry, so you call the shots, man,' said the fundamentalist impostor, before adding ominously, 'fe now.' Then he did as he'd been requested, prising the Ferret from his chair, and manhandling him out of the room.

'Well, Baz?' Dorian queried again.

'That's part of the reason I'm in London, Dorian. The Walker Museum in St Paul is considering a retrospective of my work.'

'St Paul?' Wotton appeared to be considering the physical unlikeliness of a museum's being lodged inside a saint.

'Minneapolis's twin city.'

'Minneapolis?' Wotton was still incredulous. 'Do they *have* art there?'

'Presumably they'll have some when Baz's retrospective is mounted' – Dorian put himself in an unusual, speculative role – 'or should one say "switched on" when referring to video installations?'

'It could be a real springboard for me, Dorian,' Baz said earnestly. 'If there's interest in the stuff I did in the past I can begin looking for a new gallery, finding a studio, working again . . .'

He paused. Bluejay and the Ferret had reappeared, the latter moving with the intense, studied calm of someone who has had an enormous hit of crack cocaine. The little man resumed his place and began to toy with the dessert he'd so recently head-butted. 'Oh,' he squeaked, regarding his spoon critically, 'is that treacle?'

'No,' Wotton said witheringly, 'I believe it's some of that goo you use to stick down your hair.'

'I miss your work, Baz,' Dorian went on, 'or is it simply that I dislike the untenanted space it used to occupy?'

'What are you saying?!' Baz was appalled. 'Have you destroyed *Cathode Narcissus*?'

'Oh, *that* – your little home movie of me shaking my tush. No . . . I've still got that.'

'Good, because I need to take some photographs of it; it's gonna be the centrepiece of the show.'

'I'm not sure . . .' Dorian said this with some thoughtfulness '. . . if that will be possible, Baz.'

'Why?' Baz pleaded. Everyone around the table stiffened; none of them liked pleading. They'd all done a great deal of pleading in their time and they all knew how undignified it could get. 'Surely you won't deny me this opportunity?' he continued squeakily.

'No, it's only that the thing's packed away in boxes in my attic. It'll be a fucking drag getting it all out.'

'I can do that! I don't mind doing that! Jesus, Dorian, that's a ludicrous reason – I need to see it! I need to photograph it!'

'And I,' Wotton said with magisterial unconcern, 'need a hit. Pass me your stem, Bluejay.'

'Wha' 'bout yer old lady, Henry?'

'Oh, she's still pinned down in the Balkans. Just fill it up in your hand and pass it over, man – she'll think I'm smoking a glass cigar.'

Bluejay performed the fiddly little task and passed a three-inch length of Pyrex tubing across to Wotton, who put the stem casually to his lips and ignited it with a lighter. He exhaled, and a big cloud of crack smoke boiled across the table.

After disappearing for some seconds inside this thundercloud of derangement, Dorian emerged with a change of heart: 'All right then, Baz, what the fuck. You can come and see it now.'

'Now?'

'Yeah, now – any objection?'

'It's late –'

'I don't think *any* sleep will make a beauty of you now, Baz,' Dorian snorted. 'Besides, where're you staying? I can run you back.'

'Well, actually, Batface has very kindly offered me a bed.'

'Bring your bag, then – you can crash at my place.'

'Your place?'

'Oh, come now, Baz.' Wotton sought to still this irritating vacillation. 'First you want to see the thing, then you don't. *I* think Dorian is making you a very handsome offer indeed – why are you making such a bloody fuss?'

Baz looked around the table at the shining, bleary eyes of Wotton and his remaining partners in health crime. Why was he prevaricating? This was a very dangerous place for him indeed, he knew that – could Dorian's be any worse? True, Dorian had a nasty streak in him, but at least he wasn't an addict like Henry. Baz made up his mind. 'OK then, let's split. I'll get my bag.'

Baz left the room and Dorian made the valedictory round, as urbane and unruffled as when he'd arrived. In truth, the group at the other end of the table weren't so much in the Balkans as in their cups, and Batface merely slurred a farewell, while the others waved him off. By the time Baz returned, everyone at the table had already accommodated to his loss, assuming that Dorian had done the necessary parting for them both. Baz hovered for a few instants, half-hoping that Wotton or Batface would take notice of him – call him back, even, and ask him to rejoin the party. But they seemed not to heed him at all, and after a while he put on his coat and headed up the stairs after Dorian. The last thing he saw, before the long room, lit by the dying candles, disappeared from view below him, was that the Ferret had fallen asleep again, and Wotton – with Bluejay's assistance – was forcing him to smoke a joint while in the depths of unconsciousness.

12

Once they were in the street Baz wanted to make conversation, the way normal people do when they leave a dinner party, but Dorian was having none of this. He tucked Baz into the supine passenger seat of his MG sports car, while he busied himself removing the canvas top and stashing it away. In the immediate vicinity the night-time city was quiescent, but over towards the King's Road, Baz could hear the rev and bray and hooray of wealthy fun. He felt tired, so very tired. He'd had no time for his routines today, his meditation, his infusions. He didn't place much faith in any of these procedures singly; it was the combination that let him know that he was looking after himself, that he cared about Baz. And what could this signify, this spontaneous decision to stay at Dorian's? Nothing good. Nothing *healthy*. Baz's life was now one of sobriety, of sticking to the straight and narrow. Now, for the first time in five years, he found himself cannoning on to the cold hard shoulder of existence.

This wasn't even a metaphor, because when Dorian flung himself down in the driver's seat and goaded the little car until it bucked, then flew off down the road, Baz discovered that by comparison with his protégé, Wotton was a considerate and careful driver. As the little skateboard of a car skidded around the first corner, Baz reached behind to check that his bag was shoved down tightly behind the seat; as they screeched to a halt at the next junction he fumbled to tighten his seat belt. For fuck's sake, Dorian, he shouted above the wind, slow down!

—Why?

—Because you're gonna fucking kill us, that's why.

—You're going to die anyway, Baz, but your spiritual convictions

153

will ensure that there's always a soupçon of Bazness around in the atmosphere to make everyone else sneeze.

—You're a cruel bastard, Dorian.

—Cruel maybe, but I'm very much alive, Baz – you know that better than most.

Next they were at the lights beside Harrods. It was curious how so many important exchanges between these men transpired in the shadow of this opulent mart, which now loomed out of the darkness, its lineaments picked out with glow globes. One possible explanation was that the god of Dorian and Baz and Wotton's world was a somnolent deity, who, like the Ferret, slumbered while his creations revolved in ever diminishing circles, tangling themselves up in still tighter conga lines of buggery. In the dark confines of the little car, Dorian's hand, like a pale tarantula, had crept into Baz's crotch. What's this about, Dorian? he said, capturing it with his own.

—This is about sex, Baz – you remember that? Or have the two serpents of AIDS and faith twined themselves around your cock and turned it into a useless caduceus? The lights changed, the car pulled away, the hand remained. Dorian piloted with the other. You should let me look after you, Baz, he said.

—Whaddya mean? Baz was incredulous.

—I have the money, I have the time. I'm only so nasty to you because I feel guilty about what happened in New York. It's that, and Henry's influence as well – y'know what *he's* like.

—He's bitter because he's hurting and he's lived a lie. I think there's a good man buried inside Henry somewhere.

—And you believe you can dig him up before Henry himself is buried?

—No, I don't, it's up to Henry.

—And it's up to me to apologise for the way I behaved in New York.

—No, Dorian, I was as much to blame as you; my arrogance, my envy, all my character defects were in full play – I was a using addict.

—So . . . Dorian employed the rocking of the car to draw still closer . . . *will* you let me look after you?

—I dunno, Dorian . . . I've been kept by rich people for too much of my life.

—You're an artist – I'm a patron. What you do can be astonishing, but it's hardly likely to support you – especially if you're ill. Perhaps I'm the last man in London who's honourable enough to lose money backing art.

—Yeah, maybe . . . Dorian?

—What?

—Can I ask you something?

—Ask me anything.

Baz shooed the tarantula away; this was serious. You remember that night at the Mineshaft in '83?

—How could I forget it! Dorian chuckled. It was pretty much my first landfall on the wilder shores of love.

—Y'know, Dorian, people in Manhattan . . . people on the scene . . . they say you killed a guy that night. Did you?

They'd stopped at the lights by the junction of Gloucester Road. Dorian flicked the indicator, then turned to face Baz before answering. Do I look like a murderer, Baz?

Of course he didn't look like anything of the sort; he looked innocent to the point of virginal. He seemed to Baz like some cricketing wizard of the First XI, psychically swaddled in creamy flannels, with the golden sunlight of a perpetual adolescent afternoon playing about his roseate lips.

Any part of anyone is only so strong. If the correct pressure is applied in the right places, even the toughest character will crumple up like an aluminium can. We should try to remember what poor Baz had been through, shouldn't we? We should try to maintain a certain sympathy for him as he buckles.

Baz thought to himself, why resist when the love you have yearned for for so long is at last reciprocated? He cupped Dorian's beautiful young face in his ugly old hands, and he kissed those lips.

Oh, so sweet, so very sweet. The taste and the feel of him – Baz ate and drank and even tried to *inhale* as much of the Adonis as he could. The lights changed, the cars behind began hooting, and this attracted the attention of some late-night skulkers on the pavement outside the Kentucky Fried Chicken takeaway, who began to shout, Fucking queers! and, Bum boys! One bold fellow made a little dash forward and smote the wing of the MG with his own greasy one. How suitable. It was only on hearing this oleaginous impact that the lovers broke from their clinch. Dorian grabbed the wheel, and laughing like a loon he wrenched the car across three lanes of oncoming traffic and off to the north.

Hardly anyone ever got to see Dorian Gray's mews house, and if they did they invariably arrived alone – save for the owner – and at night. Dorian was not, exactly, a homebody. Those who did happen to be invited back for a nightcap, and to have their body toyed with as if it were an anatomical model, found a domicile with all the posed artificiality of a small but expensive hotel, or the stage-set for an antiquated play. The furniture was of mahogany and leather, the standard lamps were of brass. Mirrors were bevelled, invitations were propped on the mantelpiece. There was the occasional piece of chinoiserie. The prevailing colours were russets, maroons and browns. The floor coverings were Persian kilims *on top of* carpet, which, as is invariably the case, imparted an overstuffed atmosphere – and this despite the fact that the whole of the ground floor was one single room. Fustiness was of the order of things and revival was the style, without there being any real indication of what it was that was to be revived.

Until those farceurs – Dorian and his guest – entered stage centre, or rather, Dorian tumbled backwards down a couple of stairs, because Baz was attached like a lamprey to the front of his face. They fetched up by the mantelpiece, Baz still sucking and chomping and flailing, while Dorian remained sufficiently pliant to give the impression of compliance.

Coming up for air and seeing his own contorted face in the mirror acted on Baz like a cold douche. He straightened up and rubbed his face with his hands. Have you got a cigarette? he asked and, on receiving one, lit up and inhaled big drags of bromide. He looked about him at the little house full of Little England, and his nostrils flared with the scent of rat. Dorian, he began, Henry told me about a girl on the Côte d'Azur . . . there was one, wasn't there?

—Isn't there always? Baz's host was, preposterously, pouring himself a small glass of sherry from a decanter on a sideboard.

—Henry . . . er . . . implied that you gave her the virus – apparently she died of pneumonia.

—That's absurd. It would merely be a coincidence, even if I had in fact – rather than Henry's fancy – done the deed with her.

—But you're positive, right?

—Absolutely certain. Sherry?

—No, no. Baz waved him off and threw himself down in an armchair. You know I don't drink any more – why d'you go on about it?

—Sorry.

—And you know full well what I mean by positive. C'mon, Dorian, get real.

—Ha ha. That's rich, Baz, priceless. Get real – it should be the Gray family motto. Yes, I know what you mean, and look, believe me, I feel for you and Henry and Alan, I do. All the more, I sometimes think, because I don't have the virus myself. What do they call it – survivor guilt?

—B-but how . . . ? How was it possible? Baz got up and began to pace. You had sex with Herman, you shared the works with us all . . . and yet you –

—Look, Baz, what is this? It just happened that way. It's almost as if you *want* me to be ill.

—No no, of course not, that would be disgusting! Baz had fetched up back by Dorian, and simply because he knew he could he cupped a cheek and rubbed the side of that perfect nose with his thumb. I'm sorry, he said, sorry for accusing you – it's only that there have been so many rumours over the years.

—Baz, has it ever occurred to you that most of them are a function of jealousy? After all, given the opportunity, you can feel pretty possessive about me . . .

—Yes, yes, I s'pose that's true. I'm sorry. And feeling the need to be still more shriven, Baz sought again the lips of his confessor. They took off each other's jackets and unbuttoned their shirts. Baz would have gone further, but Dorian reached for a wooden box on the mantelpiece. I'm going to have a hit, he said.

—What? Baz was appalled, incredulous.

—I'm going to have a hit, a speedball, and then I'm going to give you a blowjob like you've never had before; watch me.

—Oh Jesus, oh no, Dorian . . . I can't cope with this . . . I've been clean for years, I don't need this . . . I don't want this . . .

Dorian withdrew a glistening thing of smoked glass and steel from the box. Look at this, he said, it's an antique works, it's so finely calibrated that your blood pressure alone will flush the thing – beautiful, isn't it.

—Oh God, oh no, grant me the courage . . . Baz muttered.

—And I've got pure stuff, amps, pure coke, pure smack, just the thing.

—I've been clean for five years, Dorian! Baz wailed. Why would I want to fuck that up now?

—You've also been alone for five years, Baz, with no one to care for you. He continued methodically cracking the amps and filling the syringe. If you want to go straight back into rehab, you can – I'll pay for it – but let's have one night together of complete abandon. We can start being good again tomorrow, can't we?

—Dorian, if I shot that lot up I wouldn't be abandoned, I'd be stone dead.

But it was too late. Baz had remained within this danger zone for far too long; and now he'd countenanced the idea of drugs again, which meant that he'd as good as used them already. The points had been switched for the Baz express; nothing short of a derailment could have stopped him now.

—How much would suit? said his persecutor. Half, perhaps? As deftly as the Wotton of old, Dorian flipped off his shirt, save for one sleeve which he employed like a tourniquet. He plunged the needle into his main line. The lengthening red column quivered between them and sweat beaded along his lip as Dorian pushed the plunger in. Baz was transfixed by the fix. Here, said Dorian, giving him the hypodermic; then he undressed Baz completely, right down to his boxers. He took the phial full of the antidote to life and using his own Old Etonian tie as a tourniquet, Dorian shot Baz up. As t'were a flea / That's sucked on you and now sucks on me . . . he cooed, and looked Baz full in the eyes. Baz saw neither excitation nor revulsion, merely the cold passion of a voyeur and a lambent flicker of triumph.

—Jesus . . . oh . . . Jesus. That's strong. Baz gagged.

—I told you, it's pure, purer than baby Jesus.

—Oh . . . fuck. I think I'm gonna puke.

Half staggering, half running, Dorian guided Baz across the room and in through a bathroom door masquerading as a lacquered screen. Still-effervescent mineral water gushed from Baz's mouth. That's OK, Baz . . . that's OK . . . Dorian billed. It'll be all right . . . you're stoned, yeah?

—Righteously.

—It's good, yeah? he soothed.

—Oh yes . . . *so* good.

—And this – this is good, too?

—Ye-es.

A zipper was hauled down. The curve of Dorian's back was like the spine of some antediluvian creature, browsing in the sexual swamp. His haunches quivered as he bowed down, rose, bowed down, as if abasing himself before a phallic idol, an idol which panted and groaned and eventually cried out under the pressure of such adulation. *Nyum-nyum.* Dorian licked his lips. Still saltier than most men, Baz.

—Don't you *worry*, Dorian?

—Worry?

—About the virus?

—I think if I was going to get it, I would've done by now. Maybe I'm immune.

—I'm so stoned. I'd forgotten how when you're stoned you can lie on a toilet floor with complete equa – equa –

—Cool?

—Yeah, thass right . . . cool.

Dorian sprang to his feet. He seemed wholly unaffected by the fix, as imperturbably *cool* as ever. He padded back across the room and retrieved his shirt. Baz followed him and began to dress as well. But you still want to see it, right? Dorian said, shucking on his jacket.

—It?

—*Cathode Narcissus*.

—Yeah, of course I wanna see it. Of course. Where're these boxes?

—Upstairs – come on. The two men mounted the open staircase, and ascended through the painted heavens like villeins playing angels in a medieval mystery play. At the top of the flight, there was a single steel door pierced with more keyholes than Baz had seen since he was resident on Avenue B. With a woozy pang he thought of the three she-males and recalled their instinctive suspicion of Dorian. All of them were dead now; there was no more dressing up to be done – except in shrouds.

Dorian got out a hefty bunch of keys and began to deal with the locks. Why all the hardware? Baz asked, but Dorian merely replied, You'll see. The door swung open soundlessly, and Baz was confronted with the antithesis of the fusty repro downstairs. Here, all was empty and minimal, grey and white in the light of a full moon, which floated in the dead centre of a rectangular skylight, as if it were a line drawing in a geometry textbook. From somewhere a brassy tenor choked out the crescendo of the aria 'Nessun dorma'. Dorian turned up a dimmer switch, and recessed pinprick lights illuminated the starkness. The only furniture in the room were the nine monitors that displayed *Cathode Narcissus*, ranged in a precise crescent atop waist-high steel plinths, and an Eames chair which faced them in prime viewing position. One of the monitors was switched on and playing a tape of a concert in Hyde Park. On a giant stage Pavarotti mopped his sperm whale's forehead with a metre square of white handkerchief, while salaaming to the ecstatic crowd. The camera wavered away from this to take in Princess Diana sitting in the enclosure allotted for the blood-line.

—It's here! Baz cried out, swaying in the doorway. This is perfect, Dorian; it's like an exhibition space purpose-designed for *Narcissus*.

—That's exactly what it is, Dorian replied as he picked up a remote control and negated Princess Diana's image. I had it built when I moved in. You see, Baz, I was lying at Henry's when I was so dismissive about your work. Far from my not caring about it, *Narcissus* means more to me than life itself . . . He paused for emphasis. Baz, a most marvellous thing has happened.

—What? What marvellous thing?

—When I saw *Cathode Narcissus* for the first time, Baz, in your studio, the day you introduced me to Henry, well, I'm sure you can't remember but I wished it could be the installation that aged rather than me. I wished it could be the Dorians you videotaped who displayed all the scars of dissipation, and the marks of immorality that I already suspected my life held in store for me. Had I known about it then, I bet I would've wished that it could be those multiple images of me prancing and dancing that succumbed to AIDS.

—What're you saying, Dorian? Oh fuck, I'm too wasted to take this on board.

—Have another bump. Dorian got out a wrap and spilled a shiny white pile on top of one of the grey monitors. He handed Baz a ready-rolled note. Go on, he said, it can't make any difference now.

—S'pose not, Baz snuffled as he took a hefty snort.

Dorian guided Baz into the Eames chair, and while his solo

audience looked on he continued his exposition of the supernatural: What I'm saying is that it's happened. It's *Cathode Narcissus* that has aged and suffered, while I remain pristine. Look at me, Baz, look at me! I'm thirty-one years old. I've fucked hundreds of men and women – thousands, even. I've never used a condom in my life. Some nights I've taken it in the arse from twenty heavy-hitters. I've never stinted myself on booze or drugs, never. I take what I want when I want it. Yet I bear no marks; I look exactly the same as I did a decade ago when I came down from Oxford.

—Either you're mad, Dorian, or you're acting mad.

—I'm not mad, Baz, I'm the sanest person you'll ever meet. I tell you – it's *true*. That girl you spoke of, Octavia, it's true what Henry said . . . I can show you the letter if you like. She wrote it to me when she was dying, abandoned by her family, in the public hospital in Marseille. She maunders on about being buggered by me when she was tripping . . . and it's all true, it's all true . . . just as it's true what happened that night at the Mineshaft. Yet I don't bear a mark. I don't look like a cruel man, do I, Baz? An immoral man? I'm a dew-picked piece of innocence, a plump cherub, the springiest of chickens – wouldn't you say? And it's you, *you*, who've never looked more than skin-deep at me, or penetrated any further than my rosebud of an arsehole. It's you who're the superficial one, Baz. You.

—That's not true, Dorian, Baz managed to say. I've always loved you. I loved you when I made *Narcissus*. If you really look at it it's obvious that I loved you then – and I still do now. It's a love letter, that piece, a fucking love letter, it's not some mad fetish that keeps you looking young. I dunno what you're talking about, Dorian.

—Oh, is that so, Dorian sneered, reaching for the remote. He picked it up and pushed a button. Well, look on your love letter now, Baz; I'm returning it to sender.

The monitors whined and zigged and zagged and sprang jaggedly to life. But was it life? In place of the unchanged Dorian who stood before Baz, as fresh and youthful as the first evening he'd met him at Phyllis Hawtree's, was the Dorian Baz had for years now suspected he ought to be – an anguished figure, his face, neck and hands covered with Kaposi's, his mouth wet with bile, his eyes tortured by death and madness, his bald pate erupting with some vile fungus. And there were nine of these animated pathology plates, nine of them, haltingly disporting themselves. Concentration-camp victims forced by an insane Nazi doctor to dance.

—Ach! Baz spat involuntarily and thought he might vomit again. This is revolting, Dorian! A sick travesty – where'd you get them?

—It's all yours, Baz, all your own work. You have such a mastery of the superficial.

—Where are the tapes?! Baz shouted. Where are the fucking tapes?!

—In here . . . Dorian slid open a panel in the wall and there, neatly shelved, were the VCRs.

Baz got up and went over. He scrutinised them, ejected the tapes and examined them. He even, futilely, checked the connections between the VCRs and the monitors – but all was exactly as he remembered it. So . . . it is from within . . . he murmured in wonderment, staring once more at the moribund Dorians. How fucking bizarre . . . these images have been corrupted . . . it's almost as if sin itself were eating away at them.

—I congratulate you, Baz, you're responding to your masterwork as any artist should. Baz slumped back down in the Eames chair. When I did the original, he said, I guess I was catching the briefest moment in time, that kind of androgynous New Romantic look of the early eighties. I dunno . . . he ran sweaty hand across sweaty brow . . . maybe this version of *Cathode Narcissus* is of its time too.

—How prettily you put it, said Dorian, who, unnoticed by Baz, had withdrawn a switchblade from his pocket, snapped it open, and begun paring his fingernails. It's *so* important nowadays that an artist be able to speak well of his work.

—No – it's not my work, Dorian, it's nothing to do with me. I dunno where you got hold of it . . . S'pose it might be one of those

German guys', they do pretty wiggy stuff, but maybe it's what I'd do now, if I could . . . if I – if I had the guts, the courage to stare death in the face.

—There's no need for that, Baz . . . Dorian put down the knife on a monitor and came over to the chair, put both his hands on the arms and, bending down, breathed sweetly into Baz's face. I want you to stay here with me. I'll give you anything you want; all I want from you in return is a little technical assistance.

—Whaddya mean?

—The tapes, Baz, the tapes. They're wearing out. I need someone to transfer them all to new ones. I need the work to be maintained. Call me superstitious, but I have an idea that my life may depend on it.

—I don't think so, Dorian.

—You *do* think so, Baz, you do. Stay here, look after it! This is your life's work.

—No . . . I don't think so, Dorian . . . It's not mine, anyway . . . I've gotta . . . I've gotta go. This evening was a mistake . . . the whole thing . . . an awful fucking mistake . . . He struggled to rise from the Eames chair, but the poor old bull was penned in by its modernity. Dorian had ample time to retrieve his knife and – exhibiting all the balletic grace of a matador – plunge it deep into Baz's neck, cleanly severing the carotid artery. However, the golden boy then spoilt it all by carrying on, delving into the dying man again and again with the gory implement, as if it were a spade and the thrashing Baz unyielding ground. Blood spurted and sprayed around the two figures as the starveling ghouls on the screens cavorted and leered. Dorian howled and even lapped at the splatter.

But what of Basil Hallward in all of this? So much more attention tends to be lavished on the murderer than on his victim. Murderers remain always with us, *n'est-ce pas?* – whereas victims have a disgraceful way of creeping off into the shadows, only re-emerging in the guise of actors, who play their part for the purposes of reconstructing the crime on television. You'd have to agree that, *faute de mieux*, you would rather invite murderers to a drinks party than their victims, even if a pathetic preoccupation with self-preservation led you to hide everything sharp, including the cocktail sticks.

I've led you astray. The life-force pumped out of Basil Hallward, while the face he had loved for over a decade hovered above. It was twisted with hatred, true, but can we not say that to him it appeared as if Dorian were in ecstasy, transported by this grisly consummation? Why don't we also assume that in his final throes dear Basil was gifted that procession of precise and intimate recollection that those who have experienced 'near-death' assure us accompanies the dying of the light?

Basil aged nine, in short-sleeved Aertex shirt and wide-legged flannel trousers, tenderly nuzzling the crotch of a boy similarly attired. Or Basil aged fifteen, naughtily absconding to Paris and wandering the dappled cobbles of St-Germain, until ushered into a beat hotel to be ceremoniously sucked off by an old roué. Or Basil five years further on, sharing lodgings above a dentist's surgery in Stanmore with a merchant seaman – see him, this dull afternoon, flick through the pages of *Jeremy* (a mag for newly liberated chaps), looking for adventure while his friend is away at sea. Or see Baz the hunger artist take his first hit of Methedrine from Captain America in a closet at And*ee*'s Factor*ee*. Not intimate enough to convince? Too emblematic? Would the gland Baz found that morning when shaving – a gland where no gland should be – do the job better? Or a dust mote in Detroit or Droitwich, or a paperclip in Pretoria or Prestatyn? Many people – let's be frank – have lived too long, and of those, rather a lot have gone too far.

No. Cocaine got the upper hand even at this terminally late stage. And despite all the death he had already witnessed, the thanatos he was steeped in, Baz discovered that he'd rather not take a permanent nap. The poor sick withered Dorians danced in the darkening periphery of his vision as he grappled with this hellcat Dorian who was stapling him to the present. Oh to get away! To get back! Get off me! Baz wanted to shout, supremely irritated to be dying in such a lousy frame of mind.

The pain was bigger than Manhattan. It was as if he were being flung down on all the dagger spires and needle aerials of its skyscrapers, cut to pieces by very the city he'd so loved. So it was with acute relief that Baz realised he was dead, and stepped away from the lolling gargoyle of his corpse. He joined the wraith-like Dorians, who had stepped down from their plinths to meet him, and in the null space in the middle of the null room, the ten of them linked hands, formed a ring, and commenced a stately dance.

At last Dorian stopped, and instantly his hot face froze over. He lifted himself off the broken body, moving with his usual fluidity, as if quite unaware of the bits of Basil all down his front. He went to the door, undid the locks and disappeared down the stairs. From above could be heard the sound of a telephone receiver being lifted and digits being punched into a keypad. But of course there was no one to see him go and no one to listen to the call being made. No one save his *alter egos*, who paced around their cathode vitrines like caged beasts, returning again and again to stare out with insane eyes at the corpse of their creator.

Dorian stood with the plastic prong nuzzling his china ear. Alan? Dorian . . . Listen, I'm glad you're home, I wondered if you could come over here . . . Yuh, I appreciate that, I know it's late . . . It's just that I have some garbage that needs disposing of and it can't wait until morning.

PART THREE

Network

13

An area of Chelsea rocked back and forth as if it were a seascape viewed from the tilting deck of a ship. But this wasn't a ship – it was a building. A building of some ten storeys, seemingly caught in a gathering urban storm. As yet this was only a force 7 gale, but it was enough to allow foam sheets to form around the chimneys and television aerials of the terraces, sheets that streamed with the wind.

Up and down the deck tilted, up and down. Given that he was the captain of this vessel, it was incumbent on him to maintain his station at the bridge, his hands thrust casually in his trouser pockets to show that nothing untoward was happening. As the deck reared up below his right foot he retracted it, while allowing his left to extend. Then, when the deck tilted the other way, he reversed the process. Only for the split second when the deck became level was he able to consult the compass (a very old issue of the *Reader's Digest*), which stood upon the binnacle (an old music stand, its metal chipped and worn).

It was vital that he maintain the ship's north-westerly course through the peaks and troughs of urbanity. Due west were the chimneys of the gasworks at Lots Road, while nor'-nor'-west he could discern the shiny cliffs of the Kensington Hilton. For many years now they had not drawn any closer, but that didn't discount the possibility that one day they would. No, he must keep the MV *Block of Flats* on course towards the humped, awkward bulk of Olympia, even if she never arrived.

He had stayed at the helm through worse gales than this, force 10s and 11s, that had produced such violent pitching he could barely keep to his feet. Then he could hear nothing save the scream of his own shredded psyche through the taut steel rigging of consciousness. He knew from experience that when his own encephalogram grew spikier – with both the amplitude and the frequency of his brain waves mounting – he also observed the strange weather in the streets deteriorating. Tight isobars were ruled across the shopfronts on the King's Road and Fulham Road, while the frightening vortices of low-pressure cyclones formed over Redcliffe Gardens and Edith Grove.

Still, eventually the gales would blow themselves out. His orderly would change his trousers and underwear, wringing wet with salty urine. Some nutriment would be taken, together with the vitamin pills he needed for sustenance during this gruelling voyage. His orderly would withdraw, and he would take the helm once more, his gaze first fixed on the crenellated horizon, then falling to the heavy swell of bricks, mortar, concrete and steel that the *Block*'s prow breasted, throwing up a spume of garden greenery. With the practised eye of the mariner, he could detect and analyse the ever changing properties of this view, an urban doldrums which would, to the untutored, appear quite static: the rear of a substantial, late-Victorian terraced house set in its oblong of walled garden.

'The jiggling man's looking obscurely satisfied with himself this morning,' Henry Wotton called over his shoulder, from where he lay in his armchair peering up at the fifth storey of the block of flats through a pair of opera glasses. He drew torpidly on his Cohiba and leaked smoke, while waiting for this remark to bounce off the walls of the drawing room and enter his wife's large, pointed ears.

'What!?' Batface jerked upright, but none the less continued writing at her ugly escritoire.

'I said, the jiggling man seems bloody pleased with himself. I expect he's just had a fix of Largactil, or whatever it is they give him so as to stop the poor bugger abandoning ship altogether.'

'Ship?' queried Batface. She'd taken to randomly sampling her husband's dialogue; they had, after all, been married for well over a decade. 'He isn't *on* a ship.'

'No, no, I meant it as a metaphor for his mind, his sanity. You can see that he's completely overawed by some sense of responsibility. *I* think that his delusion is the same as mine – that he also believes himself to be meting out the seconds until we all expire, like a human pendulum.' Wotton took a slug of his morning tea, a pungent infusion Nanny Claire had been brewing from a small bale of Chinese herbs for the past one and a half hours.

'Responsibility?' Batface remained inquisitive. 'I don't know about the jiggling man, but I must sort out the aftermath of last night's party. There's still absolutely *masses* of clearing up to do; the caterers haven't even taken their stuff away yet and it's far too much for Consuela to handle. What're you doing today, Henry?' She seldom stuttered when they were speaking alone.

'Back into the bloody hospital – they wouldn't do my tubes yesterday.'

'And who will drive you? I can't, and Nanny Claire has to pick up Phoebe from school early and take her to ballet – will Basil, perhaps?'

'I don't know; he went off with Dorian, didn't he – so much for all his fine words about friendship and caring and –'

Wotton was forestalled by the clamour of the telephone ringing. It was Dorian calling to discuss last night's fun.

*   *   *

Alan Campbell had made it over to Dorian's mews house in about twenty minutes. Since being struck off the medical register in the mid-eighties, the erstwhile practitioner of chicanery had slid straight down the property ladder. When his symptoms had become too flagrant for him even to perform illegal abortions, or administer vitamin shots laced with Methedrine, he had withdrawn to a furnished bedsit in Earls Court. There, surrounded by a few cardboard boxes stuffed with mouldering papers, Campbell eked out his remaining days, listening to commercial radio while suppurating in the sweat of his own sinfulness. *De temps en temps* he phoned a call-in show simply to hear his own Strine whine complaining over the ether. So when the ring-back came to do something truly wrong, he savoured it.

They stood looking down at the corpse, which had adopted a relaxed if gory pose in the Eames chair. Why'd ya do it? Campbell croaked, and despite his own extensive appetite for gore, his guts turned over at the sight of such a large helping of person purée.

—Oh, I dunno . . . Dorian kicked Baz's corpse in the upper thigh region and it pivoted in its leather and rosewood frame like a marionette of inferior design. It was only a question of *when*, Alan, not why. He was a bore – a fucking tedious bore. He'd been threatening to blackmail me for years over some – he chose his words with care – *excesses* he was privy to in New York.

—Oh yairs?

—Yes. Dorian softly punched the mush that was Baz's face and, taking his knuckles to his mouth, licked the red stuff.

Campbell winced. This place is in an awful fucking mess, Dorian, he said.

—Isn't it.

—Are those the monitors for that piece of his?

—That's right.

—This doesn't have anything to do with it, does it?

—Of course not! Dorian guffawed. Art thefts happen all the time – but an art murder? Don't be ridiculous.

—Whatever. You want me to deal with this, right?

—That's the general idea.

—It'll cost ya.

—Of course.

—I don't s'pose you've got any of the right stuff for this kind of job . . . plastic sheeting or bin-liners, rubber gloves, some heavy cord or rope and a fucking spade – a good one?

—What're you going to do? Dorian's eyes were bright. Cut him into pieces? Dissolve his flesh with acid?

—Nah, don't be mad, dissolving a corpse needs a plunge bath and a drum of sulphuric fucking acid. As for chopping him up, I haven't the strength and you'd make a hash of it. Nah ... He looked down at Baz with a smear of pity on his snide face. We'll bury the poor bastard. So, if you've got any of that stuff – get it. I'll start stripping him.

Campbell had heard all about a good burial ground over dinner at the Wottons'. He loved to do that: pump for information a stupid and oblivious companion who'd been thrust upon him, in the process transforming them into an unwitting accomplice of a crime yet to be committed. In this case it was Chloë Lambert who'd been his mark, although he hadn't thought that her vacuous wittering about this isolated folly in the grounds of a Wiltshire estate would prove so useful so soon.

They drove down the M3 towards Andover in Dorian's MG. Dorian said, What if stupid squad stop us?

But Campbell was dismissive: Yeah, like they're looking for a corpse and not some pissed exec heading home to the commuter belt. Stay under the limit, and if we're stopped, be cool – you can do that. He could do it too; he looped an arm around the polythene-barked human log that was planted in the ditch behind the seats. A few hours before, Baz's bag had been there; now he himself was the baggage. Will anyone miss him? Just as Campbell's small talk was potential conspiracy, so he never sounded more casual than when he was actually conspiring.

—I dunno.

—I mean, does he have family?

—Family? Dorian snorted. It's difficult to imagine, isn't it? I think there was a brother somewhere ludicrous and inexistent like *Nottingham*.

—Were they in touch?

—Hardly – Baz had been abroad on and off for nearly twenty years. He was a queer, he was a junky; it's hard to picture him playing horsey with nieces and nephews climbing on his shoulders, hmm?

—Well, what about Wotton?

—Henry? Oh, don't worry about Henry; I'll take care of him.

Following Chloë's unwitting instructions, as the A303 mounted towards the escarpment of Salisbury Plain, they turned off on to a lane heading down into a valley. Within yards there was a gateway into woods. Dorian took it and killed the headlights. By the light of a sickle moon the little car crackled over old leaves and fallen boughs. Why here? he asked, and Campbell replied, Because it's remote, it isn't farmland so we won't have to rely on the silence of the fucking lambs, there's no gamekeeper so we won't be disturbed, and there's nothing much to connect us with the place if his remains are ever found. Also, according to my information we can go in by this track, do the business, then come out on a main road five miles off, without going near any human habitation.

They buried him deep and they sweated a lot. It took three hours. Dorian stripped to his trousers and hacked out the grave; when his spade hit a root too thick to be sliced, Campbell would get in and hacksaw through it. They buried Baz in a thicket of rhododendron in the middle of the wood. They buried him naked, with his jaw shattered and his fingertips bubbled with a blowtorch. They buried him so that even if he ever were found, he wouldn't be a he, merely an it. And when the killer and his accomplice were done, Dorian backed the car out of the undergrowth, while Campbell used the birch-twig broom he'd thoughtfully brought along, to sweep the leaves and humus into tracklessness.

It was dawn by the time they jolted back on to the metalled road. Campbell winced, a hand travelling involuntarily to his ribs. Anything wrong? Dorian said. No, the struck-off doc replied, I'm just not feeling too well.

At seven a.m. Dorian dropped Campbell in Boscombe, a suburb of Bournemouth where the sinister Australian had an old friend.

—Peter's a character, Campbell said, spent years doing this routine where he ponced old silver amalgam from dentists.

—What the fuck're you on about? Dorian snapped. He was gunning the engine, keen to escape this tawdry suburban strand.

—Y'know, amalgam, stuff they use for fillings. Anyway, Peter'd go round the country, collecting up all the scrapings the tooth-pullers'd put on a bit of glass.

—I don't know what a fucking filling even *is*, you idiot. Dorian groaned with exasperation.

—It all added up to something for nothing. He made enough to set up shylocking down here. Bloke's bloody loaded. You should come up and say hello –

—No. I've got to deal with Wotton. I thought we were covering our tracks – why're you holding me up?

—I've got a little present here, said Campbell, smiting the breast pocket of his alpaca jacket with a closed fist. It made a hollow, plastic 'thwock'.

—What!? What!?

—Not for *you*, for Peter. Campbell got up out of the little skateboard of a car, then bent back towards Dorian while unclasping his fist. In the palm of his hand were a dozen or so bloody molars, each with a silvery filling. Peter likes to keep his hand in, said Campbell. I'll be needing fifteen large, old notes please, Dorian – old tender for a tender old queen, yeah?

—*Hasta la vista*, baby! Dorian sang out, as he terminated the conversation by driving off. Once he was on the bypass, he let rip with a Bohemian rhapsody: I'm just a poor boy, nobody loves me / He's just a poor boy from a poor family . . .

By ten o'clock that morning Dorian was at the Fleet Services on the M3, standing in a phone booth outside a Happy Eater. It was a miserable, grey day, and the way the service centre had been bulldozed out of the surrounding coniferous plantation gave it the air of an extermination camp for drivers. 'Henry?' he said. 'It's Dorian. I need to talk to you.'

'Talk for chauffeuring,' Wotton oozed down the line. 'I need to go back to the bloody hospital this morning.'

'Talk first?' Dorian wheedled.

'You've got to be joking, you insolent young pup, get over here now.' Wotton crashed the receiver back down.

'It's Dorian,' he called over to Batface. 'He'll take me.'

'There.' She perked up. '*He* cares about you.'

'My dear Batface' – Wotton smiled as he adopted a paterfamilias's posture, one hand sunk deep in his dressing-gown pocket, the other caressing the prepuce of his cigar – 'Dorian cares for me the way an Eskimo tribe cares for its old folk – with deep respect, yes, but with an equally steely preparedness to abandon me in the frozen wastes without so much as a backward glance.' He fell silent, staring up through the bay window at the jiggling man. As he watched him, Wotton also became the captain of his own ship, swaying at first gently from side to side, but then more vigorously, until he too was mastering the motion of a force 7 gale. Batface came and went, preparing to quit the house, but recognising the intensity of her husband's reverie she merely brushed his gelid cheek with her dry lips, before leaving him to commune with his insane nemesis.

It wasn't until they reached the Middlesex that Wotton vouchsafed he would be in overnight. 'It's a general-anaesthetic job,' he explained; 'doing it when I was awake would be like changing this car's transmission while the engine was still running.' Then he fobbed Dorian off with the car, telling him to come back the following morning.

The next day there was no parking to be had and, given the complexity of the Fitzrovian one-way system, Dorian ended up piloting the Jag around an awkward, irregular polygon of a block twenty-odd times before his passenger re-emerged from the Middlesex Hospital. It was as if he were constructing a Mandelbrot set composed of many fractals of his own frustration.

Wotton stood squinting up Mortimer Street for his ride. With his empty nappy of corduroy flat on his deflated posterior, his squamous face, and his gaunt frame barely parting the front from the back of his hacking jacket, he resembled some squirearchal horseman of the apocalypse – the Honourable Pestilence Famine-War, perhaps. Dorian screeched up, leapt out, scurried round and admitted him to the Jag. He slammed the door and ran back to the driver's side, only to be greeted with the imperious complaint 'You haven't tucked me in properly – my jacket is caught in the door.'

When at last they were both properly ensconced, Dorian asked him, 'Where's the nearest place we can sit out on the pavement and get a decent cup of coffee?'

'Paris,' Wotton snapped, and set fire to a Turkish State Monopoly.

'You know what I mean, Henry,' Dorian sighed heavily. 'Somewhere we can *talk* properly.'

'I can talk properly anywhere.' Wotton's brown exhalations staggered in the slipstream before being sucked out of the window. 'But aren't you going to ask me how my trip to the hospital went?'

'Um, yeah, right . . . how was it?'

'Fucking painful. There's something exquisitely unpleasant about having a needle inserted into your body and connected to a plastic tube which is tunnelled through the skin in your upper chest wall.' He squirmed in the car seat and adjusted his moleskin shirt so that Dorian could see the plastic plug of the Hickman line. 'As soon as I get home I'm going to link this up to my morphine pump.'

'Is that what it's meant for?' Dorian's fine brow arced like a gull's wing as he hovered on a thermal of curiosity. How was it that Wotton was still alive?

'No.' Wotton tucked his plug away. 'It's *meant* for these buggers.' He pulled open the bag at his feet to reveal a couple of large plastic bottles. 'One full of Foscarnet, the other positively gurgling with Ganciclovir. These are the noble knights of the chemical table whom we spur into battle against the dreaded cytomegalovirus.'

'I don't even know what that is, Henry.'

'Nor should you, my sweetums, nor should you. It's a herpes of the most senior order – not the kind of thing that would ever afflict a cadet like *you*.'

They settled on Soho, and while Dorian deposited the Jag in the car-park underneath Gerrard Street, Wotton lingered up above, molesting the strange vegetables ranged in wicker baskets outside the Chinese grocer. He caressed the huge white lingams of the oriental radishes, he ruffled the cabbage and spruced up the sprouts. When Dorian finally emerged he found Wotton tenderly cradling a large, greenish lobe in his hand, a lobe that was evenly studded with spikes as if it were the head of a vegetative punk rocker. 'What's that?' Dorian asked, his nose twitching with distaste. Even in the stinky inky heart of tentacular London this strange fruit imposed its own sickly and faecal odour.

Wotton introduced them: 'Dorian, this is durian; durian, this is Dorian. You'll find you have quite a lot in common – both of you are delicacies, both of you taste quite exquisite. However, *you*, durian, have your pricks on the outside, whereas for Dorian here it's quite the reverse.'

They took their morning coffee upstairs at Maison Bertaux at two in the afternoon. Wotton tucked a purple lenticular pill under his greenish tongue. 'What's that?' Dorian asked.

'Morphine sulphate, twenty milligrams; it's a good breakfast opiate. Now' – he dusted the doughy dandruff of croissant crumbs from his fingers – '*why* have you brought me here?'

'It's Baz,' said Dorian. 'I want to talk to you about him.'

'Oh, *must* you? Where is he, anyway? He spent the night before last gushing over me in hospital in the most sentimental fashion. He led me to believe that we were to be henceforth inseparable.'

'Well, now he's gone.'

'Gone?'

'That's right, gone. He came back to my place and took his stupid photographs of his stupid installation. I made him up a bed on the settee, and when I got up this morning he was gone. He'd taken his bag and gone.'

'So what.' Wotton's eyes wavered away to take in the pert rear end of a perfect Day-Lewis clone, who was ambling between the tables, brushing his taut, denim-sprayed buttocks against the backs of chairs. 'Isn't it true,' he continued on another tack, 'that everyone is so much more the product of their own era than they realise at the time. I suppose it would take an immortal truly to apprehend this in any given moment. I think . . .' he paused, groping for his cigarettes '. . . I shall be compelled by ennui to kill another Kurd.'

'Henry,' Dorian insisted, 'Baz wasn't immortal –'

'What d'you mean, "wasn't"?' Wotton snapped back. 'Are you hiding something here, Dorian – have you brought me here to confess to murder? No no,' – he damped Dorian down with a handful of smoke – 'don't interrupt me; I see it all. Basil himself told me that you really had murdered that faggot in New York, and he brought me tentatively around to the view that the way you behaved with poor Octavia was tantamount to manslaughter. What would make more sense than for you to kill him in turn, hmm? After all, why else take him back to your place – you've never made any secret of the fact that you can't abide the man.'

Dorian took his time replying. He played with his cappuccino a little, dabbling with its foamy cowl. Eventually he answered, in the most subdued and choked tones, 'All right, it's true. I did kill him.'

'Oh good!' Wotton guffawed. 'Confession is such a *bodily* relief, don't you agree? It's like *shitting out* guilt – no wonder the Catholics and Freudians have made an entire system of mind control out of it. I'm so *glad* Baz is dead – although I for one always found him curiously insubstantial anyway, even when his cock was in my arse.'

'So you don't mind?'

'Mind? Of course I don't *mind*; I can see the whole scenario: he pestered you for sex, you finally snapped. It's a common enough occurrence among men of our ilk: the older importuning, the younger giving way to flattery at first, but eventually, consumed by resentment, lashing out. It's only to your credit that you realised how badly the situation reflected on you and decided to act. Nevertheless, Basil's friendship with you did have a certain artistry; it was quite an achievement for him ever to have managed to paint himself up in a good enough light for you to want to sleep with him.'

'Is there nothing you can't deal with rhetorically, Henry?' Dorian asked, a trace of wonderment in his voice.

'Nothing to do with my feelings,' Wotton replied with some seriousness. 'After all, a witticism is merely the half-life of an emotion. Now get the bill, there's a good fellow; I don't even have a half-life left any more, Dorian, and what I do have I wish to spend in a congenial, drug-full environment.'

Dorian did as he'd been bidden, but when he returned from paying downstairs and was helping Wotton to descend, he couldn't prevent himself from returning to the subject. 'So, you're being completely honest?'

'About what?'

'About Baz – about not minding about Baz?'

'Oh do shut up, Dorian' – Wotton rounded on him – 'this silliness has gone on long enough. I don't mind how you dress yourself up but don't try to pretend you're a psycho killer. Violent crimes are in astonishingly bad taste, just as bad taste is a violent crime. You, Dorian, are far too *comme il faut* to commit a murder. I'm sorry if I ruffle your feathers by saying so . . .' he stretched out a hand and rumpled Dorian's hair '. . . but it's a fact.'

14

Eighteen months had passed; it was early February. The gardens of the adjoining houses were stark and bare, yet the Wottons' walled oblong exhibited a most sinister force, which through their green fuses drove the flowers into bloom. Petals exploded from their heavy heads to lie upon the knee-high grasses of this pocket steppe, and the prickly yellow casings of horse chestnuts dangling from the leafy boughs of a tree had the semblance of Pan's own gonads, heavy with the milk of regeneration.

Two men stood in the bay window at the back of the house, looking down on to the lawn. They were watching a most bizarre game of catch. A tall, striking eleven-year-old girl, with auburn hair falling in loose waves to her shoulders, and freckles the size of petits pois squashed across her cheekbones, was standing on the area of paving that bordered the lawn. She wore the idiomatic clothing of the young; trousers and top inscribed with American catch-phrases. She flexed her knees slightly and tossed a pink tennis ball in the direction of a woman who was spreadeagled in the grass. The woman had one hand across her back, as if she were being restrained by an invisible police officer, while the other flailed in the air and missed the ball.

'Right, Mum,' cried the girl, 'now you've got to catch the ball with your mouth!'

'Oh Phoebe,' gasped Batface, for it was she, 'that's absolutely absurd – n-n-no one can catch a ball with their m-mouth. I can't even *see* because of this hayfield.' The girl ignored her, merely swishing through the grass to gather up the ball. She knelt and pulled her mother's free arm over so that it lay with the other. 'Ooh-hoo-hoo,' chortled Batface, 'that tickles, Phoebe, hee-hee, *Phoebe*!'

'One has only to watch women playing with children,' Wotton paraphrased Schopenhauer from his enclosed pulpit, 'to realise that they are themselves big children.'

'D'you think so?' The Ferret's scepticism was understandable, as to him even children seemed like big children. 'Y'know, Wotton,' he continued, 'it's bloody strange the way all the flowers in your garden are blooming just now.'

'It's global warming,' Wotton drawled, while taking a drag on the joint they were sharing; 'it's doing the most astonishing things to the biosphere.' He exhaled, doing something banal to the atmosphere.

'Hmm,' the Ferret mused, his little head aching with the unaccustomed effort of empiricism, 'if that's so, why are all the other gardens perfectly dead?'

'Oh, I don't know, Fergus, perhaps it's only local warming – does it *bother* you? Is it *interfering* with you in some way?' Wotton turned on his heel and shuffled back to his recliner. He lowered himself into the Parker-Knoll and, picking up a pair of glasses with lenses as thick and distorting as Coca-Cola bottles, began scrutinising a copy of the *TV Times*.

'Can you see at all any more?' the Ferret asked, with the brusque insensitivity that still passed for impeccable manners in England.

Wotton sighed. 'Yes, well, that other queen may have found 1992 an *annus horribilis*, but for me it resulted in an anus horribilis. We all need bacteria, Fungus – I mean, Fergus.'

'What on earth are you saying?'

'I'm saying we all need a heavily forested interior to maintain life on Planet Arse, but unfortunately antibiotics have completely logged my interior, and for months now I've been subject to the most appalling flatulence.'

'Oh Henry, *please*, spare me the detail.'

'Why? You have only to hear the words – it's I who must contend with what they describe. Anyway, you asked – and since you asked I can tell you my diarrhoea is the thing that keeps me fit; all those midnight dashes – *most* invigorating.'

'You haven't answered my question.'

'I'm getting there . . . As I say, wrestling with Mr Arse has been exhausting, but my sight has settled into a beneficent state of impairment. I have my senior herpes still; I have severe viral conjunctivitis as well. There are also the post-operative cataracts, but the net effect is most satisfying. I'll give you an example. You see the jiggling man?' Wotton waved the joint at the window.

'What jiggling man?'

'Up on the fifth storey of that block of flats – see him? He's in a fetching red woolly this month, if I'm not much mistaken.'

The Ferret went back to the bay window. 'You mean the man who's sort of rocking back and forth.'

'Jiggling.'

'Oh, all right, jiggling then.'

'Him I see with absolute clarity – I can tell when he was last shaved to within a half-hour – whereas your foul little features are blissfully blurred, Fergus. It's as if a veil of beauty has been thrown over the world – because, let's face it, the closer you get to someone the uglier they become.'

'You're unnecessarily rude,' the Ferret humphed.

'At least,' Wotton trumpeted, 'you admit that some rudeness *is* necessary.

'The fact is,' the Wotton band played on, 'that all of the initials they pump into me to treat my acronym are proving effective, the AZT and the DDI. I've been accepted for the trials of these drugs – not, you appreciate, because of my suitability, but for precisely the opposite reason: they cannot understand why I'm still alive.'

'I can't either,' the Ferret sniffed. 'Your cruelty is staggering and not at all witty any more. To think that Nureyev is dead while you continue to clump gracelessly about the world. Ugh.'

The Ferret got away with this only because at that moment Batface and Phoebe entered the room, the latter bearing a wicker basket piled with cut flowers and other garden herbage. The Ferret went up on tiptoes to kiss Batface, while Phoebe studiously ignored him by tidying the greenery with some secateurs. 'Oh, um, F-Fergus, yes,' Batface blethered. 'What're you doing here?'

'I've come to meet this friend of Henry's – he's called London, I believe.'

'Oh, yes, indeed, London; such a suitable sobriquet for a second-generation immigrant – Phoebe!' she broke off. 'Those c-clippings are going all over the c-carpet – go and ask Consuela for a vase.' The eleven-year-old stomped out of the room.

'Why?' Wotton asked. 'Why's London a good name for a second-generation immigrant?'

'B-b-because presumably he's the first of his f-family to be born *in* London.'

'Oh, that's ridiculous, Batface. It's a street name – he wasn't *christened* London.'

'But where *is* the young fellow?' The Ferret consulted his watch, a dollop of gold on a chain which he withdrew from his egregiously paisley waistcoat. 'I have a lunch at my club.'

'Oh no you don't,' Wotton put in. 'You don't get off so lightly; I have to go to the hospital to have my tubes done and *you* can accompany me. London never serves up this early; he's a drug dealer, Fergus, not an emergency plumber. We'll rendezvous with him later.'

'Thank you, dear.' Batface took a tall, flared piece of cut glass from Phoebe and began to arrange bits of this and that. 'When will you be back, Henry?'

'Tomorrow morning.' They all stood in silence for a couple of minutes, watching as under Batface's surprisingly deft fingers an anti-natural arrangement took shape, with holly berries, catkins and forsythia interleaved with roses, daffodils and snowdrops. At the centre of this thicket was the small limb of a fruiting pear tree. 'That's beautiful,' Wotton said at length. 'Very seasonable.'

'Yes,' his daughter muttered into the chewed-up cuff of her sweatshirt, 'but which bloody season?'

'Very good, Phoebe,' said her father, whose hearing was acute;

'now look for my car keys for me, will you, *I* can't find them anywhere.' He began to struggle into his new winter coat, a modish, full-length, kapok-padded number, which had the air about it of a whole-body blood-pressure cuff.

Later, in the Jag, the Ferret was outraged. 'You got me here on false pretences, Henry. First you say "now", then you say "later" – eventually you concede you're going into hospital overnight.'

'Look.' Wotton was brusque. 'If you want the crack connection you'll have to oblige me; otherwise by all means go and score by yourself on the Mozart Estate.'

'Well, *really*! And furthermore,' the Ferret huffed, 'why did you keep me waiting at your house? You know I can't abide having to talk with the womenfolk.'

'Yeah,' Wotton replied, 'because you're old woman enough for anyone. But shut up now' – he switched on the ignition and the ageing car groaned into life – 'and help me drive. If anything gets too near on your side, sing out. Other than that, tell me what you know about Dorian; I've said my piece.'

'But did you believe him?' the Ferret said, fastening his seat belt and composing his little limbs on the car seat in a stoical fashion. 'Did you think he had murdered Baz?' He took a pillbox from his other waistcoat pocket and extracted two yellow five-milligram Dexedrine. He passed one to Wotton and they both dry-swallowed.

'Of course not; he was merely striking an attitude. I assumed you saw them both out on the west coast – an American who was passing through town told me he'd run across you and Dorian there.'

'No no. I *did* see a bit of Dorian, that's true, but I haven't seen Baz since he was last here. D'you think he might have died?'

Wotton took a while to answer; he was involved in the tricky manoeuvre of pulling out on to the King's Road with less than twenty per cent peripheral vision. 'Lorry coming!' the Ferret piped up, and Wotton floored the accelerator, lurching directly into its path. There was a klaxon's bellow and a blare of abuse, but Wotton merely lowered the window and blew a kiss in the general direction of seven tons of ire. 'I love you!' he fluted. 'I love you all.' Then, turning to the Ferret, he resumed. 'For Baz to have died once would have been unfortunate; for him to die twice looks like carelessness.'

'No, I mean you don't think Dorian *did* actually murder him?'

'If he did, you'd have to *congratulate* Dorian, Fergus. After all, in the course of disposing of Baz's body, just like Nilsen, Dahmer and all those other queer serial killers, Dorian would've had to *put him back* in the closet.'

'Why are you so flip about this, Henry?'

'Three reasons. First, I don't believe he did it; secondly, even if he did, his victim wouldn't have had long to live in any case; and thirdly, Baz is so insubstantial anyway, to murder him would have all the actuality of rubbing out a bad fictional characterisation.

'I myself would *thrill* to being dispatched by Dorian. I can't imagine my nearest and dearest would behave as tediously as Basil's brother, a certain Marius Hallward, a solicitor in Nottingham – wherever *that* may be – who has written to me several times asking if I know his brother's whereabouts.

'Enough of Baz, Fergus, tell me about Dorian, tell me about LA. Paint me a picture on a taut, tan skin canvas, using only the brightest and wateriest of colours. Make it a Hockney, with sunshine yellows and swimming-pool aquamarines. I want your words to buoy me up, to lift me above all this.' He pointed at the grim outdoors. The Jag was passing the Albert Memorial, where the eponymous consort sat in his rococo rocket looking colossally constipated, as if he were about to evacuate himself into space. By the side of the road a variegated pack of dogs rootled at the frozen ground, while a professional dog-walker stood in attendance. 'Just think' – Wotton gestured in their direction – 'hundreds of thousands of years of co-evolution, and we end up paying for them to be taken out for a pee.' Beyond the dogs, on the dead brown winter grass, a small child stood fending off a kite. 'Please, Fergus' – Wotton's voice had an unaccustomed note of desperation – 'take me away from all this.'

And the Ferret obliged. 'Despite being cocooned in First Class, supine on a seat so padded and horizontal it no longer deserved the name, I still couldn't sleep. It's ironic, Henry: with this affliction of mine – not that I expect or receive any sympathy – precisely when an inability to stay awake might be deemed most useful, I find myself tossing and turning. Yes, when I'm flying, repose is as remote from me as the ground. I cruise thirty-five thousand feet above it in a jet stream of turbulent wakefulness. I try to think of the plane as an enormous *membrum virile*, absolutely full of little Ferguses, but somehow this isn't at all reassuring.

'I *yearned* for that chorus of distressed babies from steerage that meant we were coming into land. Their little Eustachian tubes are *so* sensitive they ought to invent a cockpit instrument that uses them. Were I technically minded I might devise it myself.

'Descending into LAX is like entering a vast aquarium where no one has troubled to change the water for some time. The atmosphere, Henry, it's absolutely *green* with pollution. Yet once the plane is on the ground and clunking towards the terminal one finds one's eyes have adjusted, that outside it's deliciously sunny.

'I was quite privileged that autumn (I don't like to say "fall" – it's such a brutal name for a season), because Dorian met me at the airport in one of those laughably long cars, the ones with a bar inside. He had cocaine and all sorts of other goodies, but I was only too happy to curl up in a little ball on the big seat and sleep all the way to the hotel. I knew Dorian and Gavin had met a couple of times before, but this was the first time they'd spent really *talking* with each other. I suppose' – he sniffed – 'I should've seen it coming, but one doesn't, does one? And Gavin had been so terrifically *loyal*.

'Ah well, Henry, I know you don't *do* America, but I expect you can picture the scene well enough.'

The Jag had won the race and lurched to a halt at the single yellow finishing line on Rathbone Place. Outside in the mizzle, raincoated men with the serious miens of classical-music buffs were queuing to enter a popular pornographer's. 'Oh I can,' Wotton said softly, 'I can picture it only too well, Fergus.' He lit a cigarette, and the smoke rolled out of his saturnine mouth like tiny temporal waves breaking on the beach of the present. He pictured the scene.

*　　*　　*

—Is he asleep? asked Dorian, chopping out a line on a mirror balanced on his knees.

—Yeah, I think so. Gavin did the necessary with the Ferret's eyelids. Yeah, he's out. I'll wake him when we get there. Where are we staying?

—I've booked you into the Château Marmont for the first week – but you're staying a while, right?

—Oh, I dunno – I s'pose it's up to him. He says he wants to buy a few properties; I've no idea how long that takes. Gavin took the mirror and rolled-up bill. He honked up the line, then took a slug from the Champagne flute and put it back in its plastic socket of a receptacle. I mean, he is technically speaking my boss.

—Why the fuck d'you stick with it?

—Jesus, you know nothing, Dorian, fuck all. You haven't a fucking clue what it might be like to be without money or connections or looks, even –

—You have the looks, Dorian said, and ran a finger along the smooth grain of Gavin's handsome face. Gavin grabbed it, selected a finger, bit it hard. Ow! Dorian cried. That hurt!

The Ferret stirred in his sleep. He cooed in a singsong voice, Fergus babies in the cloudy playpen.

Gavin laughed, sucking Dorian's finger. I wanted to see if you had any nerves at all. Look, I need a little time in the sun. Fergus is no trouble – all he wants is to be fed his drugs and his other luxuries, and a couple of times a week I slap him around and give him a wank. What could be easier?

—It sounds perfectly vile to me; I can't imagine how horrible his body is underneath that little suit.

—Well, it's very muscly, if wrinkled and misshapen. I'm sure you'll have the opportunity to witness it for yourself; he likes to strip off in the sun.

Oof! The Ferret ejaculated a spout of atomised saliva. He lay horizontal, on his back, at the Venice Beach open-air gymnasium. All about him bobbed balloon sculptures of the male human form; they stretched and puckered and pumped. He would've looked altogether at odds with this Olympian company – by virtue of size, age and texture – had it not been for a helper he'd acquired: a stocky little dwarf with a head disproportionately large even for his kind. From his cleft bum of a chin an oiled trowel of goatee dug into the sweaty air. The dwarf, nude save for a cache-sexe, had built his body into a veritable cylinder of sinuosity. He was helping the Ferret by adding two kilo weights on to the bench pressing bar. That's twenty keys, he said. Are you sure you can do it?

—Well – *oof-oof* – if I can't manage it *you'll* stop it *garrotting* me, won't you, Terry?

—Sure, Fergus.

—So – *oof-oof-oof-oooaaay!* – obliging. The Ferret performed the feat, sat up and took the towel Terry held out. Mopping the teensy crannies of his tiny head, he turned to his workout buddy. Um, tell me, Terry, have you always been a muscle dwarf?

—Nope, Fergus, I used to be a leather dwarf back in NYC, but that scene was so crazy and then everyone got sick, so I came out here. People are much more accepting in LA – he smirked – and I get a *helluva* lot of offers. Where are your friends?

—Oh, *them* – they're strolling along the esplanade.

—Fergus, are they, like – an item?

They certainly appeared to be an item, Dorian and Gavin, as they breasted the throngs along the roadway at the top of the beach – both of them in khaki shorts and white T-shirts, both of them in shades, both of them with the smooth, clipped haircuts of gays in the military. Yes, they looked like an item of coupled normality, while all around surged a mêlée of singular mutations: ancient hippies, with bells on their fingers and rings on their toes; snake priestesses entwined with their hissing disciples; tattooed primitives nouveaux, their patterned faces two-dimensional; punks jangling with the metal threaded through their scabrous flesh; soul dudes muffling the world with their Afros.

—I've never seen so many freaks in one place, said Gavin; these people are unbelievable! He was enjoying himself hugely. Dorian, whom back in London Gavin found arrogant, distant and hopelessly narcissistic, had been applying his formidable charm.

—Well, Gavin, in my experience it's often the most outrageous outsides that harbour the most prosaic insides, while those of us who appear fresh-faced and beautiful contain a most rotten and disgusting core.

—What about you, Dorian – what's your disgusting core?

—It's just that: a disgusting core. My looks are unnaturally preserved. Eleven years ago, immediately after I left university, Baz Hallward made his video portrait of me, and while I have remained a fresh-faced twenty-two-year-old, the installation has suffered the onslaught of the past decade. All my debauchery is now inscribed on my cathode features, while these ones . . . he broke step, turned to Gavin, took his hands, looked into his eyes . . . remain pristine.

Gavin laughed. Nice conceit, Dorian, he said; sounds like some of the conceptual works these young artists at Goldsmiths' have been working on. Maybe you should do it rather than talk about it.

—What d'you mean?

—Take Baz's installation and customise it. I know what his stuff is like – incredibly fey, laughable really. Everything's a lot more hard-edged now. You should meet some of the newer crowd – you'd like them.

—Plenty of time for that, as I'm immortal. Even if this sympathetic magic with Baz's piece doesn't carry on working for ever, I'm going to have my body frozen so that when the scientists of the future have discovered the secret of perpetual life they can boot me up again and then upgrade me.

—Are you serious, Dorian? You mean get those cryonics people to freeze you?

—Why not? That's part of the reason the Ferret is here – I said I'd introduce him to my immortalist friends; he's very keen on the idea.

*　　*　　*

In the hospital waiting room Wotton stirred. He grasped the Ferret's firm shoulder in his febrile fingers. 'I don't say hello to inverts any more, Fergus.'

'Oh no?'

'No, I say, "Welcome fellow sufferer," which is how Schopenhauer thought everyone should be greeted. Tell me, Fergus, why don't *you* have the virus?'

'Well, really . . . Henry, I don't think . . . I mean I don't *engage* in that sort of thing nowadays.'

'Perhaps you ought to. After all, if you're going to be frozen so that the doctors of the future can thaw you out, you'd be doing them a favour by presenting them with a challenge, mm?'

A woman doctor who'd been hovering nearby came forward. 'Mr Wotton?'

'That's me.' He struggled to rise and she reached down to assist him.

'I'm very sorry you were kept waiting so long; we have a bed ready for you now. Will your friend be waiting for you? It's likely you won't be conscious again until early evening.'

'Yes, he's my buddy and he's going to stay.'

'Stay? Buddy?' The Ferret was appalled.

'Yes; don't be so squeamish. They might let you watch if you're good – some buddies do. They use a general anaesthetic; all they have to do is take the line out and instal a new one. Some people I know would be delighted to witness a tube being tunnelled through the membrane below my upper chest wall. Perhaps if you cope with this you'll shape up – to be frank, Fergus, you're not much good at buddying.'

'Buddying?'

'Befriending someone with AIDS, helping them out. Look,' Wotton continued as the trio tottered down the corridor between treatment rooms, 'if you really can't handle it you can stay on the ward and sleep. The important thing is that until I actually go into theatre I want you to keep performing, keep telling me about Dorian.'

15

Way out to the east of Los Angeles, in a district called Riverside, the dry gulches of the surrounding mesa gouged down into a jumble of used-car lots, warehouses and light-industrial premises. The atmosphere here was even more bilious than in the centre of town – or was it only that the distempered air was more noticeable, having less aural and visual pollution to compete with? On a roughly trapezoid patch of asphalt outside the rolled-up steel door of a breeze-block unit stood another ill-assorted trio. (Some tales are full of well-matched couples, but this, alas, is not one of them.)

Terry, the muscle dwarf, stroked his hairy trowel and prodded at the hard ground with a sneaker. Six months in California had coated Gavin with the sweetness of good living, and this sticky layer had been caramelised by the sun. Dorian was Dorian, never more incontrovertibly himself, never more beautiful, than when placed in ugly prosaic surroundings. The three men stared up into the unit, to where, perched on top of a catwalk that ran across the top of several large, wheeled storage Dewars, stood the Ferret. With him was a scoutmasterish character, kitted out in khaki shorts, knee socks, sandals, sheathed knife, wire-rimmed spectacles, and a walrus moustache like a lip-borne token of masculinity. Wreaths of dry-ice smoke eddied from the gloom out to the sunlight. The Ferret was peering into it with the bemused expression of a genteel lady who's been told at the age of sixty-three that she is about to become a mother again.

—What are those? he asked the scoutmaster.

—Neurocans, came the reply, the canisters that contain the heads of our members who have opted for partial suspension.

—And that costs fifty thousand, yes?

—That's correct.

—While to have my whole body, er . . . *suspended* is more expensive?

—In the region of a hundred and sixty thousand dollars, sir, so yes, considerably more expensive. But as I said to you while we toured the facility, an investment in cryonic suspension isn't only financial. All of our members are fully committed to a philosophy; most are prepared to join in assisting at the perfusion and suspension of their fellows after deanimation.

—Oh, I don't know about that . . .

—Listen – the scoutmaster squatted down on his haunches and yarned on as if the dry ice were a smoking campfire – I've assisted at four suspensions now and I can tell you that in the first seconds after deanimation – when the team sprang into action and I commenced cutting down the femoral artery so we could pump in the glycerol – I felt more sense of achievement than I have in any other area of my life. And I was a marine sergeant in 'Nam – I'm no pussy, no sir.

—Um, yes, absolutely – *I* don't like to think of myself as in the least little bit feline either. Tell me, Dorian, he called down from his perch, have you gone for the whole-body suspension or only the, um, *neuro*?

—Since you ask, Fergus, whole-body – I shouldn't want to have another body cloned for me when I've been reanimated. It might not be up to scratch; they might confuse my DNA with someone else's – I could end up with my head stuck on an inferior body . . . like Terry's, for instance.

—Back off, Dorian! The muscle dwarf bridled at an invisible leash, his arms flexing invisible bolt-cutters. I don't have to put up with this crap, I'm nobody's fucking poodle.

—Boys, boys . . . the Ferret damped them down from on high . . . there's no need for such histrionics. But speaking of poodles – he turned back to the immortalist – is there any facility for, um, *suspending* one's favourite companions?

—Why, absolutely. Look down there, sir, can you see the blue linen sacks? They contain members' pets. Personally I feel certain that being greeted by our four-legged friends when we're reanimated will be a great comfort and enormously assist our integration into a future society which will be vastly more technically sophisticated than our own.

In the limo thrumming back west along Route 99, Gavin guffawed, Pets! A technology vastly more sophisticated than our own! Who do these jokers think they're kidding? Did you see their operating theatre? It was like something out of *Dr*-bloody-*Kildare*, totally hokey.

—I don't imagine you'll be laughing quite so much, the Ferret sniffed, when you're dead and Terry and Dorian and I are frolicking in a very real Elysium. Mmm, I can just picture it . . . crystal lakes and infinitely tall towers of translucent sapphire, the whole place populated by the most *divine* boys –

—Are you on *acid*? Gavin leaned over from the front seat and poked at the Ferret. You certainly seem off your trolley.

Terry, who was driving, a bulky cushion beneath his tush, a chauffeur's cap perched like a yarmulka on his pointy crown, rounded on Gavin, grabbed his arm and snarled, Don't touch the boss!

—The *boss*, is it now? Fergus, I never thought you'd stoop to such sycophancy. As for this suspension business, when they pump the glycerol into your corpse's arteries, there will be a little bit of moisture left in each and every one, and when the temperature drops to minus seventy-five they'll pop like fucking Ricicles. No matter how vast the technological advancement of the future – and frankly, the way things are going I doubt it'll get much further at all – they'll never be able to repair bodies cell by cell.

—'Course they will, the Ferret yawned; Dorian says they'll do it with nannywhatsit, little robot thingies – isn't that it, Dorian?

—Nanotechnology, Fergus – you're quite right; they'll have tiny hyperintelligent robots working in concert to repair our damaged bodies. They'll recreate you, Ferret my love, exactly the same in every detail, right down to your slumberousness. The Ferret was slumbering now, his little head lolling over at an unnatural angle on the leather upholstery, as if he were a nodding human in lieu of a nodding dog. Tut-tut, Dorian admonished Gavin, why deny Fergus his late bid for immortality, if that's what he wants?

—It's just so stupid, that's what I can't stand. Why are you doing it, Dorian? You aren't a fool.

—I suppose it's a spread bet, Gavin. I don't just belong to this bunch; I belong to a couple of other cryonics outfits too, and a life-extension group. I'm partial to the odd cult as well – there's one here called Heaven's Gate, a Japanese lot called Aum Shinrikyo who're totally gnarly. In Switzerland I belong to some dudes who dress up in delightful robes, called the Order of the Solar Temple, and when I'm in Texas I like to drop by Waco and visit a bunch dubbed the Branch Davidians. Like I say, if you put a chip on every number you're bound to win at least one spin of fortune's wheel.

—I can't believe in any of this except as an affectation, Dorian; I think you're treating your life as an artwork – of sorts. You should come back to London with me, get Hirst to preserve your corpse in formaldehyde. Put it on show in a fucking big vitrine. It'd be a kind of immortality, if that's what you want.

—No, if *you* want, Gavin. If you want.

—Yeah, well, I do *want* – more than this sad scene. It seems like Terry here is the new Californian catamite; I think I'll light out for the territory. I can't imagine I'll miss the old bastard that much.

*　　*　　*

'But *I* missed *him*, Henry, truly I did. I felt quite bereft.'

'And what about Terry?' Wotton put in, while investing heavily in a Turkish State Monopoly. 'Didn't he do the business?'

'You make it sound so *crude*. It wasn't like that at all; I think Terry *almost* loved me – he was *awfully* loyal. If he were with me in London I shouldn't have to come with you to such dreadful places.' The Ferret peered around at the dank multi-storey car-park, which, with its pissed-upon pillars and rubber-wiped ramps, resembled the interior of a pyramid constructed by an automotive despotism. The two men – one diminutive and nut-brown, the other lank and fish-belly-pale – sat in their darkened saloon as if it were a four-door sarcophagus. But all they had in the way of funerary goods was Wotton's usual Jag-load of rubbish.

'Ssh!' he admonished the Ferret. 'Here comes London now.'

A silver Honda Aerodeck – such a preposterous little vehicle, with its pretensions to a futurity that had already slid past by the time it rolled off the production line in Marysville, Ohio – came jolting up the ramp, then screeched to a halt. A lithe black guy in his late twenties, sporting a baggy maroon windcheater and baggy black jeans, shot up and out of the little car like a fighter beating a count. He had a flat-top in the current Tyson mode. He swaggered over to the Jag. The Ferret quailed while Wotton wound down his window. 'Oyez!' London exclaimed. 'S'it fuckin' 'ot yev' 'Enry.'

'Indeed,' Wotton replied, seemingly comprehending this bizarre idiolect, 'but you aren't making it any cooler with your mode of arrival.'

'Sinit 'kin 'urry up gofer over Bushmun,' London glottaled, 'an' summuv.' His head, as sharp as a sabre, slashed at the stinky air, his shoulders rolled, his knees flexed, paranoia emanated from him with such intensity that it distorted the air like petrol fumes.

'Ah well, I quite understand, London. In that case you had better furnish me with an eightball of your *soi-disant* crack. Incidentally . . .' he squirmed round to indicate the Ferret, who was now not only quailing, but so agitated – his little liver-spotted hands fluttering around his fluffy toupee – that he even closely resembled a quail. . . 'I'd like you to meet a friend of mine –'

'Issit sound an' that norv?! Issit?' If at all possible London was becoming even more agitated.

'Oh, he's entirely trustworthy, I assure you – look how *old* he is. London – Fergus Rokeby; Fergus – London. I hope you don't tire of each other.'

London had spat a dumpling of cling film into his hand, dried the spit off on his jacket and slapped it into Wotton's palm while this introduction was being effected. He took the eight twenty-pound notes rolled into a fat stogie and poked at his stomach. 'Seen you fuckiddim man I mess you good. Mess you fuckin' straightway.' And in one agitated movement he shoved the money away and flipped up a pouch of maroon nylon to expose the nacreous butt of an automatic, glistening against the taut brown skin of his belly.

The Ferret fainted dead away.

In sleep – painful to relate – the Ferret dreamed. Painful because to those tormented by a lack of sleep, who had sweated through a 'Hallelujah Chorus' of dawn choruses, the idea that the rich little bugger was experiencing a fulsome and refreshing repose as a result of his malady induced an envy of such green intensity that it threatened physically to poison.

But it was true; in sleep the Ferret dreamed, and as he slept so much his dream life was far more coherent and enduring than the content of his waking mind. In sleep the Ferret shook up the particular events of the wider world and peered at them through his own perceptual prism, to create a hypnagogic kaleidoscope of deranging hyperreality. In the Ferret's vast subconscious (as big as five thousand open-cast Brazilian gold mines, or one hundred Capris), there was ample room for Serbian concentration camps staffed by busboys, naked save for dear little breech-clouts of chammy leather; and there was plenty of *Lebensraum* for alfresco discos where all the painted peacocks of 1950s Soho could peck and flutter among the loved-up crowds of 1990s ravers. In the Ferret's cerebral cockpit, penis-nosed premiers – Rabin and Arafat, Mandela and de Klerk, Major and Reynolds – were for ever jousting. They warily circled the rose garden of the White House under the simple gaze of Bouffant Bill, their cheeks spattered with the jism of peace. While alongside this, separated from it all only by a zebra-striped fake-fur divan over a kilometre in length, marched an unending column of young guardsmen, their scarlet chests ribbed with gold braiding, their pillbox hats jigging, their waxed mustachios waving. Over all this arched the empyrean, cold bright blue, curved like the ceiling of a Byzantine church. Through the oculus at its very apex could be seen the entrance to Heaven, guarded by a slip of a St Peter, the down on his cheek burnished by eternity, the handkerchief in his belt dripping with ambrosial nitrate. Above this ascended cloud upon cloud, all gilded by sunlight. Plunging through, swarming about and hovering on these celestial cushions were swarms of well-oiled putti (bronzer, moisturiser, exfoliant, all manner of lubricants), all laughing and gossiping – 'Well, *she* said . . .' And finally, surmounting everything, inconceivably high, reclining across the very zenith of the firmament, was God Himself, who, during the latter – and more pious – portion of Fergus Rokeby's life, had assumed the form of Dorian Gray.

Henry Wotton had been, to some extent, correct about the Ferret all those years before, when they ate beluga caviar together under the stone-cold eyes of Jon the Dilly boy.

Inasmuch as any notion of the deity includes a supposition of omniscience, the Ferret was a sort of god, albeit an impotent, queeny, peeved, amoral one, who had an inordinate fondness for young men in uniform. Because the Ferret's dreams were of such duration and complexity, and because they incorporated world events that were likely to occur as well as those that already had, and because the Ferret's subconscious had a unified character (like a paternal house accessed through many different mansions), it was inevitable that, during those brief periods when wakefulness dawned across the ruched surface of his cortex, he would become aware of things currently occurring – massacres in Rwanda, coup in Moscow, earthquake in Los Angeles – that he had already foreseen (albeit incorporating a cast of multicoloured centaurs and singing seahorses) in his dreams.

So it was that awakening with his cheek pressed into white linen of a weave heavier than that of bed-sheets, the Ferret was confused for some seconds, not as to where he might be lying (he had expired on so many restaurant tables during his life that he could identify individual establishments purely by the smell of the starch their laundry used), but as to whether the conversation he was over-hearing was taking place in 1992 or 1994 or 1988.

It was the summer of 1994, and the Ferret – together with Gavin Strood and Henry Wotton – was dining in a private room upstairs at the Sealink Club in Soho. The Ferret and Wotton were only there as supernumeraries, invited along by Gavin to attend a dinner given for one of his sculptural friends, who had recently won a commission to create a world-genocide memorial, to be erected in Reykjavik.

All of this information unwound behind the Ferret's warty eyelids like televisual ticker tape continuously updating the Dow Jones. Without needing to open them he could picture the long oval white-clothed table, with its loose ellipse of night people, some in dishabille, some buttoned up tight. He could hear the sculptor – a well-bred Edinburghian, who in his cups relocated to the Gorbals – bellowing out, 'We're pure, we are – we're fucking pure!' He could apprehend, through open floor-length windows, the growl and rumble of metal tumbrels in the street three storeys below. He could register the burble of all the diners, but closest to him, and talking directly across his horizontal back, were Wotton and Gavin.

'So, Gavin, Dorian, you say he continues to plough his salted furrow across our green and pleasant land.' Wotton was hunkered so far down in his chair that his words flowed slowly on to his plate like olive oil drizzled by a sous-chef.

'As far as I know.' Gavin by contrast was upright and earnest. 'But I have a confession to make, Henry.'

'Confess,' Wotton cooed, extending his claw of a hand to be kissed as if he were a pervy prelate.

'I sneaked off from LA with Dorian . . . I suppose I stole him off Fergus here.'

'Don't be ridiculous, Gavin, no one possesses the least little bit of Dorian.'

'I know, I know, it's wishful thinking. The absolute opposite has happened – I've ended up obsessed by him . . . while he couldn't give a shit about me.'

'Join,' Wotton sighed, 'the club.'

'But that's not my confession. What eats away at me is the idea that Dorian is . . . is – I know it sounds melodramatic – is *evil*.'

'Evil is to morality as magnolia is to paint,' Wotton said after a while; 'it's an unpleasant shade of meaning, far too liberally applied, purely on the basis that it isn't white.'

'No.' Gavin swirled the wine in his glass, putting bloody bullet-holes in the tablecloth. 'I mean it – I mean that he's a murderer.'

'Oh, I've heard all *that* before – usually from Dorian himself.'

'Yes, I know; in LA he told me he'd killed Baz Hallward – I thought it was a joke too, but Baz's work has been undergoing a revival and there's still no sign of him re-emerging. Now this thing has happened to that guy Campbell as well –'

'Campbell?' Wotton cut in. 'What's happened to Alan?'

But he didn't have the opportunity to find out immediately, because the pint-of-Pinot Noir proletarian was pushing in: 'D'ye ken Baz Hallward?' he slurred. 'Och, he's fuckin' pure, man, he's fuckin' pure. That laddie was way out there in front of us all.' He grabbed for the light fitment as if intending to bring the idolatrous temple of the Sealink crashing down about their ears. 'Ah love his stuff, all that prancing about in the noddy – an' ye ken him, old man?' This last was slurred directly to Wotton, and the sculptor meant 'old' literally, for the battle between the anti-retroviral drugs and the virus itself had been waged for so long now that a no man's land of churned, scorched territory had been created all over Wotton's face. He looked twenty years older than he was; the sight in his left eye had now gone, and he wore an eye-patch as if it were a piratical affectation, although it was a medical necessity.

'Hallward . . . Baz. . . . Yes . . .' Wotton's succession of stalled words jammed the other conversation around the table. 'I know – or knew – him. Is he alive or dead? It hardly matters; the important thing is that his work remains that bizarre mixture of stupid execution and clever intentions that always entitles someone to be called a representative British artist.'

Depending on quite how saturated they were already, the members of the arty party took their time absorbing the import of this remark. Eventually the sculptor plunged back in: 'You tryin' t'be clever, pal? You tekin' the piss or what?'

'You . . . misunderstand . . . me . . .' Wotton poured oil on the Firth of Fauve '. . . my remarks were intended generally rather than specifically; they don't apply to you unless you see yourself as a representative British artist – or RBA.'

'It's not me, pal – it's Hallward I'm stickin' up for.'

'Ah, Baz – Baz . . . what can I say? He was a dull Janus; one face the nice man, the other the bad artist. It appears to me – even on our very short acquaintance – that you would prefer to be seen as the reverse.'

Wotton was ready to go on with this; after all, although he was living on mortgaged time, he had a freehold on recklessness, but he was grievously hampered by the fact that his sparring partner couldn't comprehend what he was saying. Indeed, the mental operations required by Wotton's last sentence were so far beyond the sculptor that when a waitress's bust barrelled by he simply got up and followed it like a bloodhound after a bone.

'So' – Wotton turned back to Gavin – 'Campbell – what about him?'

'Well . . . ,' he leaned still further across the small back that separated them '. . . this is all I know . . .' Gavin's words fell like seeds into the warm, damp folds of the Ferret's field of dreams, engendering the following:

—Dorian, I need to have a little word . . . Alan Campbell's voice on the phone had all the tenderness he reserved for blackmail, which was the most psychologically intimate contact he'd had with anyone since childhood. We need to talk about Basil Hallward.

—Baz, Dorian snorted, who the fuck would want to talk about that piece of shit.

—Yer forgetting the work I did for ya. I was the pooper-bloody-scoop for that piece of shit.

Dorian was sitting at his roll-top desk, toying with an ivory letter-opener, an exquisite thing depicting a miniature Hindustani army complete with howdah-humping battle elephants. How could he bother to take this seriously? Yeah, yeah, I paid you well enough for that, Campbell – what's your problem now?

—All these AIDS drugs are bloody expensive, Dorian; I can't get on any of the trials so I have to buy them on the black market. Cash is as rare around here as rocking-horse droppings – I need some more.

—Well you can't have it – I'm not a fucking charity.

—I know that, but I reckon ya might want to rent a video off me.

—What the fuck're you talking about, you disgusting old nonce? But Dorian was sitting bolt upright now, all languor expunged.

—I'm watching it right now; bloody weird thing – this bloke dancing about. He's in a bloody dreadful state, but even so, *I'd* recognise him – I bet others would too. This video could be a real smash if it were put on general release.

—You. Hold. It. Right. There. Dorian sentenced Campbell with each word, then flung the receiver down on the desk and sprinted to the stairs.

Up one flight, he fidgeted and faffed with the locks; his fingers, usually so sure, so elegant, had become numb stubs. He hadn't looked at *Cathode Narcissus* since the night he killed Baz – what need had he to? The deterioration of the tapes would only be hastened by their being played, but as long as they were intact his beauty would remain so as well. That's what he assumed to be the case. If one of the *Narcissus* tapes were in Campbell's hands – what then? Campbell couldn't possibly know the power bound up in them, but what if he destroyed this one, or, as he seemed to be

203

threatening, exposed it to public view? Like anyone who commits themselves to a life ordained by magic, Dorian now inhabited a fearful realm, where human malevolence could be exercised by a mere effort of will. He. Must. Have. All. The. Tapes.

Inside at last, he lunged for the fitted cupboard, yanked open the door, hit the eject buttons on the VCRs. One, two, three, four, five, six, seven, eight . . . one gone. One. Gone. There was one tape gone!

Back downstairs, Dorian lifted the receiver from the desk blotter and spoke as casually as if he were a middle-aged plum-gobbler ordering vintage port from a wine merchant. Hmm, yes, well, Alan, on consideration I think I shouldn't mind joining your video club. What's the entrance fee?

—Same. Fifteen large. Used notes.

—It'll take me an hour or so to get the cash – it's lunchtime; the bank'll be crowded.

—I appreciate that, mate – why don't we meet at, say, two? In front of Earls Court tube'd be just dandy.

—Fine, that will be fine.

—You be alone, Dorian.

—Naturally. Bye.

But *I* won't, thought Campbell, replacing the receiver and looking around for his overcoat. He consulted his watch. He'd hired some muscle, a nasty black pimp called Rusty on account of his Celtic-throwback hair. He'd call him on his way to the tube – best to get out of the flat as quickly as possible; he couldn't remember if Dorian knew its location. Even if he did the traffic was gridlocked at this time of the day; there was no way he could get there in less than twenty minutes.

Campbell moved slowly. He was gaunt, and had bad peripheral neuropathy. He could barely feel the things he picked up, and had to bring them before his eyes to be certain he was holding them. It took him ten minutes to get his coat on, pack its pockets with medication, find his keys and make it to the door of the bedsit.

Dorian made it over from Gloucester Road in seven. He had acquired a racing bicycle in anticipation of just such a chore. Going out? Dorian held Campbell by the throat against the door-jamb and frisked him. But where's the tape?

—It's not here – I was gonna give ya the key for a deposit box.

—Bullshit. It'll be here – you're too fucked up, old man, to put it anywhere else. He strode two paces across the urine-tinged closeness of the bedsit, punched the eject button on a VCR, which was stacked with mildewed magazines on a coffee table undeserving of the name. Bingo! he said.

—Yeah, well, whatever. Still, no need t'be so harsh, Dorian – I was gonna give it ya.

—Cack, as I believe you antipodeans are wont to say.

—But you'll give me some of the dough, woncha?

—No. Dorian started for the door. Campbell fell to his knees and, in pathetic emulation of his homeland's sporting prowess, attempted to tackle him. Get off, you dirty diseased thing. Dorian didn't raise his voice. There was a calmness and a confidence in the way he grasped Campbell's chin between thumb and forefinger, that suggested he'd acquired a personal homicide trainer. A lasso of cord had appeared in Dorian's other hand; he flipped this over his victim's head. The knot smoothly tightened. Campbell was very weak. He spluttered and foamed but barely kicked at all.

Dorian pulled Campbell's trousers down to his knees. He tied the end of the ligature around one of the corpse's legs and yanked it up against the buttocks. From his pocket he took a half-orange soaked with amyl nitrate; this he stuffed in the foaming gash of mouth. Then, confirming the accuracy of Wotton's quip, Dorian put Campbell's corpse in the closet. It was a wonky thing, with sliding doors opened by transparent plastic knobs. Over in the corner Dorian saw a black plastic bag overflowing with the polystyrene Ss used for packing breakables. Grabbing hold of its slick lip he poured handfuls of Ss out on the dead tread of the carpet. He broke some of them into smaller, curvilinear forms and then arranged them into sibilant words. 'Narcissus' was his favourite. He considered leaving the polystyrene 'Narcissus' as a signature to this figurative artwork, but then decided otherwise and merely dumped the bag of Ss on top of the concertinaed corpse.

Dorian Gray popped out of the human warren as he had popped in, looking as if he was doing an errand – especially since he was porting the mushroom-cap helmet of a serious cyclist, together with black nylon leggings, a Day-glo jacket and rubber-knuckled gloves. He didn't imagine stupid squad would search too hard for a putative killer. A Member of Parliament had recently been discovered in a similar pose, and it always pleased them mightily to find evidence of copycat behaviour. Copycat crime made for copycat policing – so much easier that way. If there was a description of a man leaving Campbell's flat and they *did* interview him, what would they discover? Dorian Gray riding a *bicycle*? The idea wasn't merely preposterous – it was grotesque.

Back at the mews house, in the locked room full of costly minimalism (too much of nothing is an expensive proposition), Dorian watched his special feature. In the three years since he'd last encountered them the Narcissi had put on a little weight. They seemed to have been annealed by the virus, so that their toughened epidermises resembled the yellowing leather of mummies.

But if they'd filled out, the Dorians had also chilled out. They now moved languidly, adopting a series of stylised postures. Their eyes were glacial with indifference, their corrupt mouths twisted with sadistic moues. Whereas the Narcissi of 1991 had been passionate marionettes, these ones were calculating killers.

The flesh-and-blood Dorian sighed, rose from the Baz-stained Eames chair, went over to each of the monitors in turn and canoodled with his own corybantic zombies. It was a Dorian x 10 Love-in. The tracking on the tapes was deteriorating, and their registration as well. Bands of prickling static appeared at the top and bottom of the screens; the images were more indistinct. But it was possible, Dorian supposed, that this very corruption of the representational medium was helping to make *him* more embodied, more at home in the world. He stretched, sighed again and drew in a great breath. He never caught cold, he never had a headache, he never experienced the slightest physical discomfort save that caused by obvious abrasions of the physical world. He hummed with vigour as a high-tension cable sings with electricity. He would go out tonight, Dorian decided, and have some serious fun.

16

'Most nights,' Gavin was concluding, 'he's to be found at that Chinaman's weird den down on the Limehouse Causeway; he picks young gay guys up in the clubs. He'll even cruise Actup or Queer Nation meetings looking for prey. Whether a chicken's high on E or ideology – it's the same to him. You know the Chinaman's, Henry?'

'I'm familiar with its whereabouts. I can't say I've ever bothered to go there myself.'

'I have,' squeaked the Ferret, his creased face parting at last from the creased linen of the tablecloth, the images of Dorian (and the images of his images) still whirling in his mind. 'I've *seen* Dorian down there. He likes to take straights with him and get them terribly confused. It's really *quite* sordid. Are we going this evening?'

'I don't see the point.' Wotton lit a Sullivan's Export and held the big white dirigible of a cigarette aloft as if it were a stupid bomb targeted at his morose mouth. 'After all, we've no one square enough in our party to be worth doing *origami* with. *You've* been as bent as a five-bob note all your life, haven't you, Fergus?'

'Well . . .' so seldom was the Ferret offered an opportunity to talk about himself that he was taken aback, but the amphetamine kicking into the flanks of his nervous system urged him on '. . . of course, when I was a lad, *Grecian* love was an absolute taboo. My father, y'know, such a *savage* man, he . . . he caught me with one of the stable lads when I was sixteen, near flayed me with a horsewhip –'

'Balls.' Wotton put in succinctly.

'No no, I *assure* you it's true.'

'My dear Ferret . . .' Wotton savoured his smoke, allowing an extravagantly curled beard of Assyrian ringlets to gather on his chin '. . . I don't doubt the paternal chastisement, I merely question whether it truly hurt you. Your taste – as you've often had cause to tell me, and with which Gavin is *thoroughly* familiar – does incline to painful pleasures.'

'Henry, you don't understand – my masochism came later on. In the thirties, desperate to conform and wishing to marry, I consulted a prominent sexologist, Professor Hilversum. This man reported great success in *curing* inversion. You young men now-adays, you can have no conception of the shame then attached to such practices.'

'Oh no?' the gay plague dog softly barked.

'Hilversum *swore* by aversion therapy; his methods were crude – vicious even – but he guaranteed success. We were put in hospital gowns and our pubic areas were shaved – rather brutally by a burly Australian sheep-shearer. Some of my fellow patients told me he would perform other services for a consideration, but I was serious about seeking a cure.

'So, once shaved, we were strapped to examination couches. An electric belt was fastened around us. There were all the trappings of medical orthodoxy at Hilversum's clinic.'

'And then?'

'Then we were shown films and photographs of naked boys and young men. It was tame enough material by today's standards, but to us then it was quite sufficient to effect arousal. However, the second we became aroused we received an almighty electric shock through the belt. And this happened even if there was no *visible* evidence – I think they must have been monitoring our heartbeats.

'Of course,' the Ferret continued in the face of his listeners' slightly stunned silence, 'the treatment was *not* a success in my case. Far from associating homosexuality with pain and rejecting the former, I came instead to enthusiastically embrace the latter and regard it as an indispensable part of homosexual love.'

There was another silence at their end of the table. A tall, gaunt man in his early thirties, short greasy hair plastered down on his spotty brow, detached himself from the drunken baying around the sculptor and came to join them. Wotton noted that he was wearing a once good Armani suit over an open-necked Thomas Pink shirt. 'I couldn't 'elp over'earin' ya,' the man drawled in fluent Mockney, 'but surely homosexuality – as in the "gay lifestyle" – is a sorta category error?' He paused and sniff-snuffled the cocaine juice around his muzzle. 'If I were in gaol, doubtless I'd become a sodomite, but as it stands I prefer invagination –'

'Hey, look!' On cue, a supremely vaginal young woman – shadow-filled cleavage, swollen red lips, minuscule dress more slits than silk – came and draped herself around the Mockney's neck. 'Are we fucking off, Cal, or *what*?' she gasped with exasperation.

'D'you know one another?' Ignoring the intervention, Gavin connected the three men with a diagram fingered in the air. 'Henry Wotton, Fergus Rokeby, this is Cal Devenish, the novelist.'

Wotton inclined his head half a degree. 'I've heard of you . . . vaguely.'

'And I of you.' Devenish took a great pull on a tumblerful of whisky. 'You're a pal of Dorian Gray's, aren't you?'

'D'you know him?'

'I was at Oxford with him. Different set to me, of course – ex-public-schoolboy dining-club wankers. Laughably crass. He hadn't even come out then, but I believe *that's* changed.'

There was another interruption, this one far more intrusive. The sculptor – like a statue of Stalin surplus to requirements – toppled across the table. 'Yairsh!' he slurred. 'We're gonna Chinaman's – you gonna Chinaman's, y'fuckin' poofs, eh?' A couple of his fabricators – who knew which side of the genocide memorial had butter on it – winched him upright and hauled him off. 'I wonder,' Cal Devenish said when they'd gone, 'if you three would like to come back to my house?' He slid a nicotine-stained hand up the dress of the girl and continued, 'I can offer you fine wines, enough MDMA powder for you to put it under your foreskins –'

'Cocaine?' Wotton entered a bid.

'Some, certainly – and believe me, anything not immediately available can be readily obtained. I have a source very close to hand.'

'In that case . . .' Wotton tipped his eye patch as if it were a small black hat '. . . who's a pretty boy, then?'

*   *   *

On the eastern fringes of that metropolitan prairie Wormwood Scrubs, Cal Devenish inhabited a small house which burrowed into the embankment of a railway line. In the dead of night, wired out of his head on cocaine, or smacked out, or sloppily drunk, or funky with skunk, Devenish would lie, wonkily tiger-striped by orange streetlights strained through Venetian blinds, and feel the shake, rattle and roll of passing trains bearing nuclear waste, while praying fervently that one would divert into his sweaty masonry pit. In the cold light of another morning, wincing from the pain of toxic bile corroding his ulcerated throat, he would clutch the sides of the bathroom sink and peer distantly into his own Chernobyl eyes, as if the disaster he could see happening in them was in a country a long way off, of which he knew very little.

Devenish had had a fair success with his third novel, *Limp Harvest*. It had gained him a major prize and reasonable sales. The kudos was sufficient to garner advances for a further five years of dissolution, but as his behaviour grew wilder and the next manuscript became more elusive, so he moved from being a young writer with promise towards the fulfilment of middle-aged failure.

In the railway house Devenish did drugs and fucked young women. Occasionally he'd invite clever people back and make himself feel tougher by drugging them under the table (there was one), and cleverer by talking them into the ground.

He and Wotton were made for each other. Wotton strode in through the front door, which opened directly into a room dominated by a great hayrick of papers. It was fully four feet cubed, and contained many thousands of pages of miscellaneous writings. Whenever a publisher sent Devenish a pre-publication proof for an encomium, or an article by him or about him appeared in a newspaper, or he received a flyer for an art exhibition, or he even completed a piece of work himself, the paper was added to this mound of pulp-in-waiting. Every couple of months, Devenish would go hunting for the manuscript of his as yet unwritten novel in this paper chase, hoping that as in a grandiose biological experiment, an alternative world might have been spontaneously generated out of these fictive enzymes. 'Haven't you heard of the paperless office?' Wotton sneered, aiming straight for the most salient chair in the room, a bizarre thing which looked like a Belle Époque throne. Gavin and the Ferret disported themselves on a sofa that had been beaten into submission.

'Drinks?' the host asked, and picking at his crusty forehead he stomped to the kitchenette at the back of the house to slop out tumblers of whisky, vodka and wine. The girl, whose moniker was Zippy (short for Zuleika, she vouchsafed, although no one could care less), brought them through and handed them round. When he re-entered the room, Devenish picked up the thread of their conversation as if seconds – rather than almost an hour – had elapsed; while filleting powdery white fish on a willow-patterned plate, he continued, 'It's been the misfortune of people who prefer sex with their own gender to be forced to regard this as some essential part of themselves. After all, homosexuality was only defined as a pathology in response to the alleged healthiness of heterosexuality. It's the great mistake of you . . . erm . . . you *gays* to mistake a mere attribute for an essence.'

'Do I look *gay*?' Wotton expostulated, taking the plate and honking up a line.

'*I'm* not gay,' the Ferret chimed in.

'Nor me,' Gavin added, and the Ferret gave his hand a little squeeze; it was so nice to see the dear boy again.

'When you have a terminal pathology like mine, Devenish' –

Wotton spoke with the full authority born of a lifetime's anomie – 'the question of whether your predilections are innate or merely assumed becomes more rarefied than any academic dispute. Call me self-obsessed, but since I've been unable to have anal sex myself, other people's arseholes seem like *hell*.'

'I'm sorry.' Devenish finished up the coke and squeegeed the plate with his finger. 'I'm being tactless.'

'No, merely a plagiarist; not everyone knows fuck all about Foucault.'

'You could try shooting up testosterone – I've heard that can have remarkable results.'

'It's too late for that, I fear.' Wotton lit a Sullivan's Export with a long kitchen match, which he waved in the air a couple of times and then threw down on the mound of paper. 'This medication I'm on puts paid not simply to the inclination, but even to the inclination to the inclination.'

'Are you on the Delta trial?'

'That's the thing.'

'I've heard' – Devenish took a gulp of his drink and began building a monumental joint – 'that it's a drug combination that significantly cuts mortality rates.'

'You seem to know rather more about it than I do . . .' Wotton sneered. 'Where's your loo?'

After he'd stomped off upstairs, those remaining sat goggling at the conflagration beginning at their feet, as match lit phone bill, phone bill ignited postcard, postcard flared up in the face of a photograph of Devenish looking younger and even spottier. At this point Gavin intervened by pouring half of his wine on the blaze. 'Thanks,' Devenish muttered, not even looking up from his craftwork.

Upstairs, Wotton had an odd encounter. As he limped out of the bathroom, trousering his sad prick, he ran into a plump, middle-aged man, bald save for a patch of ginger furze between his ears, who was exiting the room opposite with a kitbag over one shoulder. He was dressed in proletarian subfusc – jeans, trainers, sweatshirt – and had a furtive air about him. The two men stood on the gloomy scrap of landing staring at each other for some seconds, before Wotton introduced himself, saying, 'I'm Henry Wotton. I'm visiting . . . Col?'

'It's Cal,' said the ginger man, 'and,' he continued, spurting venom up into Wotton's uncovered eye from his ulterior position, 'I know you.'

'Really?' Wotton didn't do surprise any more than he did America. 'Where have we had the pleasure?'

'We 'aven't,' the other hissed, 'but about fifteen years ago I was mates with a bloke called Herman. There was this rich queer – nasty piece of work – who took a shine to 'im. This was all in Soho. Herm was a grievous fucking junky –'

'*Moi aussi* –

'An' this geezer was supplying him an' fucking him – because Herm was a renter too. Is any of this jogging your memory, *Mister* Wotton?'

'A little . . . maybe.'

'This rich queer took Herm to a party. I dunno what went down there – probably the usual fucking daisy-chain shit that kind got up to then – but the thing is . . .' and the man's voice, muted until now, choked and swelled '. . . the thing is, he wound up fucking dead. Fucking dead! I've been tracking the cunt who took him there for years now, fucking years. I know his scene, I know the other scum he hangs out with. I even know his name – Dorian-bloody-Gray – and don't forget I know your name, too.' Ginger stopped and huffed and puffed – but if he'd expected Wotton to be blown away by these revelations he was to be disappointed.

'Mm, yes: Herman – *of course* I remember him. Utterly charming. I knew him – but only carnally – in the days when I was an active homosexual rather than a passive host. It's interesting that you should blame Dorian Gray for Herman's death – and incidentally, he's told me about your homicidal designs on him – because if you

214

won't accept that your friend committed suicide, then *I* am the person you should blame for his demise . . .' Wotton, with a gesture that summed up all the fearless condescension that had characterised his life, now took Ginger's arm and, supported by the pudgy former skinhead (is it possible to call a skinhead a skinhead once he has become naturally rather than intentionally bald? Is 'being a skinhead' – like being a homosexual – a question of attribution or essence?), turned and made his way downstairs. As the two of them came in sight of the denizens of the *pays bas*, Wotton was saying, '. . . I gave him the smack that did for him . . . Still – not that it constitutes any kind of retrospective justification – Herman has had his revenge from beyond the grave . . .' He paused for effect and summoned up a ravaged sob. '*Erha!* It was Herman who gave me AIDS.'

'I see you've met Ginger,' Cal Devenish said, squinting up at them through the skunk smoke billowing around his long face, 'he's my house dealer.'

'What on earth d'you mean?' the Ferret asked.

'Precisely what I say. I let Ginger stay in the spare bedroom and in return he gives me and my friends priority service in his drug-dealing capacity. Are you doing some deliveries now, Ginge?'

'Maybe,' Ginger said, but the way he clutched the strap of his kitbag confirmed that he was.

'Well, if so, would ya serve up this lot before you go? Does anybody want anything? I can vouch for the gear and the coke; I've plenty of E, anyway . . .'

Wotton, who had been standing looking out at the empty night-time street through a gap in the blinds, chose this moment dramatically to resume his exchange with Ginger. 'I'll give him to you, if you like,' he said, his voice devoid of emotion. 'Dorian Gray, that is.'

There was silence, and the open bourse in drugs ceased trading.

'Whaddya mean?' Ginger asked.

'I'll tell you where to find him and when. Should you wish to take your time, here's his address.' He passed over a visiting card. 'I think' – Wotton savoured the sentence – 'it would probably be quite a good idea if you *were* to kill him, Ginger.' A train bearing spent fuel rods chose this moment to shake the house like a terrier at a bone. Everything vibrated; the paper mound rustled. Gavin and the Ferret looked as if they thought the rumble and crash were the fury of a deity who had finally decided to punish Wotton, but he himself appeared unaffected. When it was gone, he resumed, 'He's at a crack house in Limehouse right now. I know because I spoke to him earlier this evening.' He turned to Devenish. 'Have you an *A–Z*?'

'How do I get in?' Ginger asked, packing his unsold stock away in his kitbag.

'Simple. Tell the truth – say you've come to meet Dorian Gray. He's such an habitué of the place you'll get in. Here.' He pointed out the location in the gazetteer. 'Happy hunting.'

The quondam skinhead let himself out of the front door without farewells. 'He has a key,' Devenish muttered, as if Ginger were his teenage son heading out for an evening with mates, and these peculiar men disported about the place were really family friends enquiring after arrangements. 'I dunno why we have to have him here at all,' Zippy bleated, as she swung her tightly girded loins loosely in time to the music that infiltrated the room from covert speakers; 'it's not as if he's remotely amusing, *or* sexy.' She was trying to be provocative, but no one paid her any mind. Devenish was lost inside his stubble-burning; the others were in assorted states of shocked stupefaction. The evening, like a car recklessly driven by drunken youths over winter roads, had hit a patch of black ice. Its wheels spun, its engine screamed, the wind rushed past the darkened, rain-flecked windows. Inside, the five passengers, knees jammed against their ribs, waited in agonised silence for the inevitable impact.

'Do you imagine' – the Ferret spoke at last, in the absence of a crash barrier – 'that he actually will *murder* Dorian?'

'No,' Wotton sighed, 'I don't think so. Not tonight, at any rate. He isn't a fool, is he?'

'Ginger?' Devenish ground out his spliff. 'No, he's no fool. He's upwardly mobile in a curious way: he's putting one of his kids – he's estranged from the mother; she lives up the road in Kensal Green – through prep school on the proceeds of his drug-dealing.'

'Too many witnesses.' Wotton ignored this blether. 'I imagine Ginger's gone for a recce. He's bided his time this long; I don't think he'll want to screw things up through undue haste.'

'May I ask,' Gavin enunciated very clearly, if squeakily – the atmosphere in the room was so highly pressurised that it seemed to him as if he were breathing helium – 'why it is you've decided that Dorian should die?'

Wotton took his time in answering. He gathered the skirts of his Crombie around his thighs and circumvented Devenish's slag heap of words. He assumed his position on the curious Belle Époque throne, accepted the plate his host passed him, snuffled up the line that was upon it, took a glass of wine from Zippy and drank from it. He began to kill a Kurd. It was clear to everyone present that a speech was about to be made, as clear as if a toastmaster in a tartan waistcoat had stepped forward from the filthy kitchenette, tapped a small mallet and announced, 'My sleepy lord, slutty lady and dopey gentlemen, pray silence for the moribund Mr Henry Wotton, self-hating homosexual, drug addict and AIDS sufferer, who will now rant and rave.'

'I think we all know why Dorian must die. De Quincey didn't have it right at all. Murder shouldn't be considered one of the fine arts; rather it's one of the wilder forms of popular entertainment. In view of that I think we can agree that Dorian is becoming a comedy hoofer; he must be stopped. True, we have no definite proof that he's responsible for Baz's or Alan's death, while Octavia and Herman could be described as casualties of war. If we were to take our evidence to stupid squad they'd probably say we were suffering delusions, provoked either by drugs and disease or merely by the hissy fits of three ageing queers dumped by this Adonis.

'We know better. It isn't so much retribution we're after in seeking to get Dorian killed, and only you, Fergus, are aroused by punishment. No, it's a kind of symmetry we seek, a rounding off of events. Baz discovered Dorian over a decade ago, when he was a gauche little thing down from Oxford. Baz thought that he embodied the dawning age of "gay liberation", and that his video installation of Dorian would become an icon of all that was beautiful and true and important about the inverted "lifestyle". In fact, what has happened is quite the reverse: instead of this cathode portrait's going on show and attracting praise, it has languished somewhere in a darkened room. Meanwhile, it's the portrait's subject who has become a kind of sadistic genius, exhibiting an infinite capacity for causing pain.

'As this scourge of a retrovirus has flayed the backs of the in and the out, the queer and the queen, the faggot and the poof, this narcissistic nematode has wormed his way through the world, hollowing it out from within, while himself appearing completely unaffected. It moves me to speculate that he is a magus of some unknown kind, and that Baz's portrait of him must be a voodoo doll, which Dorian has adapted so that it usefully malfunctions, absorbing – rather than transmitting – all the marks of age, pain and disease that should, by rights, be inscribed on his oddly blank face.'

At this, Gavin made as if to interrupt, but Wotton shushed him and continued.

'I could video a portrait of him better than Basil Hallward ever did. I could capture him for you right now, as if there were a CCTV system that took in the Chinaman's den. See Dorian Gray in one of the myriad rooms of this tumbledown mansion of Morpheus. Not for him, tonight, the darkened crack den, where dwarfish figures are lit intermittently by the flare of their equipment; nor does he wish to recline in the opium-smoking parlour, where Iranian businessmen repose on carpeted divans beneath the Peacock Throne rendered in purple tinfoil. No, Dorian has brought a brace of posh, leggy, arty chicks with him this evening. He's force-fed these goslings with liver-busting pharmaceutical *foie gras*, while he himself has put a wad of MDMA powder under his foreskin, as a hillbilly might insert a chaw of tobacco in his cheek. See Dorian, then, his hands running over their silken armatures, as he and Chloë and Angela subside giggling behind dusty velveteen hangings; their six pupils large and flat and black and shiny, like a half-set of chinaware for some decadent's dinner party.

'In the remote distance there's knocking, followed by raised voices at the front door, then pounding footfalls. Feeling the draught on his exposed nape, Dorian looks up from the sweet he's been sucking, to find that it's not Angela's beading that is clicking in his ear, but Ginger's dentures. "I've seen you, Prince-fucking-Charming! I've seen you!" he snarls. "I know where you live now, you murdering fuck, and I can have you whenever I want. Whenever-I-fucking-want!" He emphasises each word with a squeeze on the divine scrotum which is close at hand. For once it is Dorian who's left moaning and thrashing about in pain, while his assaulter lets go and thuds off down the stairs, elbowing aside two saddo home boys sucking on a Volvic-bottle crack pipe. There's a distant crash – the front door slamming – and he's definitively gone. The posh girlies splutter and retch, while Dorian rocks back and forth in a foetal position, both hands grasping his bruised balls.

'Well?' Wotton aimed his monocular gaze like the barrel of a rifle at each of the others in turn. 'What say you to that vision?'

But the Ferret, Gavin and Zippy were all asleep, the two men in each other's arms, while the girl, who had crumpled where she'd been dancing, now formed a pool of dark satin on the red floorboards. Only Devenish remained in any position to comment. 'Yeah, well,' he muttered, dabbing at his side-winding spliff with a moistened finger, 'Gray was always a nasty little piece of faggotry, no mistaking. Still, this portrait riff, Wotton, I like it – it has the resonance of a modern myth. When people say youth is wasted on the young, what they really mean is that they'd like to have their health and their looks again so that they could despoil them in the full awareness of their ephemerality. Your riff captures that very well. If Gray were able to stay young and have this video installation age in his stead, he'd be *the* icon of an era in which everyone seeks to hang on to their childhood until they're pressing furry fucking teddy bears against wrinkled cheeks.' He looked pointedly at the Ferret and Gavin. 'You homosexuals are only the vanguard of a mutton army dressed as denim lambs.'

Wotton heard this out with an expression of contempt. 'Fuck you, Devenish,' he said conversationally, when the other man had finished. 'You writers only ever pay attention to events so you can set fire to them during your paper ceremonials. Suppose Dorian Gray's portrait were such a magical thing – you'd never believe it. Whatever my faults, I have at least lived my life at first hand, rather than filtering it through this paper as part of a literary experiment.' He kicked Devenish's ziggurat of tat; it rustled obligingly. 'Besides, it would be better if you avoided attempts at eloquence; in my experience the English don't weave tapestries of words, we lay prose carpet tiles.

'I myself have only one virtue – I hate every little thing and all big ideas. I loathe the so-called "art" of the twentieth century with a particularly rare and hearty passion. Would that all that paint, canvas, plaster, stone and bronze could be balled up and tossed into that fraud Duchamp's *pissoir*. With a few notable exceptions – Balthus, Bacon, Modigliani – the artists of this era have been in headlong flight from beauty or any meaningful representation of the human form. Were Basil Hallward's video of Dorian Gray to have a life of its own, it would be a fitting coda to this vile age with its spasms of isms. Yech! *Christ*, how this city sickens me. I wish the season would begin so that I could escape to the country and shoot a little smack.'

17

In the misty dawn of a steadily brightening November morning, when the grass was lucent with hoar-frost, and each gnarled, mistletoe-wreathed oak or bare beech that loomed up from the parkland had the appearance of a petrified example of prehistoric megafauna, a lone traveller who had chanced to stumble upon the country house of Narborough could have been forgiven for imagining that he had travelled back in time to some gentler, nobler age.

. Occupying a broad valley which had been dammed to create several ornamental lakes and fishing ponds, the Narborough estate had an air about it, at once foursquare and diaphanous, that would have made it an ideal subject for a set of Wedgwood dinner plates. In the late-eighteenth century, the 2nd Duke had indeed been approached by Josiah Wedgwood with precisely that aim in view, but he had shown the potter the door. A door that, like all of the main house, had been built by Vincenzo Valdrati himself, together with his travelling band of master craftsmen.

Even to call Narborough 'the finest Palladian house in England' was to demean it by association with any lesser edifice. Put simply, Narborough stood entirely alone, a rampart faced with delicious Portland stone, fully two hundred and fifty yards from east wing tip to west; the entire, sixty-foot-high façade rendered with the most edible masonry; the roof surmounted with no fewer than thirty six-foot-high rose-hued marble urns, each one bearing an individual bas-relief of fornicating fauns, salivating satyrs or diddling dryads. Surrounded by fifty acres of William Evans's landscaped gardens and a further five hundred of the afore-mentioned parkland, with its lakes and orchards and outbuildings, its conservatories and gazebos and follies, its shoots and fisheries and farms, Narborough was not so much a house as an entire world.

Which is why such a lone traveller, crunching over the gravel in the first silvery rays of a winter morning, and gaining admission to the central hallway of the house via an inconspicuous side door (the main ones, fully two storeys high, had not been opened since the visit of the last King Emperor), might have been alarmed to hear, bouncing along the milk-white marble of the main corridor and echoing off the Baldini frescos, a rousing chorus of feel-good fag-haggery. 'It's raining men!' the big black mama's voice bellowed out. 'Hallelujah, it's raining men, ev'ry spe-ci-men! Big! Tall! Short! Fat! I'm gonna go outside and get ab-so-lute-ly soaking wet!' And so on and so forth.

The next thing our hypothetical wanderer in a sea of mist might have registered as being at variance with his expectation of an aristocratic Arcadia would've been the sight of Jane, 8th Duchess of Narborough. This lady came running from the back of the house, wearing a muu-muu sewn from an entire rainbow of parachute silks, which billowed about her slender form like a psychedelic tent. Her lank, grey hair flying, she disappeared into the first of a series of enormous reception rooms. Following in her train went a retinue comprising – in order of size – a Vietnamese pot-bellied pig, a pygmy goat, a Canada goose and a Peking duck. As they traversed the hallway, feeling the cool of the marble beneath trotters, hooves and webbed feet, they all shat.

In the Hyderabad Drawing Room (which had once housed a collection of Mogul miniatures beloved of the 4th Duke, but now contained only a free calendar from a local Indian takeaway, tacked on to one of the teak-panelled walls), she found nobody save a thirteen-year-old girl in the full bloom of puberty, dancing around a boom-box, which sat on the bare parquet belting out the gay anthem. The girl gyrated in an altogether abandoned way, shaking her long auburn hair into an entire aureole of frizz, waggling her long legs in their flared jeans. She clawed at the air with painted nails and undulated her arms like a squid's tentacles. On the far side of the room from this spectacle was a marble fireplace as big as a crusader's tomb, in the very grate of which stood a quivering whippet, its flesh stretched so tightly across its bones that sunlight streamed right through its legs, illuminating the tracery of veins as if the poor beast were a living stained-glass window.

'Phoe-beee!' the Duchess ululated, and again, 'Phoe-beee!' until the girl, deigning to register the presence of the honking, grunting, ponging menagerie, snapped off the music with a naked toe. 'Oh, Phoebe,' Jane Narborough continued, 'it's *awfully* early to be having a disco down here – I don't think anyone else is up yet.'

'My dad's up; he's in the west-wing conservatory.'

'Well, that's as may be, but to be honest, Phoebe, I don't think he went to bed last night. What I'm trying to suggest – and this is only a suggestion – is that it might be considerate if you were to wait until after nine to play your pop music. My Nichiren Shoshu group will be here then – and their chanting wakes people up as it is.'

'OK,' Phoebe said with ill grace, 'but it's bloody cold in here, Jane – and this is the only way of keeping warm. It's *so* cold and I can't find any fuel; I even considered breaking up that silly whippet over there and burning its horrid twiggy limbs.'

'Um, well, I don't think that would be *too* good an idea, my dear.' Despite her legendary respect for all living things, the Duchess didn't appear too outraged by Phoebe Wotton's suggestion. 'Wystan is Narborough's dog and he's most fond of the poor beast. I myself find pedigree dogs to be evidence more of their owners' willingness to play God than of any love for animals. Your father's in the west-wing conservatory, you say? I'll go and see if he wants anything. Come come!'

This last was to her snuffling, pecking entourage, whom Jane Narborough also addressed with a smattering of what she imagined to be their respective languages, so convinced was she of their intelligence. The little ark coasted off behind its multicoloured silken sail. As soon as they were gone, Phoebe shut the vast doors and turned the boom-box back on. She resumed undulating.

The west-wing conservatory was a glass and cast-iron construction, an exact replica (one-tenth scale) of the original Crystal Palace. It had been commissioned by the 4th Duke in a fit of mid-nineteenth-century modernity, and ever since had stood alongside the stately home, tethered to it by a glass corridor of an airlock, and closely resembling a Victorian spaceship that had made one, ill-fated voyage to the past. However, it had at least this virtue: while most of the chattels from the rest of the house had been sloughed off by the châtelaine in her spasms of ill-considered and ineffective efforts at spiritual improvement, the superb collection of exotic plants amassed by the 4th, 5th and 6th Dukes remained not simply intact, but perfectly well tended.

It was logical that Henry Wotton would have fetched up here, because it was the only part of the entire property – saving the staff cottages – that was properly heated. His wheelchair stood atop one of the grilles, its wheels almost hidden in steam, while its occupant was obscured by the cascading branches of *Felix fidelis* (the highly toxic Faithful Cat tree of Sumatra). A few handfuls of conveniently-shed eucalyptus leaves lay on the lap of his Argyll plaid travelling rug. These Wotton gathered up in one of his claws-for-hands and crushed under his pitted knife of a nose.

His other hand was fiddling with a cigarette, and it was this that Jane Narborough noticed as she and her menagerie came crashing through the undergrowth. 'Henry!' she expostulated. 'You aren't *smoking*, are you?'

'No,' he replied ruefully, 'I'm not. You know perfectly well that I've given up, Jane.'

'I know you made an awful fuss about it, but what's that in your hand?'

'True, it's a cigarette; I think that *au fond* I will always be smoking – you cannot break the habit of a lifetime so simply. But I hold on to this one for something to do with my hands. If you pass me over that duck I'll cheerfully wring its neck instead.'

'Oh Henry, I-I-I think it's simply marvellous the way you keep joking in –'

'In the face of death?'

'I was going to say "in spite of your illness".'

'The illness is over, Jane; this is the endgame. I should've thought you, with your doctrine of eternal recurrence, would have less of a problem referring to it. Anyway' – he summoned himself, cast aside the cigarette and the eucalyptus and reached out for one of the Duchess's hands – 'if you are right about the cosmos I should like to be reincarnated as one of your goats; however silly you may be, you are also genuinely kind. Thank you for letting me and Phoebe stay. Just getting out of town is a balm to me now.'

'Oh . . . um . . . well . . . Henry . . . you needn't . . .' Jane was profoundly uneasy with such compliments, especially from such an odd quarter. They felt like an ill wind, but she blustered on. 'It's no trouble, truly; stay as long as you like – and Phoebe is a dear. One thing, Henry – it's Binky; they're shooting today and he . . . well . . . he's *very* particular about lunch – *placements* and so forth . . . He wanted to know if Batface would be down in time . . . and Dorian?'

Wotton gulped a few mouthfuls of the humid, vegetative air before answering, 'Honestly, Jane, it's astonishing that Binky Narborough is still slaughtering wildfowl after all these years of your indoctrination –'

'He doesn't shoot himself any more,' she put in; 'he only likes to make sure the guns are doing it properly.'

'Even so, I thought that when you trepanned him it would put a stop to the killing. You assured me having a hole in his head would unblock his chakras, or whatever.'

'Oh it does, Henry, it does,' she said mournfully. 'It unblocks them only too well. I fear he's having some sort of *dalliance* with Emma Wibberly.'

'The Bishop's wife?' Wotton queried, and Jane nodded mutely.

'Christ, it's difficult to ... I mean, he's a very *slight* fellow ...'
Wotton was bewilderingly out of character '... and she – she's
distinctly *robust* ... It must be ...' and all out of words '... it must
be –'

'Like a tomtit on a side of beef,' the Duchess snapped. 'My
thoughts exactly, Henry, and they're not pretty ones. So you see' –
she was sobbing a little – 'I'm doing my very best not to upset him
at the moment. D'you think they'll be down for lunch?'

'Jane, poor you, and a house full of people to boot. Adding
Dorian Gray to all of this is hardly likely to improve things.'

'Oh, I've never thought he was as bad as people make out, and
I'm amazed you should be one of them, Henry; I thought he was
your friend.'

'All the more reason why I should know *exactly* the sort of thing
Dorian gets up to. He called me only last night to inform me of his
latest bad behaviour.'

'Tell *me*, then.' She scraped up a cast-iron chair and floated down
on to it. 'Tell me the sort of thing. Tell me what he did – it'll take
my mind off the image of Binky and Emma ... well, y'know.'

'I'm not sure anything *could* erase that image, Jane,' Wotton said,
and then muttered, 'A tomtit on a side of beef – you couldn't make
it up.'

*   *   *

Dorian Gray liked to cruise anywhere and anything. As the years
had passed, so catholic had his cruising become that he would've
been perfectly at ease coming on to a consistory of cardinals in the
Vatican. No grouping of people was safe from his attentions:
a coachload of Mormons from the Midwest 'doing' Europe; a
housewives' club down from the North on a shopping spree; a
Sado-Masochist Pride March wending its way through the West
End. Irrespective of age, gender, race or sexual orientation, Dorian
Gray delighted in their seduction, and if he could afford the time
to ruin them into the bargain, then so much the better.

The important thing was always to stay alert. Dorian had discovered that once your conquests run to thousands it becomes increasingly likely that you'll bump into some ravaged nun, traduced traffic warden, or sinned-against civil servant from your past. It helped that Dorian remained as much of a chameleon as ever, ceaselessly adapting his style to fit his surroundings; it helped too that as the years went by from each pressing of the flesh, and the vintage aged, the vintner remained the same. In order to minimise unpleasant encounters, Dorian had discovered it was best to follow a systematically altered course through the ocean of body fluids. As for the ever present threat of Ginger, Dorian carried a gun.

None the less, there were cruising locations that were irresistible by virtue of their convenience and the variety of flesh on offer. Happy hunting grounds to which he returned again and again, where the abundance of game never declined, and the watering holes remained crowded with fine specimens. One such was London's South Bank arts complex. From the newly-opened Oxo Tower at one end to the Royal Festival Hall at the other, there was a solid strand of cafés, bars, galleries and venues. The embankment itself attracted any number of casual strollers, and the walkways of the brutalist Hayward Gallery had their own subcultures, of teenage skateboarders and street people – both of which, in their peculiar way, held an attraction for the jaded raptor.

On a Sunday such as this, when the posh people he knew were clomping in the country and the bourgeoisie were cavorting with their wretched whelps, Dorian would often take in an exhibition or attend a play or a concert. Invariably, he'd been out all night in the clubs, and a lick of his sweat alone could have loved-up another. So he prowled, on the look-out for the lone quarry, who could be separated out from the herd and brought to the dusty ground in a welter of stale intoxicants.

Dorian loitered in the main gallery of the Hayward, not bothering too much with the rusty steel pillars of Donald Judd, except as a neutral background against which to observe his true objective.

Not *him* – too ugly, too furtive, too easy. Nor *her* – too hysterical, too nervy; wouldn't get her off the premises except in a black plastic bag. Him, possibly . . . yes, very nice, very pert indeed, although the beige suede culottes are a desperate shame. He certainly looks at a loose end . . . Oh shit! A grin had split the muzzle of Dorian's intended prey. He'd seen his special friend. Silly bitch! Dorian took a few seconds to despise the young men thoroughly as they hugged and kissed, before strolling off arm in arm. He turned away from the revolting spectacle and, moving fast, nearly ran straight into . . . Helen!

He recognised her immediately, although age had most certainly withered her. Withered her, and her hips had swelled with child-bearing, inflating the puckered bag of her skin. The Eton crop Dorian remembered from fifteen years before had long since grown out, been dyed, spiked, teased, crimped and then lopped anew. Now it was a scraggy, lank pelt, with a curious lumpy, beige deposit in its fringe, the work of the baby in the buggy she was pushing, a boy of about ten months who liked to make free with his cereal.

Her eyes – red-rimmed with insomnia, the ducts cluttered with gunk – took in Dorian's trim figure in its silky black trews and silkier black jacket, then moved leadenly on to the next Judd. Not knowing quite why – except that even from the most intrinsically perverse and unpleasant experiences there was still *something* to be gained – he allowed his golden lashes to part and his clear orbs to beam recognition. His pink lips parted over flawless pearly teeth and he said, Helen, do you remember me? She took a while to answer; then her cracked lips broke over plaque-painted teeth and she said – as if pained by the recognition of him – Dorian Gray?

Helen was so fucking tired that she didn't notice the anachronism that was Dorian. Sure, he looked good, but gay men always looked after themselves. Yes, he looked rested, but everyone got enough sleep compared with her, who had a hyperactive baby both to care for *and* to support financially, with no assistance from his father or her wider family. And besides, he was rich, unlike her, who, with an inertia that defied the surrounding feel-good spend-now culture, had slid inexorably down all of the major economic indices.

Dorian Gray had solar charm, although the only people who ever experienced its full radiance were those about to die from a thrust of his short sword. He could turn on and off his capacity to beguile the way others employed light switches. It made Dorian feel as if, in a world of instinctual darkness, he was the only possessor of an intentional torch.

He complimented her on the baby, who was of mixed race.

—I should be running the fucking gymkhana, Helen said bitterly; instead I'm some Jamaican gangster's baby-mother.

—Come now – Dorian squatted, cupped the baby's cheek – it can't be that bad.

—Believe me, it bloody is. The best thing about him is that he leaves us well alone.

Dorian wouldn't leave them alone; he took them both for lunch in the café at the National Film Theatre. He assumed that with the baby she'd prefer a less formal atmosphere. He was right. He fed the baby his gloop and didn't flinch when it got on his Kenzo jacket. She surmised that he was one of those gay men who was broody, and who would make an excellent father if only given the opportunity. How affecting it was to watch him.

Dorian bought her coffees to keep her awake, and glasses of white wine to loosen her tongue. He collected her grievances up. Pass me the changing bag, he said.

—Why? She was aghast, she didn't even imagine he would know what one was.

—I want to change all the things that are bad about your life into good ones, he said, and then laughed, Seriously, I'll change him. He lifted the baby up and bore him off before she could protest. He was back in five minutes, the baby burbling and giggling and snapping Dorian's bottom lip with his chubby mitt.

Discovering that she lived in Turnham Green, Dorian was able to suggest a shared cab. He did the hailing, he did the loading, he did the directing. When they were passing Gloucester Road he proposed tea. Helen demurred – the baby, the routine . . . He pointed out that the baby was asleep.

At the entrance to the mews, a pudgy, middle-aged man sat in a car, noting comings and goings. It had become Ginger's Sunday-afternoon hobby – this Dorian-watching. He didn't know exactly what he was going to do, or when he was going to do it, but he felt confident that if the opportunity presented itself he would recognise it for what it was.

Inside the mews house Dorian fashioned a cot out of bolsters and laid the baby on the leather settee so gently he didn't wake. Helen looked about her at the conservative furniture and then at him. You're so youthful, Dorian, but this stuff is so middle-aged.

—Oh well – he was dismissive – most of it was inherited. I'm not here much; I never bothered to change it.

They had tea and delicatessen cheesecake and more wine. Helen giggled – a convulsion she couldn't remember having in months. This is, she thought, what I've needed. Old friends – stupid to have lost touch with so many; funny to think it should be Dorian – whom I thought so cruel at the time – who should turn out to be so kind. He dripped wine into her as dusk fell, and the baby slumbered on as if the claustrophobic little house affected him with some subtle soporific. In the dim yellow light of a table lamp the sight of Dorian's smooth, pale hand on her red careworn one wasn't that outrageous. What're you doing? she chuckled.

—I'm kissing you, he replied.

—Don't be absurd, she guffawed, I'm not to your taste at all.

—You are what you eat, he said, and tucked her bottom lip between his.

She whimpered – it'd been that long – and grabbed for his shoulders. So strong, so secure . . . His litheness coiled about her.

And as he pulled the chunky roll-neck sweater over her head, as he removed damp layers of T-shirt and baby-stained leggings, as he unsnapped the three poppers of her body – which was so like her

230

little son's undergarment – how Dorian revelled in the disgust he felt for her. Her underwear was flesh-coloured, but alas, it wasn't the same colour as her flesh, which, he noted fastidiously, had the alarming, greasy hue of uncooked veal, to go with the kitchen smell of her favours.

She insisted they go somewhere else in case the baby woke up, and rather than interrupt work in progress he acceded. Besides, in the sparsely furnished bedroom, with its solid-oak platform, he could assay the situation still better and decide how best to infect Helen. Performing in excess of a thousand thousand HIV impregnations had given Dorian the forensic attitude of a virologist injecting an attenuated virus into experimental cohorts. But Dorian didn't stick around to see how his guinea-pigs fared, so he had only his intuitions to trust when it came to deciding where he should put his tainted love, and how often, to ensure the experiment had a successful result.

With playmates who had no scruples about proscribed practices the whole business was so much easier, but needless to say these were not the playmates Dorian preferred. Indeed, he relished it when the condoms were brought out; there was nothing that excited him more than a challenge. Helen was going to be one of those; despite its being muzzy she kept her head at first, insisting on a cordon sanitaire. He gave it to her straight and feigned ordinary affection with the ease of a cowed, frigid wife faking orgasm. He gave it to her again. The baby woke and they dressed him, fed him and played with him. When he slept they did it a third time. Helen needed no persuasion to stay. Later, when he woke again, they bathed the baby in the black-tiled bathroom, lathering his proletarian limbs with Imperial Leather. Then they all ate supper. Then they put the baby to bed for the night. It was all so *gemütlich* at Dorian's; surely Helen could be forgiven for collaborating with the Nazi regime.

It wasn't until the small hours that he shed his rubber foreskin and downpoured her with death. It wasn't until later still that, stoned and drunk, she felt her sphincter crack like her lips, despite the Vaseline that had been rubbed every which way. When eventually she slept, Dorian went upstairs, and he spent long hours that night marvelling at the contrast between the red, careworn claws of the cathode Narcissi and his own delightful digits.

The next day Dorian effected introductions. Batface – Helen; Helen – Batface. He'd decided to keep Helen around, like a kind of trophy wife, the prize being death or its avoidance.

Batface had walked across from Chelsea. It g-g-gives me time to think about L-Lou Andreas-Salomé, she said.

Helen enquired, Nietzsche's mistress?

—I-I-I d-don't think they ever c-consummated their relationship. Batface blushed even at this, which Helen found endearing.

—Are you writing a book about her? Helen jiggled the baby, and Batface absent-mindedly twined her fingers in his curls.

—Yes, I'm interested in women not of their time, she explained. I'm a historian.

—I know, Helen said; I've heard of you.

—I don't want to be a man not of *his* time, Dorian intervened. We should go, Batface, or we'll be late.

He gave Helen the spare key and told her to stay if she wanted, make use of the contents of the fridge if she felt so inclined. What was his was hers – even if she didn't know it. Recently, Dorian had felt the angry emanations he associated with his nemesis clustering on the cobbles of the mews. He thought that maybe the presence of an older woman and a baby in the house would confuse his tormentor. It was worth a try.

In Narberton, Dorian stopped the MG so that they could buy presents for their hostess in one of the gift shops that cluttered the pretty Cotswold village.

—I say, Dorian, said Batface, it's uncommonly late for w-wistaria to be flowering, don't you think?

—Oh I s'pose so, but this place is so bloody obsessed with winning the Best-Kept Village award year on year that they've probably installed under-floor heating. Dorian bought a fake milk churn full of fudge, Batface some lavender bath cubes. It never ceased to amaze Dorian, who had been raised abroad, how the English rich would accept the cheapest, most useless trifles as house presents. Even Jane Narborough, who – as Dorian knew full well, courtesy of Henry – would shortly be bankrupt if she kept on bankrolling so many swamis, gurus and lamas. They soon won't have the wherewithal to keep up a hanging basket, he muttered.

—What?

—The Narboroughs – I said they soon won't have the wherewithal to keep up a hanging basket.

—You sound like H-Henry, Batface hiccuped, and then, Oh dear, Dorian, I told you you shouldn't leave your car there.

An irate village elder, complete with Rotary Club pin and check waistcoat, was indigesting on the edible verge. He gave them a row as they climbed in and reversed leaving chocolate furrows in his green cake. He made a show of noting down Dorian's car number. When Ginger pulled up in his Ford Sierra a couple of minutes later the old man was still fulminating. Ginger, who did deferential very well, calmed him down and then pleased him mightily by booking an off-season room in his bed and breakfast.

Lunch at Narborough, especially on the days when there was a shoot, was a most peculiar repast. It was held in a two-storey dining room, which was arrayed with the tattered ensigns of the male Narboroughs' regiments and the family's gruesome coat of arms (severed arms crossed against a field of white poppies; motto: *Semper irati numquam dormimus*), and the shifting company, who never numbered fewer than twenty-five, were on this occasion about a third oriental mystics, a third occidental huntsmen, and a third the miscellaneous hangers-on who would pitch up for any country-house weekend, no matter how strange.

Sir David Hall and his wife, Angela Brownrigg and Chloë Lambert, the Ferret and Dorian, Batface and Phoebe Wotton, all of them were gathered at one end of the cricket-pitch-sized slab of mahogany, pitchforking down great mounds of herbage in deference to their hostess. Jane Narborough sat a few yards off, together with her Buddhist pals, who were slyly sipping dal soup from wooden bowls. Henry Wotton, whose wheelchair stood at an angle from the table, and who had dispensed at last with even making a show of eating, whispered in Dorian's ear, 'Of course she's a complete cow, but fortunately I'm an enthusiastic supporter of Compassion in World Farming.'

His familiar tittered at this and asked, 'D'you want some wine, Henry? I think they've still got some passable claret.'

'I used to drink to forget,' Wotton observed, 'but now I forget to drink.'

Dorian went in search of the decanter.

At the sideboard stood a number of heavyset stereotypes of Edwardian gentlemen. They were so uniform, these men, in their tweed plus-fours and Norfolk jackets, with their roast-beef complexions and their piggy little eyes, that they could have gone on the road as a tribute band called Ninety Years After, playing their Purdey shotguns instead of Fender Stratocasters. These big guns were piling up plates with wooden sausages, slabs of ham as thickly pink as industrial floor covering, slices of game pie the size of tractor tyres. They all laughed a lot, they all swigged claret, they were all utterly revolting.

Around the Gillray calves of these characters darted the Duke himself, a peculiar figure no more than five feet in height, his bald pate fringed by wisps of white hair, his Donegal tweeds as skimpy and tight as a hairy leotard. Anyone who troubled to look down at his pate was gifted an impression of a red, throbbing depression in the middle of the ducal skull, the result of his wife's mystical manipulation of a power drill. Although the skin had long since healed over the wound, the operation had undoubtedly changed Binky Narborough. Before it he had been eccentric, but now he was flagrantly insane. 'Bip-bip-bip!' he exclaimed as he flitted hither and thither, bringing his guests odd titbits of lettuce, or a single potato, and laying these on their plates with a 'Very good! Very very good!' exclamation. 'Ta very much, Binky,' said the guns; 'most kind – lovely-looking potato.' Of course the chap was bonkers, and the wife wasn't much better. As for the son, there seemed little likelihood of the dukedom's surviving far into the next millennium. But for now, the shoot was the finest in England, and if it required a little indulgence for them to enjoy it, then so be it – they'd indulge.

Wotton, like a bitter Tiresias, was now almost entirely blind, apart from a grey aperture through which he wildly aimed his aperçus at the world. Hester Hall came over to say hello, drawing up a chair by one of his wheels. 'How are you feeling, Henry?' she asked, conscious that while he was probably pricklier than ever, it behove her not to be thin-skinned.

'I feel at one with the world,' he pronounced.

She seized on this: 'Oh good, I'm so glad you're reconciled.'

'Absolutely – it appears to have a terminal illness just as I do.' He grabbed her hand with his talons. 'I can't even stand up any more – I'm afraid of my own height; yet look at those ambulatory retroviruses by the sideboard, they're destroying the white blood cells of Nature herself!'

'Aren't you being a little extreme?'

'You think this is insignificant –?' He changed tack abruptly: 'Who's that over there?'

'The guy who's just come in?'

'That's the one, describe him for me, Lady Hall. Paint me a prose picture, albeit that the English language is a furred tongue between thin lips.'

'He's a big, chubby young man, wearing a T-shirt with a smiley face on it. His hair's all wild and he looks kinda . . . stoned –'

'Ah! Say no more; it's the heir to all of this, the future 9th Duke.'

'I've never met him.' She didn't sound particularly excited by the prospect. 'What's his name?'

'Good question. I myself have given him a courtesy title, "The Brown Bottle", on account of his pernicious – and now fifteen-year

– addiction to oral methadone. He goes into Narberton, stands by the till in the chemist's and swigs the stuff down like any street junky. You wouldn't be so good, Lady Hall . . .' his voice descended into intimacy '. . . as to gain his attention? I'd like a little of his medication for myself; you can never get too much of a bad thing.'

'D'you think you should?' This goaded her conscience in another direction. 'I understood that new drugs have been made available – you were on that trial . . . Delta, right?'

'Indeed, and it has effected an increased lifespan . . . for some. There are new methods of testing for viral load as well as new drugs – protease inhibitors, they call them: it seems that they may be on the verge of a radical breakthrough. Instead of all HIV patients' being strapped into the same pharmacological straitjacket, treatment is to be tailored to the individual. Believe me, Lady Hall,' he sighed, 'I've been keeping my wavering patch of vision trained on it. My daughter Phoebe is something of a wizard with the Internet; she researches the subject for me. It seems they have a new acronym that they place great faith in, Highly Active Anti-Retroviral Treatment. However, I fear it'll be too late for me to take any HAART.'

'Are you certain?'

'Absolutely. My other virus, hepatitis C, has enacted a pincer movement with the HIV and given me liver cancer. My lungs are finished from pneumonia, my sight is irrecoverable. I feel gothic with disease – as if Cologne Cathedral were being shoved up my fundament. No, this is the end.'

It was the end of lunch too. The sportsmen went off to gather together their hip-flasks, shooting sticks and shotguns, all the kit required for birdie-blasting. 'Bip-bip-bip!' bipped Binky Narborough, manifesting himself at this end of the table like a mad munchkin. 'Who's shootin'? Who's shootin'? Bip-bip!' Dorian went off quickly to dress, and David Hall, who despite his stroke still enjoyed winging his fellow creatures, limped in his wake.

The Ferret made his way to Wotton's chair. 'Shall I push you back to the conservatory?' he yawned. 'If it's warm in there I think I could do with a little nap. It's peculiar, but when I'm staying at Narborough on shooting weekends I find myself dreaming of the shoot.'

'Yes, all right, Fergus,' Wotton said, 'but get Phoebe to accompany us; if you conk out *en route* I don't want to find myself forgotten and freezing to death in the wilds of the west wing.'

Lying curled up like a little ferret in a hollow between the mighty roots of a vast shrub with trumpet-shaped scarlet flowers (*Rhododendron cinnabarinum*), the Ferret dreamed of shooting. He had frequently shot at Narborough himself in the time of Binky's grandfather, the irascible 6th Duke, who had commanded a regiment in the Boer War and made a secret collection of dried Kaffir penises. The Ferret supposed it must still be buried somewhere in the bowels of the house.

The Ferret knew that not least of the attractions of the shooting at Narborough was that to the north of the landscaped gardens the park mounted steadily towards the Cotswold escarpment and was fairly thickly covered. With over two hundred acres of well-stocked woodland there was no need for anyone to go short, as long as he was a reasonable shot. Gone, however, were the game bags of the Ferret's youth, when thousands of brace of pheasant, partridge, snipe and quail would be annihilated in a single afternoon, by whole regiments of the gentry, who formed up in hollow squares like their martial forefathers at Waterloo, while the peasantry flushed out the republic of the birds.

On this beautiful afternoon, which felt more like early spring than late autumn, the first drive was commenced by a handful of beaters who strolled through the poplars and ashes of Dunter's Wood, smiting the underbrush. The guns lined up in a loose rank, with all the big, serious beefcake at one end, and the irregulars at the other. Dorian Gray was on the very furthest flank. His shotgun was serious rather than flashy, and his tweeds serviceable rather than chic, yet from the tip of the grouse feather stuck in his hatband to the very toes of his lace-up boots, Dorian, as ever, exuded a lethal elegance.

The Duke ran hither and thither behind the guns, bearing his own absurdist weapon, a replica Purdey lovingly carved – by Binky Narborough himself – out of a single piece of wood. Bip-bip! he cried. Bip-bip! I say, fellows, remember, kill birds if you must, but no people please. Bip-bip! Had a fellow last year, winged a beater, very bad show. Bip-bip! Better if you all had guns like mine; still, bip-bip! Won't insist. Bip-bip! If there were to be any accidents that day, it looked as if it was the Duke himself who would cause them. But as the first pheasants whirred up into the air, levelled off, and came swooping towards the guns, he saw his son mooching along an avenue of lime trees two fields away, and cantered off to join him.

Dorian Gray loosed first one barrel, and the bird he'd drawn a bead on – a particularly fine cock – staggered in mid-air, then went into a tailless spin. It was a beautiful day, he enjoyed shooting, and last night he'd managed a particularly satisfying piece of devilry; Dorian should've been in his element – and yet he couldn't rid himself of a sense of uneasiness. There were still some birds in the air and the other guns were blazing away. Dorian had plenty of time for a second shot, but a hint of colour in the trees caught his eye and he lowered the gun. It was one of the beaters, a stocky fellow with a malevolent glare – aimed directly at Dorian. Dorian registered the pudgy features of his nemesis at the same time he heard the report of David Hall's gun by his ear. Almost unthinking, as if it were an instinctive act of self-defence, he raised his own gun and pulled the trigger. The pudgy face went bright red.

It took long seconds for the confused cries of the other beaters to silence the remaining guns, then a small bit of hell broke loose and erupted into the world above.

18

The faces of two men flickered from green to orange to blue to white in the light from a television screen. The brightness of these hues belied the tawdriness of the spectacle that provoked them. One of the watching faces was so emaciated that it had the crude features – big vertical creases, savagely undershot jaw, black button eyes – of a glove puppet fashioned from a sock. The other face was a feral little muzzle, with a pince-nez on a ribbon taking the place of whiskers.

The colours played on the two faces and spread out behind them, lighting up the serrated leaves and soaring stalks of the surrounding foliage. It was as if the two men – one wheelchair-bound and rug-wrapped, the other awkwardly poised on a cast-iron chair – were lost in a peculiar rainforest, one where electricity was available (a power point neatly implanted in a prickly pear?) so that they could scare off the animals of the night by burning an illusion.

On screen a young woman – shortish hair neatly coifed, wide eyes blackly lidded – was earnestly explaining to an earnest man how her marriage had been compromised by her husband's mistress. 'There were three of us in this marriage,' she breathed, 'so it was a bit crowded.'

'I don't call three *that* crowded, d'you, Fergus?' Henry Wotton said. 'Besides, if the transcripts of his mobile-phone calls to his mistress are to be believed, her old man thinks he's a tampon.'

'A tarpon?' the Ferret mused; he wasn't altogether there. 'Is it some kind of fishing fantasy?'

'No, you old fool, a *tampon*, the Prince of Wales thinks he's a *tampon*. He wants to be a tampon shoved up inside Camilla

Parker Bowles, so if that were the case there'd only be two full-size individuals in the marriage. Both of them, admittedly, women.'

'I didn't know Princess Di was a lesbian,' the Ferret came back gamely. 'Still, with her and the Parker Bowles woman it isn't hard to see which is butch and which femme.'

'No no no, *really*, Fergus, if you can't be bothered to concentrate there's no point in talking to you at all. Don't you realise this is a historic television moment, and therefore, *a fortiori*, an event of worldwide significance?'

The Ferret, who felt he'd been making a perfectly constructive contribution to the evening's entertainment (after all, it was he who'd wheeled the television all the way into the conservatory), lapsed into a sulky silence. But after a while he stirred himself and whined, 'You're not the only one who has an illness y'know, Henry.'

'Is that so.'

'It is. It may've escaped your attention, but I have severe narcolepsy.'

'I don't think it's escaped anyone's attention, Fergus; we've *all* been awake *all* the time – it's you who've been missing out on things.'

'I realise that many people find my condition risible, but it was never funny to begin with and now I'm getting old it's becoming a lot worse.'

'*Getting* old?' Wotton was incredulous. 'You're eighty if you're a day.'

'That's as may be, but this hormone deficiency is increasingly severe. You know all about drugs, Henry; can't you find some hypocreton 2 for me on the black market?'

'Hypocreton 2 – what the fuck's that?'

'The hormone I'm lacking. If I had enough I wouldn't sleep so much.'

'Oh *please*! That's priceless. Hypocreton 2 – d'you think that's what Fatty Spencer's on . . . ?' (In the background the Princess of Wales murmured, 'I would like to be a Queen in people's hearts . . . someone's got to go out there and love people and show it . . .') 'She certainly appears to be loved-up on something, and hypocreton 2's more plausible than E, don't you think?'

'I've no idea, Henry,' the Ferret miffled, 'and I've had quite enough of your ragging; I'm rather regretting letting you have any of *my* medication. I wonder what's happened to the rest of the party – what time is it?'

'Oh I don't know, nineish.'

'The guns must have got back hours ago. Why hasn't anybody been to see us? There's no sign of Batface or Jane, either.'

As if they were poltergeists summoned up by the petulant old man's piffle, there came a flurry of footfalls in the tunnel connecting the conservatory to the house; footfalls that announced the arrival – some minutes later, for it took him a while to locate their jungle clearing – of Dorian Gray.

'Stupid squad!' he expostulated. 'They never get any smarter, do they.'

'I assume' – Wotton, sensing Dorian's dramaturgical desires, adopted a measured tone – 'that is a rhetorical question.'

'Yeah, fucking rhetorical. I've been with the morons for nearly five hours. Five hours over a lousy fucking shooting accident!' He looked around for a patch of earth to ground his live wire, but the only vacant space in the clearing was occupied by Wotton's wheelchair and the Ferret's seat – in which the latter had, with Newtonian predictability, fallen asleep.

'A shooting accident?' Wotton killed the Princess of Wales's calculating confession with the remote. 'Who's been shot?'

'One of the beaters.'

'Fucking hell,' Wotton breathed, 'that'll be more trouble for Jane; the estate workers are almost in open revolt as it is.'

'Oh, he wasn't a local man.' Dorian produced a silver cigarette case and a lighter, and lit up. 'Nobody knows who he is at all. The head keeper only took him on for the day – found him in the pub in Narberton. What's more, his face was turned to mush by the blast, so unless someone was travelling with him it's going to take the rural plods a while to identify him.'

'How convenient.'

'For whom?' Dorian snapped.

'For whoever shot him.'

'Well, they're saying *I* did that, but it could just as easily have been David Hall – he was being bloody wild with his shooting. I don't care if he's a fucking Minister; it's insane allowing a cripple to shoot.'

'They'll find out in due course, Dorian – ballistics and so forth. Still, isn't it funny how people get dead around you.'

'What're you implying, Wotton?'

'No implication, merely an observation.'

'It was an accident – I don't know who the disgusting pleb was. I've never had any truck with anyone who has ginger hair in my entire life.'

'Is that so.' Wotton held the image of Dorian's injured innocence in his viewfinder eye, and dipped his eyelid to record the moment for posterity.

'Yes it bloody is.' Dorian ground his cigarette out on the floor. 'Look, Wotton, are you going to stay out here all night?'

'Me? No . . . no, I don't *think* so. Tell me, are you free to leave Narborough, Dorian?'

'They say I can go where I please as long as I tell them; they haven't charged me or anything ludicrous like that.'

'In that case, you can drive me back to London.'

'To London, tonight?'

'That's right. I rather think it's the place of a patrician – as it is of a *plebeian* – to die in the eternal city, wouldn't you agree?'

'What do you mean by that?!' Dorian's eyes flashed and he made as if to grab at Wotton, but the dying man merely laughed.

'I hate having stopped smoking, Dorian. My renewed sense of

taste is useless to me, and as for my enhanced sense of smell, that only seems to bring unpleasantness wafting into my nostrils, like the odour of your fear. You said "pleb", which rather implied that you knew the dead man was an urban type. Still, let's not bicker, I've no time left for that. I'll tell you something, though, Dorian, this shooting accident confirms me in my opinion. It's true that you're the spirit of the age, but it's drunk so much of you it's become cirrhotic. Drive me home, Dorian – I'm in a hurry.'

*   *   *

Despite hurrying home to die, Henry Wotton lingered until the following spring. He was right in what he'd said to Hester Hall, for although the anti-retroviral treatments introduced in the following twelve months were so effective that even very ill AIDS patients got up from their beds and walked, Wotton was not to be one of them.

In truth, Henry Wotton had always understood – at an intuitive, cellular level – that drug addiction and sexual obsession, besides being ways of making time's amorphousness measurable, were also methods of amortising the future. That for each minute or hour or day or week of abandonment purchased *now*, you would have to pay *later*. Pay with physical dissolution and mental disintegration. On this actuarial basis alone it did not surprise him in the least to wind up dead at forty.

He had this boon: terminal illness had suited him only too well. The indisputable existence of a cut-off point meant that recklessness was to be fully enjoined. Along with the drip-drip of limpid minutes, the opaque, flowing droplets of hours, the slow-moving, turbid course of days, came an unconsciousness of anything save the possibility of pain, the pain itself, and the relief at its abatement. It was, Wotton thought, like a reprise of his entire life. It was, he knew perfectly well, what everyone was waiting for. It was only that in this – as in everything else – he had demanded instant gratification.

In his last months Batface and Phoebe moved his Parker-Knoll recliner over into the bay window of the drawing room. He hadn't the sight left for his beloved television-watching, but that didn't matter because all the entertainment he required was live. They set up a high-powered telescope on a stand, and this, in combination with a centimetre-thick lens for his left eye, meant that Wotton was able to see the jiggling man's head entering and then departing the ragged grey patch of vision remaining to him. It seemed to soothe Wotton, who no longer had the inclination for anything much. No drugs save those prescribed to him, no drink save mineral water – a beverage that, in the not so distant past, he wouldn't have cleaned his car with.

He watched the jiggling man's pendulum progress. He watched the bubbles in his glass of mineral water stagger obliquely to its surface, like the rough lads with poor impulse control he used so to adore. He would sometimes take a puff on his pentamidine nebuliser in a desultory way, but apart from the most obvious palliatives, one by one he abandoned the pills and salves and potions. He preferred to await death quietly, reverently. What form, he wondered, would it take? Would it be Old Father Rim who stood by the half-open steel door and beckoned him into Hades? Possibly – although at times he thought he could hear the Latin chanting of the Brotherhood of Misericordia, as they carried his coffin along the street outside, their rubber safety vestments making a hideously lubricious noise. Or might the jiggling man himself fire a ship-to-ship rocket which payed out a rope, then come shinning down it, so he could drag Wotton's sad corpse back across to his foolish vessel?

Batface and Phoebe had his leave to get on with life – and this they did. Wotton was ministered to by people who were financially rewarded for their strong stomachs and acting ability. He didn't want for companionship, either, because the Ferret had now accepted the inevitable himself. He no longer paid to be beaten up by the lower orders, nor did he resist the waters of Lethe with the powders of Peru. Instead, he came each day to the Wottons', and in this house – which had always been out of time – he found it easier to endure his fugues. So they reclined, in armchairs side by side, long stringy Henry and short tubby Fergus. The one dying prematurely, the other in a suspended animation that might see him enduring well into the next millennium. The Ferret had no need of cryonics; he was plenty cool enough already.

They reclined and they watched the jiggling man, or else they slept and dreamed. As he nodded into nothingness, so Wotton's subconscious inland sea expanded, sending out rivulets of reverie towards the great ocean of the collective unconsciousness. In the paradoxical expanse that now lay between his narrow temples, there were the predictable white mountain ranges of crack cocaine and terminal moraines of brown heroin. There were also the inevitable lakes of Champagne around which the centaur boys cantered – so lovely! – with their thoroughbred breasts knotted with muscle, their hooves shiny, and their human countenances at once wise, farouche and trusting. And my dear . . . they're hung like *horses*.

But into this realm came other, more curious visions: scenes built, then struck with unearthly speed. This was due to the presence of the Ferret who snored alongside Wotton. Caught within the gravitational field of a far more sophisticated and accomplished dreamer, his very imaginings fell under the little man's influence. Like the Ferret, Wotton now came to inhabit a dreamscape more enduring and coherent than his waking life. Also, the Ferret brought news of the outside world, specifically Dorian Gray, and if his powers of description were unequal to the task, Wotton's subconscious more than compensated for the deficiency.

*   *   *

Dorian returned from Narborough and blithely resumed his life as before. With Ginger dead, he no longer had any need of Helen and her baby for cover, but he decided he liked having a woman in the house, and for a few weeks he was nice enough to them both to convince her that she should stay.

But having a woman in the house soon gave Dorian the opportunity to be vile in new and exciting ways. There was this benison, and also he looked forward to the time when she'd become symptomatic. Already, lying next to her one sweaty December night, a night when there was no cause for perspiration, he fancied she'd seroconverted. It would only be a matter of time, and that was a commodity he had in inexhaustible supply.

He began to betray Helen with a casual uncaring that was far worse than malevolence. He'd come back at three a.m. and let her interrupt him sucking some chicken off in the front seat of the MG. Or else he'd deliberately leave evidence of his amours – condoms, lubricants, poppers – lying around for her to find. Soon enough he stopped coming back at night altogether, and when he encountered her in the daylight, he laughed derisively in her puffy old face.

However, Helen didn't prove to be as satisfyingly distraught as he'd hoped. Unlike previous abandoned lovers, she seemed not to yearn for his honeyed flesh and his dew-picked charms. On the contrary, she began to be as repelled by him as he was by her. He awoke early one morning to find her examining his naked, prone form with a forensic eye. Jesus, she said wonderingly, you really are an arrested adolescent, Dorian.

—Whaddya mean by that! he cried, pulling the sheet over his slim, tanned torso.

—What I say, she smirked; you have the body of a young lad. She sat up on her knees in the bed, and after fifteen years he noted once again the way she held her nude self – without modesty or allure, yet with a new kind of dignity, a mature dignity. At first, she continued, I found your silky hair and smooth skin a turn-on, but to be frank, Dorian, they give me the creeps now. In part it's because I know you're putting it about everywhere you can, but I also find your baby body revolting in itself. Tell me . . . she picked up a pack of cigarettes from the bedside table, shook one into her mouth, lit it and took a drag . . . are you doing weird drugs? Is this a treatment of some kind, a blood change, whatever? Because one thing's for sure, it isn't natural.

He shot up off the pillow, gathered his clothes together, ran to the bathroom, dressed himself with trembling hands. In the bedroom he could hear the foul old harridan laughing and coughing and farting.

It wasn't a good day for stupid squad to come calling, but being the sort of people they were, they did. A rather too smooth cop – Detective Inspector MacLurie – came from the Earls Court Road station. There was the smoothness, there was the condescension of height, there was the high rank, there was a tailored suit. It took Dorian far longer to summon up his charm that it ever had before, and even then he wasn't at all certain it had the required impact on MacLurie, who smiled only once, when Helen gave him a cup of tea.

MacLurie had a lot to say for himself. His colleagues in Worcester had identified the man killed at Narborough, and witnesses had confirmed that the shot had been fired by Dorian's gun. While there was nothing at this stage to suggest that Dorian had fired with malicious intent, there were a number of things about the case that didn't add up. Dorian had said that the murdered man wasn't known to him, and yet there were certain people whom MacLurie's enquiries had turned up to whom the deceased *had* been known, and who also held the view that Ginger and Dorian Gray were no strangers to each other.

These same people, the Inspector had continued, also had interesting things to say about Dorian's relationship with a man called Alan Campbell. A struck-off doctor, whose corpse had been discovered in the early part of last year, stuffed in the cupboard of his bedsit, the apparent victim of an act of autoerotic asphyxiation that had gone badly wrong. And there was more – he sipped his tea – a fair bit more; however, there was no need to discuss it now. He'd be entirely happy to come back another day – he could see that

Dorian was agitated; presumably he was a busy man with things to do? No, there were no restrictions on him, but they'd be grateful if he called the station if he was thinking of going away for any length of time.

As soon as MacLurie had gone Dorian went to the phone. He had a very fucking good idea who was grassing him up in this fashion, very fucking good indeed. Are you all right? Helen asked. You look green. He shooed her away. Should he call Gavin Strood right away and try to put the frighteners on him? It had to be Gavin – the Ferret could never stay awake long enough to yap that much. Gavin, and also that grotty little novelist Devenish. He knew Gavin had been hanging round with him a bit, and Devenish had hated Dorian for years, ever since they were at fucking Oxford together. Maybe – and the thought occurred to Dorian as any other might think of having a bath – it would be best if he were to kill them both?

The phone rang before he could pick it up. It was MacLurie. One more thing, he said. Our sources told us about another man you were close to, a Basil Hallward.

—I knew him, Dorian admitted.

—Apparently he's been missing for several years now.

—I believe so.

—And you were the last person to see him alive.

—I don't know anything about that.

—Well, according to our information he came back with you one night to see a video installation of his that he'd given you. A video installation featuring tapes of you yourself – is it called *Cathode Iris*?

—*Cathode Narcissus*. Dorian couldn't keep the contempt out of his voice.

—Is that so. Narcissus, eh. I'm not a gardening man myself, Mr Gray. To get to the point – I'd very much like to take a look at the installation if I could.

—What for? Dorian crumpled into the chair by the desk.

—Oh, nothing specific – I'm suppose I'm intrigued.

—It's all packed away in boxes; it'd be a bloody nuisance setting the thing up.

—Well, no matter, in your own time, when you feel you can. I'll call before I come over. No pressure. MacLurie hung up.

Dorian went upstairs and locked himself in. He stared at the nine monitors on their brushed-steel plinths. He strode to the cupboard where the VCRs were kept and opened it. He ejected each of the tapes in turn and shook them one by one, as if in their plastic rattle he could discern some prophetic advice. They'd protected him all these years – surely they'd continue to do so?

But no. His enemies were closing in. Helen suspected the truth, even if she had no chance of comprehending how it was done. And now this bastard MacLurie with his cheap insinuations. Dorian would have to act, deal with the evidence. He didn't need *all* the tapes – why would he? He probably never had. One would be sufficient to keep him looking young and healthy. One hostage to his good fortune. As for the others, he didn't dare burn them or remove them from the house; *she* or even *they* might get wind of it. No, no, safer to conceal them here. Conceal them without concealing them – he tittered inanely – use *Narcissus*-concealer to keep the nasty pimple helmets away. I'll tape over them – that's what I'll do. Tape over them, and no one will be any the wiser.

He slotted one of the tapes back into its VCR and turned on the monitor. He tuned the monitor in so that it was displaying some daytime tat – dumb fucks talking about their dumb fucking problems while seated on foam-rubber pouffes – then hit the RECORD button that hadn't been touched for fifteen years. He felt a jolt in his spine – was it anxiety, or age?

Dorian spent all night up in the top room taping over the Narcissi. To begin with he was selective, trying to make it appear that this was a carefully-chosen drama he intended to watch at leisure, while that was a compilation of news clippings amassed for posterity. But soon he grew tired of this subterfuge and simply hit the buttons, then sat in the Eames chair, rocking back and forth, meting out the sixty minutes until each job was done.

In the morning, when all that was left was the one, prime *Narcissus*, Dorian descended the staircase with a regal air and greeted Helen with a slight curtsy. He felt inviolable now, beyond her or MacLurie's clutches. He felt secure as well, and altogether enfolded in the prickling glass stasis of his own vitreous insanity.

MacLurie never called to see about viewing *Cathode Narcissus*; it'd only been a throwaway suggestion. He had an idea that Dorian Gray was responsible for some bad things, but the evidence for them was sketchy. Even if such unreliable witnesses would turn up in court, it was doubtful that either they, or the strange tales they had to tell, would stand up in front of a jury.

However, Dorian didn't know this, and insanity – as he rapidly discovered – wasn't such a great place to hide after all. The police soon became only too familiar with the guilty gyrations of Dorian Gray. It was as if by destroying eight-ninths of *Cathode Narcissus* he had eradicated the greater proportion of himself as well. Every few days he'd burst, howling, into the Earls Court Road station and begin denouncing himself to the desk sergeant. Sometimes he'd have a map marked with the location where he swore one of his victims was buried; on other occasions his pockets would be stuffed full of polystyrene Ss – evidence, he claimed, of the murder of another. They explained to him, with considerable patience, that New York City lay beyond their jurisdiction. The first ten times it happened they put him in a patrol car and drove him back to the mews, where a solicitous older woman (in her mid-thirties, but still attractive) put an arm around his shoulders and ushered him inside.

Helen thought it was crack that was breaking open Dorian Gray's psychic shell; she knew the symptoms from the baby's father. Dorian had the haunted look of a crack head, and he ranted about people spying on his house who used post-boxes and plant pots for their hidden cameras and listening devices. He never seemed to sleep, only retreating to the room at the top of the staircase for the duration of the darkness. The room he kept locked and chained and bolted. She tried to calm him down, to encourage him to speak about what was troubling him. She would've confronted him with the evidence of his drug-using, but the truth was she couldn't prove anything. No dealers visited the house, and Dorian no longer left it except to visit his friends the police.

The final day she spent at the mews was terrifying. In the electric lemon of a cloudless London spring dawn she found Dorian, standing at the top of the staircase, holding her baby boy aloft by his ankle, swinging the child back and forth as if he were a human pendulum. You've got plenty of time . . . Dorian was spitting, as the baby screamed. You're so fucking young and healthy, *you've* got plenty of time . . . while I'm old and sick.

—Dorian! Helen groaned. What're you doing? Don't hurt him, oh please, oh God, don't hurt him.

—Don't worry. Dorian had never sounded closer to an absolute emotional zero. I won't hurt him; I was only using him to tell the time.

He advanced down the stairs and thrust the upended baby into her arms. Helen sank down on the carpet, her teeth chattering, as if his coldness penetrated her. I've tried to help you, Dorian – what is it? Please, tell me what it is . . . Please? *I* don't think you murdered anybody; I think you need help, perhaps a psychiatrist –?

—A psychiatrist? Ha-ha-ha-ha-ha-ha-ha-ha. He laughed long and mechanically. A psychiatrist wouldn't know where to begin – you'd be better off getting me a witch doctor. But on second thoughts, your best bet is to get the fuck out of here! Get out – go on, get out! Get! Out! He began darting here and there, picking up items of her and the baby's stuff and chucking them in a heap in front of her.

As soon as she stopped quaking enough to move, Helen got out. She hugged her child to her breast and ran up the sloping deck of this, her most titanic mistake in love.

251

In the final week, Dorian Gray sat and stared. For the first couple of days, ever fastidious, he left the room to piss and shit, but latterly he didn't bother, until, unfed and dehydrated, he had no need to. So he sat and stared, sinking down deeper and deeper into the mineshaft of his own insanity, where flesh slapped against flesh and the cloacal air was rent by the groans of the abandoned. He was left alone with the last of the Narcissi whose magical lives had guaranteed his charmed one.

He looked surprisingly good, this once beautiful, thirty-five-year-old man, who had been through a decade and a half of serious illness and survived. The new treatment was working for him, and if his skin was yellowed and smudged, it was at least unscarred. His wary eyes and mean lips betrayed the truth about the things he had done in order to survive, but weren't these things anyone would do if they absolutely had to? If they – as he had – found themselves transported to the cellular Auschwitz of AIDS?

From somewhere the *Narcissus* had got hold of a grey cardigan, which he wore over his hollow chest and swollen joints. He sat cross-legged and stared at Dorian staring at him. Occasionally – or so it seemed to his viewer – he smiled, as if remembering high old times.

On the seventh day of sitting and staring at the hated cardigan-wearer, Dorian got the switchblade out and opened it. It was the one he'd used to kill the creator – it would do for the creation as well. No, don't! the ninth *Narcissus* begged. Don't do anything foolish, Dorian . . . He backed away into the corner of his screen, looking pitifully vulnerable as, like a young girl, he tried to tuck his naked limbs up inside his woolly breastplate. Dorian chose this moment to lunge straight at the screen.

They took another week to find him, and by then, decomposition had begun. Firemen broke down the door, policemen went inside, ambulance men removed the corpse. They were all the sort of people who were disposed to play down the macabre – they saw enough of it in their work. They dealt with the naked bloated body on the floor in a straightforward way, and they dealt with the naked *Narcissus* equally directly.

—Look how old these tapes are, a member of not-so-stupid squad said; they must be from the early eighties. Who knows, maybe Gray knew this lad – maybe he was his boyfriend. The detective took another look at the monitor before turning it off. Or, it's even possible that this chicken is Gray himself. You know how poofs can't bear the whole ageing process. Perhaps he looked at the old tape of himself obsessively, loving it and hating it, and when the hate outweighed the love he killed himself.

—Creepy up in this gaff, isn't it, his colleague remarked.

—I'll say.

The post-mortem was succinct: deceased was thirty-five and suffering from manifold secondary infections associated with AIDS. Any one of them might have killed him in the long term, but instead he was cut short by a switchblade. Verdict: suicide.

The funeral was minute. The Ferret and Helen were the only mourners. Apart from utilitarian blooms provided by the undertakers there was only one tribute, an expensive but unostentatious bundle of spring flowers. The attached card – a thick slab of black-bordered pasteboard topped off with a crest of three feathers – read simply 'In fond memory', and was signed 'Diana' so girlishly that Helen expected there to be a heart instead of the dot over the 'i'. I thought, she said to the Ferret, it was part of his psychosis when he went on about knowing her.

—Oh no, he was very much the *homme du monde* for a while, m'dear. Seen everywhere – with everyone.

—What happened, then? Where are all his friends?

—'Friends' might be putting it a little strongly. When I say he was *seen* with people, I in no way mean to imply that he was *liked* by them.

If social calls had still been an option, the Ferret would have been inclined to suggest that Helen speak with Henry Wotton, but they weren't, so he didn't. They parted at the cemetery gates on the

Harrow Road; she headed back to Turnham Green on the tube, while his driver whirled him south through the terraces of Notting Hill and Kensington, to Chelsea.

Henry Wotton lasted another fortnight after hearing the particulars of Dorian Gray's death. It was as if he was worried that purgatory had the character of a waiting room, one he didn't wish to tenant with his former protégé. Best to wait until Dorian was finally on the train and then make his own way down.

The end, when it came, was curiously unexpected. For days he'd had no real awareness of the comings and goings of the Macmillan nurses, who changed his outsize nappy, or the bandages on his pressure sores. The occasional contact of wifely or daughterly lips was unacknowledged, and even the Ferret's whispered revelations were experienced as little more than a rodent-like squeaking. All Henry Wotton could apprehend was the head of the jiggling man as it entered his remaining tiny allotment of vision and left it. In and out, in and out, in and out, in and out. The poor fellow's rictus seemed more like a death's-head than his own. No, the *fin de siècle* was proving to be a killing zone for them both. In and out, in and out, in and out. Then, one afternoon, when the house was utterly silent, he stopped. The jiggling man stopped. His face entered Wotton's view and remained there.

Wotton stirred and groaned, jerking away from the eyepiece of his telescope. What the fuck was going on? He felt an arm on his shoulder and surged up in his recliner to confront . . . the jiggling man.

—Wotcher cock, he said.

—I'm sorry? Wotton was perplexed.

—I said, 'Wotcher cock,' the jiggling man repeated; it's a sort of colloquial Cockney greeting.

—Yes, yes, I suppose that's right. Wotton was rubbing his one naked eye with bewilderment, amazed that he could see clearly once again, and astonished by what he was seeing.

—I look good, don't I? Up close, the jiggling man was handsome and rugged, with the granite-outcropping features of an old-time sea captain. His woolly was beautifully intact and featured an anchor motif knitted into the weave. You were right about one thing. The jiggling man put a hand on Wotton's shoulder in an avuncular fashion.

—What's that, then?

—It was I who was meting out the seconds, minutes and hours. But I was meting them out solely for you.

—For me?

—That's right – I am, after all, your jiggling man. Now come along, old chap . . . He reached out a hefty hand and helped Wotton to rise. We'd best get under way; we've got a tricky bit of sailing left to do if we're to make port before nightfall.

—And where's that? Wotton held back a little, but the jiggling man urged him on.

—Olympia – we're sailing to Olympia.

—Oh, goody! I've always wanted to abide with the gods.

—What a shame you'll merely be with the other exhibitionists, then, sneered the jiggling man. But he sneered *sotto voce* and Wotton didn't hear him. The jiggling man opened the french window and, still grasping his charge by the arm, shinned up the line, back to the bridge of his block of flats. Wotton looked over his shoulder once at the Ferret, who lay curled up in his armchair, whimpering his way through the afternoon, then set his sights on the future.

When Batface came into the room half an hour later, her husband had gone and his corpse was already cool to the touch. Without waking the Ferret she went to the phone and dialled a number. The automatic switchboard put her on hold and she listened to the *Four Seasons* for what felt like three of them. While she waited she felt an odd apprehension, and turning to the window she saw that the unnatural force field that had surrounded the house and its environs for so long had been ruptured. Outside in the garden, as she watched, the profusion of plants, flowers, shrubs and trees adjusted themselves to the correct stage in their growing season for the early spring. Some leaves and stalks shrank, while super-fluous petals and blossoms withered away altogether. A number of birds flew off to the south, and the grass darkened several shades. It was as if the deity were tweaking the contrast controls of the very biota itself. Then the doctor picked up his extension and Batface told him the news.

Epilogue

'She had to die . . .'

The fingers holding the typescript were exceedingly well manicured, the cuticles tucked up, the hangnails executed, and rough patches of skin emery-boarded out of existence. A discreet gold ring, on the right-hand pinky, had an even more discreet diamond set in it. The backs of the hands were tanned the pleasing colour of freshly baked cookies, although if one were to have sniffed them one could be certain they would have smelled of bergamot or sandalwood or some other expensive balm. The skin on these hands was smooth and taut, but in such a way as to suggest effortful maintenance rather than easeful youth. They were the hands of a man of thirty-five, a man called Dorian Gray.

Dorian shuffled the pages of the typescript together and laid them down on the table. Well, he said to Victoria Wotton who was sitting opposite him, that really is . . . I mean to say . . . I . . . He stopped and sat in confused silence.

—You understand, Victoria said calmly, why it is that I wanted you to read it?

—I s'pose so.

—I think you have the right to know.

—To know what he actually thought of me?

—I didn't say that.

—But it's all here, isn't it? It's all here – he despised me, he fucking despised me, and af – oh, I dunno.

—You were going to say 'after all I did for him' – and you'd be right to, because you did do a lot for him, especially towards the end.

—I had no idea.

—Well, none of us did.

Dorian got up from the table and began to pace back and forth, the length of the kitchen-cum-dining room. It was only three weeks since Henry Wotton's funeral, and despite the late-summer heat the house felt chilly with the atmosphere of mourning. On his third length he paused opposite Victoria and said, Didn't you ever see him working on it?

—No, no I didn't. I suppose you think me rather odd and cold, but I left Henry pretty much to himself towards the end. He made it clear it was what he wanted, and you know better than most, Dorian, that our marriage depended on a great deal of tolerance.

—I'm sorry . . . Victoria . . . it isn't the way –

—No no, she damped him down. You don't need to apologise. I knew, of course, that you and Henry had an affair, but I knew equally well that it was long ago. Besides, the tolerance was on both sides.

—I see what you mean . . . but what about *this*, Victoria, you can't be so tolerant of this? He picked up the pile of A4 and let it fall with a thud on to the tabletop.

—Oh, I don't know . . . She poured herself some more tea from the pot, but didn't trouble to ask if Dorian wanted any . . . I'm delighted to discover that my husband wasn't entirely a wastrel. I think some of the passages are competently written.

—But – but – he always swore blind he'd never write a novel, let alone a *roman à clef*.

—Yes, he's put a joke about that in the text. His character says that the only circumstances in which he'd write a *roman à clef* would be if he'd lost his car keys. You noticed, of course, that throughout the rest of the book he is continually searching for his car keys.

—No, no I didn't notice that.

—Oh well, it's only one of the ways he plays with the form.

—Plays with the form? Dorian was incredulous. He sat down

again and swung one immaculately tailored leg across the other. He's taken colossal liberties with the truth!

—But it's a novel, Dorian. Besides, Henry also took the trouble to formally distinguish those scenes where he was present from those where he couldn't possibly have known exactly what happened.

—I'm not a murderer, Victoria – I never killed anybody.

—I know that, Dorian; don't be silly. Henry knew that too. Listen, I could've flouted his wishes and not shown you the damn thing at all. I did it because I respect the feelings he had for you.

—What feelings?

—Love, Dorian. Henry loved you. He always loved you. I think the book is a lengthy love letter . . . She trailed off. Phoebe had come into the room and was stomping from fridge to worktop, assembling the triple-decker jam sandwich of the angrily bereaved adolescent. *Pas devant l'enfant*, Victoria said, *sotto voce*.

—I'm not a child! Phoebe snapped.

—You are for the purposes of this conversation, her mother replied. But it was a measure of how upset the girl was that she didn't argue the point, merely snatching up her snack and stomping off upstairs.

When she was gone, Dorian resumed, It's a fucking odd love letter – he makes me out to be completely vapid as well as murderous. A ludicrous, narcissistic pretty boy, with nothing on his mind but sex and sadism.

—Listen, Dorian, you can't have been unaware that Henry had certain criticisms of you –

—Yes, sure, but these aren't the right ones. He turns me into a layabout – when I've worked hard ever since I left university. He makes me selfish and egotistical, when I've given a lot of my money to charity. He makes me the supreme fucking narcissist, when I've never cared about my appearance more than . . . well . . .

—Well what? Victoria smiled at him. You can't deny that you're a little bit vain, Dorian.

—I like to look good and I take care of myself – a lot of gay men do, it doesn't make us *immoral*, it doesn't make us *evil people*, prepared to sacrifice any vestige of morality in order to stay young. And that's another thing I can't bear about Henry's *roman à clef* – what he says about Baz and *Cathode Narcissus*. Henry knew full well that it was me who cared for Baz when he was dying, and who's done everything I possibly can to preserve his work since. I dunno . . . I dunno . . . even if it's some kind of allegory, this stuff – he thumped the typescript once more for emphasis – is a bit much, a bit bloody much. I understand that it was difficult for Henry, believe me, but it isn't my fault I didn't get the virus. I didn't screw around, I didn't shoot up. I didn't do these things!

Dorian's biscuity face had got decidedly bloody and it took him a while to calm down. When he had, Victoria decided to draw the interview to a close. It had been a bruising enough time recently. True, Henry's death had not exactly been unforeseen, but that didn't make it any the less traumatic. True, Henry had not been a conventional husband, and in some people's estimation he was no kind of a husband at all, but Victoria Wotton had made her accommodation to him years before. Now he was finally gone she felt the loss of him profoundly. In the last couple of years, more or less clean from drugs, Henry had done his best to improve his relationship with Phoebe, and that was the worst of the whole business.

—Look, Dorian – her voice was pitched low and her tone persuasive – he left two copies of the typescript; one is for you, one is for me. I'm going to destroy mine – if not immediately, then soon. What you do with yours is your own business, but the point is that no one is ever going to read this stuff – she gestured at the pile of paper on the table – it's a closed book.

—I'm not surprised that *you* want it that way. His manner was objectionable; in his willingness to take it out on her, Victoria saw all the ugliness of character her husband had identified in Dorian Gray.

—I don't know, Dorian, she chuckled, I rather think I come out of it better than anyone else. I've ascended a few rungs up the class ladder; Henry has made me a successful historian rather than a failed poet. I take his physical portrayal of me in good part – readers need one or two salient characteristics to hang on to. No, all in all I don't object to the text that much; I even find some of it amusing. I'm also impressed that he had the vigour and application to carry it through – he was a very ill man.

Dorian left the house resolving not to return if he could conceivably avoid it. She was envious, Victoria Wotton, that was it. She was only another *nouveau riche* Jew, after all – no matter how she dressed herself up. And there was her late husband's infatuation with him – she tried to pretend she was disengaged, but it must have hurt. Henry had been too clever for her, too sharp, too *much* in every respect. She'd probably remarry some tedious little businessman and bustle off to the 'burbs. Good riddance.

Dorian ambled along the pavement deep in thought, while his whippet, Wystan, clicked behind. Certainly, despite his poetic licence Henry had displayed a powerful turn of phrase in his writing. It would be amusing to show Fergus Rokeby his portrayal in the typescript tucked under Dorian's arm. It was fucking mean of Henry to take Fergus's tendency to drop off after a decent meal and blow it up into a major pathology. It was the same with the Ferret's harmless snobbery and his mild inclination to avoid paying his share. In every case, Henry had seized upon his friends' foibles and made them into glaring faults.

No – Dorian pulled himself up – on second thoughts, he wouldn't be showing the Ferret or anyone else this travesty. It was reaching his own car that brought the moment of clarity. Dorian prided himself on his carflesh, and this gunmetal-grey Bristol – which Henry himself had had many a lift in – was the finest of the collection. Yet in the stupid bloody *novel* Dorian was reduced to tootling about town in an *MG* – how pathetically uncool. It occurred to Dorian precisely how twisted and bitter it was of Henry, never to say anything to his face, but instead to attempt to wound him from beyond the grave.

He let himself into the car's immaculate interior and started up the engine. The muted roar of the big Chrysler V8 engine was reassuring, as was the ringing of his mobile phone. It was the office. Dorian ran through his secretary's list with assurance – ease, even – as he wheeled the big car east along the Cromwell Road. Yes, he did want to see the team working on the packaging for Valmouth Cosmetics. No, he didn't think it was necessary for him to attend the Design Awards bash that evening at the Grosvenor House Hotel. Yes, he would like to see forecasts of media spend by the top five car companies for the forthcoming year. No, he wouldn't be attending the editorial meeting for *Gray* magazine that morning. And finally, yes, he would like to see the first digitisation of Basil Hallward's video installation *Cathode Narcissus* and discuss with the website designer how it would look once it was downloaded to a PC. He said his goodbyes courteously. He liked to imagine that every member of the Gray Organisation, no matter how lowly, was valued for him- or herself.

The phone call made him think of Wotton's book again. Dorian couldn't bear to call it a novel – that suggested a certain measure of pleasurable inventiveness that this farrago was devoid of. In the book he was obsessed by his looks and lived off what? Some nebulous and unspecified private income. It was so *nebulous*, Dorian sneered to himself, because it had *never fucking existed*. Yes, he had modelled for a few years, but so what? He'd also had the guts to add to his Oxford degree with a course in graphic design at the London College of Printing. He'd started up the Gray Organisation in a room at the back of a friend's café in Notting Hill. He'd made it a success the way anyone makes a small business a success – with chutzpah, flair, and a capacity for almost limitless hard work.

Of course, Henry couldn't bear to acknowledge any of this. Instead, every single particular of Dorian's life that Henry had either experienced directly himself, or heard about from Dorian or mutual friends, had been traduced and bowdlerised in this *book*. The relationship with Herman, which had, on Dorian's part, been one of genuine – if misguided – affection; the sincere efforts he'd made in Manhattan to help out Basil Hallward; even his own grappling with his sexuality had presented an opportunity for Henry to paint him up as a sadistic pervert. The very idea that he'd given Octavia the virus was repulsive – it certainly hadn't been an adulterous relationship, and she'd died in a fucking *water-skiing accident*. Henry Wotton hated being Henry Wotton – that was the key to his *book*; and he, Dorian Gray, had been made the proxy for this monumental self-hatred. Henry couldn't abide the fact that he, Dorian, was genuinely stylish, that he, Dorian, worked hard and successfully, that he, Dorian, had, in time, come to accept his sexuality and even take pride in it. But what Henry Wotton had found hardest to take in his former protégé – and had travestied the most – was Dorian's continued good health in the face of his own gradual decline.

It wasn't simply that Dorian hadn't contracted AIDS, it was also that he'd genuinely cared for those who had. At a personal level he'd done the dawn hospital runs and the midnight bed-baths, he'd filled the prescriptions and held the hands. But more than this, he'd also worked tirelessly to help make the British AIDS charities model organisations, using all his charm, his business acumen and his social connections. He'd done all this while Henry Wotton first prated, then puled and finally succumbed. No wonder Henry accused Dorian of killing Basil Hallward, because that's exactly what he felt himself guilty of. After all, it was Wotton who'd debauched Baz when he'd turned up in London five years before, clean from drugs at last. And it was Wotton who'd derided Baz's art, together with any other examples of a creativity to which he'd aspired without any prospect of attainment.

At least Henry Wotton was in no position to impugn Dorian's latest efforts to ensure his late friend's artistic longevity. True, it was clever the way Henry had twisted the very real decay of the *Cathode Narcissus* videotapes into his perverse tale, but he'd been far too removed from the world of technological advance to appreciate that the means now existed to preserve such artefacts for ever. It was proving highly expensive to digitise *Cathode Narcissus*; doubtless if Dorian waited another couple of years it would be a lot cheaper, but that wasn't the point. The point was to ensure that anyone, anywhere, with access to a PC and the net would be able to experience what was increasingly acknowledged to be one of the most significant modern British artworks. There was a true niceness to this marriage between form and content that made the transfer of *Cathode Narcissus* from leaky videotape vessel to unsinkable digital virtuality seem an inevitable aspect of the life of the piece itself. Or so Dorian liked to think, as he steered the big, grey car up the blue canal of tarmac beside Hyde Park.

No, Henry Wotton couldn't impugn this, any more than he could carry on slinging shit at Dorian's association (to call it a friendship would be presumptuous) with Princess Diana. Still, Dorian said aloud, as he ruffled the whippet's ears, I suppose there was at least *some* honesty in what Henry said about his own snobbery, eh, Wystan? Yes, he'd admitted to this mountaineering vice, even while hauling himself and his wife on to the aristocratic heights.

Now, at last, Dorian thought of his one-time friend and mentor with pity and even a little affection. How uncannily Henry had prefigured his own wet Tuesday afternoon of an interment with his description, in the *book*, of Dorian's. The huddle of rain-wear at West London Crematorium that listened to a muttered invocation by a pathetic priest. The casket's slightly tarnished handles clutched by hired hands. Then afterwards, at the Wottons', the agony of stale sandwiches crumbling in the arthritic hands of ageing parents. Henry's shy mother and father, down from Nottingham to do the decent thing by their flagrant son, both of them incoherent with grief.

Then there was the sibling, the sensible brother, who, with his Midlands mewl and his half-baked shoes, mysteriously came from an entirely different class from Henry. Like so many gay men of his era, Dorian reflected, Henry Wotton had had a capacity for reinventing himself, but in his case there'd been overcapacity. Rather than stopping at being gay, he'd become a twisted involution of homosexual self-hatred; instead of accepting the modest elevation provided by an Oxford education, Henry had metamorphosed into a parody of a toff.

The Bristol thrummed into Fitzrovia, its exhaust blatting at the plate-glass windows of travel agencies and sandwich shops. It was true enough, Dorian allowed, catching sight of his face in the rear-view mirror, that he remained young for his age, but the book's airbrushing out of whatever impression the years had made on him was only the fictional correlate of Wotton's own pretended cynicism.

No . . . Dorian groped for the switch under the dashboard and activated the automatic door of the underground car-park . . . Henry had exhibited none of the Olympian detachment he ascribed to himself in the book. He'd been as scared of dying as anyone Dorian had seen. As scared as Baz Hallward, as scared as Alan Campbell. Scared and not a little tender, too. Dorian looked up at the five storeys of the Gray Organisation. When he'd leased the building he'd doubted his capacity to generate enough business to justify the expense, but three years on he felt a proprietorial ease. He loved its 1950s functionalism, the go-faster chevrons of the mullions, the balconies like the pulled-out drawers of a filing cabinet. As for the grey flag with a 'G' on it, which fluttered from the flat rooftop, this seemed less like a signal of imminent surrender than like a banner proclaiming an advance, no matter how tentative, into the future.

Down in the car-park Dorian opened the passenger door for Wystan. The svelte whippet undulated out and stood twitching in the gloom. The typescript of Henry Wotton's book lay on the back seat of the car where Dorian had slung it. Should I destroy it right away? he considered, but thought better of it immediately. After all, Victoria Wotton couldn't be trusted. He'd have to wait until he was certain she'd got rid of her copy, or at any rate decided definitively against revealing its contents, before he could afford to abandon his own.

With that final difficult decision made – on what had already been a far from easy morning – Dorian Gray headed for the lifts and the tidier, easier world of work.

*   *   *

That winter and the following spring were exciting times for the Gray Organisation. Alexander McQueen and John Galliano both had *succès d'estime* at the Paris *haute couture* shows, and naturally Dorian was there, both in his personal capacity as a friend to both men, and in his professional one as the publisher of an influential design magazine. He was in his element, socialising at after-show parties, arranging for features, co-ordinating shoots and even doing some of the styling himself. There was a definite vibe about Britain in the air. It seemed that at long last the world spirit of stylishness – so long absent from London – had decided to return.

And waiting in the wings there was Tony Blair, a young, dynamic leader, ready to sweep Parliament bare of the stale, bloated and in some cases rotten Tories. As for Princess Diana, with whom Dorian sat on several different charity committees, she was pushing her personal crusade in the most radical of directions. In January she was in Angola clearing landmines with the Halo Trust, and making it absolutely clear that she had no intention of allowing royal protocol to get in the way of her humanitarian work, or her personal life.

Dorian Gray was mixed up in it all, as familiar a figure around the smart West End drinking clubs as he was in the precincts of Kensington Palace, or the corridors of New Labour's HQ at Millbank Tower. Wherever he went he dispensed advice, charmed, facilitated the expansion of networks; wherever he went Wystan came trotting along behind.

Street fashion synergised with pop music, pop music energised politics, politics draped about its suited shoulders the humanitarian mantle of the Princess, and the cartoon antics of conceptual artists galvanised everybody. So what if the whole giddy rondo had the air of the *fin de siècle* about it? Because it *was* the end of the twentieth century, and after a hundred years of willed decline, there was a feeling abroad in the land that things could only get better.

*　　*　　*

That coming autumn, the Royal Academy would be staging a most audacious exhibition of the most controversial contemporary British artists. Dorian, who was involved on the publicity side, was in the middle of a planning dinner at Quo Vadis in Soho with the Academy's director, when things began to go awry.

The Director was holding the table's attention, discoursing on the scandalous situation in which he found himself – chronically hobbled by underfunding which prevented him from getting the works he'd like for the permanent collection. The other guests at the table – a sweaty art critic with fat eyes, a famous dealer with shaving-brush hair – were sympathetically nodding. Dorian was nodding sympathetically as well, when an internal voice sneered (so close to his inner ear he felt the breath tickling him from within), Fucking puffed-up little man – it isn't his money to spend in the first place, it's the tax-payers'. Dorian kept on smiling and nodding, but everyone around the table began to look different, and all that they were saying to sound different. It was all total and unmitigated bullshit.

The Director, the Critic and the Dealer were discussing the works that were going to be exhibited that autumn, when the Voice began again: Conceptual art has degenerated to the level of crude autobiography, a global-village sale of shoddy, personal memorabilia for which video installations are the TV adverts . . . I wonder if the Royal Academy gift shop is doing special offers on bottled piss, canned shit and vacuum-packed blood.

—What did you say? The Director rounded on him. Evidently Dorian had spoken aloud – but how much of what he'd said had been the Voice's words?

He made his excuses and left. At home, at the mews house off Gloucester Road, he let Wystan out to pee in the backyard and retired inside to get himself a drink.

—Fusty and dark in here, said the Voice, like some middle-aged Sloane's fucking *study*.

—That's not true, Dorian snapped; these are all beautiful pieces – I chose each and every one myself.

—Yeah, the Voice prated, but that was years ago when you were young. It's all out of date now – maybe your famous eye has deserted you, mm?

—I must be tired, Dorian said to himself; at dinner I felt so damning of everyone, but all those men are all brilliant in their fields. I need to throttle back a little, or else I'll find myself becoming bitter despite myself.

He went to call Wystan in from the yard. The whippet stood quivering on the grate of an old fireplace, which Dorian had picked up at an antiques market but never troubled to instal. The dog's flesh was stretched so tightly across his bones that the light from the lamp above the back door streamed right through his legs, illuminating the tracery of veins as if the poor beast were a living stained-glass window. We should snap those twiggy limbs and burn him in the grate he's standing on, the Voice said, and Dorian muttered, This is distinctly *unheimlich*.

—You don't even know what that means, the Voice carped; I don't believe you're up to speed in German. Best go and look it up in the dictionary – *if* you have one.

Dorian did as he was told. He flipped through his dictionary standing at the desk, the reading lamp illuminating the heavy book in a reassuring, scholarly fashion. He discovered that *unheimlich* meant 'uncanny', while *unheimlichkeit* meant 'uncanniness'. This is certainly *unheimlich*, Dorian said to himself.

—Isn't it, the Voice remarked.

—I know you. Dorian slammed the dictionary shut. You're Henry's narrative voice in that stupid book of his. I haven't thought of it in months – I haven't thought of *you* in months. All at once – could it be that he was a little drunk? – Dorian felt an urge to look at the typescript. It was locked in a cupboard in the attic room. He went straight up the stairs and reached for the door handle. The door was locked. Absurd, Dorian thought. I never lock this door, never.

—Perhaps there's something inside you'd rather not see, Henry's voice said.

—No, there isn't. Dorian rattled the handle again. If he hadn't locked it, could it have been the cleaner? She certainly had keys for all the doors in the house – but why would she lock this one?

—It wasn't the cleaner, Henry's voice insisted. It was you. You're going mad.

—No I'm not, Dorian guffawed, but I bloody well will be if I stand here all night.

He went to his bedroom and undressed. There was a mirror attached to the inside door of his walk-in closet and, as was his evening ritual, he took the time to check himself over fore and aft. Not too bad – not too bad at all. In the bathroom he used a little cleanser and a little moisturiser, and efficiently tweezed a nasal hair. He brushed his teeth with a special-formula paste for sensitive gums. He slept soundly, floating on aquamarine sheets. In the morning all memory of the Voice had gone, and he'd forgotten about the typescript as well.

*   *   *

Busy, busy, busy. Trips to the gym where broad backs, thin backs, white backs, black backs, all bowed and rose. Groans rent the air as brawny and skinny arms were pulled back to reveal oval patches of healthy sweat. At the city-centre health club where Dorian was invariably to be found at lunchtime, the rowing machines were arranged haphazardly, which gave their users – as they oofed and aahed – the appearance of slaves going nowhere on a galley rendered motionless by opposing forces. At an invisible helm, Dorian pictured a giant Nubian, naked save for a Calvin Klein cache-sexe, who with massive hands beat out the hip-hop rowing rhythm on his own, drum-tight tummy.

Busy, busy, busy at the Gray Organisation, where close involvement with the New Labour campaign meant that Dorian – and Wystan – were required to attend meetings with Ministers-in-waiting, in order to formulate the communications strategies of the new regime. And what an occasion that election night turned out to be. Dorian began at a party in Kensington and, as the evening wore on, reeled into the West End. Never normally a heavy drinker, he found it hard to resist the effervescence of victory, downing glass after glass of bubbly, as Tory after Tory went down the plughole. Dorian ended the night with the select many (this was, after all, the People's Triumph), at a massive beano on the South Bank, cheering the divine Tony as he grinned his megawatt grin. Then, on a peerless London May morn, Dorian boarded a coach with the select few, and they were bussed back across the river and issued with regulation Union Jacks. The vanguard of the future then stood in Downing Street and waved them, to titillate the entrance of the new Big Nob.

Busy, busy, busy. In May alone there were 2,456,707 hits on the *Cathode Narcissus* website (www.cathodenarcissus.com). Visitors to the site could view Baz Hallward's original installation, together with other examples of the late artist's work. Sponsored and maintained by the Gray Organisation, the site featured links to *Gray* magazine, as well as a photo-file of Dorian's own career in modelling. All of the images and the text were available for downloading free of charge. '*Cathode Narcissus* Belongs to Us All', the slogan on the homepage proclaimed; 'Download Some Perfection Today'. Dorian wanted Baz's work to become synonymous with male beauty at the end of the twentieth century. Male beauty and a new mature pride in homosexual identity – not a pride based on militant identification with an underclass, or a persecuted ethnic minority, but the true pride that came with assuming the responsibility proper to an era, when for the first time gay men and lesbian women were openly assuming positions of power.

Dorian was nothing but pleased when sequences of *Cathode Narcissus* were pirated for television advertisements and pop videos. During the first few months of 1997, the cathode Narcissi spread throughout the virtual metabolism of the culture, like a digital virus. Pulling on his trousers in the early morning, ready for another busy, busy, busy day, Dorian marvelled at the taut perfection of these limbs that had carried him thus far. True, he ruminated as he ran sharp steel over smooth chin, his moderation and carefulness had always been in marked contrast to the excess and recklessness of his peers. But none the less, to find himself, at thirty-six, looking not too much older than he had when Baz made the recordings . . . well – he smiled at himself in the mirror – anyone could be forgiven for finding this a tad . . . uncanny.

Busy, busy, busy – but not busy enough. As he bickered over the bill with friends – some gay, some straight – in a Greek restaurant by Primrose Hill one Sunday afternoon, it hit Dorian Gray with sickening suddenness, like the lintel that smacks you in the forehead as you scrupulously avoid the step. All of us childless, Dorian thought, looking about him at the edgy bantering of his social sibling-substitutes. All of us – relatively speaking – rich, all of us unencumbered with any true, organic responsibility. What's it all for?

—You've been living under an assumed identity, said Henry's voice, back again.

—I'm sorry?

—You've been living under an assumed identity, but your real name. And you're finding it *unheimlich*, if I'm not much mistaken.

—Dorian, is there anything wrong? Angela asked, her hand on his arm, her beads clicking. You look like you've seen a ghost.

—Dorian kneaded his perfect features with a galvanised hand, as if trying to remove his Dorian Gray Horror Mask. No no, there's nothing wrong.

But there was everything wrong. As Dorian trotted with Wystan along Fulham Road, Henry's voice was now strident and hectoring. It wouldn't let him alone. Whaddya want this fucking tat for? Henry sneered, as Dorian swayed by a display of miniature designer chairs in the Conran Shop. Unless, he wheedled on, you'd like to purchase that cute model Eames chair and fashion yourself a Baz dolly to sit in it for some pin-sticking.

—What are you talking about? Dorian gasped. A little wet-look assistant came trotting up: Is there a problem, sir?

—No, no.

No problem – only a fucking disaster. Out in front of Michelin House, Dorian cursed Henry roundly. The sour, bitter old bastard – wouldn't even let me have my dog; gave my dog to fucking Binky Narborough. Wystan is *my* dog, he sobbed, all my dog. He crouched on the stone floor by the caviar stall and hugged the whippet's lean grey muzzle. Yes – he kissed the velvet ear – you're my dog, aren't you, Wystan, aren't you, old boy?

—Pity his slitty little mouth's too small for you to stick your cock in, Henry cackled from beyond the grave. Dorian lunged upright, reeled across to the flower stall on the other side of the building. 'Say it with flowers' – Henry savoured the aperçu exactly as he would have had he been standing there by Dorian, his death's-head grin surmounting the velvet collar of his Crombie – what an absurd slogan it is, when all that people ever say with flowers is 'I like flowers'.

The spiral became tighter and its angle steeper. Dorian stopped going to work. It was next to impossible – driving across town with Henry Wotton second-guessing every turning he made, and forcing his foot down on the accelerator. Instead Dorian went out at night to the clubs under the railway arches at Vauxhall, where he'd lose himself in the throng of his *alter egos*, all bumping and grinding and voguing their way towards the twenty-first century. But no matter how far he threw himself into the K-hole, Wotton would always be waiting for him when Dorian crawled out again the following morning.

—No need for those biologists to bother with genetic engineering, eh Dorian.

—Why's that, Henry?

—Because you boys have beaten them to it. You're all completely interchangeable: cocks, arseholes, jeans, brains. That joint you were in last night was like a swap shop at the end of the world, wouldn't you agree?

—Shut up! Shut up!

*   *   *

In the middle of July, Gianni Versace was murdered in Miami, and this did penetrate Dorian's purple haze enough to make him think that maybe he should look for some help. He'd known the self-styled King of Glitz – or had he only imagined knowing him? Was it rather that he had flown to Miami and done the shooting himself? Cunanan – what kind of a fucked-up pseudonym was that? Utterly implausible.

The office had given up calling him. Dorian left the door to the backyard open and filled Wystan's food and water bowls when he remembered to. The whippet left streaks and blobs of diarrhoea on the carpet. When Dorian staggered by, the dog sprang out of his path. Yet no matter how hard he tried, Dorian didn't seem to be able to make an impression on his plastic-encapsulated perfection. He still looked fabulous, so regular and machined it was difficult not to imagine that there was a seam running down the back of his blond head.

Then, at the very end of August, he came back one early morning from across the river. He paid off the cab at the entrance to the mews and hobbled over the cobbles to his front door. Letting himself in, he kicked at the grey wraith that tried to twine itself between his denim knees. For no reason that he could discern – for he could discern nothing save the neon streaks and blotchy after-images of synthetic ecstasy – he lurched up the stairs instead of heading for his bedroom. The door to the attic room was ajar, and inside he saw the nine monitors ranged in their precise crescent, with the Eames chair in prime viewing position. The central monitor was on, and displaying the twenty-four-hour news channel: '. . . entered the underpass on the *périphérique* hotly pursued by paparazzi . . .' the announcer was intoning. In the background was the underpass in question, an enfilade of oil-stained concrete pillars, like the nave of the First Church of Autogeddon. Dorian slumped down in the squishy leather and tried to take it in.

And was still trying to take it in five hours later, when the same footage of ambulances speeding to the *Salpêtrière* had been shown over and over again, and the same onlookers interviewed, and the same crumpled-up Mercedes lovingly dwelt upon by the caressing camera. No, Dorian Gray couldn't take it in. Princess Diana. Dead. Impossible.

—Oh, but it isn't *impossible* . . . Henry Wotton's air of arch affectation filled Dorian's nostrils with the mephitic stench of a mass grave. On the contrary, this is one of those public events that confirms that history is nothing more or less than the confused wet dream of a humanity yoked to its own adolescent erotic fantasies.

—W-what are you saying? Dorian groaned and thrashed.

—Only this: that so perfect is this marriage between fact and fiction, so ideally *mythic*, this royal huntress slain by the paper hounds of the press, you could be forgiven for summarising the whole story with a single proposition.

—Which is?

—She had to die . . . because her name was Di.

In the mid-morning the phone downstairs began ringing, and wouldn't stop. Dorian had long since ceased to pick up his messages, and when callers heard the hideous bip-bip-bip of a full tape they gave up. But this one wouldn't. Whoever it was rang and rang and rang.

Dorian slumbered in the shocked stupor that followed months of debauchery and hours of grief. When he awoke in the early evening the phone was still ringing. Intending to disconnect it, he found himself picking the receiver up instead.

—Dorian Gray? a voice said.

—What?

—You don't know me . . . It was a deep voice, a cold voice, a harsh voice not compromised by the least vestige of humanity. My name's Peter.

—What do you want?

—No, it's a case of what *you* might want. I'm a friend of Alan Campbell's.

—Campbell? What the fuck – he's been dead for years . . .

—Yeah, you'd know all about that, Gray, all about that – but that's not what I'm calling about. I'm calling about a video you might like to buy off me.

—I don't know what you're talking about.

—You remember dropping Alan off in Bournemouth all those years ago, dropping him off to see me?

—I never did any such thing.

—Issat so? I remember it well enough. I looked down at you from my window – you were driving a natty little MG, as I recall.

—An MG? Don't be absurd – I've never driven one –

—Look, it doesn't matter about your fucking car, Gray – I've got the tape. The tape Alan gave me. If you want it, you can buy it. I want fifteen grand. Get the money ready in used notes. I'll call in a couple of days.

The connection was severed. Dorian raced back upstairs and went straight to the cupboard where the nine VCRs that played *Cathode Narcissus* were kept. He checked each one in turn: eight of the tapes were there, but the ninth was gone. Dorian had a moment of clarity in the chaos – Campbell must have taken one the night they got rid of Baz's corpse. That was what he'd meant when he said he had a present for his friend Peter. It wasn't that loser Hallward's teeth – it was the tape. Campbell had the fucking tape. He must have got it copied and left one with this Peter character. No wonder he was so smug on that drive – he was laughing at me! He even tapped his breast pocket and I heard the fucking hollow sound the thing made.

When darkness had altogether fallen, Dorian Gray put Wystan on the lead and they walked up towards Hyde Park. In the damp darkness of a late-summer night, a silent throng was converging on Kensington Palace. The throng numbered both workers and drones, but they were all animated by the same homing instinct – to zero in on the pollen of hysteria.

—She had to die . . . because her name was Di, Wotton muttered conversationally.

—Quite so, Dorian replied.

—We're all inventions of one sort or another, Dorian, Wotton vouchsafed. I don't think you should feel too bad about the way things have turned out.

—Oh, I don't.

He turned in through the iron railings. There were a lot of police about, but they stood with eyes downcast, or else directed the mourners towards the ornate inner fence that divided the gardens from the precincts of the palace itself. Even from a hundred yards away Dorian could smell the sickly perfume of a thousand thousand bunches of cut flowers, and drawing closer he arrived, together with scores of others, at the gold-crested gates. Here Dorian watched while the infantry of grief threw up a cellophane-wrapped rampart to protect themselves from the bombshell that had already fallen. Primroses, lilies, roses, carnations, daffodils, tulips, sunflowers, irises, poppies, nasturtiums, pansies, snowdrops, foxgloves, desert orchids. That they were all simultaneously flowering made of it an impossible late August.

—And yet I feel so empty, Dorian whispered to Wystan, I who actually knew her. But Wystan didn't respond, because he didn't properly belong in this context, having been Binky Narborough's dog all along.

—*She* had to die . . . because her name was Di, Henry Wotton said, but your dog was a badly-drawn touch – no one would've believed that you had one; you aren't the faithful type. And as for the *Gray Organisation*, frankly, Dorian, your fantasy of business prowess is – well – laughable.

—You – you look so different, Henry, Dorian said, staring in wonder.

—Do I? Oh well, needs must. In his new incarnation Henry Wotton stood about five foot eight inches. He was wearing light-blue jeans turned up over shiny, sixteen-hole Doc Marten boots, and a bright-red Harrington jacket. He was entirely bald save for a light ginger furze at the back of his pudgy head. Walk with me, he said to Dorian, offering his arm, and they strolled off together.

Back down the Broad Walk and then left along the Flower Walk, between the formal gardens and shrubbery. It was comfortable, walking arm in arm with Henry, now that they were a similar height. What's it like being dead? Dorian asked, but Henry merely smiled and placed a fat finger to his plump lips.

At the West Carriage Drive they passed straight over and took the Serpentine side of Rotten Row. I expect, Henry said, shifting his grip to the back of Dorian's neck, you never thought you'd be riding with the quality under such circumstances.

No no, was all Dorian could bleat in reply. It was awkward making their way over the damp sand of the ride, and if he missed his footing, or slid in a pile of horse droppings, Henry had a way of helping him to his feet with a solicitous cuff round the head, or toecap in the ribs, that Dorian found painful as well as intimidating.

They passed up the side of the lake towards the asymmetrical bulk of the Dell Restaurant. There was no one about – they had the park to themselves. I need to take a leak, Henry said; there's a place over here.

—It'll be locked, won't it? Dorian clutched at this wisp of a straw.

—So what if it is? Henry replied, opening a switchblade with a rasping click. He used it to force the door to the public toilet and dragged Dorian inside.

Standing in the piss-filled runnel of the urinal, his cheek rammed hard against wall, Dorian realised that Henry had metamorphosed back into being Ginger, and that the walk over from Kensington Palace, far from being an amiable stroll, had been more in the manner of a forcible abduction. But by now he was also coming to terms with the fact that the beautiful new tie Ginger had just given him with his knife was a warm, sticky, fluid thing, and hardly likely to remain fashionable for very long at all.